Finding Amelia
Beyond The Dark Waters
Book One

by

Graham West

To Ciarán
Hopes you enjoy
the book

Graham

Beaten Track
www.beatentrackpublishing.com

Finding Amelia

First published 2017 by Beaten Track Publishing
Copyright © 2017 Graham West

All rights reserved.

ISBN: 978 1 78645 098 2

Cover Design: Michael Gallagher

Beaten Track Publishing,
Burscough. Lancashire.
www.beatentrackpublishing.com

Acknowledgements

First of all, I would like to thank my wife, Ann, without whose encouragement this book would have remained unfinished, gathering cyberdust on a file somewhere in the bowels of my laptop.

Also thanks to my daughter, Lindsay—I could not have written a novel revolving around the relationship between a father and his daughter without her.

A huge thank you also to my editors Andrea Harding and Debbie McGowan for their support and guidance. I have learned so much in these past twelve months.

Of course, no book is complete without its cover. For that I have to thank Michael Gallagher, who took on my rather hazy ideas and turned them into a work of art while managing to make it all look so easy.

Finally, thank you to my cover model, Becky Poole who became Amelia for the day.

Dedication

To Ann and Lindsay

Contents

Prologue

THERE ARE SEVERAL things in life for which I am grateful, the first being that my parents decided not to call me Adam. It had been close, and the fact that I'm not is thanks to my father, who, having been caught in something of a dilemma, had leaned into the pram and asked his six-week-old baby boy if he would like to be named after the first man to inhabit the earth.

Maybe even at that tender age, I'd seen the flaws in the Biblical version of events, as I had, by all accounts, stuck out my tongue, which my father interpreted as a sign from the Almighty. Hence, I was christened Robert.

Robert Simon Adams.

Perhaps now you can understand why I am grateful.

Not that there is too much wrong with Adam Adams, but I prefer a name that doesn't attract unwanted attention.

You see, I just wanted a quiet life—to keep my head down, study hard, raise a family and earn enough money to get by. I'd never sought fame—not the way kids do these days. Not even the fifteen minutes' worth to which, apparently, I'm entitled.

One of the other things I am grateful for is my health. I am aware how many of my generation battle with disabilities, aggressive allergies and mental-health issues, yet I have rarely suffered from anything more than a common cold, and, according to a mystic at a local fairground, I'm going to enjoy a long and healthy life.

That was good to hear, although back then, I'd never taken much notice of those crystal-ball-gazing sideshow merchants. Spiritual things baffled me, and I generally put them to the back of my mind and concentrated my energies on the things I could actually see with my own eyes. Of course, I watched the ghost-hunting programmes if only to laugh when one of the presenters ran screaming from the old castle vault at the sound of a creaking door. Or when someone from the crew commented that they felt an icy cold draught, seemingly oblivious to the fact they were standing in a dilapidated old building with more holes than a sieve. It's great TV.

I didn't even mind watching the odd spooky movie; they always seemed to be based on true events, although I'd always taken that with the proverbial pinch of salt.

But then, something happened in my own life, and it changed everything. From my casual disregard for those who saw ghosts lurking in the shadows around every corner, I found myself on a quest to prove that we could indeed communicate with the spirits of the dead.

There are so many things I don't understand, so many questions to which I'll never have an answer on this side of the grave, but I keep my mind open. All I ask is that you do the same, because this is not a story 'loosely based on real events' nor the ramblings of a man with a mind warped by grief. It's the truth, and that's why I'm going to tell you exactly what happened—from the beginning.

Chapter One

THE MURDER OF my wife and five-year-old daughter was described by the legal system as an accident. Of course, the official term was misadventure because the suits and the wigs are programmed to categorise everything. Elizabeth and Hanna had simply been in the wrong place at the wrong time; their notes were neatly filed away and the case was closed. Me? I should be reading bedtime stories to my child, climbing into a warm bed next to my wife and breathing in the faint scent of her perfume before gently drifting away. Now I don't drift so much; I think. I think, and I watch, because there's a movie inside my head, and for the past twelve months, it has run on a loop every night.

It was mid-June and the temperatures had been climbing all week—nearly seven whole days of sunshine. Predictably, the media dragged the global warming issue into every news bulletin, and while two scientists argued over the ozone layer on the Sunday morning current affairs programme, Darren Pascoe and Kevin Taylor jumped the bus across town, hoods pulled up over their heads, avoiding eye contact with the driver as they pushed a handful of loose change into the tray and took a seat.

Pascoe and Taylor had been unlikely partners. Young Darren had been raised in the suburbs on the edge of town, a single child of Benjamin and Victoria Pascoe. Benjamin, a well-respected therapist, was a socialist of the old order and had never even considered giving their son the private education they could so easily have afforded. It was a decision Victoria—a buyer with a leading fashion retailer—suspected they might live to regret.

Taylor had been brought up on the Kirkland estate, a notorious concrete jungle surrounded by wasteland where the kids would kick footballs and shoot up with anything they could afford to buy from the local dealers. Pascoe told the judge that the place smelled like shit on hot days. Dog shit, mainly. Pets roamed the streets, abandoned by feral families. They pretty much lived by their own laws, and the police never seemed to bother with the Kirkland people, having drawn up their own no-go policy. They just drove on by, stopping only when they were asked.

The only thing the pair had in common was the school they attended, and when Benjamin Pascoe walked out of the family home, his son Darren found a listening ear in Taylor: a boy who had never known any stability in his life.

"Life is a lake of crap," he'd told Pascoe, quoting his father, a pretentious ponytailed waster. "You just have to learn to swim!"

Taylor was sixteen and already 'alcohol-dependent'—another of those politically correct terms that my old man had detested. Taylor had bought two three-litre bottles of cheap white cider from Bill's Booze—an off-licence with a fat greasy proprietor who didn't ask too many questions and had never set eyes on an ID card in his life.

The local council had poured a pot of European cash into Alshaw Park, dredging the lake and landscaping its fifteen acres. It attracted the kids during the summer months. Pascoe and Taylor spent the afternoon sitting by the water's edge, watching the girls who paraded around in their short skirts and croptops, chewing gum and strutting like mating peacocks.

That day, a few of the girls were lying on the embankment, sunbathing with their skirts hitched up to their knickers. After a litre of cider, Taylor had walked over to one of the girls and rammed his hand between her legs. She had screamed and threatened to part him from his balls, but that didn't cut much ice with a kid from the Kirkland estate. He just laughed and walked on. I discovered later that, in between his literary efforts, Taylor's father had done time for rape and possession of obscene material. His son had grown up surrounded by pornographic magazines and films.

Sometimes I wonder if the Grim Reaper actually exists in some mystic form and was already hovering in the afternoon sunlight, watching my wife playing with our beautiful, happy little girl in the back garden. I wonder if he smiled as the ice cream van turned into our road, knowing that their time was near.

Just ten minutes earlier, Sally Reston, a single mother with a wealthy father, was driving along Alshaw Road in her black four-wheel drive. It was fate. If her six-year-old kid hadn't been suffering from a bladder ready to burst then my wife and child would still be alive. It's as simple as that.

Sally would never have pulled over and hauled little Nathan over to the bushes, shielding him from public view while he urinated. Sally was a girl in a hurry, flustered by the unplanned stop. She hadn't bothered to take the keys out of the ignition. Why bother? She was less than five metres away.

But the Reaper had everything in hand. Pascoe and Taylor were heading home. Taylor loved cars. The black beast purred provocatively, and to a troubled teenager, it was sexier than all the Alshaw Park girls put together.

Pascoe rammed the pedal to the floor, and the car was gone before Sally turned. She watched helplessly as the four-wheeler took a left turn, running the red light at the corner of Alshaw Road. They were headed in our direction. No one ever asked those kids why they turned left instead of right. I guessed it had just been a split-second decision. Fate. Kismet.

I stood at my front window as the ceiling fan whirred above me. Hanna was holding her mother's hand, looking up at the pictures of ice creams on the side of the van. Her eyes danced as she jumped up and down with such innocent excitement, and in that single moment, I remember wishing that she would never grow up. I loved her just the way she was, and the irony within that wish was never lost. Hanna never did grow up.

It all happened in an instant. Elizabeth stepped off the pavement, holding my daughter's hand tightly. The ice cream was melting, and tiny rivers of pink and white liquid ran down her hand. Hanna was waving at me with frantic enthusiasm. She didn't seem to hear the screeching tyres. My wife turned in the direction of the sound. Instinctively, she stepped back behind the ice cream van just as Pascoe lost control. He swerved wildly, his hand gripping the wheel.

I can see it now. The moment. The sickening thud. Bone, blood and metal. My wife's twisted frame, the blood oozing from her mouth. She was staring up from lifeless eyes.

Hanna was under the wheel. Thank God, I couldn't see her. The paramedics covered her with a sheet. She was too badly mashed up. That's the phrase I caught the neighbours using. It seemed as if the whole world screamed when Pascoe smashed into the back of that Mr. Whirl van, and I just stood, rooted to the spot, unable to lift my feet from the floor. The window was my screen as I watched the scene unfold. I heard the frantic knocking on the front door. Someone out there was going to tell me something I already knew. Elizabeth and Hanna were dead.

***

The young policewoman sat beside me, running her slender fingers across the back of my hand. She had a voice as soft as silk and eyes of Caribbean blue. Her name was Lauren, and for some inexplicable reason, I asked her how old she was. I can't remember her answer and, to be honest, I can't remember why I'd asked. It was irrelevant. My mind was on Jenny.

She was our eldest. A seventeen-year-old with a passion for art and the classical guitar. She worked Saturdays in the local petrol station to pay for her lessons with a teacher who lived less than a mile down the road. I remember the moment she arrived home, bursting through the door, her face twisted with panic. She stared at the young policewoman holding my hand. Jenny collapsed before Lauren could reach her.

A paramedic sat with my daughter as she regained consciousness, but despite suffering what he referred to as extreme shock, she didn't shed any tears. My daughter just stared into space for what seemed like an eternity while Lauren, who had been joined by an older officer, stayed with us. They told us they'd arrested Pascoe and Taylor, who had been found running across a patch of wasteland. At the time, I hadn't the energy to hate those kids. I felt nothing.

In the days that followed, I found myself living in a vacuum while a kindly, middle-aged woman from Victim Support visited us, along with a couple of the braver neighbours who told me that their doors were always open if I needed anything.

***

I'd left a message with my sister in New York. Sophia had suffered from depression from an early age, and my father had struggled with his daughter's impulsive behaviour and violent mood swings. When she was eighteen, my sister married a New Yorker, ten years her senior, and moved out of our lives forever.

There had been no contact since, although she always sent Jenny a birthday card, unsigned, with the words, *Thinking of you xxxx*. If you knew Sophia, this would not seem unusual. Nor would you be surprised that she never returned my message. Not even a condolence card.

The man from the funeral director's visited our home to discuss the impending burial. He wore his dour expression like a mask and talked in a serene whisper as if anything louder might disturb the dead he'd buried. The minister from the local free church called a couple of days before the funeral which, I understand, was his duty as leader of a steadily dwindling flock.

I guess that he didn't get an easy ride with the recently bereaved, and at the time, God was my enemy. How could he have been anything less? The Almighty had stood by and watched as my family was torn apart and sent His servant to do His dirty work. The reverend spouted platitudes, but I treated him with the respect that my father would have demanded as an ardent supporter of the Church. The old guy would never have shaken a fist at the Almighty. In fact, he would never have even raised a question. I thanked the reverend when he left, and he vowed to call again after the funeral.

The church was full when they carried the two coffins down the aisle. The teachers from Hanna's school, young women and men responsible for the education of my child—an education she no longer required—sat with dewy eyes alongside the parents of some of her friends. Jenny and I were in the front row, staring impassively while the whole church seemed to tremble under the terrible weight of grief. The minister told us we'd coped well, but I think he knew that our time hadn't come. We were dry-eyed and numb to the very core of our beings.

I stood at the graveside with my arm around my daughter's shoulder. The minister reminded us he'd call. I smiled. His God had forsaken us, but I simply shook his hand. I wanted to crush his bony, ecclesiastical fingers and ask him what his tyrant of a God was up to, but I didn't. I didn't because my father was watching from the other side. It was for him that I held my tongue and kept my peace with the Church he loved.

***

Grief is a strange and unpredictable emotion; a ride that takes its victim through black lonely spaces into areas of light and then back to black. After three weeks, I'd still lived like a man waiting for his wife to walk through the door after an afternoon at the shops. In my heart, I couldn't accept that she'd gone. Sure, the house felt empty, and Jenny had a habit of leaving a music channel running all day just to kill the silence. Sometimes she would pick up her guitar and play a piece. It didn't seem to matter where the sound came from.

Doctor Elworth called unexpectedly, early one evening after surgery. Jenny had developed a teenage crush on the Clark Kent look-a-like when she was thirteen and would frequently feign mysterious illnesses that required immediate medical attention. He smiled sympathetically as I opened the door, an expression well practised, I guessed.

"Mr. Adams," he began, hoisting his briefcase a little higher as a statement of his professional status. "I thought I'd call—just to see how you are."

Elworth had supported Elizabeth through two difficult pregnancies and dealt with my subsequent paranoia with grace and patience. He had shown nothing but kindness towards the love-struck Jenny even when he realised that her illnesses had been invented. So, when I found him on my doorstep, I also found myself welcoming him in with an honest and transparent enthusiasm. Elworth had never succumbed to the pressures of modern medical practices, and his patients treated him like a family member.

"It's good of you to call," I said, handing him a strong coffee— in a cup of which I imagined Elizabeth would approve. Elworth removed his spectacles—Jenny informed me they were only for reading, anyway—and smiled. "You must be busy," I continued.

The doctor sipped his coffee. Clark Kent had gone with the spectacles, and now he resembled the flying, caped crusader of film and comic. "I am," he said. "I'm only sorry I've not managed to call before now. It's a terrible tragedy, Mr. Adams. Everyone at the surgery was deeply affected. They all send their sympathy."

"Thanks. I've got your card somewhere."

I recalled that he had signed it 'Doctor Elworth' and included the staff at the surgery in conveying his regrets. I'd been deluged with cards—many from people I didn't even know—and kept them all in the bottom drawer...my wife's bottom drawer, which had become a no-go area. The feel of her underwear had awakened a screaming longing inside me that could never be satisfied. Not with her. Our most intimate moments had, in the wake of death, become sacred and beautiful.

"It was the least I—we could do." he said.

A brief, uncomfortable silence followed, allowing Elworth to say his piece. "I wanted to know if I could be of any help. Are you and Jenny sleeping okay?"

I shrugged. "Sure."

It was a lie. My nights had become so restless that I awoke, tired and drained.

"That's a very short answer," he remarked with a look of concern. "Sleep is *very* important Mr. Adams."

"I don't want any pills," I said curtly, regretting my tone immediately.

Again, the doctor flashed a sympathetic smile. "Don't worry, I'd be loathed to prescribe them. I'm not a great believer in suppressants. I often advise patients to take more exercise—long walks, a swim, even a daily jog. It doesn't always go down so well, but..." He didn't finish his sentence.

Jenny poked her head around the door, blushing when she saw the doctor sitting in our lounge.

"Ah, Jenny..." There was a pause, a knowing, gentle smile. "How are you?"

Jenny was caught in two minds. Should she cut and run, excusing herself politely? Or should she stay and squirm under the gaze of the doctor's eyes? I felt for her. Somewhere inside, a flame still flickered.

"I'm okay, thanks," she said.

Elworth stopped short of inviting her to pop into the surgery anytime she wanted. The last time she'd visited, three years earlier, he'd had to explain, in a wonderfully gentle manner, that he believed she was not really ill at all, and that there were often really poorly people waiting to be seen and he really needed to attend to them. He had left his hand resting gently on Jenny's as he spoke softly, looking as if he were going to lean forward and kiss her at any moment.

Of course, Elizabeth had told the doctor that her daughter was infatuated and only a stern word from him would put an end to her virtual encampment in the corner of the waiting room. Elworth had guessed and showed no sign of impatience with his thirteen-year-old stalker. But now, that girl had developed into an attractive young woman.

They studied each other for a moment. Elworth looked uneasy. "You've certainly grown," he said awkwardly.

Jenny smiled, still unsure as to what her next move was. Elworth had been blessed, it seemed, with eternal youth, and they could almost pass for a couple. I found myself unnerved watching them as they struggled to converse.

"I thought I'd drop by and see how you both were," he explained, realising that Jenny had nothing to say.

Again, Jenny smiled. "I'm okay."

"It's a difficult time—for both of you. Don't be afraid to ask for help."

"We're okay, you know. Getting by."

He turned to me, releasing Jenny from his attentions. "Are you getting any help?"

"Just the lady from the Victim Support."

Elworth nodded. "Good. Anyone else?"

"Josie and Lou Duxbury. They're family friends."

The doctor took another sip of coffee from Elizabeth's best china. "Good friends are important. It's times like this when you find out who they are."

Jenny was still standing in the doorway, studying Elworth. "I'm just going to take a bath," she said. "Is that okay?"

We both nodded, and my daughter was gone.

Soon after, the doctor left, shaking my hand and reminding me that he would always be there if we needed him. I wondered if he really had anything to offer, but I thanked him just the same. He was a professional—good at his job even though his visit had probably been nothing more than a gesture that left him breathing a sigh of relief as he climbed behind the wheel of his SUV.

***

I expected that, at some time, the flood gates would open, triggered by a neighbour's sympathy or a song on the radio, but it was neither. I remember that Saturday morning. I was making coffee and toast, and without a thought, I'd taken breakfast up to my wife on a tray, just the way I had every weekend. I stopped suddenly at our bedroom door, staring at the empty bed and wondering what the hell I was doing. I'd never see Elizabeth's recumbent frame outlined by the bed sheet. I'd never tap her gently on the shoulder, waking her from her light, morning sleep. I'd never see her face or hear her voice. She was gone. She was gone forever.

It was like being hit by a tidal wave and tossed helplessly in its black waters. The tray slipped from my grasp, crashing to the floor as I sank to my knees. I felt the vomit hit my throat, and I prayed for a release that didn't come. Jenny found me sobbing, prostrate on the floor.

"They've gone!" I cried, repeating the words over and over in a strangled voice that I hardly recognised as my own. Jenny knelt down beside me and pulled me into her arms. I felt her body shake. I felt her tears on my neck. The pain was unbearable. I felt so hopelessly lost and desperately alone, even with my daughter by my side. We held each other, afraid to let go, and cried until the pain subsided and the numbness returned.

In the days that followed, I struggled to find a reason to rise each morning. The hours stretched endlessly before me like empty chasms filled with painful memories, my heart gripped by the icy steel claw of grief. Life, it seemed, had no point. We scoured the holiday sites online. Jenny wanted to go to Halkidiki. We'd spent two weeks there as a family, but I wasn't so sure. A pilgrimage to the old haunts, eating at the restaurants we'd enjoyed together, filled me with trepidation. We ditched the whole idea. Neither of us was ready.

On that Sunday morning, I had learned to cry, and did so frequently, cocooning myself in the bathroom and turning on the taps to drown the sound of my sobbing.

I remember the day Jenny was born, sitting with my father in the front lounge. The old man had winked at me. "A little girl, huh?" he'd said, pulling a bottle of his finest brandy from the cupboard with an air of showmanship that reminded me of a magician pulling a rabbit from a hat. "I think this calls for a nip or two, don't you think?"

We'd sat, reminiscing, as the spring sunshine flooded the room and the old clock in the corner looked on like an old friend, listening in to my father's words of wisdom.

"I never cried in front of you, son," he'd said suddenly. "It's not that I don't believe a man should cry. But in front of your children, you should be strong. If you have to shed a tear, it should be done in private."

My father had shared his homespun philosophies with grace and subtlety, and seemed unconcerned when I had questioned them. Yet, over the years, I found myself hanging onto his words. I recalled, as a child, watching him at my mother's bedside, watching his wife as she lay recovering from a stroke, interpreting her pitiful attempts at forming basic words and turning them into sentences.

He would smile stoically, holding her hand and talking about the plans he was making, ignoring the doctors and their grim forecasts. He had never shed a tear, and I realised, much later, how his strength had brought me through those dark days. I was just a kid, looking up to my father, drawing every day on his love and compassion. If I'd seen him break down—if I'd walked in on his grief—I'd have realised that he was just a man. The trauma would have floored me.

***

Jenny took up an extra guitar lesson but I'd noticed that, rather than improving, her playing was becoming increasingly erratic. She had been desperate to master a complicated piece from Handel's Messiah but had smashed the guitar across the television in pure frustration. I looked down at her broken instrument, lying in front of the shattered screen, and I started to laugh. God only knew why.

"I didn't like that TV, anyway," I said. "And that guitar's out of tune!"

The following day, we drove into town and bought a huge plasma screen TV. Jenny bought a new guitar. We watched a movie on our new TV the following evening, sharing a bottle of Friscati and a two-litre bottle of dry cider, crawling up the stairs to bed at two in the morning. We laughed and cried our way through the movie. The crying was something we'd got used to, but the laughter felt good.

The following morning, Jenny and I watched breakfast TV through bleary eyes, with the sun pouring through the lounge window and flooding the room. We decided to drive out to the woods, maybe take a walk to clear our heads. If Jenny had noticed that her friends had given her a wide berth then she never mentioned it. We were too preoccupied just keeping each other alive. We were survivors; we had each other. I wasn't going to let anyone come between us.

Chapter Two

THE MORNINGS WERE mine; they always had been. From the spring through to autumn, I'd rise with the sun, and you would find me standing in the garden with a mug of ridiculously strong coffee, breathing in the crisp, unpolluted air. While most of the population were tapping the snooze button on their alarm clocks, I was on my second mug, at peace with the world. I often wondered how many folk shared my love of the breaking day. How many of my fellow human beings had discovered the joy and peace to be found in those hours? Whatever the day held for me, I knew that I had caught its finest moment.

I remembered that Sunday morning. I recalled the clear blue sky, and wondered if the weather might hold out until the evening. Hanna loved anything cooked on a barbecue, although Jenny was prone to inspecting my efforts with a critical eye lest I poison her with undercooked meat. I poured myself a second coffee with no premonition of what lay ahead. If God could have spoken and warned me that I had only a few hours left with my wife and child, then He had my ear. But the only sound I'd heard was the familiar song of our resident blackbird.

It was almost a year ago: twelve months without Elizabeth and my beautiful little angel. I was reliving the day when the minister from my father's church called. I'd invited him in and poured him a sugarless tea, but his pious tones and ecclesiastical concern left me feeling distinctly cold. With hindsight, I'm guessing my welcome might have appeared lukewarm. I found myself with my back to the man, staring out of the window, singing lines of a song I'd always loved: Leonard Cohen's 'Last year's Man'.

The Reverend Carson studied me warily over the rim of his china cup. He looked a good deal thinner than I'd remembered, and his dog collar hung around his long scrawny neck like a hula hoop on the waist of an anorexic teenager.

"It's a line from a Leonard Cohen song," I told him. "I've always found it rather…well, interesting."

I hadn't wanted an argument, but I couldn't let the reverend go without some kind of explanation. His God had been found wanting.

He smiled gently. "And what do you suppose this…Mr. Cohen meant?"

I shrugged. "Dunno, really. I guess he was just drawing attention to the fact that our traditional binding of a holy book involves the death of an animal. A sacrifice. Blood and skin. Ironic, don't you think?"

Carson grimaced. "Well, maybe, but we don't slaughter cows in order to bind our bibles. The skin is a by-product. We kill for food, surely."

He was right, I supposed. But I had become accustomed to thinking aloud.

"Do you listen to Mr. Cohen a lot?"

The minister's question took me by surprise.

"Not really. The line just popped into my head."

Carson grinned. "Good!" he quipped and elegantly placed his cup on the table. "Because I fear you are already growing increasingly antagonistic towards the Church…or maybe God Himself."

I hadn't been prepared for a direct challenge. I'd tried, obviously, without much success, to suppress my feelings about God. "I'm not antagonistic," I lied. "But I fail to see the Almighty in any of this."

"I know it's hard," Carson began.

"Hard? Hard?" Something snapped inside of me. "Mr. Carson, I watched my wife and daughter get crushed by two thugs. I can hear their bones snapping. I can see the blood! It haunts me every waking moment! Hard? You don't know the meaning of the word!"

Carson blushed. His God had forsaken him, leaving his servant alone to do his dirty work. "I know, I know," he said in little more than a whisper. "I can't begin to understand how you must feel. But Elizabeth and Hanna's deaths are not the work of God. You must believe that."

"So why do ministers talk about Jesus calling people home? Why Elizabeth? Why Hanna? What the hell did God want with my wife and kid when there are homes full of people just wanting to die?"

Carson shifted awkwardly in his seat. "It's a term we use to give folk comfort. Personally, I don't believe God calls people. He merely receives them, just as I trust He will receive me should this disease take its toll."

I stared at the minister, realising suddenly that, like the dog collar, none of his clothes fitted him. He saw the look in my eyes.

"I have cancer, Robert. Bowel cancer. Unfortunately, it has already spread to other organs, although the treatment seems to be buying me some time." Carson smiled. "So, you see, I, too, have questions."

The ailing minister, on the cusp of discovering if his faith had been built on a firm foundation of truth, chatted breezily, refusing to dwell on his own fate. He told me that I had coped well, steering my daughter through a traumatic time with all the skill of a loving father. But in truth, I had failed her.

Just two months after Elizabeth and Hanna's death, Jenny had found me sitting cross-legged at the grave in the rain, surrounded by empty beer cans. I'd been missing all day. Jenny had managed to pull me to my feet and taken me home where I'd crashed into the chair and fallen asleep in rain-soaked coat. It was that night I'd heard her sobbing uncontrollably in her room. It was the wail of a broken heart, and my blood ran cold as I lay in the darkness of my room.

"Dad?" I whispered. "Please help me. What would *you* do? What would you say to Jenny? Just tell me!"

I listened. I listened with an intensity that made my head ache, but heard nothing. Maybe I knew the answer already. I needed to be strong; I needed to be there for my daughter. I needed to be as much a father to her as my old man had been to me. I needed to stay away from the bottle.

I woke at six the following morning and found Jenny sitting at the kitchen table with a glass of fresh orange juice. I wanted to take her in my arms, but she was watching me from behind an invisible wall, clearly embarrassed at having discovered her father in a moment of private grief. I returned to my bed and picked up the Bob Dylan biography I'd started three weeks earlier. I managed three pages and gave up. My heart ached and my whole body felt weary. My bones were tired, and I wondered if this was how old age felt. Doctor Elworth told me that grief affects people in different ways. I had aged thirty years in just a few months.

As for young Darren Pascoe's father, Benjamin, he had lost his son, not to death, but to something he might have considered far worse—a life of hopelessness mixing with the dregs of society. Three months after his son's incarceration, he took to his bed with a bottle of whisky and a handful of pills. They found him two days later.

***

Josie Duxbury still called me nearly every day. Jo ran The Dog and Keys with her husband Lou. She was a born earth mother who took on life's problems with lead-lined boxing gloves. Elizabeth and I had often spent a Saturday evening listening to Josie belt out black soul and blues at the local clubs. She was 'the white Aretha Franklin', according to the little balding compère who introduced her each weekend with childlike enthusiasm.

Lou was a big guy with hands like shovels, a ruddy complexion and short, insanely white hair. He cut an imposing figure and was worth two pit bulls when it came to deterring potential burglars. He insisted on hugging me every time we met. It was like being mauled by a bear and then dropped, winded, on the floor.

It was Lou, an innately passive man, who had offered to go looking for Pascoe and Taylor, and I'd never seen a man filled with such rage. "I'll tell you sommat, Rob, if I catch those fucking bastards I'll tear them apart, I will. I'll rip them limb from fucking limb."

I knew it wasn't idle talk. Something inside told me that if Pascoe and Taylor walked through the door of The Keys at that moment, they'd be carried out in a box. Lou's face was almost purple with anger. I'd heard him swear twice. That was rare for the guy. He was one of life's true gentlemen who would, even in these liberal days, warn the punters about their language frequently; towering over them at six foot plus, he rarely got an argument.

***

Josie had given up the clubs and taken up psychology at St. Mary's College. Lou had never liked the idea of his wife breathing in the smoke that drifted like a creeping fog across the stage, and when her doctor had advised her that it was affecting her vocal chords, she decided to give up the stage for a quieter life.

I suppose that I became Josie's patient. She was a skilled listener who would analyse every word. I'd called in for a drink to escape the emptiness of the house but discovered that I couldn't. It was there when I woke and remained throughout each day.

Jo placed my whisky on the table and looked at me with that stern mother-like look that she reserved for these occasions. "So, Robert Adams, how the hell are *you?*"

"Lonely," I replied. "Unbearably lonely."

"You have Jenny," she reminded me.

"I know. But it feels as if we are one. We're lonely together—it's hard to explain."

Josie smiled. "Doesn't Jenny have any friends?"

I shrugged. "She did, I suppose. But they seem to be giving her some space. Maybe they just don't know what to say."

"What about boys?"

"Well, there's a lad sniffing around her at the garage," I told her. "But I don't think Jen's interested."

"Have you seen him?"

"I took a peek."

"And?"

"He seems like a nice kid. Very polite."

"Good-looking?"

"Yep, he's good-looking!"

Josie smiled, and I suppressed the urge to lean forward and kiss her. I wished, in that moment, that I could have buried the past along with the pain the memories brought with it. I wanted to begin again, cleansed of the grief that held me in a vice-like grip.

Chapter Three

Jenny and I visited the grave the day after the first anniversary, both hurting like hell. We drove with the radio switched off, alone with our thoughts; neither of us uttered a word until we reached the gates of the cemetery.

"I want to speak to Mum," she said in a tone that sounded more like a demand.

"You want some time alone?" I asked. "I'll sit in the car for a while."

Jenny looked at me as if I was crazy. "No! I want to speak to her—you know—actually speak!"

I pulled over and killed the engine. "How?" I asked, unable to mask my frustration.

Jenny shrugged. "One of the girls in school lost her dad. She went to see this medium—"

I should have let her finish, but the word *medium* sent my mind into a spin. "No! You're not."

Jenny stopped, looking as if she'd been hit in the stomach by a cannonball.

"We're not going to see a medium, Jen. It's out of the question."

I saw the tears forming in my daughter's eyes, and I remembered how fragile she really was.

"Look, sweetheart," I continued, softening my tone, "it's a dangerous game. Let's just stay well clear. Hanna and your mother are still with us. You have to believe that. You can talk to them in your heart."

Jenny turned. "Bullshit! That's what people say when they don't believe in life after death!" My daughter wiped a tear from her

21

cheek, her eyes blazing. "So you believe Mum and Hanna are just rotting in that grave? Is that it? We die and get eaten by worms?"

"I didn't say that."

"Then what *do* you believe?"

My head felt devoid of an answer yet the words tripped off my tongue. "I'm not sure. I'd like to think—"

"Well, Granddad always talked about God—what happened to you?"

I swallowed hard as another tear trickled down Jenny's cheek. My own father would have put his arm around his granddaughter's shoulders, and the words of comfort would have flowed like honey. I placed a reassuring hand on my her arm, but she pulled away. "Mum and Hanna aren't dead," she snapped. "Not really." She glared at me. "It doesn't matter whether you believe it or not, does it?"

"I want to believe, sweetheart, honestly. I'm just not as sure as I once was."

Jenny huffed and turned away, staring out of the passenger window.

"But I really don't want you to start that talking-to-the-dead stuff, okay?"

She didn't answer. The conversation was closed.

***

The following Friday, Jenny and I had lunch with Josie and Lou at a table they had dressed in the corner of The Keys. The white embroidered tablecloth seemed to glow under the light from the window, and as Jenny pulled out her chair, her eyes fell on the two red roses in the centre. "Mum and Hanna," she whispered to herself.

Josie smiled softly, but Lou looked a little embarrassed.

"Thank you," I said to him, trying to put the big guy at ease. "That was a nice thought."

Lou relaxed immediately and nodded. I swear I saw a tear form in his eye. The meal was on them. Josie ordered a bottle of champagne, although Jenny grimaced at the mere sight of it. I knew she still felt there was nothing to celebrate. For several months, she had kept herself hydrated but had barely eaten and had dropped several pounds. Josie had noticed, and I was guessing she wanted to see how my daughter dealt with a plate full of food. I could read that woman like one of her many books. The word 'anorexia' would never have passed her lips, but it was there in her mind.

Jenny ordered the chicken with pasta, and Josie seemed to relax, realising that it wouldn't have been the first choice of a girl who was starving herself. I settled for the haddock in a fancy sauce and potatoes with fresh vegetables. Jenny and I both cleaned our plates, and Josie slipped my daughter a glass of the champagne. "It won't do you any harm," she whispered. "Just don't tell your friends, okay?"

The teenage obsession with alcohol had bypassed Jenny. Too much drink made her ill, and she had experimented only a couple of times and then backed off. Maybe God had granted me one favour—a daughter who wasn't going to waste her weekends throwing up in the street outside the city clubs.

That afternoon at The Keys passed quickly. Lou bought another bottle of bubbly to the table, and we talked well into the early evening. Jenny seemed to thaw as the afternoon wore on and seemed happier than she had since she lost her mother and sister. Maybe the drink was kicking in, but I believed that there might be a future for both of us. The wounds were still open and raw. We would still ache and cry. We would still wake to empty days when the sun shone on everyone but us and left us feeling so desperately cold inside. But somewhere in my soul, I felt a faint stirring of a new life, and Jenny obviously felt strong enough to bring up the contentious issue of life after death.

"What do you think about mediums, Aunt Josie?" Jenny asked casually, pushing an empty plate away.

Josie frowned. "Mediums? Well, I'd exercise extreme caution."

Jenny seemed to accept the reply, nodding thoughtfully. "But if you found someone genuine, someone—"

"That's the whole point, hun," Josie cut in. "How do you know?"

Jenny smiled. "Well, I'd put on my best poker face. They wouldn't be getting any clues, so if my mum came through, I'd know, wouldn't I?" Jenny took a sip of water. "I'm not some silly kid. I'm not going to get taken in by some crazy old crow with a crystal ball."

Josie laughed, shaking her head. "Just be careful, hun, that's all."

I resisted adding anything to Josie's warning, having decided that the conversation would move on a lot faster if I kept my silence. When we arrived home, Jenny took herself up to her room and I took a bottle of red wine from the cupboard, intending to treat myself to a glass while watching the twenty-four-hour news channel. The glass turned into a bottle.

***

The following morning, I washed and shaved as usual, although sometimes, even this seemed like a waste of time. Who was going to worry whether I was clean shaven and smelled of soap? Who gave a shit whether my hair was greasy? Elizabeth was gone.

The metallic aftertaste of red wine remained on my tongue despite several rinses of mouthwash, and I vowed to stick to white in future.

Jenny was watching an American sit com with a coffee in her hand, suspended in front of her lips, and looked up with a cursory smile as I walked in. She had on her rose-petal pyjamas—the ones her mother had bought her for Christmas—and my heart lurched in my chest. Suddenly, we were all back together, watching Hanna rip the wrapping paper from her gifts and squeal with excitement. It was the first Christmas she had really understood the whole Santa thing. I had no idea it would be her last.

Chapter Four

I T WAS LATE summer and I thought about taking a camera and stopping off at the old church on the way to the grave. I might have got lucky and snapped the sun as it dipped behind the steeple, catching that elusive picture that would find its way onto the cover of a glossy monthly.

My relationship with photography had always been uneasy; the resulting images always appeared lifeless and uninspired. Even the idea of changing my old camera for an all-singing, all-dancing contraption failed to inspire me to get back behind the lens, and I found myself driving past the church without so much as a sideways glance.

I reached the gates of the cemetery just as the sun sank behind the trees, casting long, dark shadows across the graves. I stopped the car near the entrance and pulled on my jacket. Sometimes, when the mood took me, I found myself reading the epitaphs on the headstones. Each time, I'd take a different route, stopping at any grave that caught my eye.

There was a history engraved in every stone, lying between the lines. What, for instance, did Constance Penworth die from? Aged thirty-two and loved only, it seemed, by her husband. No other name appeared on the old white stone. No children. No brothers. No sisters. Maybe their love had begun as an illicit affair—an affair that had left them ostracised and destined to live the rest of their days alone.

I wondered if Constance was watching me as I stopped at her grave. Did the spirits of the dead gather there, hovering in the ether above their bones? Was Elizabeth waiting for me, holding Hanna close to her side? *Here's Daddy, my darling; he's come to see us.*

Jenny would talk to her mother every time we visited the grave; she would chatter freely, almost as if they were standing face-to-face. I longed for her faith, the unshakeable belief in the afterlife that would allow me to converse with my wife and child free from the restraints of my own scepticism.

I hadn't bought any flowers; the visit had not been planned. "I just thought I'd drop by, darling," I muttered uneasily, casting my eyes across the inscription bearing my name.

Beloved wife of Robert...

There was a space underneath—a space that would be inscribed with the date of my own demise. I shuddered, the reoccurring fear of being buried alive passing through me like a cold wind.

I stood over the grave for several minutes, alone in a landscape littered with bones, wood, stone and earth. Yet I felt at peace there, a member of an exclusive club which allowed me to walk freely amongst the dead with impunity. I would nod and smile in the direction of others who attended, with an understanding hanging between us. They were my brothers and sisters in grief, in loneliness, in longing. We needed no words, no explanations and no apologies.

***

When I arrived home, Jenny was in her room. Not that it would seem unusual to find a teenager sitting on her bed and watching TV, but my daughter was not a bedroom girl, preferring to sit at the kitchen table, surfing the net and chatting to friends on social media. I left her. Maybe she needed some space.

But over the following days, I found her spending more and more time alone, venturing down only to make herself a coffee before disappearing again. She was pale, and had that look of a rabbit caught in the headlights of a car. I felt the storm clouds gathering, I swear. Was it a premonition, or was it an inert sense that since the deaths of Elizabeth and Hanna, everything in my life was destined to go wrong?

On the night it all began, Jenny had, as far as I can recall, eaten nothing but a piece of fruit and a diet drink. I'd started to wonder if Josie's suspicions had been well-founded. Maybe she might have taken to one of these starvation diets and was staying out of my way. Maybe she needed something she could control: the image that stared back at her from the bedroom mirror.

I had a glass of whisky, my thoughts lost in the TV screen as I wondered if my decision to leave my job at a local investment company had been a wise one. Elizabeth's life insurance had paid out handsomely, and I'd cashed in my shares, leaving me with enough money to live on providing I didn't live like a lottery winner. But I needed something to fill my days—to occupy my mind. Maybe I could give Martin a ring in the morning and see if there were any vacancies.

By the time I'd emptied my glass, the day had been planned. I took a few gulps of cold water and turned off the lights. I didn't bother to undress but collapsed onto the bed, falling into a hazy sleep as soon as my head touched the pillow.

At two in the morning, I was wakened by a scream.

I ran to Jenny's room to find her sitting up in her bed, shaking violently. She was staring in my direction, but I knew that she wasn't focusing. Her eyes were filled with what I can only describe as pure, unadulterated terror.

"Jenny!" I cried, fearing to approach her. "What the hell…"

My voice seemed to cut through her semi-consciousness. She blinked, fell back onto her pillow and sighed deeply. "A dream," she gasped. "Just a dream…" Her eyes closed. "I'm okay…go back to bed."

The following morning, I attempted to elicit some kind of explanation from my daughter, treading like a barefooted man through broken glass. But Jenny would offer me nothing, claiming that she couldn't remember. I didn't believe her. I could still see the fear in my daughter's eyes.

***

"She's hiding something from me," I told Josie the following day. "I just can't work out what it could be."

Jo thought I was imagining it all. "It's probably just a phase," she told me with a reassuring air of confidence. "And as for the nightmare—well, that ain't rocket science, is it? She's probably reliving the accident."

"Then why couldn't she tell me?"

Josie just looked at me as if I'd grown another nose. "Come on, Robert, you're not that stupid. The kid isn't going to risk upsetting *you*, is she?"

When I left Josie, I felt a little happier. It was all part of the grieving process—the loss, the loneliness, the memories of that Sunday afternoon which haunted me every day. I had never relived the moment in my dreams. I'd been spared the terror of watching my wife and daughter dying all over again.

I didn't call Martin. I'd only be talking to an answering machine, and my ex-boss was never that good at returning calls anyway.

***

We visited the grave together the next weekend. It was the first time my daughter had ventured outside of the house in nearly two weeks, but her mood hadn't changed. It was as if she had given up on life, choosing to wallow in her own misery. I'd tried to talk to her, but the replies barely formed the basis of a sentence, and I'd hoped that the visit to the grave might at the very least provoke a conversation of some kind.

We stopped at the florist and bought a bunch of flowers—pink and white. Jenny nodded her approval as I placed them on her knee and slid back behind the wheel and fired up the engine. The journey was undertaken in silence with the radio playing low. I turned it off as we drove through the gates of the cemetery.

"I don't know why we bother coming here," Jenny mumbled. "Mum and Hanna aren't here, so why are we?"

I turned. Jenny was staring ahead of her. "Because the grave is here, that's why we come."

"Wrong!" Jenny spat. "Their rotting flesh and bones are here. Mum and Hanna are with us—all the time—every day!"

We were back on the subject of my scepticism, and it was eating Jenny up.

"So where do you suggest we go to place flowers and pay our respects?"

Jenny shrugged. "Does it matter?"

"It does!" I retorted angrily." It matters to me!"

I pulled up and killed the engine. "Look, Jen, I don't know what this is all about, but for the past two weeks—"

She didn't let me finish. "What? You think I should be out clubbing, getting pissed and shagging anything with a pulse? Would that make you happy?"

"No, I didn't say—"

"You want me to be happy? How? How can I be happy?"

"Jenny...I—"

"Dad!" She glared at me with a hatred in her eyes that was like a stab in the heart. "Why don't you just stop fucking with my head?"

Jenny flung open the door, pulling free of my hand as I reached out to stop her. She was gone before I'd drawn breath. I watched in desperation, never having heard my daughter use even the mildest of swear words. Her grandfather had instilled the old-fashioned values he had held and lived by. He believed that there was nothing as vulgar as bad language, and only in extreme circumstances could it be forgiven. Maybe this was one of those occasions. I didn't know.

I stood at the grave alone, waiting, hoping. But Jenny was nowhere to be seen. I spent the whole afternoon searching, texting and calling while wandering between the graves, nodding in the direction of my brothers and sisters in grief and asking if anyone had seen a teenage girl. No one had. I drove home expecting to find Jenny in her room, but her bed remained unmade and the curtains were still drawn. I called Kelly Dawson's house. If she had needed a friend, Kelly would have been top of the list. Mrs. Dawson answered the phone.

Kelly's mother was a petite blonde who pretty much lived in Lycra. I'd met her at a couple of parents' evenings and mistaken her for Jenny's teacher. She ran keep-fit classes at the local gym, which she conducted with an enthusiasm that left her subjects exhausted and debating if they would return the following week. Despite this, she had a warm manner.

"Jenny?" she said. "No, we haven't seen her for some time. Is there a problem?"

"It's nothing, really. She's probably out walking, trying to clear her head."

Kelly's mother laughed. "Aye, probably. I'm sure she's okay. Jenny's a sensible girl."

I replaced the receiver and flopped back into my chair. I was weary, yet to close my eyes was an invitation for the demons who would be lingering on the other side. I flicked the remote and the TV burst into life like a faithful old friend.

And on tonight's programme...

A young woman in her mid-twenties stared out at me from the screen. In the background, children played at the water's edge while their parents basked in the Mediterranean heat. My mind slipped back. Suddenly, I was standing on the beach in Kos, watching Elizabeth at the water's edge holding Hanna's hand. Jenny was riding the waves, a fourteen-year-old girl in a skimpy white bikini, unaware that several boys were watching her as she climbed onto the cheap plastic dinghy. My daughter had grown into a young woman overnight, and I'd only just noticed.

The phone rang, abruptly interrupting my thoughts. It was Kelly Dawson's mother.

"Mr. Adams? I've spoken to Kelly. She's going to try texting her...just thought it might help."

I thanked Mrs. Dawson profusely, feeling a wave of warmth towards this woman for her concern. I could hear the scream ringing in my head. The scream that rang out in the night—the look of terror on my daughter's face. Mrs. Dawson listened as I told her about Jenny's dream and her reclusive behaviour. We had something in common; we both had teenage girls. Josie might have been the psychologist, but neither she nor Lou knew what it was like to bring up a child, and right now I needed a little guidance.

"If I was you," she said softly, "I'd back off. Let her come to you. That's what I've always done with Kelly, and invariably she opens up when she's good and ready."

I thanked Mrs. Dawson again and replaced the receiver, knowing that I could do nothing but wait for Jenny to return. When she did, I'd make her a large cappuccino and a plate of hot, buttered toast. I'd ask no questions. As far as I was concerned, the incident at the graveyard had never happened.

But by eleven that night, Jenny hadn't returned. I tried to suppress the fear that was rising within me. My daughter had, after all, walked off in the heat of an argument; she was teaching her father a lesson and she just might stay away long enough to make sure I learned it.

I didn't sleep. The whisky did nothing but burn my throat, leaving a thick coating on my tongue that tasted like the hide of a wild boar. I showered and shaved the following morning, taking several swills of mouthwash and brushing my teeth until the sour taste of stale alcohol had been drowned by peppermint.

The radio presenter was quizzing a caller on his taste in music while I poured myself a fresh orange juice from the fridge. That's when I heard Jenny's key in the door. My heartbeat quickened. *Say nothing. Remember the plan. A coffee and a plate of hot, buttered toast. Okay?*

There was a welcome sound of footsteps on the stairs. It didn't matter. I'd take her breakfast up and leave it outside the door—just like a hotel. I'd be her waiter until she was ready to treat me as her father. Then, I'd listen the way her mother listened, and I'd resist the urge to shake her into unconsciousness for being an eighteen-carat little bitch.

I left the toast and the coffee on a tray outside her door and called through before leaving. It was several minutes before I heard any movement. Jenny stayed in her room for the rest of the day while I continued to serve food and hot drinks, never breathing more than a word to let her know that there was a tray on the other side of the door. My heart ached; it ached for Elizabeth. It ached for Hanna. It ached for Jenny. I longed for my father; I longed for his faith, his ever-present God, because I was useless at coping with life on my own.

I left a cup of hot chocolate at her door that night before taking to my bed with Bob Dylan's autobiography. I managed another chapter but the words were lost in a fog. My head ached and my eyes were heavy, yet when I dozed, it was nothing more than a light and fitful sleep. The bedside lamp remained on and the book was still in my hand as the sun rose in a cloudless sky, illuminating the blanket of frost that covered the ground. Hanna would have been screaming in delight, "It's snow, Daddy! It's snow!"

I wandered downstairs, my eyes still heavy. Why did this feel like the mother of all hangovers when I hadn't even touched a drink? I went to open the fridge but stopped suddenly. On her fourth birthday, Elizabeth had bought Hanna an alphabet of brightly coloured plastic letters that decorated the fridge door. They reminded me daily of my baby's love of colour, but now I stood rooted, staring at the words they formed.

FIND ME

It could only have been Jenny. She must have ventured downstairs during the night while I'd slept. Was this a cry for help? *Find me?* What did she mean?

I called softly though her bedroom door and waited before tentatively opening it. Jenny was lying in her bed, staring at the ceiling. "Jenny?"

She turned her head, looking at me with eyes that told me nothing. She was so pale—almost white.

"I saw your message on the fridge…"

Jenny frowned.

"The letters—you spelled out a message."

Something inside me froze. My daughter knew nothing about it. I could tell before the words left her lips.

"What letters?" she asked drowsily. "I haven't even been downstairs!"

Back off. Mrs. Dawson's words had never left my mind. I simply nodded my acceptance and tried to mask the confusion I felt. I told Jenny that I was taking a walk and would be back later that morning. She nodded without a hint of a smile and closed her eyes.

I walked for several hours, along the maze of footpaths that took me through the acres of farmland stretching from the borders of our suburban haven. I stopped at the old church to spend a half an hour feeding my morbid curiosity. I had become something of an obsessive grave reader. When I returned, Jenny was still in her room. The silence disturbed me. No music, not even the faintest hint of movement. I prayed that Mrs. Dawson was right, and my daughter would finally feel the need to confide in me.

I continued to play the hotel waiter for the next two days, serving Jenny her food on a tray and grateful that the plates were returned clean. At least she was eating; small mercies and all that. Finally, I found the courage to ask if she was okay, attempting to sound as breezy as I could. Jenny just nodded and flashed me a fake smile that vanished almost before it had registered. Her TV was on but the sound was down. My daughter turned away as if she couldn't bear to look at me for more than a few seconds at a time. I left her watching the flickering images on the screen.

The plastic letters on the fridge... I'd resisted the urge to remove them altogether. But on the Thursday morning, after a night of high winds and battering rain, I found they had been rearranged again. A single word.

HYPOCRITE

I could hear the scream inside my head. I wanted to sweep the letters away and run. It was nine—too early for a whisky, but I needed a drink. I called Josie and set off for The Keys, where Lou made me a strong coffee and sat me down in the corner. Josie slid into the chair opposite and listened as I tried to make sense of the thoughts bouncing around in my head.

"Well, if it wasn't Jenny, and it wasn't you..." She hadn't felt it necessary to finish the sentence.

"Yeah, I know—we have a ghost!"

Josie smiled. "I hate to state the obvious, but you must know in your heart that this is down to Jenny and her state of mind."

"She's not crazy, Josie."

I tried to sound casual but failed. I was the typical worried father who had woken suddenly to find he had to start using a skill that had lain dormant for years. Elizabeth had been adept at dealing with our children's tantrums and moods. I had managed, like most men, to slink into the shadows until the storm had passed.

"Of course she's not crazy," Josie said peaceably. "She's grieving, she's confused, she's crying out for help. Maybe she doesn't even realise it."

I took a mouthful of coffee, almost emptying the cup. Josie sipped hers as if to remind me of how civilised folk took their drink. "I think she may need some professional help," she said, treading softly across my male ego. "It doesn't mean that you're a bad parent. You're a fantastic dad—really, Rob, you are. But Jenny needs to talk to someone who isn't so close—someone trained to deal with this kind of stuff."

I nodded slowly. Josie was right. An annoying habit of hers. "I'll look into it."

"Maybe I could have a chat. It may be better coming from me."

She was right again. I couldn't even imagine how Jenny would react if I suggested she should see a shrink. I'd be dodging a few flying plates, that's for sure.

I hadn't mentioned the word I'd found on the fridge that morning, and I'd not been able to work out exactly why I was supposed to be a hypocrite. I'd left Josie, agreeing to keep a low profile around my daughter, but that night, I was wakened by voices coming from her room.

I raced up the stairs, flinging open the door. Jenny was sitting on the edge of the bed, her face lit by the flickering images on the TV screen, her eyes wild with fear. I stood, frozen, wondering what the hell I was supposed to do and instinctively reached out and turned on the light. The bulb exploded, the noise catapulting Jenny back into the world.

At first, it seemed as if she didn't even know who I was, recoiling in fear as I approached.

"Sweetheart, it's me!" I sat beside her, tentatively placing an arm around her shoulder. "Jen, we need to talk."

There was no reply, but at least she wasn't pulling away. That had to be a start.

"These dreams," I began. "Can you tell me about them?"

Jenny shook her head. "I'm sorry, Dad." Her voice was little more than a strangled whisper.

"You're seeing Mum and Hanna, aren't you? Look, don't worry—I can handle it."

Jenny shook her head. "It's not about them," she whispered, staring down at her clasped hands.

I was making progress, and I wanted to push harder for some kind of explanation, but Jenny wasn't ready. I left her briefly and returned with a cup of hot chocolate. Josie would have been proud of me. Robert Adams, a man who normally stormed over people's sensitivities in clown's boots, was tiptoeing around his daughter's emotions with the grace of a ballet dancer.

"You know where I am…whenever you're ready."

I left her cupping the mug in her hands and went to bed, opening the Dylan book at chapter nine. I wanted to be awake if Jenny decided to talk, but by three in the morning, my eyes were closing. I looked in on Jenny and was relieved to find her sleeping peacefully. The TV continued to flicker on the rolling news channel.

***

I woke with a start later that morning, realising immediately that I'd slept late. The sun blazed through the window, and I could hear Jenny moving about in her room. It was nine-thirty. I washed and shaved, looking in on my daughter, who was busy surfing on her phone. She shot me an absent smile, and I resisted the temptation to glance over her shoulder, deciding it might be better to leave and make myself a strong coffee.

The letters on the fridge door caught my eye.

**AA BB CC DD FF GG H JJ KK LL M N OO PP QQ RR TT UU VV
WW XX YY ZZ**
S H E I S M I N E

I stared at the letters. *She is mine? Jenny?*

I called Josie from my mobile, standing under the tree at the bottom of the garden. "She is mine? What the bloody hell's that supposed to mean? Why is she doing this stuff?" I was talking an octave higher than normal, sounding, even to myself, like a chipmunk caught in a trap. Josie was trying to calm me down.

"Listen, Rob, you mustn't say anything to Jenny—promise me?"

"Sure."

"This could be nothing more than a game. She might be trying to freak you out!"

"But why?"

"Because she's angry. It may be totally unfair, hun, but she might be blaming you for Elizabeth and Hanna's deaths."

"*My* fault?"

"No, hun, I know it *wasn't* your fault, but she's grieving, and grief can twist people's minds. She's just a kid—you need to remember that."

I sensed that Josie did not want to elaborate.

"Anyway, if it is a game then she'll grow tired of it if you just ignore the whole thing. Just keep showing her plenty of TLC."

I walked back into the house and poured a coffee. I had a choice. Did I leave Jenny's message for her to alter in her own time? But then she might think I hadn't noticed it.

S H E I S M I N E

It was an aggressive statement—a kind of *hands off*—but what the hell was she trying to tell me. Who was she pretending to be? Elizabeth?

She is mine.

I slouched back in front of the TV and turned on the BBC's twenty-four-hour news channel. A political analyst with a face like a squashed tomato was assessing the chancellor's tax reforms and the possibility of an early election. I killed the sound and turned on the hi-fi.

It was Frank Sinatra at his best, digitally re-mastered and sounding as timeless as ever. I closed my eyes and let the music wash over me, feeling totally helpless and way out of my depth. I imagined that I was drowning, allowing the water to fill my lungs as I surrendered my soul to the ocean.

There was nothing I could do but wait until my daughter had worked this thing out, and if there was any counselling to be done then it would be down to the professionals.

Chapter Five

JOSIE CALLED TWO days later to ask after Jenny, but there was nothing to report. Her mood had changed little, and our exchanges had remained courteous but brief. I'd replaced the bulb that had blown and rearranged the letters on the fridge door; the alphabet had been restored. Jenny ventured down a couple of times to pour herself a glass of milk, looking as pale as the liquid she emptied into Hanna's plastic beaker. Jenny hadn't given the letters a second glance.

I'd left her only to take in some fresh air, returning to a home that was becoming a prison to my daughter. I longed to know what was troubling her, but each time I'd looked in on her, I'd seen something in her eyes that told me to keep my distance.

Josie was trying to sound upbeat. "Lou wants to know if you two fancy coming over for a meal."

I cupped the handset, keeping my voice to little more than a whisper. "I'm not sure. I can't get Jenny out of her bedroom—I'd have to literally drag her over the doorstep."

"It's worth asking. Don't worry if she's not up for it, hun, we'll understand."

Josie was, in her own words, a lapsed Catholic, while Lou was brought up as an Anglican and had spent his boyhood singing in the choir. They were what my father affectionately referred to as God's prodigal children. But before we had said our goodbyes, Josie had promised to reacquaint herself with the Almighty and pray for me.

That afternoon, I answered the door to find one of my neighbours standing on the step. She greeted me as if she was relieved to discover that I hadn't thrown myself under a train.

"Hi, Mr. Adams. Good to see you! Just called to see how things are going."

Caroline Unsworth. I hadn't seen her for some time but recalled that she worked for the Samaritans. She had a ruddy, farmer's wife kind of complexion, with a mop of almost stylishly unkempt hair. I invited her in.

"I hope you don't mind me calling," she said, hovering over a chair, waiting for the invitation to sit. "I always think this can be quite a difficult time…people think you are starting to move on…"

Jenny appeared suddenly at the door. She stared at Caroline and then at me. "What's going on? Did you invite her?"

If Caroline Unsworth had become accustomed to dealing with raw human emotion then Jenny had caught her off guard. My daughter glared at me, her eyes red-rimmed and almost manic. Caroline's jaw dropped. She, too, was staring at me. *How have you allowed this to happen?*

"Mrs. Unsworth just dropped by…to see how we were doing."

"Well, I'm fine," Jenny hissed. "If I wanted to call your lot, I would have done it by now, so you two can talk all you want. I'm going back upstairs!"

"Jenny!" There was an authority in my voice that I barely recognised. "We have a visitor! Don't be so ignorant!"

My daughter stared at me. What was that I saw in those eyes? Hatred? No. It was confusion. Confusion and fear.

Caroline smiled warmly at her as Jenny slumped into a chair without a word.

"Now, who's for a coffee?" I asked and left before either had a chance to reply.

My heart was thumping hard as I strained to hear what was going on in the other room. The sound of a boiling kettle all but drowned the beginning of a stilted conversation.

"So how have you been, Jenny?"

"Fine."

"You don't look fine…"

Silence.

"Jenny?"

"Well, I am fine…"

I hadn't wanted my daughter to give Caroline an easy ride. I wanted this rather pleasant professional counsellor to understand that Jenny's problems couldn't be resolved with a few well-chosen words, so I waited a while.

When I walked back into the room, Caroline was sitting on her own.

"I'm sorry," she said, looking up wearily. "But it was no use… She's not ready."

I handed her a mug of steaming black coffee with no sugar. "I was advised to give her some space," I said, feeling vindicated by my daughter's exit.

Caroline smiled and sipped her coffee as I recounted the tale of my daughter's reclusive behaviour—the phone call from Kelly's mother, the nightmares and the terror I'd seen in her eyes. She nodded, listening attentively. I felt as if I was telling her an old story—a story she'd heard a million times over—that was, until I started telling her about the messages on the fridge door.

FINDME
HYPOCRITE
SHEISMINE

Caroline looked perplexed. "And she really doesn't remember anything about it?"

"Well, if she does, she's good at acting dumb."

"It sounds as if she's imagining that her mother is talking to her. Maybe that's who the messages are supposed to be from."

"Then why is she asking me to find her? And why is she calling me a hypocrite?"

Caroline thought for a moment. "Has Jenny been trying to contact her mother?"

"She wanted to. That's all I know."

"That might explain the *find me* message"

"And the *hypocrite* thing?"

Caroline smiled sweetly. "That would be between you and your daughter."

***

I managed another two chapters of Bob Dylan that night, before drifting into some kind of semi-consciousness that was as close to sleep as I could hope for. Maybe it was an inner sense that left me so restless, because at ten minutes past two, I was wakened by the sound of breaking glass.

Fear propelled me from my bed, dreading what awaited me on the other side of the door. My blood runs cold even now. I still dream. I still see my daughter standing there, lit only by the glow of the bedside light, her eyes wide, blood dripping from the hand that gripped a shard of glass.

Had this been anywhere else, I would never have recognised my own child. She had the face of a demon, her hair as wild as her eyes.

"Jenny?"

The same beautiful girl who had emerged from the ocean in her bikini, looking like a goddess only a few years earlier, had been transformed into a being from the other side of hell itself.

"Stay away from me," she hissed.

I hardly recognised the voice that seemed to emanate from her belly. Even her eyes, those beautiful brown eyes, looked as black as night.

She took a step towards me. "Hypocrite!" Her breath was stale—a smell I knew but couldn't quite recall. "Hypocrite! Hypocrite! Hypocrite!"

Her voice grew louder as I stepped back. "Jenny!"

Shout louder. Scream at her!

"JENNY!"

I lunged forward and grasped her shoulders. The shard of glass dropped from her hands, landing at my feet as her eyes rolled. In that moment, I believed that I'd lost my only child.

Jenny crumpled, slipping from my grasp and falling to her knees. The lids closed on her lifeless eyes as she crashed forward, her head hitting the floor with a sickening thud.

I saw the blood trickling from her mouth as I knelt beside her and frantically searched for the heartbeat I was afraid I'd never find. I whispered her name, stroking her hair as I felt the gentle throbbing signs of life through my fingers. She had a pulse. She was alive.

Had anyone walked into the room that night, they would have sworn they had stumbled upon a tragedy: a sobbing father hovering over the body of his daughter. Her skin was cold to the touch—so cold that I wondered if I was imagining the pulse I had felt in her wrist. Her hand was bleeding from the gash. The glass had cut deep into the flesh of her palm.

"Jenny?"

I called her name once more, willing my daughter to open her eyes. "I'm so sorry, sweetheart. If I've let you down…I'm sorry!"

It was almost as if I'd uttered the words she had been waiting for. Her eyelids flickered and her bloodied hand moved.

"Jenny?"

Her eyes opened.

"Jenny?"

I saw the faintest of smiles that told me my daughter was back. *Be careful. Don't rush her!*

"It's okay, darling. Everything is going to be just fine."

My words carried the conviction that I felt at that moment. I was convinced we would find that elusive peace that lay like an oasis in our barren hostile world of grief. It was a journey we had to make together, supporting each other. We didn't need the help of anyone else. From now on, it was just the two of us. If only I'd known how wrong a man could be.

Chapter Six

I DROVE JENNY to the Accident and Emergency early that morning and watched as she sat impassively while the nurse tended to the wound. Jenny needed twelve stitches, but there were no questions, and that suited me fine.

We headed home in silence—a world that I had become accustomed to. At least I had my daughter with me—what more did I want? Conversation? An Aretha Franklin track was playing on the iPod I had plugged in. I turned it up just as the radio tripped in, and Lenny Trent—a presenter with a heavy Northern accent who considered himself to be 'the voice of the people'— piped up…

Did anyone see that psycho freak on TV last night? What was his name?

Someone in the studio called out.

Ah, yes—that's it—Orson Pennyworth! Well, waddya think? He hears voices, right? Dead people talk to this guy. Okay—we all know about mediums, but this bloke takes the biscuit! They speak to him in his dreams, and then he goes looking for them! Well, what would you say if some nutter turned up on your doorstep and told you that he'd been talking to your old man?

Jenny leaned forward and turned the radio off.

"I was listening to that."

My daughter looked at me as if I had just slithered from under a stone. "He's an ignorant prick. Why would you want to listen to that drivel?"

45

Jenny turned away, and I decided it was one of those *least said* situations. It was true, Lenny Trent did seem like a man who liked the sound of his own voice, but he'd touched a nerve. Trent had talked about a man who heard dead people communicating with the living...in their dreams. Was Jenny hearing the voice of her mother? Did she think Elizabeth was talking to her? And, if she was, what was she saying?

But I had seen the look of terror in my daughter's eyes. Could that have been the result of a dream about her own mother?

I drove home on autopilot, trying to construct an opening line that I could deliver to my daughter without arousing the demons that lurked within her. I had turned into a father who lived on the edge, fearful of his own child and consumed by the need to regain some kind of control.

When I closed the front door behind us, Jenny kicked off her trainers and headed for the stairs.

"Jenny."

I had hoped to find an edge in my tone, a hint of authority that she might respect, but my voice cracked, and all that escaped my lips was a sound that resembled an expiring frog. It sounded weak, but my daughter heard a voice, thick with emotion. She stopped and turned. In that moment, our eyes met, and I saw the girl I thought I'd lost forever.

"I want to help, sweetheart."

A tear trickled down Jenny's face. "But you can't help, Dad. That's the problem."

I felt a burning sensation in the back of my throat as fresh tears formed in my eyes. "I can't go on like this, Jen. I'm going crazy!"

Jenny turned and continued, treading the stairs heavily. My heart sank. I was losing her again.

Give her some space.

I thought of my father; his grace, the depths of wisdom on which he could call. He would never have told me that he was going *crazy*! I had longed to walk in his footsteps but knew that I'd forever be living in his shadow. A feeling of utter hopelessness and failure consumed me. "Sweetheart," I called after her. "I can never be the man your grandfather was. He would know exactly what to say, and if he was here today, I know you would be with him now."

Jenny stopped dead. For a moment, she stood without flinching. I waited, knowing the love that existed between my father and his granddaughter. The mere mention of his name would bring tears to her eyes as the memories flooded back.

"This isn't about words, Dad. It's gone beyond that."

My daughter turned, lowering herself onto the stair, and sat facing me. "You can't talk away the dreams. You can't stop her!"

In the dim light of the hallway, I saw the look of despair on her face. "You're talking about your mother?"

Jenny shook her head. "If only."

"Then who?"

Jenny remained silent for a moment, but when she answered, her voice was on the edge of breaking. "I can't tell you."

I sat down beside her. "Jen, however frightening—they *are* just dreams…"

Jenny shook her head. "No, Dad, they're not. When I wake, I still feel her, as if…as if she's inside me! I feel her in the room!"

"Who? Who is it? You have to tell me, babe. You have to."

The words that escaped my lips were empty, for in my mind, I was standing in front of the fridge door looking at the messages that had appeared: *find me.*

"It's my fault, Dad." Jenny began to sob. "It's all my fault!"

My daughter stood and continued up the stairs, leaving me sitting alone. I heard the bedroom door close. *Dad,* I whispered, *for God's sake, help me!*

The silence left me feeling cold. What had I come to expect from the dead? A voice? A vision? A message on the fridge door? I found myself almost running through to the kitchen, praying that the plastic, multicoloured letters would form a sentence, a revelation. But they remained as I had left them. The alphabet. Every letter in its place.

I watched TV until I passed out, and woke with the dawn chorus, my neck aching and my eyes confronted by a young presenter reading the early morning news. I passed Jenny's room on the way to the bathroom; her door was open. I stopped and peered in. The bed was unmade, clothes littered the floor. But Jenny had gone.

I called Josie later that day, convinced that Jenny would be sitting in Kelly's bedroom clearing her head.

"I wouldn't normally advise you to do this, hun, but maybe you should start your own investigations."

"Investigations?"

There was a pause, as if Josie was having second thoughts. "Yeah, you know...have a little scout around."

"You're talking about her bedroom?"

"Well, that would be the best place to start."

"I can't...it's..."

"Yeah, yeah, it's an invasion of privacy and all that shit! Listen, Robert, if my kid was wandering around the house leaving weird messages on the fridge and waking up with broken glass in her hand, I wouldn't be worrying about space and privacy. I'd wanna get the thing sorted, okay?" Josie sounded exasperated by my wariness. "Look on her phone. You might just get some clues, hun. If she's been spending days stuck in that bedroom, it's quite possible she's been up to something."

I paused only briefly outside Jenny's door, afraid, even in her absence, of what I might find on the other side. The hinges seemed to squeak as I pushed on the handle; I closed my eyes, wondering if the weight I felt in my stomach was tension or guilt.

I glanced through the window, checking that Jenny wasn't walking down the road. The whole place, the house, the world outside, seemed eerily silent.

I shuddered, surveying the bookshelf. *Narnia. Bridget Jones.* A couple of chick-lit paperbacks, but no diary; no schoolbooks. I turned anxiously, expecting to find my daughter watching me with cold, stony eyes, before cautiously pulling open the top drawer of her bedside cabinet. *Great—underwear! I'm actually trawling through my daughter's knickers and bras!*

The second drawer was full of CDs, and I was about to close it when I caught sight of a box. I remembered Elizabeth arriving home with the set of six CDs her last Christmas: a presentation set of virtually everything Elvis had recorded. Jenny had just discovered the King of Rock 'n' Roll, and my wife had swooped on the special offer in a closing-down sale and proudly presented it to our daughter who, thinking it had been my idea, threw her arms around my neck.

I was no detective, but I knew the CDs were loose amongst the others in her collection. *Elvis Live! Elvis Love Songs. Elvis Rocks.* They were all there. All the music would have now been on her iPod; the discs and the player were clearly redundant. I pulled out the box, glancing once more out of the window. No one. Not a soul. The place was like a ghost town. My hands shook with nervous anticipation as I pulled open the lid.

Inside, and quite obviously intended for no one's eyes but her own, was a lined notebook. It was pink, about the size of the exercise books she'd used at school. I touched it, half expecting to be struck down for my transgressions. I was grossly uncomfortable with my intrusive behaviour no matter how necessary or well intentioned it might have been. In my quest for an answer, I'd secretly hoped to find nothing more than a few innocent sketches and teenage ramblings, but I was to be disappointed.

On the first page, a sketch of what appeared to be a couple of young boys hanging side by side from a crude wooden gallows. I'd almost forgotten Jenny's artistic prowess; her A* grade in art was achieved with little effort or even, I suspect, interest.

I stared at the pencil drawing. She'd captured the likeness perfectly. Darren Pascoe and Kevin Taylor's bodies hung lifelessly from their nooses, staring back at me from the page. I shuddered. My daughter had never even mentioned their names, and I'd considered this as a sign that she had somehow accepted that the death of her mother and sister had been an accident.

Now, I realised that Jenny had found comfort in a sketch depicting Pascoe and Taylor's execution, knowing that in reality, they would never have to pay for what they'd done. I turned the page to find my daughter's erratic, sloping scrawl—untidy enough to have merited a note from the teacher in my day. Although she had omitted an address in the top left-hand corner, the page had been set out in the form of a letter.

Dear Mum. It began. I shuddered. It were almost as if the temperature had dropped ten degrees in those few seconds. I read on.

> *I guess there's nothing I can tell you, is there? You see everything now though I don't think dad really believes this. He is not like Granddad who taught me about God and the eternal soul. Why do you think this is, mum? Why has he lost his ability to believe in anything he cannot see? This is surely the curse of the materialistic, not my own father.*

I felt a jolt, like a knife through my gut.

> *Forgive me, Mum, but sometimes I wish I was with you, wherever you are. I miss Hanna like crazy. Sometimes I swear I can hear her laughing. Maybe I*

can…I'm always listening, Mum—always—so if you can come through, I won't be afraid… Look after Hanna, won't you? Love, Jen. xxxx

I flipped the page with a physical ache in my stomach.

Dear, dear Mum,

Dad went ballistic when I suggested that we tried to contact you! I know that Granddad was sceptical about mediums—I seemed to remember that it said something about them in the Bible…like STAY AWAY! But he would have understood. Dad doesn't! I don't think he even believes in an afterlife anymore but if you would give him a sign—anything—then he might just change his mind. I love you, Mum…wherever you are…Jen. xxx

I closed the book, my hands trembling, and sat for a moment. Jenny had two parents. One dead. One, alive. Yet she had chosen to unburden her soul to the one who was lying six feet under a slab of stone. I had never considered myself to be a *bad* parent— sure, I'd made mistakes and I could have listened harder when she was a kid with an aptitude for incessant chatter—but I never considered myself second to the deceased.

I must have sat, sinking further into the mire of self-pity for nearly half an hour before finally picking up Jenny's macabre journal. I flipped another page.

Dear Mum,

Last night, I had a dream. It WAS a dream, I know that. But it was so real. I saw this girl—or was it a young woman? She was in this really gloomy room. It was awful—like a prison… She was sitting at on old wooden table, looking out of a tiny window, and there was a book in front of her. The page was blank, and beside the book was a pen and an inkwell. She turned towards me as I stepped into the room. She had huge eyes like that Scream *painting that they use for Halloween masks. She looked like a zombie and was shaking violently too. Her whole body was trembling like someone had plugged her in.*

I wanted to run but my feet wouldn't move. She stared at me for ages, and I tried to scream. I wanted to scream, but all that left my mouth was a rush of air. Then she spoke to me. 'So, you have come at last, my child!' Her voice was low and rasping, like someone was choking her. Then she turned away, looking out of the window and began to cry. I can hear her crying... even when I'm awake! What does she want, Mum? What have I done...?Jen xxxx

***

I pulled up in the only empty space in the car park at the back of the local library. Jenny's notepad lay on the seat beside me, filled with everything I needed to know, but without the luxury of time, I was unable to study.

There was a faint scent of wood and leather that I found strangely comforting as I walked into the library. The middle-aged woman behind the desk, who looked as if she had been born to the job, glanced up at me over her thick-rimmed spectacles and flashed me an officious smile.

"Photocopier?" I asked.

"Over there." She pointed at the machine underneath the sign that said 'photocopier' in large blue letters. "Just bring your copies over here when you're done."

I thanked her and pulled Jenny's notebook from my pocket. I wasn't that good with copiers, but that afternoon, the place was empty apart from a couple of young girls sitting in the corner, bent over a desk full of books. I had the space, if not the time, to press the wrong buttons without an impatient queue behind me.

The instructions on the lid were mercifully simple—as if written for fools like me. I folded back Jenny's pad and laid the first page face down. The copier was wonderfully quick, and in no time at all, I had presented the librarian with twenty sheets of A4, paid up and was back behind the wheel.

When I arrived home, there was still no sign of Jenny. I replaced the notepad in the box and slid it back underneath her personal things, praying she had not inherited her mother's powers of observation. Then, creeping out of my own home, unable to rid myself of the feeling that I had just burgled a stranger's property, I climbed back behind the wheel of my car and set off for Alshaw Park.

Chapter Seven

THE DARK THUNDEROUS rain clouds had gathered overhead, threatening to break at any moment. The first spots hit my windscreen as I pulled up under the cover of a large oak tree in the leaf-strewn car park. This was the place where men brought their mistresses in the late evening. It was the place where the middle-class wannabes parked up four-wheel drives as their golden retrievers looked longingly out of the window, anticipating the freedom of the open parkland.

Today, with a storm forecast, I found myself sharing the gravel-covered, potholed parking area with a rusting Jeep and a souped-up Toyota. I had the space and the time. No screaming kids, no barking dogs. I killed the engine and, with a mixture of anticipation and dread, began to read my daughter's private ramblings.

> *Mum. I must be driving Dad insane. He's leaving food outside my door. I'm so sorry, Mum, I know you wouldn't want this, but I can't face anything. Every time I close my eyes, I see HER eyes! What does she want?*
>
> *I feel trapped here—that's weird cos the door is open. Even when I go for a pee, I feel this thing gripping me. It's like fear—a voice screaming and telling me to get back in my room. I'm going mad, Mum, and I'll end up in one of those loony bins with a straitjacket! They'll talk about me as the girl who thinks she's possessed.*

*People don't believe in all that devil stuff these days.
You're either sane or insane, a regular kid or a psycho
case. xxxx*

My father had always considered humankind's obsession with
therapy to be a substitute for the faith it had lost. The art of prayer,
and the peace it brought to the troubled spirit, had been buried
beneath a wave of scepticism. I wasn't sure if God, in whatever
form He existed, would be listening but it was worth a try. After
all, I owed it to the old man; I owed it to my girl. So I closed my
eyes and began to pray.

If God merely existed in the mind and we were quite capable of
summoning Him in times of need, resulting in an overwhelming
sense of comfort and well-being, then it was still worth a try. It
was an exercise in self-healing. Maybe they were right, but I found
myself hoping that a greater power existed—someone who was
watching over us, waiting for a call.

Chapter Eight

Dear Mum,

I was there again last night. In the room. I walked in this time—right up to the window, but I can't remember if I bothered to look out. I felt as if she was there, watching me. The book was open on the desk. It's a diary, Mum. I tried to read the page but my eyes wouldn't focus. Then her voice came from the corner of the room.

She was so weird. "It is not yet time, my daughter," she said—funny how I can recall her exact words as if they are recorded in my head. Why did she call me her daughter? Is she an ancestor trying to reach me? What does she want? When I turned, she just smiled, but it wasn't a normal smile. It was really creepy. "You can only read my words in the world in which you now exist."

When I looked back, the diary was closed, and this time I could read the words on the cover: THE DIARY OF AMELIA ROOT. I woke up shaking. I've let her in. I'm so sorry, Mum xx

The rain washed down the windscreen as I flicked the page.

Mum.

I'm going crazy. I saw myself in a white padded cell with the ghost of Granddad pacing up and down. He was crying, and I felt so bad. It was only a short dream. I must have drifted off reading some stupid novel about a girl who can't stop shopping. Anyway, I tried to stay awake last night. I was too scared to sleep!!! DIDN'T WORK! I watched a couple of movies, but even they couldn't keep me going all night. I must have passed out at about three in the morning and Amelia was waiting for me.

Honestly, Mum, these aren't just dreams. I know it sounds mad, but I feel like I'm walking into another world like those kids in Narnia. I loved those books, by the way—guess you remember how I made you read them to me every night and I'd fall asleep dreaming that you and Dad had brought me a pet lion!!!!!! I wish I was that kid again.

Amelia didn't say anything to me last night. Her eyes were red and her face was so white. The room smelled like a drain. I didn't know you could smell things in dreams, but I did. There was a mattress in the corner. I hadn't noticed it before. It was where she slept, and I think that was all she wanted me to see. When I turned back, her face was blue and rotting. I screamed but there was no sound. Then she vomited but it was just like water. She's showing me something different every night, hoping I can build a picture. I can't tell Dad. He'll just tell me that I'm having nightmares cos of losing you and Hanna, and I can't tell him about the stuff at Kelly's, can I???

There were no kisses, just a picture of a pair of eyes that sent chills running the length of my spine. What was the stuff with Kelly? What had she done? I turned the page.

Mum.

I'm so scared!!! Please help me. I'm trapped!!!! Last night, I was there in the room. Amelia was lying naked on her mattress, her head covered by a sheet. There was blood on her thighs. As I bent down, she reached up and grabbed my hand. Her nails were long and sharp as hell. I screamed. It was so horrible. I pulled back the sheet to find a skeleton with skin hanging off the bones. I tried to scream once more, but this time I coughed up bile. When I woke up, I found a cut on my hand. The room was freezing, but when I felt the radiator I burned by hand. xxxxx

I couldn't get warm. She'd followed me. I could feel her in my bedroom. I could even smell the damp. She wants something from me...but what? And why? Do you remember those horror movies with Freddie Kruger? Do you think something like that could really happen? xxxxx

My heartbeat had quickened as I read the untidy scrawl of a girl who had won a neat handwriting competition only two years previously. Freddie Kruger, strangely enough, flooded my mind with pleasant memories of those evenings sitting in front of the TV with a heavily pregnant Elizabeth covering her eyes as a succession of wary teenagers met their maker on the end of Freddie's bladed hands.

We had been, in our own opinion, good parents, but to our eternal shame had lapsed, occasionally allowing a young and restless Jenny to snuggle up next to us on the sofa and watch the mutilated murderer as he embarked on his killing sprees. I read on.

> *Mum. The only comfort I get is that I know that there is a life after death! I know that the ghost of Amelia Root has found a way through. Last night, I had a long and dreamless sleep, yet this afternoon, I dozed off listening to some music. She was waiting for me. She was kind of normal this time. Her skin was pale and smooth. She called me her 'only child'. What does she mean? Maybe I look like her daughter, because she looks so young! I need to know who she is! I've researched on the internet—nothing!*

The car shuddered as a sudden clap of thunder shook the ground. The rolling black clouds seemed to be within reach of my fingers as I opened the window, feeling the rain cool my face. I wound the window back up and sat for a moment with my eyes closed as the water ran down my cheeks. I had remained sceptical of people's obsession with spirits and ghosts, but in truth, I held a deep-seated and healthy fear of all things to do with the unknown.

Now it appeared that there could only be two explanations for Jenny's bizarre behaviour: either Amelia Root really did exist and my daughter was being stalked by her spirit, or—and in many ways, this was worse—Jenny was suffering some kind of mental breakdown.

Five years ago, I had been a helpless bystander, watching the gradual decline of Jack Jessop, a regular at The Keys. Jack was one of those eternally buoyant characters who seemed to be top of everyone's guest list when they threw a party. Jack drew people like a magnet, and I often listened to him telling his tales with a natural wit and warmth that I admired yet left me with an irrepressible jealousy.

He was approaching forty when he lost his two daughters in a car crash, but everyone thought, as I did, that if anyone was equipped for coping with such a tragedy, it was happy Jack. In the months that followed, it appeared we had all been correct. He had, after all, recovered from the death of his wife five years earlier, but no one had questioned why a youthful, good-looking man had never found anyone else.

We had never considered that he'd been living for his two girls. In them, he had seen his wife, his future and what was left of his world. He still managed to smile and regale us with stories of his daughters' adventures with an element of the old wit and charm. But it dawned on me that Jack was beginning to talk about his precious girls in the present tense. Then he began to buy them presents.

We all watched on, praying that Jack would stumble through his grief and appear on the other side in full mental health, but it wasn't to be. Six months later, I saw him walking along the road and arguing violently with his daughters, but of course, there was no one there. I wanted to pull over and drag him into the car, away from the eyes of the public, who were looking on with varying degrees of amusement and pity. I wanted to rescue him yet to my disgust, I drove on by.

Jessop had ended up in a home and died two years later. When I visited him, he'd dropped three stone and looked like a man who was waiting for the end. He believed I was his son-in-law and asked after his daughter over and over again, begging me to tell her that she was forgiven and he wanted to see her.

Jack's decline had been gradual, but few of us who drank at The Keys had not felt complicit in his downfall. We had considered him the eternal optimist with an inherent ability to find a chink of light at the end of every tunnel. We had forgotten he had no family—no brothers, no sisters—and the relatives he did have lived on the other side of the country. Looking back now, his slide into madness was almost inevitable when he was surrounded by friends who found it easier to turn a blind eye to his eccentric behaviour.

Jack's face haunted me, isolated in a failing mind, swallowed by confusion, yet as he looked up at me from the chair that had become his prison, I felt that somewhere inside the decaying shell, the seed of the old Jack was reaching out. The young nurses had all, at some time, been mistaken for his daughters and had found themselves looking into old eyes, filled with paternal love.

It was not a physical illness that took him. It was grief. And I couldn't allow Jenny to walk the same road. This time, I would step in. I thought of Josie and her fascination with the human mind. I thought of the shrinks sitting in their leather armchairs, studying my daughter over the tops of their horn-rimmed spectacles. Jenny, I knew, would not bare her soul to any of them.

Chapter Nine

I RETURNED HOME, negotiating the lanes under a leaden sky, with the copies of Jenny's makeshift diary hidden under the back seat. I felt vulnerable, sitting in a small metal box while all hell let loose around me. It was, apparently, the worst storm to hit the North in five years and a relief to finally reach home.

When I walked through the door, the phone was ringing.

"Mr. Adams?" The voice was that of a well-spoken man whom I guessed was in some kind of authority.

"Speaking," I replied.

"Mr. Adams, this is Reverend Francis."

He paused. I hadn't heard the name before. My stomach turned.

"I'm the minister at St. Jude's in Tabwell..." He paused again. People only pause when they have bad news. "I have your daughter here, Mr. Adams."

I should have felt only relief, yet it had never occurred to me that anything could have happened to Jenny. She was a smart kid with an instinct for spotting potential danger.

"I think maybe you should come on over."

***

Tabwell was a small and affluent town lying on the borders of Cheshire, renowned for its ageing middle-class population who continued to embrace the fading traditions, played the stock market during the week and stepped across the threshold of God's house each Sunday morning to thank Him for their profits and find comfort in their losses.

St. Jude's was the backdrop to many model brides who graced the covers of the various glossy wedding magazines that lined the newsagent's shelves. Its gardens had been exquisitely maintained by the Barrington family for the past hundred years, and throughout the summer, the local ladies would raise money holding tea-and-cake afternoons on the lawns.

I arrived just as the evening sun appeared from behind a black thunderous cloud. Pulling up outside the stone archway, I wondered what awaited me. The minister had refused to go into any detail on the phone, but his concern had been almost tangible.

The entrance to the church was shaded by two large beech trees, their branches forming a natural leafy arch, and as I stepped into the porch, the smell of old pews and flowers drifted on the stale air. Inside, Reverend Francis was waiting for me. He was small, around five-four, and balding.

"Mr. Adams?"

I nodded as he extended his hand. His face was surprisingly youthful while remarkably pale. I half expected him to smile and reveal vampire teeth as he shook my hand with flimsy cold fingers.

"Jenny is in the back. She's just had a cup of tea."

He spun on his heels with an ease that belied his rotund frame and strode off down the aisle at a pace that almost had me running through the patterns of light cast across the red carpet. He stopped suddenly just before the altar and spun to his left. *Definitely been a dancer,* I thought as we reached a large stained-glass window depicting the Virgin Mary cradling her child, surrounded by myriad angels.

"I found Jenny standing here with a knife in her hands," he explained. "At first, I didn't see what she'd done."

Francis wasn't looking up at the window; his eyes were fixed on the statue of St. Peter who appeared to be looking down at the stone floor. Then I saw the word sprayed across the wall behind the statue. *Hypocrite.*

"When she saw me, she dropped the knife," Francis continued. "She seemed agitated and terribly confused."

My own confusion must have been apparent.

"I don't suppose you can shed any light on why she considers St. Peter a hypocrite?" he asked.

I shook my head, but the reverend wasn't convinced.

"You look as if you've just seen a ghost, Mr. Adams."

"I'll pay for any damage," I replied meekly. "And I'll make a donation—"

The minister didn't allow me to finish. "There's no need." He patted my arm gently. "A scrubbing brush and little elbow grease will sort this out." He paused. "I'm guessing you have enough problems of your own."

He beckoned me to follow him, stopping briefly as we reached the door of the vestry; his hand hovered over the brass knob. "I'm sure Jenny will be all right..." Looking me directly in the eye, he smiled warmly. *No vampire teeth.* The door creaked as it swung open.

The whole place felt heavy with a history of which I knew nothing. Jenny was sitting in a leather chair, her hands shielding a mug. As she looked up, our eyes met. I stared into the face of a frightened, confused child. Jenny studied me for a moment, as if checking I was really there and not part of a dream.

The reverend was also watching me, gauging my reaction, and I wondered how much he knew.

"It's okay, Jen. Whatever's happened we can sort it out."

I reached over and placed my hand over hers. "Just talk to me. Tell me why I'm here."

My touch opened the floodgates. Jenny began to cry.

My father was a patient man. If I had something to tell him, he was prepared to hold his tongue until I was ready. Jenny was still sobbing, gulping the air until finally, the tears stopped. I allowed her to take a sip of tea and waited.

"I don't even know how I got here," she said. Her voice was strained and barely audible, the darkness in her soul visible in her eyes. She looked so vulnerable, surrounded by the trappings of her grandfather's faith. The stone walls, the silver challis in the corner, the framed wooden cross above the door. "I can't be here. I can't be here—I want to go home!"

The minister sat down beside her. "Jenny," he whispered.

My daughter wiped a tear from her cheek.

"I know we find it difficult to understand why God allows these things to happen, but I couldn't stand before my congregation each week if I didn't believe He loved us."

Jenny looked down at her trembling hands. "How can you say that? If He loved me, I wouldn't be going through this!"

The reverend placed an arm around Jenny's shoulders. "Jenny, do you believe that God loved His own Son? Do you believe He loved Mary?"

Jenny looked up. "Of course I do."

Francis continued, his voice barely above a whisper. "Yes, he did, yet Mary stood and watched as they took her son, stripped and humiliated him, and then beat him until his back resembled a ploughed field. She stood by as they hung him from a cross, and watched as he died in agony, crying out to a God who had forsaken him. God's love doesn't absolve us from suffering."

***

I left the reverend standing under the arch of his church. I'd insisted on sending a donation and apologised for the damage. He shook my hand and gave me God's blessing. Jenny flashed him a brief smile but seemed determined to put distance between herself and the church as quickly as possible. She climbed into the seat beside me with a look in her eyes that reminded me of a girl who had just woken up in a strange bed and was wondering how she'd got there. There was no point in asking her, but the history of the place held the answers, and I knew this wouldn't to be the last I saw of St. Jude's.

***

Josie was wearing that familiar look of motherly concern that left me feeling like a child about to receive a lecture.

"I'm really not happy about this, hun," she whispered, glancing around her lest the couple sitting more than five metres from us might overhear. "Jenny needs help—professional help."

I had told Josie about Jenny's diary, the letters it contained and the dreams, but it was clear that after eighteen months of studying the human mind, Jo had become sceptical, and that scepticism reared its head whenever I mentioned the spirit world.

The emphasis had been on the word *professional*, and Josie was in no doubt that the task was beyond me. "You can't cure her by chasing ghosts from the past, hun."

She might as well have slapped my face and kneed me in the testicles.

"I'm not taking her to a shrink," I said defiantly. "Even if Jenny agreed!"

"What about the doctor? She'd go to him."

"Elworth?"

"Sure. Didn't she have a bit of a crush on him a few years ago?"

I recalled the unease that permeated their last meeting. "I don't think it would be such a good idea. She's still a little embarrassed by the episode."

Josie grinned." Well, she's grown into a real looker, your Jen. I'm guessing Dr. Dish might be quite flattered if he thought she was still smitten."

"She isn't. That's why she won't go."

Josie shrugged. "I guess he couldn't help, anyway. It's hardly a medical problem, is it?"

"Not unless it's some kind of brain tumour—you hear about these things, don't you? People start having hallucinations and stuff like that."

"And headaches, usually. Has Jenny had—"

"She hasn't said."

"Let's put it this way, hun. I'd rather see her visiting a shrink than a surgeon!"

I hadn't really considered the possibility that my daughter's behaviour had been caused by something growing in her head, but it tripped off my tongue before I'd had a chance to stop it. The internet would have allowed me to research the tumour subject privately, but when I arrived home, I found Jenny sitting cross-legged on the floor, watching the History Channel on TV. I asked her, as nonchalantly as possible, if she had been suffering from any kind of physical pain. She shook her head and turned up the volume.

Jenny was looking for Amelia on the TV; I was sure of it. It was a documentary on ancient churches, and I was tempted to sit with her and pry. Maybe she would open up and tell me about the dreams. Maybe she would let me into her head—more likely, my interference would send her scuttling back into her bedroom.

Instead, I busied myself in the kitchen, arranging glasses and cups the way Elizabeth used to in her spare time, and hoping that my daughter would find the tools to break down the barriers she had erected.

I made two phone calls the following morning, the first one to Doctor Elworth's surgery, where I managed to make an appointment for the following day. Reverend Francis answered my second call and sounded relieved to hear my voice.

"Mr. Adams," he said breathlessly, as if he had picked up the phone at the end of a hundred-metre sprint. "I'm so glad you called—I'm afraid I mislaid your number. How's Jenny?"

"She's not said anything about the incident."

"Have you asked?"

"No. I'm hoping she will talk to me when she's ready."

I wasn't sure if the reverend would agree with my hands-off approach, but I told him everything I knew about my daughter's state of mind. It had all started out of the blue, after she began talking about mediums. I kind of guessed that would get any self-proclaimed servant of God listening.

I was allowed to tell my story without interruption—I occasionally had to stop to check he was still on the other end of the line—and when I'd finished, the reverend cleared his throat.

"I'm not really into all this demon possession theology," he began. "To be honest, I absolutely detest those awful so-called God channels on satellite TV, but I do believe that we can leave ourselves open to evil forces."

"You think Jenny is possessed?" My heart began to thump.

"I'd hesitate to make such an assumption at this point..."

"My friend thinks she needs a shrink."

Francis hesitated. "I wouldn't discount that possibility, either. As I say, I think some of our more enthusiastic Evangelicals blame mental illness on the Devil and his minions, but I do feel this could be a spiritual thing."

"The spirit of a dead woman?"

Again, Francis hesitated, but when he spoke, there was an authority in his tone. "Yes. If this woman actually existed." There was a brief silence. "I think Jenny needs a lot of prayer."

I knew better than to ask my daughter to go back to St. Jude's. It was out of the question. But I agreed to return on my own later that week. I liked the rotund, balding minister. He was easy to talk to and, unlike Josie, didn't seem to believe my daughter was ready for the asylum. That alone made him worth a visit.

***

Doctor Elworth greeted me warmly as I walked into his surgery. "Mr. Adams. How are you?"

He stood to shake my hand with his Superman-like grip. Pictures of his wife and baby stood in silver frames in the corner of his desk. No chance for Jenny, then.

"Take a seat," he invited, flopping down into his leather swivel chair and tapping the keyboard. My details fired up on the screen. "How have you been keeping?"

"We seem to be surviving," I replied, feeling that the word *fine* was an insult to Elizabeth and Hanna's memory.

Elworth was staring at the screen. "So, how can I help?"

"It's about Jenny."

He smiled. "Ah, Jenny. She's a credit to you."

"Yes—thank you—she is—but…"

"She's not coping well?"

"I don't know. It's complicated."

With that, I repeated the tale I'd told the reverend the day before. Elworth listened attentively, just as the minister had done, but unlike Francis, he believed it was all down to the stress brought on by the tragedy.

"I can refer Jenny to a counsellor," he suggested, turning to face me. "But I would have to talk to Jenny first."

"God! No!" I blurted unintentionally.

Elworth raised his eyebrows. "Oh?"

"She wouldn't come. I know she wouldn't."

"It would all be confidential. Someone would speak to your daughter—a phone call. Then they would assess the situation and take it from there."

I felt my face flush. "The thing is—she doesn't know that I've read her diary. I'm not supposed to know about this Amelia Root woman."

Elworth looked concerned. "But the fact that she wandered into a church fifty miles from her home with a knife and a spray can… That might be enough."

The doctor was right, I knew. Dismissing his advice seemed irresponsible. "Look, I'll have a go—but I wouldn't hold out any hope. She'll go ape shit, I'm telling you."

I left the surgery under a cloud and drove home with the lunchtime phone-in blasting out on the radio. I felt close to my father when those things were on—I could almost hear the old guy muttering as some idiot called with an ill-conceived argument.

When I walked through the door, Jenny was waiting for me, her face red and tear-stained.

"Where have you been?" she snapped angrily.

"Out."

"Out? Where?"

"Just a run—you know—fresh air."

Jenny glared. A tear trickled down her cheek. "Liar!"

The hatred in her voice startled me. "Why?" I asked meekly.

"You've been to see Elworth!"

I felt as if someone had just punched me in the stomach. "Well, yes."

"What about? Me?"

"No, of course not, darling. I was getting headaches…"

"Liar!" Another tear trickled down her other cheek. "Why don't you tell me the truth, Dad? Why?"

"I am telling you the truth."

"No! No, you're not. You went to Doctor Elworth telling him how I was going crazy…how I walked into a church and vandalised it…how I wake up screaming in the night!" Jenny's eyes flamed with hatred. "Well, thanks a fucking bunch, Dad! Why don't you just throw me in a padded cell and forget about me! Then you can bring your cheap tarts home to Mum's bed and I won't even know! Is that what you want?"

"Tarts? Where did that come from?"

Jenny burst into tears. I moved towards her, but she backed up. I stopped.

"Jenny! That is the last thing I want. I'm scared, honey. This is just getting out of hand. I'll do anything I can to help, but you have to let me in."

"There's nothing you can do. I'm going crazy," Jenny said, stifling her tears.

"You're not. I'm going to prove it!"

Jenny looked up. "How?"

"I'm going to find this Amelia woman!"

As soon as the words left my lips, my insides turned and my heart seemed to stop. In that moment, it seemed that the whole world gasped. Jenny had never mentioned Amelia!

I was met with a look of disbelief. "WHAT?"

I tried to form a reply, but there was nothing to say. I just waited.

"You—you've been in my room. You've been in my room—through my things!" Jenny's voice rose to a scream. "You sneaking bastard! How could you?"

Before I had time to react, Jenny was on me, her fists flailing, her ring splitting my lip, further blows raining down on my chest. I managed to grip both of her wrists and hold her as her eyes blazed, cutting through me like lasers, but I could do nothing about the stream of sputum that flew like a missile from her mouth and caught me in the eye.

In shock, I let her go and felt the sickening crack of bone as her clenched fist slammed into my nose. The pain was excruciating, and I felt myself staggering backwards. Only the doorframe stopped me from falling. Blood poured from my nose as Jenny thundered up the stairs.

"You and me—we're over!" she screamed. "Go and fuck yourself!"

I watched, dazed by the anger. My angel had turned in into the Devil before my eyes.

Chapter Ten

LUCKILY, MY NOSE had not been broken but I cancelled my visit to Tabwell, explaining to Reverend Francis that I had a more pressing appointment and would be in touch soon. I drove to the graveyard early the following day, having had no further contact with Jenny, who had not ventured from her room even to make herself a drink.

Neither of us had eaten, and the only thing that had entered my mouth was a toothbrush. That morning, I'd not even bothered to shave. My left eye was turning a rather violent shade of purple, and I couldn't face either Lou or Josie and give them the old *walked-into-a-door* story. Besides, I didn't even want to *start* lying to Josie.

The tranquillity of the cemetery was my only option—a place where I could walk in peace. The graveyard was, in many ways, a haven of rest to the living as well as the dead, yet as I sat behind the wheel of my car, I found myself wishing my father was sitting beside me. I had a million questions.

Jenny had never morphed into the teen from hell. She had been spared the effects of raging hormones and remained balanced and remarkably mature, and I'd been proud of her. She was thoughtful, eloquent and chose her friends well. Her closest friends—Kelly, Ellen and Laura—all had aspirations above those of their classmates. They had little time for the celebrity culture that gripped the youth of the day.

But now, she had developed a volcanic temper, hence her attempt to rearrange my features. Terrible thoughts raced through my aching head. I'd never seen such rage on my daughter's face—a rage that left me wondering what else she was capable of. I couldn't risk leaving my photocopies of her diary in the house and decided that they were best hidden under the mat in the boot of the car. If she only knew. I shuddered and pushed the thought from my mind as I turned into the cemetery and parked up.

The watery mid-morning sun reflected off the marble stones as I walked down the narrow tarmac paths. As always, I stopped several times to read the epitaphs—the verses of love and grief. I was so busy reading the lament to a lost love on a newly placed expensive headstone that I'd not noticed the man standing at Elizabeth's grave.

From the back, it was difficult to tell his age; his gender was the only thing his attire revealed: a dark grey fedora, a maroon scarf and a long dark overcoat, which hung low on his calves, revealing a little of a pair of black trousers and casual black loafers.

I approached in silence, but, as if he had heard my almost inaudible footsteps, he turned when I was nearly fifty metres away. He smiled, as if he were expecting me.

"Mr. Adams?" he said as I arrived at the grave.

"Er…yes."

He was in his late seventies, at least. Wisps of fine grey hair poked from beneath his hat, and his face was lined by age, but his eyes—and they were a quite remarkable hazel brown—were as bright as a child's. He held out his hand and I shook it. His grip was as firm as Elworth's.

"My name's Sebastian Tint—unusual, but I'm stuck with it." His expression softened. "I'm sorry to intrude," his baritone voice was almost musical, "but I have often stopped here." He paused and studied the epitaph for a moment. "Someday, I hoped I would meet you."

I wondered if I should have been worried by the news this old eccentric had been visiting my wife's and daughter's graves, yet the man had an aura—believe me, I wasn't into the whole aura thing normally—and a serenity that was comforting.

"You lost your child and your wife," he continued. "Tragically, I presume?"

"Yes."

"A car accident?"

"An accident-cum-murder," I replied.

"Oh."

"Two kids out joy-riding ploughed into them. Crushed against the back of an ice cream van."

"Good Lord! I'm so sorry." He was thinking, shaking his head. Clearly, Sebastian Tint wasn't given to making idle talk; that was obvious even at this early stage in our acquaintance. "Are you on your own?" he asked.

"I've a seventeen-year-old daughter—Jenny."

He nodded. "Good. She'll keep you going."

"She does," I replied with a rueful laugh. "There's no doubt about that."

Tint smiled. "So, that's it," he said.

"Pardon?"

He looked stunned. "Oh…nothing. I was—"

"You said 'so that's it'—what did you mean?"

The old guy sighed. "I'm sorry. Sometimes I think aloud."

I let it go. He was just a casual acquaintance, after all. A man I'd probably never meet again.

"I lost my wife nearly fifteen years ago," he said, staring down at the grave. "We had no children." He pulled out a wallet and flicked it open, revealing an old black-and-white photograph of a young woman, standing in front of a huge rock, the sea tickling her feet, her skirt hitched above her knees. "Honeymoon," he explained. "Her name's Joyce."

"Did you never want children or…"

Tint laughed. "Want? In those days, it was not your decision. It either happened or it didn't. Family planning was frowned upon."

"So, you would have liked children?"

He nodded, and for a moment we stood in silence, both staring at the epitaph to my wife and baby girl. Tint drew breath, inhaling the morning air. I knew it was the prelude to an explanation—the reason he was here.

"Mr. Adams, could you humour a strange old man for a few minutes? If, after that time, you decide I'm a fool, then I will never trouble you again. Nor will I ever cast a shadow over the grave of your precious wife and daughter."

I agreed and Tint waved me forward. "Shall we take a stroll?"

The old man walked without the aid of a frame or stick. He was willowy and athletic, even in his dotage, and I guessed he could still tackle a few Lakeland fells if he chose.

"I was drawn to Elizabeth and Hanna's grave," he said. "It is on the route to the bench I often use when I come here to reflect. But each time I passed…" He paused. "Each time, I had to stop. I sensed something."

I remained silent, waiting.

"It's a long story, Mr. Adams. I have a sixth sense. Me! I was a man of science who frowned on religion and ridiculed those who professed they talked with the dead."

"You're a medium?"

"Good Lord, no!" he gasped, as if the very word might choke him. "I don't make a business out of it. I doubt if I could summon a dead person if I tried."

"But you believe in the afterlife?"

"I have no choice, Mr. Adams. I do not pretend to understand the spiritual world or why I was unable to pass by your wife's grave. But I know you need help, and I'm guessing that somewhere in this turmoil, your daughter is right there—the centre of this storm."

I felt the blood draining from my face. A part of me wanted to walk away. I was being drawn into another world—a world which I, like the old man, didn't understand.

"So, Mr. Adams," Tint said softly, "tell me what's troubling your daughter."

I was uncertain where to begin. "She's stressed—grieving for her mother and sister."

"Of course she is. But that is not why I'm here, is it?"

If I had not seen the rage on Jenny's face the day before—if I had not felt so desperate—there was no way I would have revealed her secrets to a stranger that morning. But I felt our meeting was more than chance.

We sat on the bench Sebastian Tint had funded and dedicated to the memory of his wife, overlooking the acres of green littered with marble and stone, and I told him everything, beginning with the dreams—the nightmares—and the woman who waited for Jenny every time she passed into the unconscious world.

When I'd finished, the old man stayed silent for many moments, reflecting on the things I'd told him, before he asked, "Do *you* think that Jenny needs *professional help*, as your friend so delicately puts it?"

"I don't know."

Tint hummed thoughtfully. "Dreams always fascinated me. They often reveal our deepest anxieties."

"You think this is all to do with Jenny's grief?"

Tint smiled. "Oh, it's not as simple as that. I believe it is easier for spiritual energies to connect with our subconscious."

I nodded. "Which would suggest that she has somehow contacted an aggressive spirit."

"Maybe. I know it's difficult to overcome the natural scepticism that we harbour. But if you wish to help your daughter—and I know that you do—you have to decide whose help you will enlist. The psychotherapist's…or mine."

I didn't answer.

Tint pulled a card out of his wallet and handed it to me. "Think about it, Mr. Adams. This is an important decision and you must be quite sure. This is my name, address and phone number. I do not run a business—I'm not a medium—but I can help."

I glanced down at the slip of plain white card: *Sebastian Tint. 122 Heyworth Garden Lane. Patchton.* There was no code, and the telephone number was so small, I could barely read it without glasses.

"If you decide to enlist my help, you can call tomorrow. I shall be in all morning." Tint rose and turned, raising his head. "And if I do not see you again, I shall wish you well." He smiled warmly. "Feel free to remain here. The seat is yours."

***

The following day, I found myself at the old man's house. He looked pleased, almost relieved, as he waved me through the door with an extravagant sweep of his arm. I ventured forward cautiously, like a child being ushered into the headmaster's study. The room suited him. It was almost as if I'd known what to expect. My ageing host could never have survived in a dwelling that did not somehow reflect his eccentricity.

It was large, gloomy and the walls were lined with books from ceiling to floor. An old brass lamp lit the corner, casting eerie shadows across the dusty crimson drapes that hung across the window at the far end. On what I assumed to be the dining table, partially hidden by a clutter of Sunday supplements and old journals, was an old typewriter. I was hardly surprised to find such a museum piece in his possession. Indeed, if old Tint had any relationship with modern technology, it would have astounded me.

He was watching me; sometimes I was sure he could read my mind.

"It serves me well," he said, smiling affectionately at the machine. "It's a family piece passed down by my father. He treasured the old beast. Old Bessie still looks wonderful, don't you think?"

I nodded. "You write?"

"A little. I've penned a few articles for those editors who bother to ask. The ones who appreciate the less sensational view of the paranormal."

As he spoke, my eyes drifted over the shelves, crammed with titles from Shakespeare, Dickens and Roust to Darwin, C. S. Lewis and Tolkien. A King James version of the Bible had been placed mischievously alongside a couple of modern works, including *The Holy Fiction*—a controversial book written by a young media-conscious scientist who believed religion was the root of all evil.

Tint's eyes fell on the same book. "It took me two days to plough through that drivel," he said witheringly. "It was a complete waste of time. The man is an utter fool, and his work—because it fails in that which it sets out to do—does not *prove* there is no God." He paused to shrug, cloudy eyes glittering with amusement. "So I placed it alongside the Bible."

I laughed, because I could hear my father laugh. Somewhere, somehow, I sensed his approval of this strange old man.

Tint's face flushed, waving his finger in the direction of the book. "Of course, I do not take everything in the Bible literally, but I have drawn great strength from it over the years." He turned to me. "I have no argument with the sceptics. Only with those who seek to disprove that which cannot be disproved.

"You, my friend, are nothing more than a sceptic, and I'd wager that even if you did not believe, you would leave others to their faith." He paused again. "I want to show you something."

I felt a strange sense of anticipation. Tint's words carried the weight of experience and an intelligence that wrapped the listener in a warmth a child might feel upon being swept up into its father's arms. If he had something to show me, it was worth seeing.

"You don't have an aversion to dogs, I trust?"

I shook my head, and he left, closing the door behind him.

I was alone, the silence broken only by the ticking of an old wooden clock sitting over the fireplace. Yet the room was peaceful and comforting. I felt like a young boy, hiding from the modern world in a time capsule that possessed an energy of its own. I wanted to stay here, protected from the warped minds of the politically correct and the moral decay that confronted me every time I turned on the TV.

"This is Ricky," Tint said, finally returning with a huge German Shepherd dog that looked like a cross between a wolf and a bear. Ricky cocked his head, eyeing me with caution.

"It's time for his walk," Tint informed me. "Would you accompany me?"

I smiled, instinctively taking a step back and giving Ricky some space.

Tint grinned. "He's as soft as putty," he said. "He's probably more scared of you than you appear to be of him."

Somehow, I doubted that.

Tint's dog stayed obediently at his side as we walked around the back of the house and took a footpath that led us onto lanes bordering acres of flat, open farmland.

"I'm so pleased you agreed to pay me a visit," Tint began. "I felt a great burden as I stood by your wife's grave. I trust you were not alarmed by my gift of flowers."

I didn't get the chance to reply.

"You see, we humans are all cursed by greed. That's why I offer my services free of charge, though it is costly to keep that old house on its foundations. I have never taken any, even when it has been offered, so you can rest assured that you will never have to dig into your pockets or consider a gift of any description…

for it will be fervently refused." Tint smiled. "I like to make that absolutely clear from the start."

Ricky sniffed the air as we passed an old stone cottage on the left.

"I'm really nothing more than an old man still grieving the only woman he ever loved. I have never understood this modern attitude to marriage. We seem to have such a casual acquaintance with the sacred vows and family life. Morality is constantly being questioned by these so-called activists. We have, I've noticed, become overrun by modern thinkers with a predilection for perversity, afflicted by political correctness and bound by the letter of the law."

"My father would have loved you," I said, almost vomiting the words in my head.

Tint barely flinched. "I'm sure we would have found much common ground, Robert. You are his son, and I feel an affinity between us. A spiritual bond if you like."

Tint must have noticed my alarm, because he smiled and added, "Oh, I'm not talking about love. At the very core of our beings, beyond the interference of those things we watch and read, we possess beliefs that we can either nourish or suppress. I'm suggesting that we share those beliefs. You are an honest man, I know that. I pray to God that I can guide you out of this darkness."

Tint fell silent for a moment as we approached an old oak tree that stood alone, its branches overhanging the road like menacing tentacles waiting for an unsuspecting soul to wander beneath. As we approached the tree, Ricky stopped suddenly. Tint pulled, but the dog strained against the lead, his paws spread out in front of him.

"Come on, boy, come on," Tint urged.

I watched as Ricky, now almost on his belly, began to whimper.

Tint turned to me. "He sees something in that tree. I've never been able to get him past it." He bent down and patted the dog. "Let's go home, boy," he whispered.

As we turned to walk back, the old man explained, "After Ricky refused the second time, I suspected something, so I did a little research. The library is a great place for local history—a whole section of it." Tint pointed at the old stone cottage we'd passed earlier. "You see that place? A young woman lived there—1989, I think it was. The poor lass was found hanging from that tree early one Saturday morning. Apparently, according to the girl from the local stables, they have trouble getting the horses past the old oak as well."

I looked up at the gnarled branches silhouetted against the silver blanket of sky, wondering if I concentrated hard enough whether my sixth sense would kick in there and then, revealing whatever Ricky saw. The ground on which I stood was the same ground that this poor young woman had walked, rope in hand, heart heavy. I felt a weight in my chest, as if, for a brief moment in time, I was sharing her grief. Yet I saw nothing.

***

Tint poured me a brandy fished from an antique cabinet in the corner of the living room. We had not discussed the paranormal during our walk. Tint had, instead, preferred to talk about the desecration of the local farmland and the new breed of landowners who sold out to the developers at the drop of a hat. I thought he'd probably been allowing me time to digest what I'd seen.

He lit his pipe. "I've heard it all, Robert," he said. "We all dream. Some of our dreams are lucid and real, while others are quite bizarre. I know that many believe our subconscious infiltrates our conscious under certain conditions, such as stress and grief." Tint turned to me. "I was a teacher. An atheist. A man so sure of the progression of nature that I taught it to my students. They embraced my theories the way you would expect the spawn of an immoral, restless society to do. That was until I met Kieran Porter."

Tint hesitated, inviting me to take a seat in an old, brown leather armchair facing an ancient TV set in the corner.

"Porter was my favourite." A wisp of smoke rose from his pipe. "I loved the boy's enthusiasm—his pure, youthful energy..." Tint stared into the middle distance. "I think he knew...we had an understanding."

"And he convinced you that there was an afterlife?" I asked.

Tint smiled ruefully. "Oh, yes. But not with words."

I was intrigued. "What happened?"

Tint blew a cloud of thick swirling smoke into the air. "It was a Friday afternoon, and I dismissed the class early—it was a particularly warm day, late June. I figured if they wanted to revise, they would be better doing so in the fresh air. The class filed out, grunting their appreciation as they passed my desk.

"I continued writing for some time after they'd gone, and when I finally looked up, I saw Porter sitting in the far corner, staring at me. He smiled warmly and rose in complete silence. He stopped briefly at my desk and looked at me with a strange, distant sadness. 'You are wrong, Sebastian,' he said. 'You are so wrong.'

"I looked down at the papers strewn in front of me—only briefly—and when I looked up, he had gone."

I frowned doubtfully. "And *that* changed your mind?"

"As I said, it wasn't his words."

I was staring into the face of an old man ravaged by age, yet with eyes still brimming with the passion of youth.

"I walked out of the university grounds to find the road sealed off by the police. There had been an accident. One of my students came running over to me, cheeks streaming with tears. She told me Kieran was dead.

"My blood ran cold as I embraced the young student, holding her the way I would have held my own daughter. She was still sobbing as she informed me he had been killed in a road traffic accident on his way to the lecture."

Tint sighed. "I thought the girl must have been mistaken, of course. I told her so. Porter *had* been in the lecture. I'd seen him. But this young girl gazed at me as if she were looking into the eyes of a complete fool. That's when I realised."

I thought I saw a tear in the old man's eye as he paused to take another draw on his pipe.

"I was shaken to the core," he continued. "I grieved for that young man, yet I could not accept that he had appeared to me after his death. It wasn't possible—not to a man such as myself. The voice of sanity in a world steeped in superstition and spiritual ignorance.

"I checked and re-checked the time of Kieran's death, and questioned my own experience, but I knew in my heart that that young man had stood before me. There was no plausible explanation—at least, none that didn't sound more ridiculous than the theory that there might just be a life beyond the grave."

A rueful, crooked smile crossed Tint's craggy features. "The very foundation of my beliefs crumbled, and I was left with nothing. My dear wife believed I had taken young Porter's death badly but, of course, I was also grieving for my theories, too. Theories which had died with him. What arrogance! What utter bigotry!"

He cast a loathing glance at the scientist's book that now sat on his shelves like an imposter. "I should burn that book at some stage," he mused. "Then again, I would probably have continued to live in similar ignorance had Porter not…"

Tint's voice faded as he blew another cloud of smoke into the air. "It took me nearly three weeks before I finally told my wife about Kieran." His eyes filled with tears. "That dear, sweet woman just looked at me. I remember her very words. 'My dear,' she said, 'I have prayed for this day!'"

"So, your wife was a believer?"

Tint smiled softly. "Indeed she was. And I never knew. You see, Robert, I loved her dearly, but I had never stopped to consider that she might not share my dismissive attitude toward the spiritual life. I was filled with remorse, and in an effort to right the wrongs, I offered to accompany her to the local chapel."

Tint was back there in his head, remembering with affection. "It was a long, slow process, but I figured that if there was a life after death, then maybe God himself existed in some form or other. That, I suppose, is how it all began, although I would hardly call myself a fundamental believer—in the accepted sense of the word."

I took a sip of brandy and felt the smooth liquid warm my throat.

Tint continued, "The Reverend Jenson, a good and godly man, I concede, does not approve of my gift. He believes that mediums—although I do not consider myself to be one—are of the Devil. He watches me with a keen Evangelical eye, anxious in such a sweet way that I do not contaminate his flock." Tint laughed. "I toe the line, of course. I think the young reverend and I have reached an understanding."

"So, what exactly do you believe?" I asked.

Tint sighed. "That is precisely the word I have trouble with. *Exactly* means just that; exact. It is a word I would never use when it comes to spiritual things. I believe in God, but not in the conventional sense. We must remember that He is a spirit—a force—not some benevolent, old, grey-bearded man sitting on a golden throne. But beyond that, all is shrouded in mystery."

"And Christ?"

Tint nodded slowly, smiling as if he had wrestled with the question his whole life. "If you are asking me if Jesus was the Son of God, then I have to ask you, in turn, if anyone can be sure. It is a matter of faith." Tint paused. "I would like to think that He walked this earth with that spiritual energy within Him, but I am not so sure about the virgin birth. I like to believe that Christ was adopted by God to carry out His work on Earth." He grinned. "That is just my own opinion, of course."

Tint took another sip of brandy. "Anyway, I have told you something of my life. I am assuming that now you want to discuss your daughter—is that right?"

I smiled. "Sure."

Tint pulled a crisp, white handkerchief from his shirt pocket and dabbed his lips. "Let's assume that this spirit—Amelia Root— is real. Jenny is a troubled girl wishing to connect with her mother and sister. I believe we can open ourselves to the spirit world just as we can choose to close ourselves to it." Tint pointed at the bookshelf. "Just as our friend chose to do."

He clasped his hands tightly, considering his words. "Jenny believes that Amelia is an ancestor—of her own bloodline— so think of it this way: if Amelia is an ancestor, then her spirit may just have been waiting for an opportunity to come through. Like someone waiting on the other side of a door. Your daughter merely opened it."

"And you think her desire to see her mother—"

"Was the door? Perhaps." He smiled. it all sounded so logical. "Jenny obviously has a sensitivity to paranormal activity even if she, like me, was not aware of it until now."

"So, what do we do?"

Tint emptied his glass. "I know a genealogist. He's retired, unfortunately, but he loved his job, and I'm sure he would be quite happy to trace your family's ancestry. We need to find out who Amelia Root *is*—then, maybe we can find out what business she has with your daughter."

It sounded good to me. Tint was practical—I liked that; I liked the lack of hocus-pocus.

He shook my hand as I left. "I'll be in touch. In the meantime, try to build a few bridges with that girl of yours."

***

I drove home feeling lighter in spirit. Sebastian Tint reminded me of an old prophet whose words were weighted with wisdom. If he'd told me the world was flat, I would have believed him. Of course, I knew in my head that he was no more than a man with a wise brain and a big heart, yet there was something about him that I warmed to. Even if he could not help Jenny, I wanted him in my life.

I arrived home to find a used plate on the draining board. At least Jenny had eaten. There was hope; a faint, flickering light.

I slept well that night, a peaceful, almost blissful sleep, undisturbed by dreams.

Chapter Eleven

TINT CALLED EARLY the following day, suggesting that it might be wiser if I allowed Jenny some time on her own. "Don't aggravate the girl. It's much better that we wait. You'll know when she's ready."

I told him I had no intention of telling my daughter that I had spilled the contents of her diary to a complete stranger. One black eye was enough.

The old man chuckled. "I'll have a word with Jack—he should be in contact with you shortly."

I was sceptical. *Shortly* could mean days but it could also mean weeks; however, the following morning, I received a call. It had just gone nine.

"Robert Adams," I said sharply, gulping down the last of another cup of coffee.

The caller introduced himself with an air of military formality. "Hello. Staple here!"

"The genealogist?" I asked, feeling a tightening in my stomach.

"Retired," he quipped, "but happy to help."

There was a pause. "So…what happens next?"

"We need to meet—perhaps we could discuss this over a drink—you know—oil the wheels?"

"Sure. Where?"

"You choose."

"Do you know The Keys? Fulwood Road?"

"I think so. Anyway, I'm okay with my satnav—I'll find it."

"How about tomorrow lunch—say twelve?"

"That sounds fine."

"What shall I bring?"

Jack cleared his throat. "Everything you know about your family tree—and that of your late wife. If this Amelia Root existed, we will find her. I don't give up easily!"

Chapter Twelve

THAT NIGHT, JENNY had another nightmare. I lay awake, praying that my decision to enlist the help of Sebastian and his sidekick was not a mistake. Josie had cast a shadow of doubt over the whole affair.

"And if you can't find this Root woman, what then?" she'd asked, and then smiled and patted my hand. "I'm sorry, Rob, but I think you might be better having a word with a therapist."

I hadn't realised how much I valued Jo's opinion—how much I longed for her approval. She clearly believed that I was grasping at straws, unable to face the fact that my daughter needed a shrink. I had stormed out of The Keys like a petulant child, refusing to reply to Jo's calls and messages. My mind was spinning after spending the evening digging for information.

My knowledge of Elizabeth's family tree took me back to her great-great-grandparents: they'd had two children and had lived in Ireland in virtual poverty before arriving in England in early 1885. Beyond them, I knew nothing.

My own great-great-grandparents, Henry and Grace Adams, had lived in Cornwall. Henry, a fisherman lost his life at sea, leaving Grace to bring up her only son, Anthony, alone.

I had scribbled the details down with a rough tree, along with any details of marriages that I'd managed to glean from the photos and documents, which Elizabeth had filed in three red boxes and stored in the loft.

I spent the evening wading through the contents while listening for my daughter's footsteps on the stairs. She'd made herself a coffee, breezing past as if I wasn't there. I'd held my breath, hardly daring to make a sound. My very existence riled her, and any attempt at a reconciliation would have been pointless.

I spent a restless night listening to my daughter caught in her dreams. Her breathing was hard and fast as she tossed restlessly on her bed. Amelia was there, I was sure, but there were no screams and no sounds of footsteps on the stairs. There would be no cryptic messages on the fridge door.

***

The following evening, Josie greeted me with an enthusiastic embrace and a kiss that told me yesterday was forgotten. We were friends, and sometimes words were unnecessary, although I wondered if my love for Josie was on the cusp of something deeper. I took my seat, and she smiled, her eyes filled with a compassion that made me want to pull her into my arms.

Jack Staple stood at the bar-room entrance with an expensive-looking briefcase under his arm. He was a stocky man with a face like a bulldog and a head of hair that was either dyed or purchased. I caught his eye, raising my hand. He smiled broadly, revealing a mouth full of teeth that weren't his either.

Jack had a predictably firm handshake that suited his pugilistic demeanour. "Robert Adams, I presume," he said with a penetrating gaze that suggested he could see the Adams ancestry in my eyes. Josie hovered in the background, wiping tables that gleamed with her repeated attentions.

"The Adams family," he said wryly, pulling out a chair. "They should make that into a TV show!"

I managed a half-hearted laugh and asked the old bulldog what he fancied to drink.

"Pineapple juice will be fine. I've done the drink-driving thing. Had the ban, got the t-shirt."

I shrugged. It didn't matter to me. If he found Amelia Root somewhere in the annals of my history, he could be supping blood with the Devil for all I cared.

There was a silence as Jack Staple glanced over the documents and other hastily sketched details I'd thought might be useful. He nodded slowly, sipping his pineapple juice.

"This is good," he said finally, slipping the papers back into the large, brown envelope with fingers heavily stained with nicotine. I could smell the stale smoke on his hands. "I'll start on this first thing in the morning."

We made small talk for half an hour before he rose from his seat and shook my hand. "I'll be in touch."

I wished him luck. I meant it. Jack smiled warmly. He was, I guessed, in his late fifties and, in spite of his seeming lack of care for his health, looked like the kind of man who could wrestle a gorilla and win. I liked him only because I wanted to like him, and I trusted him for the same reason.

***

Filled with a renewed hope, I sat down that evening and began to write.

> *My Darling.*
>
> *I am so sorry. I totally understand your anger, but it is important that you also understand I'm on your side. At the risk of angering you further, I have no alternative but to tell you I have enlisted the help of a genealogist who is tracing the family tree. We need to find out who Amelia Root was and, more importantly, what she wants with you. I pray and hope with all my heart that we can sort this out.*
>
> *I love you, Jen. Let's do this together.*
>
> *Dad xxxx*

I pushed the note under Jenny's door and waited in front of the TV for the thunder of footsteps on the stairs. An hour passed. No slamming of doors or drawers. No loud music. Nothing. I waited till midnight before I went to bed. The room was cold as I reached through the darkness for the bedside light, and under the amber glow, I saw a note on my pillow. It read simply: *I love you too.* Beside it lay a pink notebook.

My daughter's diary.

Chapter Thirteen

IT WAS TWO days before Jenny and I spoke. She walked past me and asked if I wanted a coffee. I'd not opened the diaries, believing that such restraint might impress her. We would go through them together, maybe with old Seb, if Jenny agreed. We sat, with our mugs, in front of the morning newsreel. She smiled when I thanked her, but said nothing, even though she must have been longing to know who was on the team. I guessed she was still smarting…still afraid…still confused, and still grieving for her mother and Hanna.

That afternoon, I joined her in the garden as she watched a resident blackbird hopping along the lawn and listening for worms. Jenny didn't acknowledge my presence at her side, and we stood for a while in silence. When she finally spoke, her words choked me.

"Dad," she said softly, staring down at her feet. "I'm sorry, too."

I flung my arms around her. "Jenny!" I whispered, "I love you—I love you so much!"

We held each other the way we had done the day it dawned on me that Elizabeth was never coming back. We spent the evening sitting with our arms around each other, and after watching TV presenters wade through celebrity interviews, makeovers and lifestyle tips, we decided to order a pizza and catch a couple of movies. It was well after midnight when the final titles rolled and Jenny looked at me.

"Dad?"

"Yes?"

"This is going to sound really odd—and I wouldn't ask if…"

"It's okay, Jen. Ask away."

"It's not that simple, honestly. It's going to sound weird but…"

"What?"

"Can you stay with me…in my room?" She gave me that old hang-dog look. "There's a camp bed in the loft." She sounded apologetic. "I know it's not that comfortable but, well, you could be there…to wake me if…"

I nodded. "Tell you what, let's get that weapon of torture out right now."

A huge smile broke across her face. It felt as if the sun had escaped from behind a thundercloud and lit up the sky. Jenny would never understand how much it meant. I would have slept on a bed of nails if she had asked.

***

The camp bed wasn't quite as bad as a bed of nails, but it came pretty damn close. Each morning, I would rise, leaving Jenny in her bed, thankful that she hadn't caught me hobbling towards the bathroom and massaging the base of my spine. To her, Amelia Root had become as real as me, although it was still unclear what this apparition really wanted.

On the Saturday, we took a drive down to the Nature Reserve six miles away, and followed the Lakeside trail through the pine woods. It had been six days since I'd given Jack Staple my family history, leaving him with the task of finding the woman with the bulging eyes. I was growing impatient.

Jenny and I hadn't talked about the nightmares or how she had found herself in St. Jude's, defacing the wall behind St. Peter. I kept my silence under strict instructions from Josie, who believed my daughter was waiting for the right time.

We picked our way over the carpet of pine, our eyes firmly on the ground, avoiding the mammoth roots. Jenny pushed her arm through mine.

"Are you sleeping all right?" she asked casually.

"Yeah, sure. Why?"

"You look beat."

"Thanks."

"No, really—you do."

"I'm okay, Jen, honestly."

"You can move back to your own bed if—"

I placed my arm around her shoulder and pulled her to me. "Listen, I've hated the past few weeks. I've hated seeing you so unhappy...so scared...so angry. I'd have slept in hell itself to—"

"I'm still scared, Dad," she cut in. "I'm still unhappy, and I'm still angry. I'm angry with myself, for letting Amelia in. I'm angry with those bastards for killing Mum and Hanna..."

"And you're angry with me?"

She shook her head. "I was, but to be truthful, I don't have the energy and..."

Jenny paused, stepping over a trailing root. She rested her head on my shoulder. "I was wanting Mum back. I wanted to wake in the middle of the night and find her standing at the bottom of my bed. Then I got angry with you because I couldn't talk it out, and in some weird way...I dunno. It kind of made it all your fault."

I thought about that for a moment. I had to ask. "Maybe it was. If I hadn't gone ape-shit the moment you mentioned a medium— but you mentioned Kelly in your letters to Mum—what was *the thing* you did?"

I could almost feel the tension. I had invaded her space, and the hurt came flooding back.

"I can't tell you," she hissed. "I know you were just protecting me...I know why you did what you did—"

"I'm sorry," I replied quickly, desperate to avoid another argument.

"I'm sorry, too, but I just can't tell you."

As much as I longed to know, the consequences of pressing my daughter for an answer terrified me. The girl who walked beside me with an arm through mine was living on the edge of something no one understood. An unknown world we referred to as the paranormal—or was it mental instability? Either way, treading carefully was my only option.

Jenny kicked a clump of wood, watching it fly several feet into the air. "You haven't asked me about the church thing," she said. "I thought that would be messing with your head big time!"

"Oh, I've plenty of questions." I laughed. "But I'm not sure you have the answers."

She smiled and shrugged her shoulders. "Maybe not. I still don't remember how I got to that church. I was just following something. As if there was a device inside me. I wasn't sure if I was dreaming the whole thing cos when I got on the train…I wasn't sure why. I just knew it was the right thing to do. Does that sound weird?"

"It sounds scary," I countered.

"And when I got off and caught a bus—well, it felt like the *right* bus…"

Jenny stopped, as if her recollection of the event was becoming clearer.

"The bus," she said slowly. "It stopped outside the church, and something inside me said, 'Here!' It wasn't a voice—just a feeling—but I remember running down the aisle and feeling a can in one pocket and a knife in the other and something was screaming, 'Hypocrite! Hypocrite!' in my ear. I stood in front of the statue and it spoke to me."

"What did it say?"

Jenny sighed. "I can't remember. I've tried so hard, but it won't come back to me."

"This whole thing," I replied, "the church thing—did you remember anything about it after I picked you up?"

Jenny shook her head. "Nothing. It's like I woke up there."

"Then it's slowly coming back to you, isn't it?"

Jenny nodded. "But what if it happens again, Dad? And what if the next time...what if I use the knife?"

I didn't tell my daughter that she wasn't the first to ask that question. I shuddered at the thought. From her lips, the words had chilled me, but I tried to lighten the whole subject. "Maybe we need to find out who this hypocrite really is. They sound like the one to be worried!"

***

When we arrived home, the red alert on the answering machine was flashing. Instinctively, we both reached to press the button, our hands colliding. We stopped cold as Jack Staple's voice filled the room.

Hello, Robert. Jack here. Could you call me back? Thanks.

I flipped the card that lay by the phone and dialled his number. Jenny looked on anxiously.

"Jack? It's Robert Adams. Got the message—how did you get on?"

Jack smoked heavily, and his voice was as thick as treacle. He cleared his throat. "You have an interesting ancestry, Robert, but I haven't been able to trace anyone by the name of Amelia Root anywhere—either on your side or your wife's."

"I see." My heart felt like a stone in my chest.

Jenny saw my face and turned away, flopping into the armchair.

"But I'm not giving up," Staple continued. "It doesn't mean that the woman never existed."

"So...what next?"

"Maybe we could meet again. I've had your family trees printed up—you might like them, anyway—but Sebastian and I would like to talk with Jenny, if that's possible."

"Sure. When?"

"How about The Keys? Tomorrow lunch?"

***

Tint and Staple were waiting at the corner table when we arrived. The two men were deep in conversation and well into their drinks. A brandy suited Tint with his sophisticated air while the shorter, more robust genealogist was clearly more at home with his pineapple juice. Both men looked as if they should have a cigar hanging from their lips.

Sebastian spotted us first and immediately rose from his seat to greet the young lady he knew to be my daughter. Jenny had seen enough period dramas to know that this was how gentlemen used to behave.

The old man bowed his head. "And you must be Jenny." He reached out and took her hand briefly.

Jack Staple rose, too—with less grace, but with a gentle smile that put Jenny at ease.

"Good to meet you, Jenny," Staple said gruffly, shaking her hand.

The moment we sat, Josie was there like a genie appearing from a bottle.

"Yes—and what would you like, kind sir?" she asked mischievously.

I ordered a pint of beer. Jenny opted for a cola.

Staple dug out his briefcase and presented me with a large brown envelope. "That will tell you everything about your bloodline, going back as far as 1745."

"Bloody hell! Really?"

"Sure. When I say everything—I mean births, deaths and, in most cases, occupations. Obviously, I don't know what they ate for breakfast."

"That's great. Thank you."

Tint took a sip of his brandy. He was wearing glasses today and studying Jenny over the top of them. "You must be a little disappointed," he said, addressing her with a sympathetic smile.

Jenny nodded and smiled ruefully.

Jack Staple pulled a pen from his briefcase, along with a cheap writing pad—the kind you get from the supermarkets in a bumper-pack deal. "Like I said, this does not mean that Amelia Root never existed..." He paused, looking directly at Jenny "It's a little difficult. You say that she called you her *flesh and blood?*"

"They're the words she used," Jenny confirmed.

"And that is the only clue you have to her identity?"

"Yes."

"I'll be absolutely honest with you, Jenny. I neither believe nor disbelieve in the spirit world. I don't know what to think about your dreams. This woman could be in your head. A complete figment trumped up in your subconscious."

I looked at Jenny, her face showed no emotion.

"That is what makes this whole thing so fascinating. I *want* to believe in the supernatural. I want to find this woman's name somewhere in your ancestry. I want to prove you're right!" Staple glanced at the envelope I was holding. "But the details are sketchy. We don't really know what century she is from. We don't know where she lived. Sometimes people slip through the record books, but if we are to do any digging, we need to narrow the whole thing down—times and places."

Josie arrived with the drinks. Jack Staple handed her a note. "Keep the change," he said with a cursory nod.

Jenny was thinking hard. "The room is empty—just floorboards, I think. And a small window with a table by it."

"Can you recall what the table looks like?" Tint asked. "It could give us a clue as to the era."

Jenny frowned. "I can't—it's just a table. It was the diary I noticed."

"Could it be possible that the diary belonged to someone else?"

"No. No—she was the only one in the room—I know that it was hers."

Jenny's emphatic reply satisfied Tint, who nodded thoughtfully. "Do you remember what she was wearing?"

"A white gown."

Jack Staple shrugged. "That would cover several centuries."

"Do you have anything else?" Tint asked.

Jenny placed her shoulder bag on the table, pulled out her notebook and handed it to the old man. "That's everything—up to three days ago. There's a sketch of the room and a couple of Amelia. I drew them almost as soon as I woke up."

Tint took them with the kind of reverence with which one might handle an ancient document.

Jenny smiled and looked at Jack. "You can keep hold of them for a while. My number is on the front if you have any questions."

Tint opened the book as Josie sidled up to the table. "Any food, gents and beautiful lady?" The picture on the open page caught her eye. She hummed. "They are enormous eyes."

Tint looked up. "Apart from that, she's quite a pretty girl, though."

"That's the other thing," Jenny added. "She sometimes…shakes really badly."

"A bad case of hyperthyroidism, I'd say," Josie said.

We all stared at her.

"Why do you say that?" Jack Staple asked.

Josie shrugged. "Those eyes—it's a classic symptom. My sister's cousin-in-law had it." She looked perplexed. "Why? Who's this supposed to be?"

"Just a drawing of someone," Staple replied casually.

Josie caught on. Her expression altered as she recalled the things I'd told her. "Well, tell her she needs treatment," she said, recovering admirably.

None of us had any appetite, and Josie left us with an empty pad.

"This is good!" Tint said. "Amelia had a medical condition."

"I'll check it on the web," Staple said, writing down the word *hyperthyroidism* in his notebook and emptying his glass. "I have work to do, gents." He stood and picked up the notebook, holding out a hand to my daughter. "Lovely to meet you, Jenny."

Tint waited until Staple was out of earshot. "Jack's a good man," he said softly. "And quite charmed by your daughter," he told me. He smiled at Jenny. "Understandably." He took another sip of brandy. "He has always been sceptical when it comes to the paranormal, but he is a fair man. He never dismisses anything, so don't be afraid to talk to him."

Jenny flashed a brief, polite smile. "I won't—thanks."

"In the meantime, I shall study your books while Jack tries to trace your ancestor."

"Good old Josie," I said.

Tint nodded. "I wonder sometimes how much influence the spirit world has on our daily lives. Do they—*can they* interfere?" He glanced over a Josie, who was sharing a joke with a regular over the bar. "If she had arrived a few seconds later…"

"You think Amelia wants something?" I asked.

Tint nodded. "Restless spirits are restless for a reason."

Jenny exhaled and closed her eyes. "But why me? Why did it have to be me?"

***

The next two days dragged on endlessly, and on the third, Jenny and I decided to treat ourselves to coffee at a new bistro that had opened up by the local shops. We took the fifteen-minute walk with our mobile phones on vibrate in case we missed a diverted call.

The coffee shop served light lunches, cakes and a rich variety of drinks that left us confused.

"What about the Columbian?" Jenny suggested, tapping on a line of the menu.

"Might be too strong—I'll settle for a cappuccino."

A young girl, fresh out of school, took our order and smiled sweetly.

Jenny grinned mischievously as the girl walked away in her short black dress and black tights with pink bows on the heels. "Well, ain't she just cute enough to put in an apple pie?" she said in a perfect American accent.

I smiled. "Ain't she just!"

The smile died on Jenny's face. "I haven't had a dream for two nights," she said. "In fact, I've not had a really bad nightmare since you moved in."

"That's good, isn't it?"

But it seemed to bother my daughter. "It's as if…" She paused. "Well, when you're there, she doesn't come to me."

"Isn't that what you wanted?"

"Kind of. But why would the spirit of a woman be frightened of you?"

I shrugged.

"Maybe it *was* all in my head."

Jenny looked downbeat. It was time to change the subject.

"Hey," I said, looking over her shoulder, "chin up, kid. The cute kid's back with our coffees."

The girl's tag told us her name was Helen. She smiled again. "Enjoy your drinks," she squeaked, placing the bill on the table. Jenny was right. The kid really was good enough to eat.

"Girls didn't look like that in my day," I said as she left.

"Don't be perving, Dad. She's the same age as me!"

I hated that word *perving*. Kids overused and misused it every day, but Jenny wasn't being too serious, so I playfully slapped my own wrist and let it drop.

Jenny grinned. "Well, I'm not sure I should tell you this, but there is a girl sitting in the corner, and she keeps looking over at us."

"Really? What does she look like?"

"About my age—brunette. She's pretty…dark eyes…"

"And she's looking at us?"

"Yep."

"Are you sure?"

"Well, she's not staring but keeps looking over here, so she's either a lesbian or she's really into older men."

I laughed, resisting the urge to turn and look, but then quite suddenly, Jenny's eyes widened.

"It's my phone," she said, reaching into her pocket. "Hi! Jenny here."

She listened for a moment. "Yes, he is. Just a moment."

She passed me the phone. "It's Jack," she mouthed.

Staple had news. No, he hadn't found an Amelia Root yet, but he had discovered that the hyperthyroidism not only caused bulging eyes but also tremors and high anxiety.

"That might explain the violent shaking Jenny described," he said.

"Sure."

Jack sounded perplexed at my lack of enthusiasm. "But don't you see? Jenny could not have known that there was a link between the bulging eyes and the shakes, so she could not have dreamed it, either. It certainly adds weight to the theory that Amelia Root did exist and had a very real medical condition."

I covered the phone with the palm of my hand. "Jen—is there any way you might have read about hyperthyroidism in school sometime?"

Jenny shook her head. "No. I've heard about thyroid problems cos some girl in our class had it and dropped three stone after she started on the drugs."

I returned the phone to my ear. "You're right," I said. "Thanks for calling."

"No problem. I'll be in touch."

We paid, up and left, and I turned to catch a glimpse of the girl in the corner. As Jenny said, she was pretty. Our eyes met briefly before my daughter ushered me through the door. "Come on, Dad. She's too young for you."

***

Over the following weeks, Jenny slept soundly, although she woke crying one morning after dreaming that she had been pushing Hanna on the garden swing, but even with red-rimmed eyes, my daughter looked a whole lot healthier.

I had moved back in to my own bed with a degree of trepidation, wondering if the nightmares might begin again. They didn't. Jenny started to laugh again. We watched some reruns of the old classic comedies with a monster meat pizza from the local takeaway sitting in a cardboard box between us as we began to talk about the rest of our lives—as if the bad times were behind us. But we were merely resting at an oasis, ignorant of the storm brewing on the horizon.

Sebastian Tint called one morning and invited us for 'a spot of lunch'. Jenny agreed reluctantly, having indicated that she would rather hold any meetings on neutral ground, but Ricky the German Shepherd swung it. Jen adored dogs, and Ricky bounded up to my daughter as if he sensed that she would be putty in his paws. He gave me a cursory lick—an indication that I was welcome—but it was clear my daughter was his new best buddy.

Tint laughed and waved us into his front room. Jenny followed behind me, to be met with a scene from a historical TV saga.

"Guess you think you've just stepped out of a time machine," Tint said with a smile, reading the expression on Jenny's face.

My daughter was as tactful as ever. "It—it's lovely." She eyed the wall of books that faced her and then spotted the typewriter. "Cool! How old is that?"

Tint seemed genuinely pleased that a young girl should be interested in his antiques. "Whoa, I'd say at least seventy years. I've had it for fifty."

Ricky was sitting at Jenny's side, waiting patiently for more attention. He raised a paw, catching my daughter's hand, and all interest in the time-warp room and its contents was lost.

Tint laughed. "He loves the ladies," he said, beckoning us to sit. "Such a Romeo!"

We sunk into the brown leather settee as Sebastian disappeared.

"This place is amazing," Jenny whispered. "I bet he's read every one of those books…"

The old man caught me perusing his library when he returned, minutes later, with a tray of tea and an assortment of biscuits. "Half a century of stuff," he said, following my gaze. "You can't beat the smell and feel of a book." He placed the tray on a Queen Ann coffee table—the sort that fetched a fortune on *The Antiques Road Show*. "Jack doesn't bother—say's they're too expensive. He seems to rely on the internet. Just types in a word on that…what's-its-name—bubble or something."

"Google," Jenny corrected.

"That's it. Well, we have many interesting discussions about the merits of both forms of research and learning, but we never come to any sort of agreement. Once an old dinosaur, always an old dinosaur!" Tint smiled at Jenny. "I'm guessing you'll be a computer girl?"

She smiled and nodded. "But I like books, too."

The old man looked impressed. "You read much?"

"A little."

"Modern or classics?"

"Both. We did *Pride and Prejudice* and *Wuthering Heights* in school. I loved them. The language was so, so graceful."

Tint nodded. "It would be foolish to suggest they were better times. The wealthy lived well in those days, just as they do now—but the poor...that was different." He poured the tea into china cups "We have a greater social conscience these days, it seems."

I didn't wish to enter into a debate with such an educated man, but I thought about the Kirkland Estate and the human scum it spewed out. Then I thought of the leniency of the sentence those kids had received and the pious look the judge wore when Josie gasped and voiced her disapproval. *Don't question me, woman—I know what I'm doing!*

Jenny guessed what I was thinking and flashed me a sideways glance. *Academics, eh? What are they like!*

Tint passed us the plate of biscuits. We politely took the plain biscuits, leaving the mouth-watering chocolate assortment. "I've taken a look at your notebook," he said to Jenny, returning the plate to the table with a clatter. "The sketch was very interesting."

"Any conclusions?" I asked.

Sebastian nodded his head slowly, inviting us to take our cups. "Help yourself to sugar." He retrieved a hefty tome from the lamp table beside him. "This is not quite as old as it looks." He patted the cover. "It's called *The Science of the Soul,* and it's by an American professor called Edwin Colbert." Tint gazed at the book reverently. "A fine man whom I had the pleasure of meeting ten years ago. It's a signed copy."

Jenny and I were waiting.

"Anyway, he says that if you believe in the soul, then you must believe in life after death, and if you believe in life after death, naturally, you believe in spirits." Tint paused. "Therefore, the only argument is: do we believe that we can communicate with them? Of course, my summary of the book is just that. Colbert uses science as well as many well-documented cases to back up his arguments. It is quite compelling."

"So…" Jenny said," where do I fit into this?"

Tint flipped the book open to a well-thumbed page. "It could be spirit attachment."

"Attachment?" I repeated, voicing Jenny's thoughts.

Tint nodded. "It is not the same as spirit possession, and occurs often when the person—the living person—is in a vulnerable state. In other words, they are *open*. It is rather like having a stalker, only the stalker is a spirit and therefore can have a greater influence on the subject, because you can hardly lock your doors and call the police, can you?

"Dreams are an ideal vehicle for these spirits, according to Colbert. And that would seem to be confirmed by your own experience."

Jenny looked at me. *Should we tell him?* I was reading her mind.

"The thing is," I began, almost as if it were to be a confession, "Jenny hasn't had *any* dreams for over two weeks now."

Tint's eyebrows arched. "None at all?"

Jenny shook her head.

Tint glanced down at his book. "Mmm."

"Is that unusual?" I asked casually.

The old man didn't answer for a while. We sat waiting, listening to the ticking of the old clock over the fireplace.

"It may not be," he said slowly. "But I am surprised."

It was difficult to know what a man like Sebastian Tint was thinking. Had Jenny been released? Had the spirit of Amelia Root flown, finding another victim?

"During this time..." Tint was choosing his words with care, "you felt alienated from your father—is that right?"

Jenny nodded.

"And now, peace has resumed?" I saw the faintest of smiles on the old man's face.

"Sure. We're okay," Jenny replied.

"Did the nightmares stop after or before?"

Jenny frowned.

"Before you made your peace," Tint clarified.

My daughter thought for a moment. "It was after."

Tint looked like a man who needed another couple of days with his book. "Jack Staple called yesterday," he said finally. "He said he had drawn a blank—his words. There's no record of an Amelia Root in your ancestry—no record of anyone with any medical condition that might cause bulging eyes or violent tremors."

Tint seemed to be apologising, almost as if he, too, was starting to doubt. "We have to reassess this."

"You mean, I've been imagining everything," Jenny said defensively.

"No. But we may have to consider that she is not in your ancestry."

"Then what does she want with me?"

Tint smiled sympathetically. "That's what we need to find out. But I'll be honest with you, Jenny. If these dreams have stopped, and you're no longer vandalising churches and leaving messages on the fridge door, I'd say a prayer of thanks to God and be done with the whole thing!"

It made sense. Anyone in their right mind would have nodded in approval, yet I felt betrayed. I was hooked into this whole thing, wanting the answers. Now, it seemed, Sebastian was throwing in the towel. Did he think Jenny was making the whole thing up? Was she merely craving attention? Was that why he asked if the dreams had stopped *after* we had made our peace?

If Sebastian had not thought that then Jack Staple certainly did. He called the following day to tell me the search was dead. He had explored every possible branch of history and given up. "If she's not in your ancestry, we have no way of tracing if she actually existed," he told me. "Although it is possible that her birth was not recorded—it may have happened but we can't be sure."

When I mentioned that the nightmares had stopped, he sounded cold. "Maybe she's getting the attention she needs."

The comment winded me, almost literally.

As if Staple had realised that I might have been offended, he added, "I'm sorry, that sounds heartless. Jenny's a lovely girl—been through a hell of a lot. You both have."

"Sure," I said weakly.

"I wanted to find this Root woman, more than you'll ever know. So if you get anything more—you know—info that might help find out if she—"

"Exists, " I said curtly.

"Well…yes."

"Then I'll contact you. Thanks for your help. Goodbye!"

I left Staple hanging onto the receiver at the other end, slamming the phone down hard and storming into the kitchen with the anger boiling up within me. I stood for a moment, my hands resting on the breakfast table, unaware that Jenny had crept up behind me. She wrapped her arms around my waist and told me not to worry. It was over. I should have treasured the moment, believing that we could now get on with our lives. But neither of us could possibly have known what lay ahead.

Chapter Fourteen

THE RESPITE LASTED two more days. We shared a takeaway from the local Chinese and watched a Ben Stiller comedy on DVD. Jenny took herself off to bed just after eleven; I stayed up for an hour longer, staring at the flickering shapes on the TV screen. My eyes were closing, and I began to drift into another world—a world in which Elizabeth and Hanna had slipped beneath the grasp of the Grim Reaper. My little girl played happily in the back garden while my wife sat flicking through the pages of a magazine. During those moments, I believed it was the past twelve months that had all been a dream and I had woken from a peaceful afternoon nap to find that life was good. The sun was shining. The nightmare was over.

That's when I heard the scream.

I raced up the stairs, taking three steps at a time, and shouldered Jenny's bedroom door. The dim light from the bedside table threw a shadow across the wall. Jenny was standing by the bed. If she had been lying down, I would have thought she was dead. Her face—indeed her whole naked body—was white.

I stood, frozen. "Jenny!"

She opened her eyes—eyes that were wild and unblinking. Instinctively, I took a step back, knowing that she wasn't awake, and reached behind me to quietly close the door. My heart raced. Despite the coldness I'd felt in my bones, perspiration was running down my back.

"You want me?" she hissed. "I'm just meat to you! Meat!" Her eyes were so full of hatred.

"Jenny! You're dreaming!" I shouted as loud as I could.

My daughter blinked and collapsed back onto the bed, motionless.

I waited, afraid to leave, afraid to take a step closer. Then suddenly, she looked up at me, a flicker of recognition in her eyes.

"What…what are you doing here?"

There was no anger in her voice, only confusion. "You've been dreaming, babe. Get back into bed."

That was when she realised she was naked. "Oh my god!" she screamed, pulling the duvet around her. "Get out! Please…just go!"

Amelia Root was back.

***

I waited for Jenny to appear the following morning, my eyes heavy from lack of sleep and my face thick with stubble. I took several gulps from a carton of fresh orange juice to drown the taste of stale coffee and scanned the local free paper to fill the time. The words on the pages failed to filter into my consciousness, but I'd become accustomed to reading things that my brain could not process.

My ears were trained, though. I longed to hear the creak of a floorboard, the slamming of a door, yet there was no sound from Jen's room. I knocked on her door at eleven and slowly eased it open to find her sitting up in bed. When she saw me, she began to cry.

I sat on the bed beside her. "I know, sweetheart, I know," I said, taking her hand.

So, now that all this attention was about to stop, hey presto! The ghost is back. Let's crank up the gears. Let's get everyone running around after her again.

They weren't my thoughts, but I sure as hell knew that's what other people would be thinking—that my daughter was having some kind of crisis and it had nothing to do with the paranormal.

"Look, I'll move back in," I said.

Jenny dried her eyes on her sleeve the way she'd always done as a small child. "You sure?"

I squeezed her shoulder. "Anything, sweetheart. Like I said, we're in this together!"

I left her to shower and dress, and then we sat at the kitchen table, drinking coffee and listening to the morning phone-in on the radio, but I sensed Jenny was uncomfortable outside her zone.

We visited the graveyard to place flowers that afternoon. Jenny was, at least, prepared to venture over our doorstep, but she remained pensive throughout the trip. Interrupting her thoughts would not have achieved anything, so I decided not to tax her with questions and let her talk when she was ready. We remained together in an easy silence, arm in arm at the graveside, neither of us knowing what the night would bring.

***

"Mind if I read for a while?" Jenny asked as I flopped onto the camp bed in the corner of what was, thankfully, a reasonably large bedroom. It was a rhetorical question, merely informing me that the light would remain on for the best part of the night. I didn't care too much, happy just to lie staring up at the ceiling, listening to the sound of rustling pages. I heard Jenny chuckle at something she read—that was the last thing I remembered.

I woke in complete darkness with an immediate sense of foreboding. I reached for the light only to find the sheets from Jenny's bed crumpled on the floor. It was two-thirty. I waited, listening for a sound and ignoring the tightening in my chest. I rose and crept towards the top of the stairs.

I'd hoped to see a shaft of light that might suggest Jenny had simply woken with a thirst and I'd find her by the sink with a glass of water. But the whole place was in complete darkness. I shuddered—not with fear. It was a cold breeze, and after having lived in the house for so long, I knew it meant only one thing.

I took the stairs three steps at a time and ran out through the open door, stumbling over a pair of old walking boots, sending them flying like skittles across the path. I shouted my daughter's name over and over again, but there was no reply, just the rustling of a cat in the bushes. I stopped, gathering my thoughts. Where was she? Where was I supposed to look?

There was a noise behind me. I turned.

Jenny was standing in the doorway, staring at something over my left shoulder. Her eyes registered nothing. No fear. No recognition. I took a nervous step towards her. She continued to stare beyond me at something that only existed in her subconscious. I reached out to touch her…

It were as if someone had switched on a light. Something caught my eye, a flash. I looked down and saw the blade in her hand.

She raised her arm. I tried to step back but it was too late. The knife sliced through my shoulder. The pain felt like a fire in my veins, and I screamed, stumbling backwards, holding my shoulder as the warm sticky substance—my own blood—trickled over my fingers.

Jenny was staring at me with venom in her eyes. "No more!" she hissed. Then, without another word, she turned and walked back into the house.

At that point, I thought I was going to pass out. My head was spinning, and I had the sour taste of bile in my mouth. Still clutching my shoulder, I fell against the wall, wincing with the pain.

What do I do now? What if she's waiting for me?

My sleeve was soaked in blood. *Please, God, don't let anyone know about this.*

I lurched forward and got myself into the hallway. The sounds from Jenny's room told me that I was safe for the moment, but my whole body felt incredibly cold. *You're in shock. Just get to the sink. There's bandages in the middle drawer on the right-hand side.* The voice was there in my head, but it didn't sound like mine. I pulled off my top and began to bathe the wound with a wet sponge, watching as the water mingled with my blood and swirled into the drain.

Elizabeth ran what could only be described as a small pharmacy in the kitchen drawer: pads, bandages, slings, plasters of every conceivable size with clearly marked antiseptic creams and lotions, plus a packet of ultra-strong painkillers. I dressed the wound the best I knew how and downed a double dose of the little capsules with a glass of water. There was a clean shirt hanging over the chair. I struggled into it, shivering so violently that I didn't even bother with the buttons.

The process of drinking became a greater effort than it was worth. I took deep breaths and tried to steady my heartbeat. It proved useless but, at least, after twenty minutes the pain in my shoulder became a dull ache. I took two more painkillers, went upstairs—to my own room—and passed out on top of the duvet. When the morning came, the physical discomfort would be the least of my problems.

Chapter Fifteen

THE BLOOD WAS beginning to seep through the dressing. What story would I concoct? Had I accidentally stabbed myself or wandered absentmindedly into the path of a knife thrower at the local fairground?

Jenny was sleeping peacefully when I looked in on her at nine that morning. I left a note by her bed. *Jen. I've pulled my shoulder out. Fell awkwardly and it's really painful. I'm taking myself to A and E. You know what those places are like. See you later. Dad xxxx*

The nurse at the station didn't believe me. "You say your daughter did this?"

I nodded. "It was my fault. I was late back and forgot my key. I didn't want to wake her so I climbed over the fence and got through the window at the back of the house."

"And your daughter thought you were a burglar?"

"Yes."

The nurse frowned. "But didn't she recognise you?"

"It was dark."

Somehow, as feasible as my story sounded, I wasn't convincing the staff at the hospital.

"Well you're a lucky man," she said. "If your daughter had swung twelve inches lower she would have stabbed you through the heart!"

The thought chilled me. I'd never given a moment's thought to the possibility that I could have died. I felt the blood draining from my face and the room began to spin.

"Mr. Adams? Are you okay?"

"Yes," I replied, telling her that I'd just felt lightheaded. I should have been glad to be alive—but I wasn't. My blood pressure was high according to the nurse. She advised at least one full day of rest and relaxation and I wondered if a day in bed with a book and a few painkillers might not be such a bad idea.

Jenny looked up at me as I walked through the door. "Is everything okay?"

"Sure."

"You look like a ghost!"

"Jenny. We need to talk."

"What about?"

"Last night. What did you dream?"

Jenny looked puzzled. "Why?"

I pulled back my shirt, revealing the bandage.

"Wow! Did you cut yourself as well?"

I sat down opposite her. "What happened in your dream last night?"

Jenny stared at me. "Dad? What's wrong?"

"I lied, sweetheart. I didn't fall. This is a stab wound."

I felt as if I'd just punched my daughter in the stomach. "No! Who? Who?"

I saw the pain in her eyes and wondered if somewhere, in the dark recesses of her troubled mind, she knew.

"You were sleepwalking last night," I replied. "I approached you and—"

Before I could finish, Jenny let out a howl of anguish, burying her head in her hands. I watched helplessly as she rocked backwards and forwards. "No! Jesus Christ! No! no! no!"

Leave her!

I waited until the tears had stopped. Until she found the courage to look at me, the tears still running down her cheeks. Then I asked her. "So—are you going to tell me?"

Jenny nodded slowly, wiping her eyes. "I was in the room," she began. "Amelia wasn't there but when I looked down—I realised." Jenny hesitated. "I was dressed in a white gown—I *was* Amelia!"

"And how did you feel?"

"Angry. The door was open. For the first time. I was walking through it and he was there."

"Who?"

"I don't know—I don't know but I feared and hated him."

"And you stabbed him?"

"I think so."

"Did he die?"

"I don't know—he fell backwards. I walked back into my room and I can't remember any more."

Jenny looked up at me, angst-ridden. "I'm going crazy, aren't I, Dad!"

I felt as if someone had reached into my chest and wrenched my heart from behind its cage of flesh and bone. Jenny needed my reassurance but any inner strength that remained had evaporated.

"I could have killed you—I could have killed my own father and I'd be like one of those weirdo serial killers who hears voices…" My daughter was sobbing and all I could manage was a supporting arm around her trembling shoulders.

***

I left Jenny sleeping on the couch and called in at The Keys looking pale enough to arouse Josie's concern. "You could make a fortune on Halloween!" she joked.

I found it difficult to raise a polite smile. "It's not funny, Jo. Have you got a minute?"

The bar was too busy for any private conversations so Josie led me through the back, up a flight of narrow stairs and along a corridor strewn with cardboard boxes until we reached the lounge which looked more like a storeroom with a few leather chairs thrown in.

"You look awful, hun," she said, sitting down.

"Jo, I don't know what to do."

"We're talking about Jenny, I presume."

I nodded. "I've got to tell someone…"

Josie sat, perched on the edge of her easy chair and listened as I trawled through the events of the previous night. I saw the tears forming in her eyes and finally escaping, leaving tiny trails of black mascara down her cheeks. Was she crying for me or was she crying for Jen? I didn't know.

"Jenny thinks she is going crazy," I told her. "And I really don't know which way to turn."

Josie dabbed her eyes with a handkerchief. "I know this is hard, hun," she said, composing herself. "Look, hun, I'm just new to all this psychotherapy stuff, but Jenny really does need help. She's displaying all the signs—"

"Signs?"

Josie nodded, soaking up another tear as it coursed down her cheek. "You've not found any trace of this spirit woman in your ancestry, have you?" she asked.

"Not yet." I hesitated. "But you said *signs.* What signs?"

Josie looked at me. I thought the woman was going to break. "Psychosis," she whispered. "Or possibly a case of borderline personality disorder." She studied me as if the very word might carry a curse with its utterance. "That kid is like a daughter to me, and I'm telling you, Rob, this is serious shit!"

***

That afternoon, I cleared the kitchen of any sharp implements, wrapped them in old newspaper and hid them under the bed. Jenny had woken while I was away and was sobbing uncontrollably when I walked through the door.

I didn't bother to ask her what was wrong. I just held her.

"I had another dream," she said, eventually managing to stem the tears. "And I saw another message on the fridge."

I knew that was an invitation to go and look for myself. The innocent plastic letters spelled out an ominous message.

THESAINTBURNSINHELL

"Do you know what this means?" I asked.

Jenny shook her head. "I was standing at the fridge…in some kind of dream. I wasn't in my own clothes and…and I was hurting…"

"Where?"

Jenny looked embarrassed. "You know…down there. In between my legs."

"You don't remember moving the letters?"

"No. I wasn't thinking. I just felt rage—and pain."

She looked at me, her eyes heavy. "I'm so tired. I sleep but when I wake…"

Her voice faded, but I knew. She looked weary and confused.

***

We made an effort over the following couple of days, determined to mingle in a world of which neither of us felt a part. We had breakfast at a local farm shop and dined at an Italian overlooking the fountain in the centre of town. It was difficult to find any common ground beyond the grief and loss we shared, beyond our desire to break free and escape from under the clouds that hung over our lives. We tried. We eat late at a country inn and headed home beneath a cloudless sky and a full moon.

Jenny slept, untroubled by any dreams for the following two nights, and foolishly, I slipped into a state of apathy and left a pair of scissors in the bathroom.

Jenny was taking a bath while I watched a documentary on the life and loves of common garden insects. I'd assumed that Jenny had taken to her bed after a long soak, but when I looked in, the room was empty. I felt my chest tighten—a sudden pain exploded behind my ribs, and I stopped for a moment, leaning against the wall. *This is not the time! Not now—not a heart attack!*

I looked up as the pain subsided. The bathroom door was closed. I knocked hard and called her name. No answer. I'd seen this on the TV so many times. I almost knew what I was going to find as shouldered the door, bursting the lock and splitting the frame.

Jenny was lying in a bath of blood-red water, her eyes closed as if in a peaceful sleep. I heard myself screaming her name, carrying her naked body to the bedroom. She opened her eyes—I knew she was alive. I must have called an ambulance but remember little. Her eyes remained open—open and lifeless. She tried to speak but no sound escaped her lips.

I watched helplessly as the paramedics wheeled my daughter down the path under a flashing blue light. I was shivering violently despite the coat that someone had draped over my shoulders.

"Jenny appears to have cut her wrists with a pair of nail scissors," the ginger-haired girl in the green uniform told me. "But she hasn't severed the artery—I don't think it's an attempt." She continued with one eye on the ambulance. "She has a very weak pulse." She patted my shoulder. "Don't worry—she's in good hands."

I knew that the questions would begin as soon as Jenny was stable. I could almost see them gathering with their white coats and serious expressions. Jenny would make several professional friends over the next few weeks. Friends with faces filled with concern, who talked in soft tones. They would want to win her trust—to climb inside her head and do a little rewiring.

***

I called Josie from the hospital the moment the doctors had told me that Jenny was stable and sleeping peacefully. My news was greeted with a stunned silence. "She's okay," I added quickly. "The doctors say she'll be fine."

"Why? Why did she do it—I thought she was..." Josie's voice broke. I heard a door slam; the rumble of conversation and clinking glasses died. "I'm coming over, Rob," she said tearfully. "Meet me by the door."

The phone went dead before I had time to reply, but sure enough, Josie was there within the hour. We greeted, embracing like lovers, and held each other, sobbing like children as the world turned without us. For a brief moment, and to my shame, I wanted her. It was a stronger feeling than the surge of affection that had taken me by surprise in The Keys. I wanted to feel her flesh next to mine. I wanted the comfort of intimacy to numb the pain.

Then Josie pulled back, almost as if we were both feeling the same passion.

"I'll buy you a coffee," I said.

Jo smiled and leaned forward, kissing me gently on the cheek. "You keep your money, hun—this one's on me."

The hospital's snack bar felt like an oasis in a desert of pain and death. We sat and talked about the good times, the nights when Lou, Elizabeth and I had sat in dark smoky clubs as Jo had belted out her Tina Turner numbers. She would shimmy by the tables, winking at the guys and shoving the mic in front of their faces as they sang a line, hopelessly off key. Occasionally, she would throw in a line: "Honey, I bet you *talk* out of tune!"

Josie always ended up sitting on my knee, stroking my hair as my wife looked on with unbridled glee at my embarrassment. We would stumble home with our Chinese takeaway in a plastic bag and swill it down with a bottle of white wine. Elizabeth and I rarely got to bed before three the following morning.

Josie smiled, her eyes met mine. "I'm thinking of taking up the act again."

"What? Singing? The clubs?"

"Sure. Billy Kinsella called me the other day. Wanted to know if I was interested in a residency at a club he's opening."

"Kinsella? Isn't he dodgy?"

"Well, he's kind of known to the police, but I'm not marrying him, hun—just singing at his pit!"

I laughed. Josie grinned but then leaned in and patted my hand. "If it happens, I could get Jenny in. You could come together. Kinsella wants it to be classy—good food and champagne, smart dress and pug-nosed bouncers!"

She shrugged. "I know my act isn't going to blow Jenny's problems away, but I just think it might be a distraction…"

"I know—thank you. It'll be good."

I paused, remembering how carefree we had been. "They were good days…who could have guessed what was coming?" I stared down at a rather unappealing drink in a Styrofoam cup.

Josie squeezed my hand, her eyes brimming with tears. "You deserve a break, Rob," she said. "And if this God of ours is all he's cracked up to be, then there must be some good times ahead."

***

We took the lift back to the third floor and were greeted by a young male doctor who approached us with a sympathetic smile. Josie nudged me in that *be strong* manner. "Ask him," she whispered.

I didn't need to.

The doctor stopped directly in front of me. "Mr. Adams?"

A cursory, nervous nod sufficed.

"Jenny is still sleeping—if you'd like to sit with her for a while…"

Josie wiped a tear from her cheek and checked her reflection in a glass door. "Come on, hun," she said stoically, "let's do this!"

Jenny looked pale, almost angelic, and as beautiful as I'd ever remembered her. The room was softly lit and warm—more of a bedroom than a private ward.

"I wouldn't mind a couple of nights here..." Josie began but stopped short as Jenny stirred.

"Jen?"

My voice was almost inaudible, but my daughter seemed to sense my presence. Her eyelids flickered, closed and then opened wide. She re-entered the world with a weary smile.

"Hi, Dad," she said with a husky, almost unrecognisable voice. Her eyes roved, taking in her surroundings. "Where am I?" Her voice was clearer but still strained.

Josie raised her eyebrows. "Hospital. You're in hospital, babe."

Jenny frowned. "Hospital? Why?"

I reached out, taking her hand. "You don't remember?"

I watched as my daughter continued to gaze around the room, confused by her surroundings.

"Remember what?"

Josie looked at me, shaking her head slowly. *Easy, hun, tread carefully!*

"What was the last thing..."

Jenny hadn't checked her wrists. "I was taking a bath..." Her voice disappeared, trailing away into the distance.

"And then?" Josie prompted softly.

"I must have fallen asleep..."

Neither of us spoke, both watching as Jenny's look of confusion deepened.

"I had a dream...a nightmare..."

"Amelia?"

"Yes...but..." She paused, and her eyes narrowed. "I *was* Amelia—again. I was...drowning. I was in this stinking water...

there was blood. My blood…" My daughter's eyes flashed. "That's why I'm here, isn't it? I nearly drowned…"

Josie was looking at me. *What the hell do we say now?*

We didn't have to say anything. Jenny caught sight of her bandaged wrist. She glanced quickly at the other arm to see the red marks across the ball of her hand and stared at me, her eyes wide with fear. "The blood," she said. "It was real…the blood was real."

"You cut your wrist, hun," Josie said suddenly. "You used nail scissors…"

The sound of my daughter's sobs turned my stomach and clawed at my heart. I gave Josie a look to kill; *What the hell were you thinking?* She shrugged as if there had been no option. *What happened to the taking-it-easy plan?*

Josie looked away, reading my anger. I understood why relationships were often destroyed by grief. Jo and I had been friends for nearly twenty years. We had enjoyed an understanding that was deeper than many married couples enjoyed, yet at that moment I almost hated her.

The weight of my daughter's sobs was crushing me. I was helpless, unable to reach out and stem the tide. I turned to Josie who sat like a target, waiting.

"Look what you've done!" I hissed

Josie looked up, and the pain in her eyes felt like a knife between my ribs. She tried to say something, but the words escaped her, and I watched helplessly as she ran from the room. I sat holding my daughter's hand, stroking her fingers with my thumb and waiting for the tears to stop.

"I didn't do it, Dad—I didn't… I fell asleep—dreaming—just dreaming…"

I squeezed her hand, pulling it to my lips and gently kissing her fingers. "It's okay, sweetheart, it's okay."

She looked at me through puffed, pink eyelids. "But it's not, is it? It's not okay at all! They won't believe me. They won't believe all this stuff—dream stuff!"

I wished I could have reassured her, but I couldn't. They would only see a troubled teenager with issues.

***

I spotted Josie sitting on a plastic chair in the corridor. She looked up the moment she heard my footsteps, which seemed to echo in the silence. It had just turned midnight—Jenny was sleeping, and the nurse had suggested that a couple of hours' rest wouldn't do me any harm either.

Josie stood, so small and vulnerable in her surroundings, the dark tracks of fresh tears staining her face. On stage, this girl could strut like a rock star, but now she looked like a street waif. "Oh, Robert—I'm so sorry," she sobbed, launching herself into my arms. "I wasn't thinking—I really wasn't thinking."

My anger—if it really was anger—melted away. "It wasn't you," I said, hugging her so tightly that I almost heard the air leaving her lungs. "I just got stressed out—seeing Jen so upset."

I released Jo and pulled a paper handkerchief out of my pocket. "Have I ever mentioned that you look like Alice Cooper?"

She flashed me a weary smile. "I need to freshen up," she said.

We walked the empty corridors and took a lift down. Josie gasped at her reflection in the window of the hospital shop and dived through the door marked *Ladies*. She appeared ten minutes later looking like the woman I knew.

I smiled and put my arm around her shoulder as we negotiated the revolving door. "I know a late-night diner that serves horrible coffee and stale cakes," I said casually.

"Sounds great," Josie replied without a flicker of a smile.

***

Tammy's had been famous for its *heart-attack-on-a-plate* food and caffeine-loaded beverages that attracted truckers and young families from surrounding council estates. We arrived to find that only the name had stayed the same. The old greasy-spoon tables had been replaced by designer chrome and wood furnishings, and the walls had been stripped of their wood panels and re-plastered and painted a fresh cream colour.

We stood in the doorway, breathing in the heavenly aroma of expensive coffee and fresh bread, staring at walls lined with frameless modern art. Nothing remained that would remind the customers of the old *eat-if-you-dare* retreat. The tattered linoleum had been ripped from the floor and replaced with dark-grey flagstones; the fluorescent strip lights had gone, and the diner was now lit by series of halogen lights suspended on chrome rods that hung from the ceiling. From the miniature speakers set into the walls, Neil Diamond serenaded us with an appropriate, 'Hello, Again, Hello'.

Josie looked at me. "I don't think the coffee's going to be that bad after all," she whispered. The state-of-the art machine that hissed away behind the chrome-and-glass counter suggested she might be right. The smell made me feel hungry. Behind the glass, a healthy-looking array of fresh cakes and slices remained. We sat in the corner by the window and picked up a menu. *Welcome to Tammy's place.*

Josie grinned. "There's a slice of chocolate fudge cake with my name on it," she said in a low voice that was heard by the heavy-set man sat less than ten feet away.

He lowered his paper and winked. "I can recommend the cheesecake," he said with a grin that revealed a set of teeth that suggested he might have been better giving the sugar a miss.

Josie blushed and thanked him. "Now I feel like a pig," she whispered.

"Jo, treat yourself. No one is going to know but trucker guy and the waitress."

She nodded and shrugged. "And *you*, of course."

An attractive young woman in a crisp white blouse and knee-length red skirt sidled up behind us from the shadows. She turned out to be the wife of the new owner and seemed happy to talk us through the whole makeover. Apparently, Jim Steen had an eye for opportunity and saw the potential in the ailing café that had little respect for the working-class people who no longer wanted to die via the plate.

They were doing well. Business was good. They closed at two and opened at six for breakfast—continental or cooked but, she insisted, still healthy. Josie settled on her chocolate fudge and a Brazilian coffee. I tried the cheesecake and a hot chocolate.

Laura Steen winked and slipped us a money-off voucher. "Everything is made from fresh ingredients," she said, "so it's kind of healthy in a calorific kind of way... Enjoy yourselves." She smiled sweetly.

We left at two-fifteen and promised to do the whole Tammy's thing again. I kissed Jo on the cheek and said goodnight as she climbed into her car. She reminded me that it was morning and we laughed. Yes, I loved Jo. I had always loved her.

Later that day, I found myself sitting in a perfectly square room with white walls and a dark-green carpet. The hospital's Styrofoam cups of coloured water couldn't compete with the stuff we'd been treated to at Tammy's diner. I found myself thinking about Josie, and our reminiscing, trying to find some kind of hope for the future.

***

The nurse was dressing Jenny's wound and I had been asked to hang back for a while. Admittedly, as waiting rooms went, it was pleasant. They had dispensed with the portable TV, replacing it with a wall-mounted plasma screen, although the faces of the daytime presenters looked as pale as milk. I picked up an old copy of some trashy celebrity weekly and thumbed through, looking at overweight, underweight and just-right soap stars in their bikinis before a rather haughty female voice cut through the boredom.

Dr. Grace was an attractive woman with deep-brown eyes and a Mediterranean complexion that belied her advancing years. She called me through to a room that smelled of fresh paint and invited me to take a seat in front of a rather jaded looking desk.

"I spoke to Jenny, Mr. Adams," she said, with a warm smile.

I looked at her suspiciously.

"Don't worry—we just had a very informal little chat."

My stomach did some kind of flip as she glanced down at a lined notepad on the desk.

"You lost your wife and other daughter last year, I see."

"Yes."

"How are you coping?"

The doctor studied me. What was she expecting me to do? What was I supposed to say?

"I'm just taking one day at a time." It was the best I could manage.

Dr. Grace nodded. "Have you spoken to anyone? Professionally, I mean."

I shook my head. "Only the Victim Support lady."

"Well, they do a very worthwhile job, however—"

"I don't want a shrink!" The word escaped before I could stop it. "A psychiatrist, I mean—sorry."

"Don't worry—we hear worse. You'd be surprised how many people regard psychiatry with suspicion." A slightly crooked smile put me at ease. "But there is no stigma these days. There is nothing to be ashamed of—just think of it as a health issue."

"Is that what you think Jenny needs? A psychiatrist?"

Dr. Grace crossed her hands, and the smile faded. "We would like to keep your daughter with us for a while longer. She doesn't remember cutting her wrist—she claims to have fallen asleep."

"I know."

"She told me about the dreams," Grace continued, her eyes never leaving mine.

"Yes, they've—"

"I'm a little concerned, Mr. Adams. If she is self-harming in her sleep, then obviously, we have to take this seriously."

"What are you going to do?"

"We will need a professional assessment. We need to get to the root of the problem. And we can't sort this out on the operating table, can we?"

"I was thinking…maybe a holiday…"

"Mr. Adams," the doctor said softly, "your daughter needs help. She cuts herself and writes messages on the fridge—messages from an ancestor who does not appear to have existed. She is becoming more and more unpredictable and is clearly a danger both to herself and possibly to you. Don't you think it's time we stepped in?"

I felt my face burn. Jenny must have told them everything—*everything*—even the knife attack? "What do you mean, *unpredictable*?"

Dr. Grace glanced once more at the notepad. "The incident at the church?" she replied, as if she might be questioning my memory.

"I don't want her sectioned."

"Sectioned?" The doctor laughed. "What do you think we're going to do, Mr. Adams? Put your daughter in a padded cell and throw away the key?"

I didn't. But I feared for my daughter's sanity.

"She will talk to someone who is trained to help people like her, and we will go from there."

"She'll be on drugs?" I asked.

"We can't say." Dr. Grace saw the look of dismay on my face and smiled sympathetically. "I'm not the one assessing her, but I can assure you that she will be in good hands."

I nodded.

"Don't worry. We will just talk with her," she continued. "It will be an assessment—to find out how she feels about things. It will feel like a chat, that's all."

***

Jenny was sitting up in her bed, humming along to something on her iPod. Again.

"I've just spoken to Doctor Grace," I said, trying to sound nonchalant.

Jenny pulled the headphones from her ears and nodded. "Yeah, she said she'd have a word…"

"You told her everything?"

My daughter stiffened. "Well, yes. That's okay, isn't it?"

"Sure. What did she say?"

Jenny relaxed. "She just asked about stuff."

I waited. Jenny read my discomfort.

"I couldn't lie, Dad. I had to tell the truth—surely you can see that."

I shrugged. "Sure…I know but…"

"You'd rather them think that I tried to kill myself?"

"No, but…"

Jenny's cheeks flushed. "You didn't want me to talk about Amelia—you didn't want them to think you had a crazy daughter!"

The indignation erupted within, suppressed only by the knowledge that my father would have dealt with his granddaughter with love and patience. "How could you think that?" I asked, my voice higher than normal. "All I ever do is worry! Worry about you and where all this will end!"

Jenny looked away, her eyes flooding. "Well, maybe it would be better if they did lock me away."

I couldn't answer. I had come so close to losing her—losing my precious daughter. I could almost hear them talking in The Keys—*Shame about Jenny Adams, wasn't it?* The pain swept through me, and for a moment, I was there, staring at a marble slab with my child's remains six feet below.

"You don't mean that, Jen," I said softly. "I know you don't." I sat at the edge of the bed. Jenny looked at me and began to giggle. "What?"

I saw the mischief in her teary eyes, but it was too late. Jenny bounced herself hard and watched with childlike delight as I slid to the floor. The girlish giggles turned to laughter, and seconds later, a confused nurse burst in to find two overgrown children engaged in a pillow fight. Caught in the act, we dropped our weapons, looking sheepishly at the girl who was, I guessed, not much older than my daughter.

To our relief, Ursula had a sense of humour. "I'm not too sure if beating each other up is part of NHS policy." She beamed.

Jenny pouted and pointed at me. "He started it!"

"I can believe that. Now, if you tell me what you want to drink, I'll let you get on with your fun!"

Jenny opted for a cola—I was offered a coffee and accepted gratefully. I'd forgotten how much of a thirst you could work up with a pillow.

I called Josie that evening. She seemed relieved.

"Everything will be okay, hun," she said after listening to a rambling account of my day. But the house felt empty as if the very heart of the place had been ripped out. I needed my daughter back—whatever it took.

Chapter Sixteen

I WAS WOKEN by a call at eight. Reverend Francis apologised for the early hour and asked how Jenny was doing. I hadn't the energy to go into all the details and told him that she was okay.

There was a pause. "Anyway, I've been meaning to call you about the graffiti…"

"Yes—I'm really sorry…"

"No, no," the reverend cut in. "It's just that when one of our wardens was cleaning it off…well, he noticed something…" Francis hesitated. "The word hypocrite wasn't referring to St. Peter at all. In fact, it was so obvious that I'm not sure how I missed it!"

"Missed what?"

"There was an arrow sprayed under the word—pointing down."

"To what?" I asked.

"To the grave of The Reverend Allington," Francis replied. "He was the minister at St. Jude's, 1870 to 1880. A great man, apparently. He founded the church school and did a great deal of charity work around Tabwell. He was laid to rest beneath the statue as a mark of the respect. Anyway, I just thought I'd let you know."

***

I called Sebastian Tint immediately. "I think we can date Amelia Root," I blurted without bothering to introduce myself. There was a pause.

"Oh, Robert. Hello. Yes, carry on," he replied, sounding preoccupied.

137

I told him about the call from Francis. "It still doesn't make sense, but we know that this Allington bloke was the minister at St. Jude's between those dates. So that must mean Amelia existed around the same time."

"Have you spoken to Jack about this?" Tint asked.

"Not yet."

"Then I'd let him know and then call Francis back. They should have records. It's worth a look—you don't know what you might dig up. In fact, it might be worth you paying the old church a visit."

After leaving the details of my discovery on Jack's answering machine, I called the reverend, and within the hour, I was taking the fifty-mile trip southwards with the unmistakable sound of Ella Fitzgerald drowning out the lorries as they thundered past. I was there in what felt like a few minutes; I'd made the entire journey on autopilot, my mind preoccupied. Who was this Allington? What had he done?

***

I followed Reverend Francis up the path and through the gardens to the manse. The old house towered above the trees that surrounded its walls and had lost none of its grandeur despite having been turned into a meeting centre for young mothers and local pensioners.

Cork boards covered in health notices and postcard adverts for prams and stereos lined the entrance, which had been knocked through into a large reception and painted a rather unappealing beige colour. A young girl with a pushchair looked up from her plastic seat as I walked in. She smiled at the minister, who greeted her cheerily. "Hi, Andrea. How's things?"

"Oh, much better, thanks," she replied breezily.

I followed Francis up the newly carpeted stairs.

"We've spent quite a bit of money on this place," he told me a little breathlessly. "It's been empty for fifteen years. I'm not sure what's taken the council so long."

We reached the narrow stairway that led to the attic. My heart was thumping hard. The minister had said nothing that would dash my hopes. Francis fiddled with a bunch of keys as my impatience grew with every second. "We have kids in this place, too," he said. "We have to keep it locked—you know what they're like for rooting around!"

At last, he found the key, twisted it in the lock and pushed open the door, which groaned like a sick animal. The darkness seemed to spill out as the reverend reached in, feeling for the light. A sixty-watt bulb, hanging in the centre from a wooden beam, cast a dismal light across a musty room lined with old plastic chairs and cardboard boxes.

The wooden floorboards creaked as I entered.

"Not a particularly pleasant aroma," Francis said. "And I'm not sure what's in all theses boxes."

"History, I'm hoping," I said. "Is it okay if I have a look?"

"Well, that's what you're here for." He must've seen the *where the hell do I start* look in my eyes, because he elaborated, "I seem to recall that all the documents were put into one box, more than twenty years ago, but it's everything from old hymn sheets to council letters. You're going to be some time." He smiled. "How about a coffee?"

"That would be great."

The first box I opened was on a pallet in the corner of the room and contained documents stuffed into two plastic bin bags. I had opened the first and emptied its contents onto the floor when Reverend Francis returned with a large plastic cup. Steam swirled into the damp musty air. "There's a machine in the reception. Help yourself when you want another."

He placed it on a chair next to me and looked at the mountain of paper on the floor.

"Good Lord," he breathed. "Let's hope all this is worth your while!"

I was thinking the same. The task ahead of me was daunting. I took a gulp of the warm, sweet coffee and began, but it was nearly an hour before I came across anything that might be of interest. Much of the bag contained nothing more than general church business, along with sheets of children's drawings. There was nothing I would have dated earlier than 1960.

The envelope that caught my eye was yellowing and handwritten. *For the attention of Rev H Penworth*. It was dated April 1902. I pulled the neatly folded paper from the envelope and carefully opened it. The writing was beautifully neat.

> *Dear Reverend Penworth,*
>
> *It is with regret that I write to inform you of the death of my daughter, Helen. She passed peacefully into the arms of the Lord early on Sunday morning. I know that you held her in your thoughts and prayers during her illness and would beseech you to continue to pray for our family. I have entrusted this letter to Mr. Granger, who has assured me that he will deliver it as soon as he arrives in Tabwell.*
>
> *Yours faithfully,*
> *Ann*

If the letter had raised any hopes, they were dashed when the remains of the bag proved to be nothing more than old balance sheets and church magazines from the early seventies.

I emptied the second bag to find more of the same, and after two hours, with the paper junk returned to their bags and re-boxed, I fetched myself another coffee from the machine in the reception. I passed Reverend Francis on the stairs.

"Any luck?"

I shook my head. "Nothing," I said gloomily.

He gave me a sympathetic smile as he continued on his way. After several seconds, I heard his voice.

"You could try the old metal trunk under the blanket," he suggested. "It has some old biscuit tins in it. I've never looked in any of them."

***

The lid of the old trunk was covered in old children's annuals. I stacked them carefully on the floor and eased the trunk open to be greeted by what appeared to be a toy box. Old teddies, dolls and boxes of jigsaws along with an array of old games had been thrown in together. I delved through the mountain, careful not to displace any lids. At the bottom of the trunk were two large and very old tins.

I opened the first and my heart sank: old pencils, sharpeners, erasers and crayons. I returned the tin to the bottom of the trunk and pulled out the other. Inside was a plastic bag which, it turned out, contained what appeared to be a batch of letters. But they were nothing more than parish newsletters that had never been sent out.

I returned everything to its place and stood, stretching my legs and patting the dust off my knees.

The remaining boxes contained only bric-a-brac. I opened each one, peering in and moving on to the next. I glanced at my watch; I had been there for over three hours and decided that was enough for today. I thanked the reverend and asked if I could return the following morning. Francis was more than happy to give me the freedom of the room, so I made the journey home with hope still stirring in my heart.

I sat at Jenny's bedside, recounting the events of the day like a man trying to break the world record for words-per-minute. "It's good news, isn't it?" I said excitedly. "We know that this has something to do with this Allington bloke!"

Jenny seemed in good spirits, despite my failure to find anything at the manse. I was determined in my quest, and my daughter believed in me. I wasn't going to let her down.

That night, I slept well and took the fifty-mile trip back to Tabwell early the following morning.

Francis greeted me warmly and handed me the keys. "Help yourself, Mr. Adams."

I found nothing in the first two hours, and the hope that I'd carried in my heart began to fade. I returned a set of dusty parish accounts to a cardboard box and was about to take a break when, in the far corner, half hidden by the largest of the storage cartons, I spotted something beneath a large, grey blanket.

The old sideboard stood about a metre in height and about two metres in length. I studied it for a moment. It could easily have graced the home of a family in the eighteenth century. The antiques shows on TV had not exactly turned me into an expert, but I'd seen something similar dated to the time when the Reverend Allington would have been in his pulpit.

It had four panels of eight drawers—a piece of furniture clearly designed to hold small household items. I pulled open each drawer but found nothing in any of them. I tried again, this time pulling each section out and checking it fully. By the time I reached the top drawer of the final panel, I'd become accustomed to the length of each one. But this particular drawer was at least six inches shorter than the others.

I bent down and peered into the empty section that had housed the drawer and saw, at the end, a small silver clasp. I reached in, undid the clasp and the wooden lid dropped into my hand. Behind it, I felt what I knew immediately to be a batch of envelopes.

I sat down on the plastic seat with the naked bulb dangling above me and released the rubber band. The letters were all addressed to Mary Allington. I took a deep breath to steady myself, but my hands trembled uncontrollably. *Mary Allington. Wife of Reverend Charles Allington.* I pulled out the first letter and began to read.

Chapter Seventeen

My dearest Mary,

I fear you are more troubled by recent events than you saw fit to divulge in your recent letter. Naturally, I understand that it is no business of mine to question the activities of a man of God. Charles is an eloquent man, and a servant befitting his position in the Church, and I am sure that his frequent visits to the Stanwicks should not be of any concern to you.

My darling daughter, I do not need to further impress upon you that as a minister's wife, it is your solemn duty to God Himself that you support your husband with all your heart and soul.

As you are aware, I find it difficult to write. My hand tires so easily these days, but I shall ask of you only one more thing. Do not raise your doubts. Do not give them a voice or allow them to trouble your mind, for you are also a servant of God.

Your Mother.

With the first letter, I'd discovered a link with the Stanwicks. Who were they? Why was Mary Allington so concerned that her husband was visiting them?

There were five letters. I opened the next.

Dear Mary,

How I would love to see you. My heart aches when I bring to mind your beautiful face. I am relieved that you have resisted in confronting your husband, for it is not the place of a wife to do so. Such a confrontation will bring no reward or peace of mind. I fear you may not be spending enough time with the Scriptures, my dear. You are leaving your mind open to the Devil and his lies. I pray that God may lift you in His truth and guide you in His ways.

Your Mother.

I returned the second letter to its envelope and opened the third.

Dear Mary,

I am so relieved that the cabinet has met with your approval. Mr. Jamison is a fine Christian and a skilled craftsman whose furniture, I'm sure, will grace the homes of the nobility, one day. I could not think of a more fitting gift and trust that you both feel it was worth waiting for.

Your Mother.

I took a sip of warm coffee and pulled out the fourth letter.

Dear Mary,

My dearest girl! What wonderful news. With such joyous an event, it has not been difficult to forgive you for keeping a secret from your mother. If only I were well enough to travel, I should be making arrangements without delay. I fear, however, that

*I shall never see my granddaughter, yet I rest in the
knowledge that the hand of God is upon her. Give my
regards to the Reverend Allington.*

Your Mother.

The letters had all been short and straight to the point, written
in a day when ministers and policemen could do no wrong.
But what had troubled Mary, I had not been able to determine.
Until, that is, I took the final letter from its envelope and noticed
immediately that the handwriting had deteriorated. A sign of
failing health? I began to read.

Dear Mary,

*My dear child. The news reached me this morning
and I felt compelled to leave my sick bed and write
immediately. If I had not learned of this through such
a worthy source, I should never have believed that you
could have disgraced yourself and that dear man in
such a way.*

*I trust that you have prostrated yourself before God
and begged His forgiveness by the time this letter
reaches you…*

I blinked hard, trying to decipher the following sentence.

*It is beyond reason that you should question your
husband or, even for a moment, lend your ear to
the ramblings of a mad woman. Is it true that this
demented creature entered the house of God and
spewed forth this bile as you consecrated your precious
child? Did you ever really consider her claims?*

145

Oh, Mary. How could you believe that a righteous man could behave in such an unseemly way? May God forgive you, for I cannot find it in my heart to do the same. I will pray for your Soul.

Your Mother.

I stared at the letter. My stomach rolled and my heart thumped. I re-read it, over and over again, scarcely able to believe that I'd found it. But it was true. It had to be.

I folded the letter carefully, as if it were a winning lottery ticket, and slipped it back into the envelope. I heard footsteps on the stairs and looked up to see Reverend Francis standing in the doorway. "You've found something?" he asked, reading my expression.

I nodded and held the envelope in the air. "This is the first—maybe the only—written evidence."

Francis frowned. "Evidence? Of what?"

I managed a weak, tired smile. "That Amelia Root existed!"

The minister eyed the envelope suspiciously. "What is it?"

"A letter—five, in fact—all written by Charles Allington's mother-in-law to her daughter, Mary."

The reverend stepped into the room. "You found them in the trunk?"

I shook my head and pointed towards the corner of the attic. "They were in the old sideboard."

Francis peered through the gloom. "Goodness—I thought that was empty."

I smiled. "Mary had a secret drawer," I said, tapping my temple. "It seemed Allington knew nothing about it."

***

I drove home with the letters on the passenger seat beside me, occasionally glancing over to check that they actually existed. The details within them were sketchy, to say the least, but my mind was working to fill in the gaps.

Mary Allington had been suspicious of her husband's behaviour. That was beyond doubt. She was questioning his visits to the Stanwicks' home—that, too, was quite clear. But why? Was it the frequency of those visits? Had this particular family been disreputable? Had Mary believed that her husband might be having an affair with someone within that household?

It had been the fifth letter that left me totally confused. I was convinced that the graffiti on the church wall was referring to the Reverend Allington, which suggested that his wife's suspicions might have been founded. But that was all they had been. Suspicions. Then, if I had got this straight, a mad woman had interrupted a service of consecration with accusations of abuse.

Had the reverend made sexual advances? Had he raped her? Or, had this woman—the one I believed to be Amelia Root—really been crazy? Had her advances been rejected by Allington? Had the birth of his child pushed her over the edge and left her seeking a terrible revenge?

By the time I arrived home, my mood had changed. Had Amelia Root been an institutionalised lunatic, well known in the parish? Maybe it was among the duties of the minister to visit the asylum, and that was where he'd encountered Amelia. I poured myself a coffee and laid the five letters on the table in front of me. I had promised to return them when I'd finished reading between the lines.

I scanned the letters onto my computer and printed off several copies of each. Then I sat down, with Frank crooning in the background, and read through the originals over and over again. My head ached, but I knew that there was little chance of a nap.

Instead, I saw, in my mind, the church with its suited congregation, and the Reverend Allington, standing proudly by the font with his wife and baby—a scene of eighteenth-century middle-class civility portrayed in one of those expensive period dramas. Then, quite suddenly, the peace was shattered. I could almost hear the crashing doors—the people turning to see a howling wild woman running down the aisle, her arms flailing as she vented her vitriolic accusations in the direction of the minister. I could see the wardens rushing to restrain her, wrestling her to the ground.

Mary, already paranoid and suspicious of her husband, in a moment of confusion had given some credence to those accusations, incurring the wrath of her mother. Had she raced to the woman, questioning her as she writhed like a trapped animal? Or had she questioned her husband at home, resulting in a violent argument?

I might never know, but I was coming to the conclusion, with nothing more than five short letters to go on, that Amelia Root was insane.

***

I called Sebastian Tint early the following morning and, with nothing more than a cursory hello, launched into my tale of discovery. I didn't stop to draw breath until I'd reached the fifth letter.

"Then I came to this," I said, pausing for effect before beginning.

Sebastian listened without a word, waiting patiently for me to finish.

"What do you think of that?" I asked, placing the letter back on the table.

Tint hesitated. "It sounds interesting," he said. "At least we have something."

"Interesting?" I said, feeling deflated. "It's more than that! That mad woman—it has to be Amelia Root! It has to be!"

"Let me see the letters," he said. "Can you come tomorrow afternoon, around three?"

"Sure."

I replaced the receiver and fired up my computer and typed the word *Tabwell* in the search engine. Where I was going wasn't clear. Maybe the village would have its own paper with an online archive. Perhaps there would be a collection of local books covering the history of the area.

Tabwell Arts Association topped the first page, which also told me that there were another one hundred and twenty eight entries featuring the word. I scrolled through but found nothing of any interest. After nearly an hour, I gave up and called Jack Staple, leaving a short message on his answering machine.

"Jack? It's Robert Adams. I have *another* name. Could you call me?"

I poured myself a glass of fresh orange and read the letters again. Mary Allington had hidden them in a secret compartment in a piece of furniture commissioned by her mother as a gift— probably a wedding present. But what had happened to the other furnishings in the Allington house, and why had this one survived?

I called Reverend Francis and put those questions to him.

"Your guess would be as good as mine, but I'd imagine that the quality of the cabinet was the reason no one wanted to scrap it."

"It is an antique, though. Someone could have made a wad of cash."

Francis chuckled. "If only! Whoever moved into the manse would need the permission of the parish council. It would be regarded as the property of the Church."

"So, there would be no more of the Allingtons' furniture around?"

"I doubt it. It would have either been scrapped or donated to various charitable organisations over the years."

I thanked the reverend and went back to my letters, waiting for Jack Staple to return my call.

***

Jenny began to cry when I told her the news that evening. She looked so pathetic, sitting up in her bed in her white gown with a copy of *Hello* on her side table. "It must be her," she said emphatically. "She *looks* crazy, Dad. Anyone would think she was a mad woman."

"But you don't?"

"I...I don't know. Perhaps she is... But..." Jenny hesitated. "There's more to it. She's so angry—so restless...but she's not a bad person. I just know in my heart."

My daughter read over the fifth letter and looked up at me. Her eyes flashed in anger.

"That priest—that Allington bloke—he was guilty as hell!"

"We don't know that for sure," I replied with little conviction.

She tapped the letter angrily with her forefinger. "His wife knew something was going on. It's obvious! And then this woman appears from nowhere, accusing the vicar of something, and his wife believes her! Why?"

I shrugged. "Because she's crazy?"

Jenny glared at me. "Men! You're all the same. Listen, Dad, he was up to something. She suspected him! There must have been a good reason."

I didn't argue. I didn't even *want* to argue. Jenny's theory was hardly watertight but it was quite possible. She closed her eyes and sighed wearily. "The thing is, Dad...where do we go next?"

"Jack Staple might be able to shed some light on the Stanwicks," I said brightly.

Jenny looked thoughtful, her hazel eyes fixed on the letters that lay strewn across the bed. "There's something I need to ask you, Dad," she said. "And I want you to tell me the truth."

I couldn't have possibly known what was on my daughter's mind, yet I felt the strength drain from my legs. "This sounds serious," I said, lowering myself slowly onto the bedside chair.

She pulled out a note pad from under her pillow. "I asked for this," she said. "I keep it beside me, just in case Amelia gets inside my head and…"

"Like the fridge alphabet?" I interrupted.

"Yep…something like that. Sometimes I just go into a kind of daydream…"

"And is there anything? Has she contacted you?"

Jenny looked at me. "I think so."

"Are you going to tell me?"

Jenny nodded and opened the notepad "It's just a name…I found myself writing a name." She paused, as if the question was being torn from her lips by a force beyond her control. "Dad, who is Melissa?"

There was no hint of accusation in my daughter's tone, no look of mistrust in her eyes. It was just a question to which she had no answer. But now Jenny was watching me squirm under her gaze. It was no time for lying. If we were going to get through this, I had to tell her the truth.

Chapter Eighteen

ELIZABETH AND I had been married six years and had managed to scrape enough money together for our first holiday abroad. Most of the money we earned had been spent on the house—installing a new kitchen, replacing old furniture passed on by well-meaning family, and installing a new central-heating system. We had worked well as a team. We were happy.

Two days before we flew out to Cyprus, Elizabeth decided that I needed a haircut. My regular barber was away, leaving a rather gawky, acne-faced youth in his place. I decided to give him a miss and opted for the unisex salon at the local shops. I had been assured that these days, men could frequently be found in these establishments.

I found myself seated in front of a wall-sized mirror with a room full of females and, after a young girl who sounded as if she had only just finished school offered me a coffee, I began to relax. The coffee was good—free—and I was halfway through it when a young woman appeared behind me.

"Mr. Adams?" she said brightly. "I'm Mel. What can I do for you?"

There was a seductive air behind the breezy tone that captivated me. She was beautiful, and yet it was almost as if her appearance was of no consequence to her. Her shoulder length raven hair framed her perfect face—a beautiful, olive complexion—and there was no visible sign of any make-up. Her skin smelled dusky and sweet, and her eyes…I still recall those eyes.

Melissa Ingram had spent much of her time travelling, trotting the globe by any means of transport she could find. She told me about tiny Nepalese villages, African huts, New Year's Eve in Sydney, and Summer in New York, the bohemian quarters of Paris and a cottage in the highlands of Scotland where she lived off the land for nearly three months. I listened, wondering if there was any part of my life worth mentioning, but before my input was required, the job was done. My hair was short, my eyebrows trimmed and my neck brushed.

"There you go, Mr. Adams," she said, patting my shoulder. I paid up, and gave the girl a generous tip, but in the days that followed, her face haunted me. Throughout the holiday, Elizabeth held my hand, infused with the romance of the Mediterranean sunsets and the soft salsa rhythms—but in my mind, it was Melissa's hand I held, and my imagination ran wild each time we made love. I could only feel the soft raven-black hair of the girl who I imagined had never given me a second thought.

With time, the memory would fade—that was what I believed— but I was restless in the knowledge that this mere woman had only been elevated to the status of a goddess in my mind. Maybe if I saw her one more time it would confirm that she was no more than a pretty girl on a good day. Two days after arriving home, I made my way to the salon.

It was a Friday, just past lunch, and the kids were going back to school. I pulled up outside the unisex salon and waited. Three girls arrived, opened up, and closing the door behind them as they disappeared inside. There was no sign of Melissa. I left, returning at lunchtime the following day, and went to the cash machine, punching in my code and waiting for the machine to process my request. That's when I felt a hand on my shoulder; I swear to God, I recognised that touch.

"Mr. Adams, isn't it? Remember me? I cut your hair."

Remember her? If only she had known. "Of course. Melissa. The globetrotter!"

She laughed, looking pleased with my powers of recollection. "I'm sorry about that, but I love a captive audience. Just don't ask to see the photos!"

I couldn't think of an answer. My mind was playing tricks, and the super highway connecting my brain and my mouth was gridlocked. Melissa was looking past me.

"Er...hadn't you better—"

"What?"

"Your money?"

The machine gave up on me just as I reached to grab the wad of cash, snatching it back with an impatient mechanical whir.

Melissa laughed again. My goddess, as beautiful as she had ever been in my mind. The madness of love, of infatuation, of obsession. It had brought down presidents and kings, and now, for the first time, I understood why. Melissa began to walk away, but I couldn't let her go.

"I wondered if..." I called after her.

She stopped and turned.

"I'd like to hear some more...you know...about your trips..."

She frowned. I was losing her. "Really?"

The brief silence that hung between us felt like a lifetime before finally she shrugged her shoulders and said, with little enthusiasm, "Sure, why not?"

***

And that's how it all began. Melissa pulled me into her world of Eastern mystics and ancient Mayan tribes. I loved her free spirit. She was beautiful, intelligent and engaging. We made love for the first time in her modest two-bedroom flat on a Saturday afternoon and, as in everything else she did in life, it was with an energy and passion I'd never known.

We lay naked on her bed as the early evening sunlight streamed through a gap in the curtains, and I believed that my life had begun again. It was love, but it was a destructive love—a beautiful tree that blossomed at the expense of everything that lived within the radius of its roots. I began to resent Elizabeth. Then I began to hate her. She had little ambition, accepting her life, tied to the home and the routine it demanded. I no longer saw the need. Melissa was free, having somehow escaped the clutches of a society that demanded we settle in our little brick boxes. The banks sold us their mortgages, the high street their furnishings, the garages and their cars, trapping us in a world that led us to believe that our worth was measured by the things we possessed. Before many of us reached thirty, we were chained to our jobs, trapped by our own materialism.

Melissa had seen it coming. As a girl, in her late teens, she had decided to reject the life her parents had chosen—parents who had rarely ventured beyond the shores of their own island.

My days at the office grew longer, my temper shorter. The idle gossip of my colleagues drove me to distraction; the girls, with their obsession with silicone tits and plastic faces, filled me with despair.

I needed to escape. I drove to the salon after work, calling Liz to tell her I'd be late. Melissa was surprised to see me.

"I need to speak to you," I said as she climbed into the passenger seat beside me.

Mel frowned. "Is this bad?"

"No. I don't think so, anyhow."

There was a silence before she said, "Go on, then—shoot!"

I explained that it could wait until we were back at her flat. We'd have a couple of hours before the girl she shared it with returned. That would be enough. I felt the ring in my pocket and I prayed.

***

The flat was typically untidy. I'd almost grown to like that. "Make yourself a drink, I'm going to get into something more comfortable—then you can tell me your news!"

I poured myself a mineral water from a bottle in the fridge and sipped it, trying to clam my jangling nerves. Melissa didn't take long, and it was obvious what was on her mind as she stood before me in a see-through negligée." OK. What is it?"

I took a deep breath. "I'm leaving Liz!" That was it. The news was out. It was the beginning—the beginning of the end. If I'd expected Melissa to throw her arms around me and play the grateful mistress, I'd totally misjudged her. The memory of that icy glare chills me even now.

"You what?"

"I—I thought you'd be pleased," I stammered, feeling a bead of sweat trickle down my neck.

"Pleased? Why would I be pleased?"

"We can be together—married—I want to marry you."

Melissa could have struck me dead with her withering look. "Oh, I get it! I can sign a form and become your property, just like Liz!"

She killed the stereo with the remote and flung it on the chair. "You really don't know me at all, do you, Rob? I'm not wife material. I don't even understand the concept of marriage! Why should two people vow to share their love with no one else for the rest of their lives? Why? Can you tell me?"

I shook my head meekly as my world began to fall apart.

"And you're hardly an advert for the constitution, are you?"

My shock turned quickly to anger and then to lust. She stood before me, the outline of her body tantalisingly visible beneath her negligée. I reached out, pulling my mystic princess towards me, and our rage melted. If I had nothing else—if there *was* nothing else—then I had this. Our love-making was frantic and almost violent, but inside I knew it was the last time I'd ever touch her.

***

Liz had watched me turning into a monster, lashing out, fighting for his freedom, and that evening, I'd hardly spoken to her, choosing to skip tea in favour or the whisky bottle. I felt physically sick. I needed a shower but knew that I would be washing away Melissa. I took small comfort in breathing her scent and hoping, with time, she would return.

I found Elizabeth crying in the kitchen. She spun round when she heard me pouring another glass. "Who is it, Robert?" she said, spitting out the words. "Who the fuck is it?"

"Her name is Melissa," I replied before I could stop myself.

Liz staggered back, gripping the handle of a cupboard to steady herself. The colour drained from her face; her lips moved but formed no words. Then, quite suddenly, she closed her eyes, turned to the kitchen sink and threw up. I had never felt so utterly wretched, dealing with my own pain while knowing that I was destroying the woman I once loved.

There were no words. Elizabeth pushed past me, throwing herself on the chair, sobbing uncontrollably. It was at least fifteen minutes before she began to ask the questions every wife wants to know. Why? How? Where? I spared no detail, I couldn't. It was best that she knew the truth. I was not going to give up on Melissa. Not yet, maybe never.

***

The following day, I rose early and drove round to Melissa's flat before work. I had more news for her. I'd told Elizabeth about us and we were starting divorce proceedings. But when I pressed the buzzer, it was Rose, Mel's flat mate, that called me up on the intercom.

I was greeted by a heavily set woman with a bob of mousy-blonde hair, dressed in a white blouse and navy pleated skirt. She looked flustered as she waved me through the door.

"I'm sorry," she said, glancing into a small wall mirror and flicking her hair. "You must be Rob. Have you left something?"

"Left something? No. I've come to see Mel."

Rose turned, looking perplexed. "Mel? Didn't she tell you?"

I felt the knife twisting in my gut. The same knife that Melissa had plunged into my stomach the day before. "Tell me what?"

Rose shook her head. "Typical! Bloody typical!"

"What?"

"She's gone! She said she was going to tell you!"

"Gone? Gone where?"

Rose looked exasperated. "Oh, for Christ's sake, Rob, stick a pin in the fucking map—I haven't got a clue!"

"You mean anywhere? Anywhere in the world?"

"Yes! And she's gone with three weeks' rent! I'll tell you something, Rob, she's left me in the shit. I'll have to find that money and a new flatmate pretty damn sharpish or I'll be out on the street!"

She looked at me accusingly.

"Why did you have to get so serious? I mean, marriage for God's sake! Marriage!"

"I thought that's what she'd want…we were good together, you know…"

Rose smiled sarcastically. "Sex? Well, maybe Mel just wanted to fuck a nice guy for a change!"

She saw the look of confusion on my face. "Nice?"

"Yeah. Nice. I'm nice, too, Rob, but you want to know summat? You and me—we're like chocolate-box paintings in a modern art exhibition. The kind that everyone stops and admires but no one wants to take home." She shrugged her shoulders and smiled sadly. "They want excitement. Vibrant colours and energy." Rose sprayed some perfume into the air around her, breathed in and continued. "So guess what happens to us? We stay stuck on the fucking wall, that's what!"

For the first time, I sensed sympathy.

"I can tell you're a nice bloke, Rob. There's something about you. Even though you've done a really shitty thing, you're basically decent. You wouldn't be the first guy to get trapped in Melissa's web. But you need to go back to your nice wife and build a nice life with her. Have some nice kids and take them to Disney. I'll still be here, looking for some bloke who doesn't need a good-looking bird to boost his ego!"

Rose opened the door to what I assumed was a bedroom and disappeared. Drawers slammed and curses drifted through the walls. "Shit! Shit! Shit! Fucking keys!"

A notepad lay by the telephone but the scrawl drew my attention. It wasn't a list of numbers but a kind of poem.

I lie by his table
I lie waiting. Like a dog
For what?
Scraps from his plate?
Scraps of what?
Of friendship? Of love?
He would smile, occasionally.
But offer me nothing on which my heart could feed.
His indifference destroyed me.
It was worse than hatred.
If only…if only he had hated me.
I could have learned to hate him too.

I turned to find Rose staring at me, framed by the light pouring through her bedroom door. She smiled, and I saw the gentleness that lay beneath. "You see, we all have sadness in our lives, Robert," she said softly. "We all have to deal with heartache."

***

I must have walked for hours, my world shattered. Melissa had broken my heart, and the pain was physical. I left the marital home a day later and arrived on my parents' doorstep with battered suitcase and an ache in my gut. My father could not bring himself to speak to me for at least two days. He would avert his reddened eyes every time I walked in the room, and when he did finally find his voice it was only to tell me that he was ashamed to call me his son.

The words choked him, and we both cried. I hated hurting my father. He had goodness running through his very core. He would never have been unfaithful, I knew that. I knew it with every fibre of my being, and his presence made me feel like a snake.

My mother would look at me with hope in her eyes; she possessed an inner strength that had brought her back from the brink of death with nothing more than a limp to show for it. Now, she was praying that her son would find the strength to put everything right. She asked about Melissa. Who was she? What did she do? What did I see in her? Was she worth all the pain? But she ate little, if anything, during my four-week stay, and by the time Liz and I had decided to give our marriage another chance, she was looking pale and gaunt.

I spent the first few weeks in the spare bedroom. Liz could accept nothing more than an arm around her shoulder, and often it felt as if the physical side of our marriage had gone forever. But as my obsession with Melissa faded, I found that my love for Liz was still there, lying beneath the turbulence of an uncontrollable passion. I saw Mel for what she was: a girl with no roots and no responsibility.

Liz and I made love eight weeks after I returned home. It felt awkward, and for her, I sensed, it had been an exercise born of duty rather than desire. Six weeks later, Liz told me she was pregnant. Jennifer Helen Adams was born nine months later, weighing eight pounds, two ounces. Now that child had turned into a beautiful girl and was staring at me, listening patiently and trying not to cry.

"I never thought you were capable, Dad," she muttered. "Thank you for being honest, but I don't want to talk about this anymore." She tore out the page bearing Mellissa's name and screwed it into a ball, launching it across the room. "I don't want to hear her name," she hissed. "Ever again!"

***

Sebastian Tint studied the letters carefully, reading each of the five several times. I remained silent, sipping my tea out of his best china while Ricky the German shepherd lay by the door, watching his master with mild interest.

"Well," he said finally, removing his glasses and looking up. "I have to say, I'm relieved. We might not have a name for this woman but, as you say, she could well be our Amelia. We know, of course, that Reverend Allington existed, but this Root woman has proved rather elusive."

"Do you think she was mad or just angry?" I asked.

Tint replaced his glasses a glanced down at the letters. "We can only speculate—but she certainly seemed to hate this Allington person."

Tint paused, his finger running along the lines on the page in front of him. He stopped and tapped. "We need to find out about the Stanwick household," he said. "Where they lived, what they did, and, above all, what connection they had with the Church. Then we can speculate a little more accurately."

***

The phone was ringing as I walked through the door. It was Staple. I told him about the letters and gave him as much information as I'd gathered. "I just need to know where his descendants are," I told him. "I know I'm clutching at straws here, but—"

"I understand," Jack cut in. "Sebastian told me about your daughter. I'm really sorry. I'll get onto it straight away."

We didn't talk for long. Staple sounded preoccupied, almost as if he had now taken upon himself the responsibility for my daughter's welfare. I wished that my life had a remote control with a fast forward or maybe a rewind, which would take me back to that Sunday morning when Pascoe and Taylor were eyeing up the girls in Alshaw Park.

The feeling of restlessness led me to Elizabeth's grave, where I remained until visiting time approached. I'd eaten nothing, but despite my lack of appetite, I stopped off at the hospital shop and bought an overpriced sandwich which I ate as I made my way down the long soulless corridors.

Jenny looked up as I entered the room. She was pale and drawn but seemed relieved to see me.

"Jack's onto the Allington thing," I told her, trying to sound upbeat.

My daughter nodded but didn't answer. I could see that she had been crying. I didn't want to bring up the subject of Melissa Ingram.

"Look, Jen," I said, sitting on the edge of her bed, "everything is going to be okay. We'll find Amelia."

Jenny shrugged. "If she exists."

"You don't think she does? What about the mad woman at the church?"

"I don't know. I'm not sure about anything anymore."

I felt anger surging inside. Jenny had only been here for a couple of days and had started to believe that this was all in her head. "Let's just see what Jack drags up," I said, trying to ignore her dark mood. "I've a good feeling about this."

***

My instinct served me well. Jack called two days later. Days during which I watched helplessly as my daughter struggled with self-doubt, sinking into a mire of despondency.

"Robert—I have some news!" He paused. "You might like to sit down for this."

My heart quickened. "I'm ready. What have you got?"

"I've traced the Reverend Allington's family tree. They had a daughter called Rebecca, who married a Joseph Laycock. They had two children, Louisa and Thomas. Thomas fell ill and died, aged twenty, while Louisa went on to marry an Arthur Pensby. They had one child, Ellen, who married a certain—wait for it— George Pascoe!"

I felt a chill travel the length of my spine. "Pascoe?"

"Yes. They had one child. Benjamin."

I flopped back into the chair.

"Hello? Robert?"

"I'm still here," I replied. "I just don't quite know what to say."

"Well, if I were you, I'd go and drop in on his wife for a chat. Then I'd see if any of his family might have any stories or, better still, photos or letters. You just never know what they might dig up."

I thanked Jack and replaced the receiver, allowing the music from the radio to drift over me. Had I been dreaming? What would Jenny's doctors say when I told them that she had walked into a church, fifty miles from her home, and vandalised the grave of Darren Pascoe's great, great grandfather? I didn't really understand the spirit world, but only a fool could consider it a coincidence.

I needed to talk to Victoria Pascoe. It would, at least, give me time to think.

***

Jenny stared at me. "Pascoe? That little bastard's father?"

"The very same."

She seemed to stiffen, almost as if she had placed her finger in a light socket. "I can't believe it—not..."

Her voice trailed off as she stared into space, her face drained of any colour.

"What's wrong?"

Jenny's eyes were red, her face almost grey. I guessed she wasn't sleeping too well.

"It doesn't make sense."

Jenny was addressing herself, not me. I could have walked out of that room and she wouldn't have even noticed. I left after half an hour. My daughter, absorbed in her own confusion, had not wanted to talk.

I walked like a man bearing the weight of the world, hardly recognising my reflection in the glass doors. I could only hope that the Pascoe family had some answers.

Chapter Nineteen

I T DIDN'T TAKE too long to find the Pascoes' home. I pulled up outside and waited, having already decided against revealing my identity. My name was now Peter Norris, and I was writing a book on life in the eighteenth century. I had been studying certain people I believed to have been her ancestors.

Mrs. Pascoe had sounded amiable enough when I'd called that morning and had agreed to talk, although she wasn't sure she could be of much help. I wasn't so sure either, but curiosity took over. I wanted to meet the woman who had given birth to the kid who had robbed me of my wife and child. Perhaps it could be described as a morbid curiosity, but I couldn't have cared less.

The woman who opened the door to me was younger than I'd expected. She wore a black silky top and tight fashionable jeans. She smiled warily. "Mr. Norris?"

I nodded, feeling a pang of guilt. The woman, after all, was innocent. Maybe it had something to do with the physical attraction I felt as I followed her into the room. It was difficult not to notice that she still had her youthful figure and her face showed little sign of age.

The room was modern—the kind you see on these TV makeover shows. Cream walls, wood floor, modern art hanging over an artificial coal fire set into the wall and lit by remote control. The plasma TV screen towered in the corner. Mrs. Pascoe flicked the remote and the picture died.

"Coffee? Tea?" she asked, standing with her hands on her hips, flashing a couple of inches of bare midriff.

I smiled. "Coffee will be fine, Mrs. Pascoe. Milk and one sugar."

"Call me Victoria," she said with a smile before disappearing into the kitchen.

I sat back, uncomfortable with the fact that I already liked the woman whose child had killed mine. How many tears had she cried? Her world, too, had fallen apart. A broken marriage. A son locked away. Would she have given up all the trappings of success just to have her life back? Was this something we shared? Something we had in common?

"I've not really taken much of an interest in family history," she said, handing me a mug of instant coffee. "I never seemed to find the time."

"Not many people do," I reassured her. "It seems to be the occupation of the retired, these days."

Victoria nodded. "So what's bitten you?" she asked.

I'd not really considered an answer to that one but surprised myself nevertheless. "Probably too many period dramas," I replied. "I just found myself looking over old sepia photos of life in the late eighteenth century—the old houses, the workhouses and the servants. It's fascinating."

"So what brings you here?"

"I traced your family from the Reverend Allington, the minister of St. Jude's in Tabwell in around 1870. According to the records, he did a great deal of good work amongst the poor and founded a school with the intent of providing a good education for the local kids."

Victoria Pascoe nodded. "Nice to know we came from decent stock, at least."

"Ah, but did you? You see, we found letters suggesting that Allington may have had a few skeletons in the old cupboard. Apparently, at the christening of his child, the service was interrupted by a crazy woman."

I went on to tell Victoria the whole story—or everything we knew from the letters I'd discovered in the attic—about the rocky relationship that seemed to exist between Mary Allington and her fiercely religious mother.

"Interesting ancestors," she said with a faint smile. "Almost as colourful a life as ours…" her voice trailed off.

"Really?"

Victoria smiled. "It's a long story."

***

Our meeting lasted little more than an hour, during which I had looked at some old family photographs of Victoria's side of the family. I'd taken them, feigning interest and promising to copy and return them the following day. I'd drawn a blank—a kind of dead end—or at least I thought I had. Victoria handed me a slip of paper just as I was leaving.

"If you want to know about my husband's side of the family, I'd go and talk to his mother. If I remember rightly, she has a house full of old letters and documents. She lives in a bit of a time warp herself, if you ask me."

I looked at the slip of paper. *Ellen Pascoe.* The name had a phone number scrawled underneath it.

"If she wants to talk to you, she'll give you the address—but be warned, don't bullshit her. She might be elderly but she's as bloody sharp as a razor."

I drove home wondering why Victoria had thought that I might even attempt to *bullshit* her mother-in-law. Did she doubt my story? Had she been humouring me all along? I knew that the woman was no fool. She had a good job and had married well—a man, if my memory of the newspaper articles served me well, who must have been at least fifteen years her senior. Benjamin Pascoe was in his early fifties. Victoria, even if she had been under the knife, could only have just hit her mid-thirties.

I wondered if I'd been forewarned by a disgruntled daughter-in-law. I sensed little affection in Victoria's tone when she talked about the old woman, so I called her that afternoon anticipating an abrasive old grandmother to pick up. Instead, I'd found myself talking to a rather sweet, eloquent woman who dealt with the call from a stranger with humour and grace.

"Ah, an old crusty historian! How wonderful!" she exclaimed. "So much more exciting than those double-glazing salesmen."

I laughed.

"And you say that Victoria recommended me?"

"Yes. She said you have a house full of family history."

"Yes. Much of which that girl would have tossed out, along with half of my possessions, if she'd been given half the chance!" the old lady said with a chuckle. "That girl's home looks like no one lives in it!"

Ellen Pascoe was not only bright but very active, and she agreed to see me after her local coffee morning in two days' time. I wrote down the address and thanked her, already having decided to arrive with a bunch of flowers, although I had a feeling that a bottle of gin would have been just as welcome.

***

When I saw Jenny that evening, I failed to disguise my lack of animosity towards Victoria Pascoe. She stopped me mid-sentence, staring coldly. "Good to see you're making new friends. Mum would be so proud!"

If she could have slapped me and got away with it, she would. But Jenny knew that her behaviour was being monitored, and if she could not control what happened in her sleep, she sure needed to watch what she did while she was awake.

"That's not fair, Jen," I protested. "I could hardly be unpleasant to the woman, could I?"

"I can read you like a book, Dad," she whispered as a nurse hovered at the door, scribbling something on her clipboard. "I can tell by the way you're talking about her. Doesn't Mum's life mean anything?"

"She didn't kill Mum, Jen."

"She was responsible for her son. She obviously didn't seem to care who he was with or what he got up to!"

"It's not always that simple," I protested

"It is when you want it to be," Jenny replied with an accusing glare.

***

I left the hospital that evening with my daughter's words laying heavily on my conscience. She now saw me as a bed-hopping middle-aged womaniser. It wasn't that I didn't understand how she felt. Victoria was a Pascoe, after all. She may not have been behind the wheel of the four-wheel drive that Sunday afternoon, but I'd felt comfortable in her company and that was enough to anger Jenny.

Sometimes people found the capacity to forgive others for the most terrible acts of violence. I'd often wondered how they overcame the natural human reaction to wallow in hatred. Perhaps my ability to accept Victoria's innocence, and my inability to find her complicit in the death of my wife and daughter, meant that I was just a good guy at heart.

I was at peace with myself by the time I arrived home but the answering machine was flashing ominously. I hit the button and waited. Sure enough, it was Victoria.

"Hi—Victoria Pascoe here—please ring me ASAP."

There was none of the warmth in her tone—in fact, she sounded agitated. I picked up and dialled her number immediately.

"Hi, This is—"

Victoria cut in. "You've left your wallet."

I felt my stomach tighten.

"Thank you—I'll come over now."

***

I ran a red light with my foot hard to the floor, praying that Victoria wouldn't open the damn thing and discover my identity. When I arrived she was watering the plants that overflowed the terracotta containers either side of the door.

She pulled the wallet out of the pocket of her denims as I approached. "Mr. Robert Adams, this says." Her eyes were cold.

"I know—I'm sorry…"

"Why did you lie? What do you want from me?"

"Look, I can explain. My daughter—"

"I thought your face was familiar. I just couldn't place it. Then I remembered. It was plastered across the front pages of the local news. How could I have been so stupid?"

"I'm sorry. I just—"

"Want blood?"

"No, I thought—"

"You thought that you'd lie, wheedle your way into my life, and then exact some kind of revenge. What did you have in mind, Mr. Adams?"

"Mrs. Pascoe, I'm not after revenge. I don't intend any harm. Please believe me."

Victoria stood, her arms hanging limply by her sides. "Then what *do* you want?"

"It's a really long story."

"Five minutes," she said. "After that, I don't want to see you again!"

The spark of attraction I'd felt yesterday burst into a flame.

"One sugar, isn't it?" she called from the kitchen.

Stop this! I chided myself. *Stop this now! Think about your daughter!*

Victoria Pascoe watched me warily as I sipped my coffee. "Okay," she said calmly. "What is this all about?"

***

Victoria had come from a long line of agnostics and found the whole spirit thing a little hard to swallow. She looked flustered as she listened, fidgeting incessantly throughout and saying little. When we shook to say farewell, I'd noticed her palms were damp.

"I don't wish to be rude, Mr. Adams, but I think it would be better if you didn't contact my mother-in-law. The whole episode nearly destroyed her. Darren was the love of her life."

"Elizabeth and Hanna were the loves of mine, Mrs. Pascoe. I deserve some cooperation."

Victoria blushed and averted her gaze. "Yes. Yes, I'm so sorry— that was thoughtless…" I saw the guilt in her eyes. "I just feel that it might be too much…"

"I'll call her back. If she says no, I won't push."

Victoria shrugged and smiled weakly. "If you have to. But I'll be calling her to let her know exactly who you are."

***

I flicked on the early evening news and lay back on the couch while a local politician bemoaned the escalating cost of fuel. I groaned and stretched, glancing at my watch. It was four—plenty of time to shower and visit the grave on the way to the hospital.

The sun was sinking low on the horizon as I arrived at the cemetery gates, bathing the land in a glorious golden glow. A solitary blackbird sat perched on the branch of a cherry tree leading the evening chorus. The whole place looked so wonderfully peaceful—a resting place for the dead and those they left. I had come laden with guilt—guilt that could only be shed at the place where my wife and child lay.

Once again, I read the inscription: words penned by a man who had fallen into the bed of his mistress and broken the heart of a woman who truly loved him. I began to sob, sinking slowly to my knees and drowning in remorse. I missed Elizabeth. I missed her love—her body—the smell of her skin. Melissa could never have replaced the woman I'd lost and the beautiful little girl she had presented me with.

I left having made my peace. I climbed behind the wheel of my car and turned up the radio, wondering once more what I was going to find behind the hospital doors.

***

Jenny was sitting up in her bed, listening to her iPod as I walked in. She smiled, pulling the wires from her ears. "Hi, Dad," she said breezily. "Guess who I'm listening to?"

I shrugged. "I'm guessing it has to be something you downloaded."

"Yeah, ages ago—when you got me into that swing stuff. I'd forgotten about it."

Given the fact that Jenny's iPod could hold about three months' worth of continuous music, it wasn't hard to believe.

"Tony Bennett rocks!" she said with a wide grin. It appeared that my encounter with Victoria Pascoe had been forgotten. "Do you reckon he's better than Frank?"

I shook my head. "Hey, girl, watch your mouth. Sinatra is the King!"

Jenny laughed and tucked her iPod under the pillow. I'd not seen her so upbeat for a long time, but somehow her mood unnerved me.

"You're looking well," I said airily.

My daughter shrugged as if she didn't really understand it herself. "I've been talking to Dr. Grace today. You know, about Amelia and all that stuff."

"About Allington and the mad woman?"

Jenny nodded.

"And what did she say?"

"Nothing, really. Just asked more questions about my dreams and wrote things down."

"But you felt good, just talking?"

"She believed me, Dad. She doesn't think I'm going crazy."

"She said that?"

"No. She didn't need to. I sensed it. No, I knew it. Don't ask me how."

I smiled. "That's great, Jen. Let's hope she has some clout when it comes to getting you out of this place."

We talked some more about Frank and Tony, and I promised to introduce her to Dean Martin sometime soon. I left her with spring-heeled shoes and a dancing heart, convinced that our luck had changed and Ellen Pascoe would complete the jigsaw leading us to Amelia Root.

***

I called the old girl the following morning, just to check that our meeting was still on. It wasn't. "I can't help you, Mr. Adams. My heart aches every time I think of the poor man who lost his wife and little girl. It was my boy—my grandson." The old woman's voice sounded suddenly frail. "I could not bear to look at you when I still have love in my heart for the boy who caused you so much pain."

I tried to reason with her. "But I could never blame you, Mrs. Pascoe. How could any grandparent stop loving their grandchildren?" My words echoed in my head, hollow platitudes that seemed destined to fail.

Ellen Pascoe sounded tired, as if my very name had been a weight in her heart. "I'm sorry, Mr. Adams," she said. The silence that followed left me with no option but to apologise for bothering her and hang up.

Dead ends. I hated them.

Chapter Twenty

OVER THE WEEK that followed, Jenny slept soundly at night, untroubled by dreams of any kind. She seemed relaxed and happy, spending her days listening to music and reading a chic-lit novel.

Josie invited me over to the local church hall to watch her run through a set with the old band she used to sing with. "Not sure when it's going to be, hun, but I just want you to tell me if I've still got what it takes," she said with an air of confidence that suggested she had no real doubts.

The invitation lifted my spirits, and that evening, I picked up a bottle of Argentinean white at the local late shop. The day had been mild, with not even the hint of a cloud in the sky. I missed Elizabeth and Hanna so much on these days. We would go walking together along the local footpaths with a picnic stuffed into a backpack.

I sat out late that night and fired up the patio heater, listening to the water trickling into the pond I'd built as soon as Hanna had reached an age where she understood the dangers of even the smallest expanse of water.

By ten-thirty, the sounds and the smells of autumn evenings had stopped, leaving me alone in my own world. The garden had been designed for this. Peaceful days and silent nights. I sat with my bottle of chilled wine, staring over a lawn lit only by the moon and a few garden lights, thinking through the past few months and wondering what lay in store.

I had never understood the supernatural or, if I'm honest, ever had any desire to investigate its role in our lives. People who immersed themselves in such things seemed to see spirits everywhere they looked. I didn't. Maybe that was why I was so convinced by what I witnessed that night.

It was eleven thirty, and despite being three-quarters through my bottle of wine, I felt stone-cold sober. I sat back and closed my eyes, allowing my mind to drift away from the turbulence of life into an unusually peaceful state. When I opened my eyes, I found myself staring at a tree in the neighbouring garden. The only thing I knew about this tree was its size; it was large enough to cast a shadow across our lawn every sunny summer afternoon.

Now, silhouetted against the moonlit sky, it had taken on a different shape. I saw the profile of a woman's face. She was old, her hair tied in a bun. The forehead was long and the eyes deep set, the nose straight and the mouth...I stared. The mouth was open wide and moving in a wind that didn't exist. In my mind, I heard the wail of anguish that wrenched at my soul. I knew this woman. I knew her even though I'd never set eyes on her in my life. It was Ellen Pascoe.

That night I dreamed. I saw the shape of the old woman's face in the tree again. Water dripped from the branches, leaving pools that reflected the moonlight from a cloudless sky. Even now, with the passing of time, I can recall the image vividly. When I called Ellen the following day, to ask her to reconsider her decision, I knew she would agree to see me. She sounded tired and almost on the verge of tears. The call was brief. She agreed to see me that evening, anytime after seven.

I spent the day in the garden, staring at a tree which now appeared to have no shape whatsoever.

Chapter Twenty-One

ELLEN PASCOE PEERED round the narrow gap between the front door and its frame. "Mr. Adams?" she enquired in a frail voice. The old lady dropped the chain and opened the door.

Darren Pascoe's grandmother stood no more than five foot with a shock of thinning grey hair tied into a bun. I saw the same forehead, the same nose, but now the mouth formed a wistful smile. She looked every one of her eighty-eight years, yet there was a youthfulness in her manner that time had not dimmed.

"Do come in," she said, waving me through to a narrow hallway that was somewhat overpowered by a heavily patterned blue, gold and red carpet. "I'll go and put the kettle on." She pointed through an open doorway to her left. "Make yourself comfortable."

Mrs. Pascoe motored on with her Zimmer and disappeared into the narrow kitchen facing us as I walked into an Aladdin's cave of porcelain ornaments lining every surface of a cluttered room. The walls were lined with photographs and old prints in yellowing frames. A youthful Benjamin Pascoe smiled down at us in his cap and gown, next to some old photos of a young child— Benjamin, I presumed.

The prints protected my eyes from a hideous flock wallpaper that looked like a surplus stock from a local pub. I scanned the walls, looking for clues of which I found none, apart from a couple of small pencil sketches of a tree-lined pond.

Mrs. Pascoe popped her head around the door. "Tea's ready. Would you mind getting your own?"

I sat down with our mugs of milky warm tea, wondering if it would be possible to leave without drinking it.

"Mrs. Pascoe, I'm really sorry to bother you," I began, "but I thought you might be able to shed some light on the family history."

Ellen Pascoe smiled. "Well, dear, I'll certainly try. What is it you want to know?"

The old lady peered through her bifocals, her eyes unnervingly magnified by the angle of her head.

"I know this might seem a strange request," I began, "so I might as well tell you the whole story, right from the start. At least then you'll understand exactly why I'm here."

Mrs. Pascoe nodded slowly. "That would help, dear."

Bright as a button! I thought.

***

I began on the day my wife and child lost their lives before moving on a year to Jenny and the nightmares. As the story unfolded, I saw the change in the old woman's expression. The look of mild interest disappeared, and her eyes grew dark. I told her how the Reverend Francis had called us from St. Jude's. I told her about the graffiti and the discovery that the word hypocrite was, in fact, referring to Reverend Allington.

The old lady's eyes closed as she shook her head but said nothing. When she looked back up at me I continued, explaining how we had traced Allington's ancestry in our quest to discover the link between Jenny and the spirit of a dead woman.

Mrs. Pascoe shifted in her chair, her hands crossed neatly on her lap. "Well, you certainly have been through the mill, my dear," she said. "But I'm not sure how I can help. I might have some old photos, but I don't think that they would tell you much."

I knew the woman was lying. "I'm sorry to impose, Mrs. Pascoe, but we're desperate—"

"This woman," the old lady said, interrupting me mid-flow. "The one in the dream. Does she have a name?"

"Amelia Root," I replied.

Ellen froze, and the colour drained from her face.

"Are you okay?" I asked nervously.

"Yes! Yes!" she replied, quickly composing herself.

"Mrs. Pascoe… That name…it means something to you, doesn't it?"

Ellen nodded, her hands trembling. "I have something you need to see," she said, rising unsteadily from her chair and shuffling across the room before exiting without a word.

***

The old lady had been gone some time, and when she finally returned and pushed an envelope into my hand, there was sadness in her eyes. "No one at St. Jude's must ever hear about this," she said. "I beg you."

There was no threat in her voice, and I could do nothing less than give her my word. I looked down at the old envelope.

"It is a letter my own mother left me," she said. "Along with a letter from my grandmother…"

It read simply: *Dear Ellen. To be opened after my death.*

I pulled out a letter, beautifully written and filling two pages. Within the envelope was another one, smaller and addressed: *To Louisa. Upon my death.*

I pulled out my glasses and, with the room now eerily silent, began to read.

Chapter Twenty-Two

My dearest Ellen,

I have considered, many times, revealing the contents of this letter face-to-face, yet I feel that the printed word will, in effect, carry more weight. Much that needs to be said is within the letter my own mother left for me, and you will find this enclosed. Please do not read it until you have considered my own requests.

Your great-grandfather lies interned at St. Jude's, beneath the statue of St. Peter. He was a much respected man who founded the church school and provided an education for many children who would otherwise have grown up illiterate.

I only remember that those around the parish remember him with affection, considering him to be a true and righteous man. Hence I, as his granddaughter, lived my life, striving to keep his memory alive through my own dedication to the work of God, and in many ways, I considered that he might have approved of my life.

I was a small girl of about eight when I heard my grandmother, Mary, sobbing in the company of my own mother, who discovered me listening on the other side of the door. She scolded me and I was sent to my room immediately. However, in the days that followed, I noticed that my mother's disposition had changed, and she talked little, often waving me away when I approached her, telling me that young girls should not be so inquisitive. I saw little of her after that and learned nothing of their dark secret until the day she died.

You are now free to read the letter I read many years ago and would request of you the same that she, my own mother, requested of me, should God bless you with children. I beg of you this one thing.

Your Mother, Louisa.

Mrs. Pascoe sat, impassively, watching as I opened the next envelope. The writing was large and sloped, heavily suggesting that Rebecca might have been shortsighted.

Dearest Louisa and Thomas,

You are, and will remain, my beloved children, and I consider it my duty before God that I, Rebecca Laycock, wife of Joseph Laycock, reveal the truth of your ancestry.

As you know, I was raised by Mary Allington, wife of Charles Allington, who was the long-serving minister at St. Jude's, a man considered by many to be a saint. One day, my mother came to me in great distress and informed me that she had lived with a terrible knowledge for many years. Sometimes, I wished she had never shared that knowledge.

For months before my birth, my mother had long suspected that her husband had been attracted to the young school governess employed by the wealthy Stanwick family at The Grange, after his not infrequent and unnecessary visits to their home. She had confided in her own mother, still living in Ireland, writing several letters, but received no comfort in reply.

The Stanwicks were not God-fearing people, and rarely attended church, but my father claimed that they were generous and made many donations to God's work, hence his visits. My mother's fears were allayed and the letters to her mother ceased. However, God had not blessed them with the child they longed for, and my father was beside himself with rage. Why should a servant of God be treated thus? He blamed my mother, claiming her sins, whatever they had been, had left her barren. His absences from the house grew longer and longer until one day, he asked my mother to come to his study. He had some good news.

"We can have a child," he told her. My mother, quite naturally asked how this could be. "To the world outside, it will be our child. No one knows of your inability to conceive. You will feign pregnancy and remain out of sight until I bring the baby home."

My mother believed that this was the will of God, an answer to prayer, and that to question such was to insult the Lord himself. So she waited the term, venturing out only when necessary, until the night my father arrived home with a local doctor and baby girl, swaddled in a blanket.

"This is Dr. Ellis," he announced. "Dr. Ellis delivered your baby tonight."

With that, he placed me, a three-hour old child, in my mother's arms.

I cannot imagine how she felt, but she loved me from that moment, having convinced herself that I was a gift from the Almighty.

It was ten years later that a woman arrived at the door of the manse in a state of distress. She quickly introduced herself as Sarah Bell, governess to the Stanwick family, and my mother, concerned that the woman might require spiritual guidance, invited her in.

The woman revealed that she had carried a dark secret with her for many years and now, unable to live with the guilt of compliance, had wished to unburden her soul. She handed her a letter, several pages in length. "Please read it," she said. "For I fear that I should not be able to tell my story without a great deal of distress, so I have chosen to write."

The woman left, refusing to put a foot over the doorstep. My mother handed me the letter and sat in silence as I read it. I cannot tell you how wretched I felt when I learned the truth. The man I believed to be my father—a man who had been respected and loved. I wept for days, taking to my bed and refusing the food my mother offered me. I had no appetite. Even as I write this, my heart is heavy.

Your Mother, Rebecca.

"Where are you up to?" Mrs. Pascoe asked.

"The governess is about to tell her tale," I muttered.

"This is the part you won't believe," she said, handing me another letter while peering into my half-empty mug. "I'll fetch some more tea."

Sarah Bell's account was written on bonded white paper with pale fading ink, almost as if it had been watered down.

"I would make yourself comfortable," the old lady said, pulling herself to her feet. "I have shorter novels in my possession!"

She had a point. The letter was several pages long. I began to read.

My name is Sarah Bell, a woman compelled to document the truth that I have lived with for so long. I am guilty of silence and compliance. These are sins for which I have begged God's forgiveness and the reason I am writing this letter. I could talk of my time with the Stanwicks for many hours, yet my words would die with me, forgotten in time. I cannot allow this to be and beg you to preserve this letter, allowing it to be passed down through the generations. The reason for this request, you will understand as you read on.

I was raised by a strict mother and a prudent father who, despite longing for a son, treated me well and invested heavily in my education. I taught at the local school before taking up the position of governess at The Grange in the employment of the wealthy Stanwick family.

I was made most welcome by Harriet Stanwick, the lady of the house, an immaculate and handsome woman who introduced me to Clara, her daughter, informing me that this was the young lady in my charge. Clara stood, resplendent in a blue velvet dress with exquisite lace cuffs. She had inherited her mother's fairness of face but I was told that she was preoccupied with much that would hinder her education and would require a firm hand.

I saw little of Mr. Stanwick, a large man with heavy jowls and dark eyes that seemed to lack any trace of human kindness. He made no effort to welcome me. Indeed, I was a servant and not worthy of his attention. I could see nothing of him in his daughter.

Clara proved to be a delightful child but was indeed boisterous by nature and would beg me to take her to the woods were she would run and hide from me, giggling incessantly. We would retire to the drawing room for lessons but Clara was tireless and lacked concentration. I would often retire, and take to my bed, weary from my efforts.

I was, however, happy at The Grange and Mrs. Stanwick would spend much of her leisure time with me, often treating me as a sister rather than an employed hand. One particular day, during one of Mr. Stanwick's frequent prolonged absences, she took me into her confidence.

We sat in the drawing room while Clara occupied herself in the library. "I have a matter to discuss with you," she told me. "It is with regard to your duties within the house."

It was then that Mrs. Stanwick revealed that, during one of her husband's frequent and prolonged absences, she had become intimate with another man. "We spent many hours together, walking in the grounds. He was intelligent and self-educated, with impeccable manners and a kindly heart. I loved him and one night he came to me."

Mrs. Stanwick's mood was solemn. That is when I learned that she had become pregnant with her lover's child. As the governess, I felt it was my place to listen and not to enquire, but having encountered the rather unpleasant Mr. Stanwick, I was slow to judge the woman, despite having found myself unable to disguise my shock.

When Mr. Stanwick learned of the pregnancy he beat his wife so badly that a doctor was called. He was, however, unrepentant and made it clear that he never wanted to set eyes on the child and left the house, remaining abroad for several months. It was during this time Mrs. Stanwick gave birth to a girl.

She had arranged for medical assistance and insisted that no one beyond the walls of The Grange should ever hear of the birth. The baby was not to be registered. Stanwick insisted that it was to be raised in the attic room at the top of the house, and his daughter, Clara, was never to know of its existence, although I am at a loss to know how this was kept from her during the nine months she was with child.

"And that is everything you need to know," Mrs. Stanwick said, rising from her chair. "And I think you know what I am going to ask."

It was with much trepidation that I followed Mrs. Stanwick up a narrow flight of stairs to a wooden door. She turned briefly. "It is not my choice," she informed me coldly. "I have taught the child as much as I know. I owe her an education." With that, she turned the key and pushed open the door. The room was small and bare, with only a tin bath tub, a bed, a wooden trunk and a desk, where a small girl of five sat staring out of a tiny window.

The child, her black hair tied back into a bun, turned as we entered. "This is Amelia," Mrs. Stanwick told her. "She has beautiful eyes."

I gasped, for indeed, her eyes were unusually large. I was alarmed by the paleness of her skin yet when she smiled, I knew that I could learn to care for that wretched child.

I committed two hours of each day to the education of little Amelia who, unlike Clara, seemed anxious to learn. She spoke well and took great delight in recording almost everything I told her in a diary that her mother had provided. She had a beautiful hand. She addressed me as Miss Bell but corrected me when I referred to her as Amelia Stanwick. "My name is not Amelia Stanwick," she told me. "My name is Amelia Root."

I enquired as to why this was. Amelia smiled. "That is my father's name," she said in a whisper. "He works in the gardens."

Amelia's father would visit every few days, taking her into the gardens. I, too, would take Amelia out, careful that Clara was not present. Amelia would wonder at everything. The trees, the breeze on her face, the blue sky and white, rolling clouds. She would sob on her return to the room and take solace in her books and her diary, where she would record the things she had seen and would often sketch the world beyond her tiny window from memory alone.

I feel only joy when I recall those days, watching the little girl as she grew into a young woman in the body of a child. She was small, developing little, but when she closed her eyes, I realised that there was an unusual beauty in that face. Her mind was sharp and I loved her. I loved her as if she were my own child, and it is with a heavy heart that I relate the following.

On Amelia's seventeenth birthday, I was asked to inform her that the minister from St. Jude's was to pay her a visit. Amelia was perplexed by the news, wondering what a man of God could possibly want with her. Just after lunch, I heard Mrs. Stanwick arguing with a man at in the main lounge. I considered it wise to move into the garden and take an afternoon stroll.

Later that day I passed the Reverend Allington on the main stairs. The man appeared extremely agitated and barely acknowledged me. I found Amelia sobbing uncontrollably, but the girl would not be pressed as to what had caused her distress, and I felt it was prudent to let the matter drop, choosing not to report the incident to Mrs. Stanwick.

Reverend Allington visited Amelia several times over the following weeks, and it troubled me to see the change in her quiet and friendly disposition. The girl would begin to cry over the most simple matters and would frequently leave her food. On one occasion, I found her standing in the tub, naked and scrubbing her body with a brush, her skin raw and bleeding.

Eventually, I brought my concerns to the attention of Mrs. Stanwick, who promised to look into the matter. It was shortly after this that one afternoon, Clara became unwell and, with no further duties that day, I decided to visit Amelia. When I arrived at the attic door, I heard sounds from inside. Fearing that Amelia might harm herself, I pushed open the door.

It was with horror that I saw the figure of the Reverend Allington forcing himself on Amelia, who was naked, her legs wrenched apart, her screams muffled by the pillow held over her face. The minister turned, his face the colour of a ruby. "Get out!" he bellowed. "Get out now!"

I slammed the door shut, fear overtaking my desire to come to Amelia's rescue. I waited, consumed with hatred and guilt, until the Reverend Allington appeared minutes later. He addressed me curtly. "This is God's will," he said, "and it is no business of yours. Should your tongue ever be loosened, you will never set foot in the house of God again." He smiled grimly. "And your soul will burn in hell!"

I discovered shortly after this that Mrs. Stanwick had knowledge of the Reverend's visits. "The Reverend Allington and his wife are childless," she told me tearfully. "We have an agreement with them, arranged, quite naturally, by my husband, who cares nothing for Amelia's welfare."

"But why? Amelia is protesting!" I told her. "She is resisting his attentions and she is becoming increasingly distressed." Mrs. Stanwick raised the palm of her hand. "Say no more! There is nothing I can do!"

I discovered the Reverend Allington learned of Amelia's existence and had been visiting for months without my knowledge, offering spiritual guidance to Mrs. Stanwick, but his kindness was to be rewarded with a child.

I continued in the service of the Stanwick family only for the sake of Amelia, who, ten months later, gave birth to a baby. A certain Dr. Ellis delivered the child while the Reverend Allington waited in the lounge. Ellis passed the child to Allington at ten past five in the evening, assuring him that the baby was healthy, and agreed to accompany him home.

I was allowed to visit Amelia after two hours and found her sitting up in her bed, her eyes closed. At that time, I felt as if my heart would burst with sorrow and shame. Amelia opened her eyes and I have never seen such grief. "They have taken my baby," she said. "They have taken my poor baby!"

I could not console her, and over the following weeks, she became impossible to teach. Ellis would visit Amelia to salve his own conscience but cared little for his patient. Then, one day, I found that Amelia was not in her room. I immediately reported this to Harriet, and we both searched the house and gardens for several hours, but Amelia was nowhere to be seen.

We came across Jacob Root in the lane, and Harriet, still clearly smitten with her gardener, asked him if he had seen Amelia. "She will be at the church," he said. "For the christening of her child."

Harriet was taken aback and asked how Amelia had found out. Jacob looked angry. I could tell that he now despised Harriet. "I informed her," he replied. "It is, after all, her child."

I was not there to witness the moment Amelia intruded upon the ceremony, with her claims that were dismissed by the congregation and indeed the whole community, as the ranting of a mad woman, but I remember the Reverend Allington calling at The Grange the following day, his face contorted with rage.

Amelia had returned and, ignoring her mother's rebuke, taken to her room. I tried to stop the Reverend Allington, but he shook me away like a child's doll. I followed him, up the narrow flights of stairs, until I reached the open door. Amelia stood when she saw him. He stepped forward.

"You ungrateful child of hell," he muttered. "How dare you enter the house of God and accuse me in front of my flock? You came from hell and it is there you shall return!"

Amelia stared at him. "Sir, I have read my Bible through. It is the same Bible that you read yet fail to understand. It is you who will stand before God on judgment day and it is you who will have to account for your actions."

This enraged the Reverend Allington. "How dare you speak to me of such things, you daughter of a whore!" With that, he grasped Amelia's shoulders and pushed her hard. I saw her falling backwards against the desk. I tried to intervene but again, reverend Allington pushed me aside. Amelia stared up at him. "Leave me be," she hissed, her eyes fixed on the minister.

The Reverend Allington was furious and, with a single hand, took her by the neck. I swear before God that I could have done nothing to prevent the events that followed, for I didn't notice her hand on the knife I'd used for peeling apples from the garden lying alongside her diary.

"God has put you on this Earth for a purpose," he roared. The Reverend Allington tightened his grip on her neck just as Amelia raised her arm high in the air and plunged the knife into his chest with a force I had never imagined she possessed. I screamed as the Reverend stepped backwards. He looked at me, his eyes filled with terror, and I watched helplessly as he collapsed upon the floor. Amelia ran from the room as I remained, standing over the Reverend Allington as his eyes closed. I called for Mrs. Stanwick, who was quick to summon Dr. Ellis. But by the time he arrived the minister was dead.

Dr. Ellis told the Parish that their minister had died of a heart attack. I find it difficult to believe that such a thing could remain a secret, but not even his wife knew the truth. Jacob Root went looking for his daughter later that day, followed by three rather uncouth looking men who Dr. Ellis had ordered to find the girl. They never found Amelia, but I overheard one of the men telling Mrs. Stanwick that Jacob Root had been dealt with and his actions avenged. To this day, I believe they killed him. Harriet would not allow me to mention Amelia's name, and I left two months later and with a generous remuneration in exchange for my silence. No one must ever know that Amelia Root existed.

I have borne the guilt of my silence for too long and would beseech you not to destroy this letter. It will serve as the only written evidence of Amelia's pitiful existence and the inhumanity of those who profess to serve God. I, an undeserving soul, have found employment abroad and shall be leaving these shores within the week. May the Lord forgive me. Amelia may have no grave on this earth but she will always remain in my heart. Sarah Bell

Ellen Pascoe watched me as I folded the letter and replaced it in the envelope. "So now we know," I said. "Amelia exists."

Mrs. Pascoe nodded. "Yes dear. And it's quite a story isn't it!"

I wanted to smile. I should have felt elated, relieved that my daughter had been right all along, yet, I felt strangely burdened. "One thing that bothers me..." I said, staring down at the gold swirls in the carpet. "My daughter believes that Amelia is her ancestor...but she can't be...she's yours."

And that is when I saw it in the old woman's eyes. Knowledge. If I had not addressed her face-to-face, I'd have missed it but however fleeting that look might have been, I'd no doubt. "What is it, Mrs. Pascoe? What am I missing?"

"Missing?" The old lady replied wearily.

I leaned forward, meeting her eyes "I have an incomplete jigsaw here. There are pieces missing!"

Ellen looked down at her frail hands and shifted forward. "I can only offer you advice," she said, her voice breaking. "You have found out all you need to know. Let it rest."

"But I need to see the complete picture," I replied continuing with the jigsaw analogy.

"If you find those pieces, Mr. Adams, the picture will change. Please leave it alone." Ellen Pascoe stood, signalling that it was time for me to leave.

"Last night," I began as I left the room behind my host. "Last night...I heard you crying."

Mrs. Pascoe spun round with the agility of a woman half her age. Her eyes fixed on mine. "Last night, Mr. Adams, I was sound asleep!"

I saw fear. "At half past eleven, last night, you were crying."

The fear turned to anger. "How could you know that? How? This is silly, Mr. Adams. I have helped you as much as I can, and I am beginning to regret it. Now, please go. Please."

The look in Ellen Pascoe's eyes haunted me, and as hard as I tried, my efforts to dismiss it as a mere figment of my overactive imagination failed. Conjecture is always a dangerous thing, leading its victims up blind alleys and abandoning them in dark places. My father had always taught me that you should only work with fact. Anything less was a waste of time. That night, I prayed for his strength.

***

Jenny could see the look in my eyes. I had always been an open book—heart-on-my-sleeve kind of person—and this was good news. I was a father with a gift for my baby.

"We've found her!" I said, slamming the door shut behind me.

Jenny sat upright in her bed.

"I spoke to Mrs. Pascoe. She had letters…"

My daughter listened patiently as I told her the story, starting with the tree and ending with the last words of a guilt-ridden governess, but Jenny was troubled by the same thoughts as me.

"But why did she call me her daughter? Why should everything else I've seen be right, yet this one thing…"

"It could have been a term—like women call each other 'sisters.'"

Jenny shook her head. "She was inside my head, Dad—inside here—my heart. I know what she meant."

A young male nurse interrupted us with profuse apologies and took the empty tea tray from the bedside table. Jenny waited until he had gone.

"I need to get out of this place, Dad. Amelia *wants* me out." She stared ahead at the wall, as if a great burden had come to rest on her shoulders. "This will not be over—not until we find her body."

Chapter Twenty-Three

I CALLED SEBASTIAN Tint the following morning. He sounded bright and cheerful, almost as if the news of my visit to Ellen Pascoe had already reached him on a strange, spiritual wind.

"I'm so glad," he said after I'd told him the story. "I'm about to take a walk—maybe you could come with me."

I had never felt quite so enthusiastic about such simple exercise—or maybe it was the company. I felt at ease with the old guy. He was eloquent and wise, yet the years had shaped him into a man of compassion, and it seemed to me sometimes that no one else on Earth could have filled my father's shoes.

We walked for nearly an hour, taking public footpaths through fields and over streams, a man and his hound at peace with the world. I told Tint how Jenny had confronted me with Melissa Ingram's name, which meant I then had to tell him the whole tale of my infidelity. The old man nodded, deep in thought.

"Have you asked yourself why the spirit of a dead woman would want to reveal such a thing to your daughter?"

I hadn't.

"You see, Amelia wanted to bring this affair to light—therefore, it must have some relevance."

"To what?"

"Well, that is what we need to find out."

"But Jenny hasn't had any dreams recently—"

Sebastian cut me short. "Because now she is speaking to *you*." He raised his eyebrows. "The face in the tree?"

I had sailed through my brush with the spirit world without having stopped to consider its relevance. Had those leaves and branches really formed themselves into a shape? Or had it all been a figment of my imagination, infiltrated by a restless spirit? Nor had I questioned whose face it had been. I knew. I knew without question and acted instinctively.

We walked for over an hour, stopping at a canal-side inn for a drink, leaving the subject of the paranormal alone in favour of lighter subjects. Ricky lay patiently, looking up occasionally to check that his master had not managed to sneak any food onto the table when he wasn't looking.

***

I felt unusually optimistic that afternoon and arrived at Jenny's bedside in a buoyant mood.

"You drunk, Dad?" she said with a frown.

"I had a drink with Seb," I told her. "Only one...but I had a couple more at home."

"A couple?"

"Don't worry, I took a taxi...and I'm here!"

"So you are."

"I'm just happy, that's all."

"About what?"

"Because I know it's all going to be okay—I just know."

Jenny grinned. "How much have you had...really?"

"Two pints with Sebastian and then, when I got home..." I had to think. "Erm...a bottle of beer and...and...wine. That's it. Wine."

"How much wine?"

"Well, there wasn't a lot left in the bottle...I don't think so, anyway."

"How much exactly? A half? A quarter?"

"Erm...kind of a...well...I suppose...nothing, really!"

Jenny giggled. The alcohol had kicked in and my head had started to ache. *This*, I thought, *is why I shouldn't drink during the day.*

***

The alcohol spun me into deep and beautiful sleep that night, having topped up my levels with a rum and ginger just to make sure I wasn't awake when my demons paid their customary visit. When I woke, the autumn sun was filtering through the curtains. It was mid-morning, the longest sleep I'd had since Elizabeth and Hanna had died. It meant something...yes, *something*. But I wasn't sure what.

Despite my buoyant mood, October loomed like an ominous storm cloud over my life. It was a dour month which, if it had a face, would be heavy eyed, deeply creviced with the thick jowls of a fearsome headmaster. I had always hated autumn, as beautiful as it could be. The crimson and gold had turned to brown mulch under busy feet, and I saw only death and decay. It was a month that heralded the onslaught of long cold nights and cheerless mornings—the beginning of hibernation.

Usually, by the time December arrived, as dismal a month as it could be, we had become accustomed to the dark nights and looking towards the festive season as we gathered around our fires and grew fat on beer and TV snacks. Elizabeth and I had always started the Christmas shopping by then. It was routine. Routine. You only miss it when someone takes a sledgehammer to your life and it shatters like a cheap wine glass.

I called Josie, who answered against a background of raucous laughter and jukebox music. Something inside me stirred when I heard her voice.

"Hi, Rob!" she said brightly. "How's it going?"

I told her about my walk with Sebastian and my subsequent drunken visit to Jenny's bedside. She laughed and told me that we should go out for another late-night coffee sometime. The idea sounded good. Even better than a long walk with my geriatric friend. When I called off, I told Josie that I loved her. It wasn't planned, it just happened. The words were out before I'd had a chance to stop them. There was a brief silence.

"I love you too, hun," she whispered. Then the phone went dead.

I *did* love Josie. Was it just a platonic thing? A love that existed between two friends? No, it was more than that, yet I failed miserably in my efforts to categorise those feelings and eventually settled on the fact that very few people objected to being loved. Josie would probably be quite happily pulling pints for her jukebox jivers at that very moment.

***

My relationship with Josie and the feeling of warmth that I felt each time I thought of her did nothing to distract me from the need to dig deeper into the mystery surrounding Amelia Root. Jenny could not find a link to the wretched woman in her ancestry but Ellen Pascoe knew something I didn't, and as hard as I tried, I couldn't come up with any answers. What secrets was she hiding? What *was* this whole picture? *The picture will change…let it rest.*

I could never understand why people revealed that they were holding onto secrets if they really didn't want anyone to find out. Something compelled Ellen Pascoe to dangle the carrot, inviting me to dig while warning me of the consequences. I thought that Sebastian had probably thought the same thing but had not wanted to encourage me to push the old lady.

I sat scanning the morning paper with Frank Sinatra crooning away in the background. *I've got you…under my skin…*

He was singing that line when I made up my mind, killed the sound and picked up my car keys. Within twenty minutes, I was outside Victoria Pascoe's front door.

Her manner was less than welcoming. "Mr. Adams. What do you want?"

"The truth."

Victoria Pascoe was an intelligent woman, immaculate and organised in every part of her life. She would not suffer fools gladly. I had to stand my ground. She would spot any weakness.

"You're hiding something. Something I need to know."

Victoria frowned. "I'm sorry, I really don't know what you're talking about."

My heart sank. The woman looked genuinely bemused by my approach. Maybe she really didn't have the whole picture, either. *Don't give in...don't back down!*

"There is a link between my daughter and your ancestor. I need to know what it is."

I was sure that Victoria was about to close the door.

"Mrs. Pascoe...please. This is destroying me. It's destroying Jenny. Mrs. Pascoe, try to put yourself in my shoes."

It didn't work. "I'm sorry—I can't help you."

"Ellen told me that I should stop asking questions...something about the whole picture changing. What did she mean, Mrs. Pascoe?"

Victoria glared at me. "I haven't got a clue! Look, she's old and she gets confused..."

"I need to know. Even if it means paying Ellen another visit."

I'd known from our first meeting that the faintest whiff of a threat would be like throwing a cigarette end into a barrel of gunpowder. It wasn't that I minded a blow-up—just not in my face.

"You set foot on her doorstep and I'll have you arrested!" she hissed. "Now stop stalking me, okay?" She paused, only for effect. "I can make this very difficult for you, Mr. Adams. If you want to play hardball then check out your opposition first!"

I knew exactly where this was going. I held my hand up in temporary surrender and walked away, but I wasn't defeated. The mother of my wife's killer only had the law on her side—a flawed legal system that frequently parted company with the most basic concept of human morality. But I had God on mine. That was how it felt. Maybe God was not a being, either sprit or human. Maybe He was just the inner knowledge—the understanding of evil. The appreciation of goodness.

Behind me, a door slammed shut but in my mind, a bell rang. I was a boxer. It was the next round.

Chapter Twenty-Four

I SAT AT the window that night, sipping slowly on a malt whisky and watching the trees shifting lazily in the evening breeze. Ellen Pascoe appeared to be my only hope of finding the answers I needed, but she had become almost as hostile as her daughter-in-law when I'd asked too many questions. Yet, she was troubled, and a troubled old lady with time on her hands craves a listening ear.

I poured myself another malt while an old compilation disc of Elizabeth's played in the background. I closed my eyes as the last track played. After this, I'd vowed to take to my bed. Then I heard what must have been a bonus track—the ones that you find hidden away on the CDs—a girl with a gentle voice that sounded like a melodic whisper. *I have a picture of you, I see a picture of you and I cry,* she sang. *That picture of you made me cry—made me cry—made me cry—made me cry.* Her lament was interrupted by a sound coming from the lounge.

I rushed through from the back room, my heart thumping, praying that I wouldn't find myself confronted by some thug with a baseball bat looking for easy pickings.

The room was still—that awful stillness that only the parting of a loved one leaves. I glanced around. Jenny's youthful face looked back at me from a gold photo frame. The picture itself was intact, and so was the frame. But the glass had shattered.

I felt a clawing coldness in my bones. There was something—someone in the room with me. I knew that it was nothing I'd be able to see of touch. I felt no malice in the presence, but I wanted to run. I wanted to run from the room, to run from my life yet my legs felt like lead.

"What do you want with us?" I whispered. "Why can't you leave us alone?"

There was no answer. I picked up the photograph, running my fingers over the broken glass. Slowly, the warmth returned to my body and the presence faded. I emptied the glass into a plastic bag and removed the photo from its frame. The music played gently in the background. If I remembered correctly, it was the first track playing again—Tony Bennett singing about his heart and San Francisco. I opened another bottle of malt and poured a glass. It was five past midnight.

The old compilation CD played through and I'd finished my third glass of malt when the final track began to play. I recognised the plaintive female voice. *Over the rainbow...* I'd been mistaken. This couldn't be the final track. This wasn't the song about a picture. *I have a picture of you. I see a picture of you and I cry.* It was track 19, and there were only19 tracks on the CD.

I peered through the glass-fronted cabinet at the display on the player. The green numeric display was clear. Track 19. I picked up the plastic case. The final song was 'Over the Rainbow' by Judy Garland. The song I'd heard was nowhere to be found on the CD. I flicked through with the remote, checking each track until I was sure that 'Picture of You' was not hiding somewhere.

I punched the song title into my laptop and waited for the results and then scrolled through the pages looking for an artist whose name I didn't even know. I could live with the tree with its changing shapes, I could live with the subtle brushes with the paranormal. But this was heavy stuff. Where had that song come from? How could I have heard it, and what did it mean?

Jenny's photo lay on the table beside me as I shut the laptop. My head ached, my eyes stung like crazy, and I felt a compulsion to throw up the whisky. My mind whirled until the tiredness kicked in. I turned on the TV and flicked through to the rolling news channel, and after five minutes felt myself drifting. Maybe all this would make sense in the morning light.

***

I called Josie just as she was opening the door of The Keys for the lunchtime drinkers.

"What's up, Rob? You sound awful."

Frankly, I was relieved to find I wasn't talking to Lou. I felt guilty making small talk with a bloke when I'd rather be talking to his wife. "I'm okay. Just some weird stuff happening here. Can we talk?" It was a rhetorical question. Of course we could; Josie was always there when I needed her.

"Sure, hun. Lou's got his mate Sammy giving him a hand today. We could meet for coffee at that late night place. I fancy a slice of death by chocolate!"

I laughed. I laughed because Jo could always make my world feel brighter. "Sure. But I'll give the chocolate a miss."

Within the hour, we found ourselves sitting across a table in the revamped diner with two large coffees and a calorie-ridden slice of chocolate cake. Josie sat eying the dark mountain of decadence with childlike joy. "I've lost three pounds," she said, sinking her spoon into the mass. "I deserve a treat."

She took a mouthful and closed her eyes, savouring the flavour while I waited and watched. Maybe chocolate was better than sex…for Josie, anyway. She opened her eyes and smiled.

"Okay, hun, what's up? Shoot."

She listened to my tale of phantom tracks and splintering glass, replacing the spoon by the side of her plate and pushing it to the centre of the table.

"Maybe you should call Sebastian about this," she said, resting her chin on her hands.

The old guy would have been top of my list, but it was Josie's company I'd craved as I'd woken that morning. "You're prettier!" I said.

Josie grinned. "Gee, thanks, Robert. Prettier than an old man in his late-seventies? Are you sure?"

I nodded. "And prettier than many girls half your age."

I hadn't meant to throw her a line; it just seemed to slide off my tongue. Josie blushed.

"I'm sorry. That sounded really cheesy."

We both laughed and Jo fed me a spoonful of chocolate. The young waitress eyed us from behind the till and probably thought we were lovers, both married, but not to each other.

"Anyway," Josie said as the smile faded. "You have to ask yourself if there is any rational explanation for all this stuff. I mean, if you had a cat then that would explain the broken glass but wouldn't explain the phantom song. That could have been just a dream, of course."

"There isn't a rational explanation for the picture, Jo, and even if I had been dreaming, isn't it a coincidence that I was listening to lyrics about a photograph?"

Josie shrugged. "I know what Sebastian would think."

"What?"

"The same as you're thinking. That picture of Jenny is the key to something."

"So, what do I do?"

Josie took a sip of her coffee and laid her hand across mine. "Put it in your pocket. Take it with you wherever you go."

***

I called Sebastian that afternoon. He sounded downbeat on the phone but told me I was welcome and the door would be on the latch. "Just come in," he said before hanging up prematurely. My head ached. I was afraid. Afraid of the world I'd been caught in.

Afraid that I was falling in love with Josie Duxbury. I swallowed two painkillers and set off for Sebastian's house with the radio on low.

Carly Simon was singing 'You're So Vain'. I looked in the rear view mirror and saw the reflection of an unshaven old man. Whoever she was singing about, it wasn't me.

Sebastian's door was ajar. I crept in like a burglar. "Hello? Hello?"

A strained voice seemed to echo down the hallway. "In here."

I opened the door to a room I felt I knew so well to find the old man kneeling over his dog. Ricky, the German Shepherd who bore more than a passing resemblance to a mountain bear, lay motionless as Sebastian looked up with tears streaming down his face.

"Sebastian?" I stopped in my tracks. "What's wrong?"

The old man shook his head slowly, unable to form a single word. He patted Ricky's head gently.

"Is it the dog? Is he ill?"

Sebastian didn't answer. I took several tentative steps forward and reached over to stroke the recumbent animal. Sebastian began to sob yet the dog didn't stir. The old man looked up at me "He's dead, Robert!" he wailed. "He's dead!"

***

After half an hour or so, I was allowed to lift Ricky onto the floor and pour his master of fourteen years a brandy. *Don't forget. To you, Ricky was just a dog. To the old man, he was a friend and companion. They loved each other.*

I could hear my father's voice. It was as if he was standing behind me, watching as I poured a measure into a crystal glass. *Let him do the talking.*

So I did. Sebastian drank four brandies and two coffees and we agreed to bury his dog together. "I don't want a ceremony," he said. "I just want a burial marked with a rose bush. Can you sort that for me? I don't feel up to visiting a garden centre."

I was actually leaving before the old man stopped and shot me a look of surprise. "Oh no!" he said. "I haven't even asked you what you came here for!"

I smiled. "It can wait," I replied.

***

The following day, we buried Ricky in the far corner of the garden he had shared with his master, and I placed a rose bush to mark his grave. We sipped a brandy and I stood with my arm around Sebastian's shoulders as he wept. We both knew loneliness, and we both knew grief, so I spared him the platitudes. He just needed the company and was happy to talk.

"So what's been happening with you, then?" he asked as we sipped another brandy. "It's okay, fire away. I need to keep my mind occupied."

The photograph was the key. Sebastian had no doubt. Josie was right; I should carry it with me wherever I went.

***

I didn't tell Jenny about the phantom track or the photograph. I'm not sure why. Maybe it was my father's influence, his ability to know when to speak and when to stay silent. I thought about him as I drove home through the driving rain and wondered if a Hollywood producer ever made a movie of my life, he'd have placed the ghost of my father in the back seat. I felt him watching, silently wishing I could, just for a moment, catch a glimpse of his dear face.

Chapter Twenty-Five

THAT EVENING, THE weather girl cheerily informed her public that parts of England were on flood alert, and as thick black clouds rolled in over the Irish sea, the nation braced itself. I had already decided to visit Elizabeth and Hanna's grave, come what may, and the journey itself became something of a pilgrimage.

The rain had not stopped since the previous evening, and the sky was eerily leaden, plunging the whole cemetery into semi-darkness. As I stood over the grave, the fear of loneliness gripped me like a cold steel claw around my heart. I wanted to believe in a heaven, but at that moment, it was no more than a children's fairy tale. My wife and child lay six feet beneath me, and I would never see them again.

I couldn't even bring myself to talk to Elizabeth the way I'd done before, but her voice—her voice and Hanna's laughter echoed around my head. I wanted to scream. I wanted to scream because there was nothing I could do about the past. I wanted to scream and block out the voices—the voices and the memories. I didn't. I just sobbed, my heart and spirit broken.

Time meant nothing. Nor did the fact that the drizzle had turned to a driving rain and the clouds seemed so thunderous and low that I swore I could reach up and touch them. I drove home through the traffic, negotiating the flooded roads, listening to a James Taylor disc. When I heard the opening chords of 'You've Got a Friend', I thought of Josie. I pulled over and called her.

"You sound bloody awful!" she told me. "Where are you?"

"In the car. Just been to the cemetery."

"What? In this weather?"

I didn't answer.

"Look, hun, why don't you come on over? I'll make you some lunch, OK?"

I muttered something and hung up, firing the engine and pulling back out into the traffic.

***

Josie had made me a club sandwich that defied the human jaw span, but I was desperately hungry and anxious to drink myself into oblivion a soon as possible. The coffee wasn't particularly welcome.

"Anything stronger?" I asked casually.

Jo shook her head. "Just go with the coffee, sweetheart," she said looking through me the way Elizabeth had when she was reading my mind. My jacket was drip drying in the cellar, and Lou had thrown me a fresh towel to dry my hair. My eyes were red rimmed, but the weather had been so bad it would have been difficult for anyone to have guessed that I'd been crying.

Lou came and sat with me for a while, making small talk. He asked about Jenny and told me what a beautiful girl she was. I nodded with a mouthful of sandwich, wiping salad cream from my chin. I still felt that cold steel claw. I still felt empty. I needed to get my Jenny back. The Jenny I'd waved goodbye to that Sunday as Darren Pascoe slipped on his trainers and headed off to the park.

I thanked Lou and Josie for the lunch and went home, picking up the phone and calling Ellen Pascoe as soon as I stepped through the door. She answered immediately but sounded stern when she heard my voice. Even in her dotage, the old lady could be fearsome.

"Mr. Adams, please don't call me. I can't help you."

I braced myself. "But you *can,* you just don't want to! There's a difference."

The old lady bristled. "Well, you should respect my decision, whatever you believe."

"I will, but Mrs. Pascoe, will you just do one thing for me—just one?"

"What is it?"

"When I hang up, will you just sit down, close your eyes and imagine you are me. Concentrate. Put yourself in my shoes. I've lost my wife, my child, and I'm losing Jenny. I can't rest, Mrs. Pascoe. I can't rest because I don't know. Even if the truth—this whole picture—is ugly, I need to see it. I need to come to terms with—"

"I don't think you understand, Mr. Adams…"

I replaced the receiver gently and wandered into the kitchen. My heart was racing as I stared at the kettle. A half bottle of whisky stood within a few feet of it. Decisions. I poured myself a glass and sat down, flicking on the TV to drown out the sound of the rain beating relentlessly against the windows.

***

I called Ellen Pascoe back at seven. "Very well," she said wearily, "You can come round if you wish, if only to talk things through."

I climbed behind the wheel of my car and set off. I was dressed in a t-shirt with joggers and a pair of old trainers, but I wasn't out to impress the old lady with my fashion sense. I was wondering how I was going to get the stubborn old woman to spill.

"Don't tell Victoria that you've been here," she said, greeting me with a dour expression that told me I wasn't exactly welcome.

The house smelled of fresh bread so I made some casual comment about the delights of home cooking. Ellen cast me a look. "I've always baked my own," she said. "Benjamin loved it, though judging by his weight, a little too much, I'd say."

I smiled, remembering that this old lady was probably lonely, too, and if I played it carefully, she might actually begin to enjoy my company. I made some comment about the weather, glancing over at the window. Ellen Pascoe smiled.

"They never seem to get it wrong when it comes to the rain," she said as I followed her through into her lounge.

The room was gloomy, lit only by a small lamp in the corner. A local newspaper lay open on the table next to her chair and the TV flashed its pictures silently.

I took my chair, wondering if we were going to make polite conversation all evening, and wished we had a bottle of brandy to share rather than the weak tea she placed in front of me. "I'm afraid I've nothing stronger," she said, reading my mind. "I've never been a drinker...most alcohol tastes awful." Ellen Pascoe smiled gently, as if she really had made an attempt to put herself in my place. "Sherry is the only thing I can stomach but I don't really bother."

"Maybe I should take a leaf out of your book." I laughed. "I'm inclined to drown my sorrows, although they always seem to resurface the next morning."

"You and a million others," Ellen replied with a reproachful look.

A silence hung between us, as heavy as the clouds that had rolled over England for the past twenty four hours. I had to begin somewhere. "I'm lonely, Mrs. Pascoe. I'm lonely and confused."

The old woman looked up at me, "Well, maybe you and Jenny should get away somewhere. It doesn't have to be abroad. Just away from—"

"I can't, Mrs. Pascoe. I can't escape."

"And does Jenny feel this way?"

"I think so."

"Maybe you should ask her." Ellen looked frail and her voice sounded strained. "Like I've told you, I can't help. You should concentrate on your daughter."

"I need to know the truth."

"No, you don't!" There was a determination in her voice, but Ellen's eyes betrayed her. I saw a longing, maybe even fear. "Jenny needs *you*. That's the only truth that matters!"

I instinctively reached into my pocket and pulled out the photograph of Jenny and handed it to the old lady. "This is my daughter."

Ellen looked as though I'd cast a hot coal into her lap. She stared at me. *Why are you doing this? Why?* It was as if I was gazing into her soul. Her lips never moved but the words were written across her face. Finally, she glanced down at the picture resting on her lap. I watched as she lifted the photograph closer to her failing eyes with trembling hands. "She's...she's beautiful... So beautiful..."

I waited. Ellen Pascoe looked up. "She has his eyes... His eyes..."

"Whose eyes?" I asked.

She didn't answer, glancing back at the photograph. "Oh, she is so lovely...so..."

The old lady began to cry, and I could do nothing but watch helplessly. She was in her own world, and nothing I said would have registered in her mind. *The picture of you...I have a picture of you.*

I heard the song again. *The picture is the key!* The voices echoed in my head. Elizabeth—Hanna—Sebastian—Josie. They sang like a choir as Ellen Pascoe wept.

"Whose eyes, Mrs. Pascoe—whose eyes does she have?"

Ellen looked up at me as the tears rolled down her face, drawing a paper handkerchief to her mouth as if she were preparing to stifle the words that might have escaped in a moment of weakness.

"She's lovely..."

"Whose eyes?"

The old lady looked at me, pleading. *Don't ask me again. Please don't ask me!*

Her skeletal fingers stroked Jenny's cheek. I fell silent, leaving the old lady alone in her thoughts. It felt right. *The picture is the key.*

"Can I see her?" Ellen's voice was as weak as her tea, but the question came like a thunderbolt out of a summer sky.

"You want to see Jenny?"

Ellen nodded slowly, still holding the paper handkerchief to her lips "If that would be all right with you…and Jenny, of course."

I was in control. My opponent as old and stubborn as she was, had found herself on the ropes. I delivered my final punch. "Mrs. Pascoe, I'm sure she would love to meet you, but if I agree to your request, you must answer my question. It's as simple as that."

Ellen looked at me, her face already having surrendered to the years, now wearing the expression of a defeated soul. She didn't answer at first, choosing to gaze once more at the photograph. My heart was racing again, my palms were hot and damp.

"If you want to see Jenny, you will have to tell me the truth. The whole truth."

Ellen didn't look at me. She placed the photograph on her table and pushed herself up onto her feet. I watched as she moved silently, the world resting on her ageing frame. An old lady who, it seemed, was growing visibly frailer as I looked on. She returned five minutes later with an envelope in her hand. "Here," she said curtly. "If this is what you really want."

I pulled out the letter, oblivious to Ellen's gaze, and began to read.

***

Now I wish I hadn't. I wish I'd listened and walked away. But I also know it had never been an option.

I remember nothing of the drive home—the red lights, traffic islands or junctions. My head reeled and my heart continued to thud like a bass drum in a marching band. I threw off my coat and flopped into the chair. My hands shook violently as I opened the letter that had been addressed to Benjamin Pascoe, praying that I had misread the whole thing. But I had recognised the handwriting immediately. It was Elizabeth's.

I closed my eyes for a moment, praying to my father's God for strength. This couldn't be true—Elizabeth was not capable of such deceit.

Dear Ben,

I had to write to you, I'm so sorry. Robert has been home for three weeks now, and I know we will be okay...at least, I thought so. I could have got through the guilt of our brief affair because, after all, my husband's fling with that hairdresser was the reason I came to you for therapy in the first place. I might have even told him eventually, just to get it all out into the open.

But something awful has happened and I'm not sure I can live with it. I'm pregnant, Ben. It has to be your child. I cannot abort a life, so don't ask because it's not an option. I don't want any money from you and I don't want you in the child's life. Please respect my marriage and I will respect yours. Just let me know how I can deal with this. Should I tell Robert? I don't want to lose him, Ben. I love him and hate the whole idea of watching him bring up your child in ignorance.

I think I know what you will say. He will be a better father if he thinks the baby is his, and I should consider the welfare of the child above everything else. Again, I'm sorry. I have no one else to talk to about this. No one.

Elizabeth xx

I sat for three hours as darkness descended on the room, numb from my feet to my head. Jenny had never been mine. I had no one. Hanna had been my only child and she was gone. How was I going to break the news to that girl lying in the hospital bed? The girl I'd shared the last seventeen years with? Who was she? Her half-brother had killed my wife and child…Hanna, my baby.

I vomited, taking to my bed and lying in the darkness as the world continued without me. The truth was unbearable. I had owned up to my affair with Melissa, but Elizabeth had taken her secret to an early grave.

I called Josie at two that morning. She sounded hazy, but I detected no anger in her voice.

"Jo, I need to see you…now."

"Robert? What's up, hun? What's happened?

"I can't say…I need to see you."

There was a pause. "Stay where you are, sweetheart, I'll come to you."

***

Josie arrived half an hour later. She had thrown a housecoat over her nightgown and left a note for Lou. I'd made some coffee and switched on the TV, but the moment she stepped into my space I instinctively pulled her into my arms. Jo held me, remaining in my embrace until I felt able to release her.

"This sounds serious, hun," she whispered, kissing my neck gently.

"It is," I replied. "I'm living in some kind of nightmare."

I poured our coffee, wishing I could shake myself awake and discover I'd been in bed all along, but it hadn't been a dream.

Jo read the letter several times over, and she remained with her head down for some time before I realised she was crying. I took her in my arms once more with nothing more than a deep need to hold, to comfort and to be comforted. I tried to thank her for being there, but Jo pressed her finger to my lips and kissed me passionately. My need for comfort turned to desire.

It was grief, frustration, love and confusion that took hold as we tore at each other's clothes. I needed to belong. I needed contact. We made love as the twenty-four-hour news channel rolled in the background. When it was all over, I rolled onto my back. "I can't believe we did that," I whispered.

Josie rolled back towards me and placed her arm across my chest. "You regret it?"

"No—but it feels weird—we've been friends for so long."

I lay for a moment, listening to my own heartbeat, suspended in a surreal world as Jo slipped on her housecoat. I remained, staring at the ceiling as she poured us a brandy, wondering what the future held. I had lost a daughter and gained a lover...or had I just lost a friend as well? I wondered where Lou fitted into all this. How was I going to face him?

Jo returned with the brandies looking troubled. She knelt down beside me, gazing into her glass.

"You know what this means, don't you," she said darkly.

I didn't answer but Jo continued. "It means that unless you believe in coincidences—and I *mean* coincidences—of the million to one kind..."

"What?"

"I don't think it was an accident...Darren Pascoe goes joy riding and kills two people...his father's mistress and her daughter..."

I don't understand why it had not occurred to me in those hours following my visit to Ellen Pascoe's home, and yet it was obvious. As obvious as Victoria Pascoe's reluctance to help me. It had not been in an effort to spare me the pain—it had been all about Darren.

Josie downed her brandy. "What if that kid had found out about Elizabeth...maybe even discovered that letter? Maybe the marriage broke down because Victoria discovered that he had another child. Darren would have blamed Elizabeth…"

I lay naked, the perspiration from our love-making drying on my skin. Josie patted my arm.

"Go and get a shower. You smell like shit."

I rose obediently, like a child obeying its mother, relieved that someone was taking control. The exhaustion was debilitating, leaving me weak and unable to reason. Maybe that was a good thing. I was able to concentrate on the sensation of the warm water cleansing my body. My mind, at that moment, felt like a vacuum, and each time Pascoe's name entered that vacuum, it vanished into the darkness.

I found Josie pouring another brandy. She glanced at her watch and handed me my glass. "I'll call Lou in the morning and ask him to open up at lunch."

"You'll stay?" I asked.

Jo nodded and smiled. It was one of those smiles that fades quickly and is usually followed by tears. Josie bit her lip. "I couldn't leave you, hun—not at a time like this—I mean, this is…" She shook her head. "This is just…shit!"

I hugged her clumsily and our glasses clinked.

"I should be telling you that you are still Jenny's father, that you've been there for her since she was born and that's what parenthood is all about, but I can't…it sounds so…"

"Feeble?"

Jo shrugged. "I guess."

She slumped back into the chair and raised her glass wearily. "Cheers, anyway!"

I sat next to her, wondering if the painkillers that Elizabeth had been prescribed months before her death would live in harmony with the brandy—and even if they didn't, would it really matter? Jo seemed to read my mind.

"Look, sweetheart, I know you're a stable kind of bloke but all this shit… Well, it can be hard to take." she reached out and closed her hand over mine. "Just don't do anything stupid, okay? I mean, even if it enters your mind for a nanosecond—tell me."

The truth was simple. There was nothing to live for, but I had never really possessed the strength—or the cowardice?—it takes to die. Sure, I'd thought about it, yet the knowledge that I could never swallow that pill, pull that trigger or throw myself from any height, swung like a safety net beneath me.

I nodded and Jo smiled. "I'm sure you wouldn't. I mean, think what it would do to Jenny."

I sighed. My head banged like crazy. "I need to do something… something positive…"

"Sleep on it, hun. Just sleep on it."

***

Sleep came three brandies later, and I woke at eleven like a twisted corpse, my head propped up on the arm of the couch. Josie was making coffee and I smelled toast. She breezed by, as the world came slowly into focus, and pulled back the curtains. I blinked as the room flooded with light.

"It's black coffee," she said, disappearing into the kitchen only to reappear moments later with a tray of toast, honey and cereal and a silver pot I hadn't seen in years. Josie placed the tray on the coffee table and perched herself on the arm of the couch, waiting for me to stir.

"What's this in aid of?" I asked, trying to raise my reluctant frame from the sofa.

"Breakfast is the most important meal of the day," she announced, sliding into the space beside me as I finally achieved an upright position. "I'm just making sure you get some decent food down you."

I smiled wearily. "You're a bossy bitch—has anyone ever told you?"

"Well, Mr. Adams, a bossy bitch is just what you need right now!"

"Right. What else have you got planned for me—after the four star breakfast, that is?"

Josie poured us both a coffee and I watched as the steam rose and swirled from the cups.

"Actually, I have got something planned."

"Does it involve us being naked?"

The words slipped out before I could stop them

Josie blushed, which was in itself unusual. "Actually, no. It involves you going around to Victoria Pascoe's house with that letter."

My heart lurched. "What?"

"Let's move this forward. Ask her if she thinks it's just a coincidence that her son managed to mow down his father's mistress."

"I can't. She'll—"

"What? Get the police?"

"I was going to say that—she'll just deny it."

Josie turned, and there was anger in her eyes. "She's covering for her son, Robert. She's an intelligent woman, and you can bet that she knows exactly what happened that day—and why he drove up your street."

"But shouldn't I go to the police?"

"No. Pascoe couldn't have stage-managed the accident. He couldn't have known that Hanna and Elizabeth would have been standing behind that ice cream van just as he turned into your road. Even if he knew what Elizabeth looked like—even if he had recognised her from two hundred meters away and drove at her in a moment of fury..." her voice trailed off. "It would never hold up, hun."

"You think it was an accident, then?"

Josie shrugged. "I don't know what I'm thinking. Maybe he just wanted to check out the house—check out his half sister. Maybe it was just curiosity. But maybe he had something else in mind. That Taylor kid was an evil little bastard, and Pascoe was obviously influenced by him."

Half sister? My Jenny and the Pascoe kid? I felt numb. Jenny wasn't mine but my heart could not accept the fact.

"Go and see Victoria. You need to keep active—do something!"

I stared at Josie. She was serious. I buried my head in my hands. Part of me wanted justice, whatever the price, and if Pascoe had deliberately mown down my wife then I wanted him to rot. But Josie was right. He was a kid in emotional turmoil, devastated by his parents' divorce and looking for answers.

I felt Josie's hand brush my arm. "You have nothing to lose, Rob. Nothing at all."

As Josie was leaving, she smiled slowly. "Don't worry about us—you know—making love."

I looked at her quizzically.

"I mean, don't start beating yourself up over it—you've got enough on your plate without feeling guilty. Lou and I...are okay...it's not what you think."

"Meaning?"

"I'll tell you sometime...when things settle down."

Josie climbed behind the wheel of her car and waved, but Jenny was on my mind. I remember walking back into the lounge and catching sight of a picture of her on the bookshelf. My stomach tightened and lurched. I was looking at Benjamin Pascoe's little girl. Jo was right. I had nothing to lose.

Chapter Twenty-Six

SLEEP BROUGHT WITH it a certain peace, and I drifted off for an hour or so in front of the TV while watching a rerun of a house makeover programme. I dreaded seeing Jenny, wondering how she was going to react to the news. I remembered seeing a photo of Benjamin Pascoe in the local paper, the day after he had taken his own life, and thought how he had looked like a young Marlon Brando. It was a blessing that Jenny looked like her mother everyone told us so, and I guess she did. It was all in the eyes.

I opened the fridge door, recoiling at the cold draught. I'd not bothered to stock up properly for some time, and the very thought of food turned my stomach, so I took a swig from a can of cola and wandered out into the fresh air, telling myself that Benjamin Pascoe had been nothing more than a sperm donor. It didn't work. Jenny was his, and I couldn't get past the fact.

My mind raced as I drove over to see Victoria. There had been no point in calling first. I was willing to take a chance on her being at home. Something told me she didn't step out much these days, and by the time I arrived on her doorstep, Darren's face was imprinted in my mind.

Victoria glared at me for several seconds. I held the letter up and waved it in front of her face. "Okay, Victoria, let's have the truth."

I could have been a serial killer—maybe Jason from those insufferable Friday the 13th movies. Victoria recoiled. "You... Who gave you—"

"Jenny's grandmother gave this to me, Mrs. Pascoe. But you know that, don't you."

"Why are you here?"

"To find out what else you know."

"I don't know anything."

"That's bullshit!

Victoria looked as though I'd just taken a swing at her.

"Listen, you could keep me here, standing on your doorstep, while you explain how your son just happened to end up on my road behind the wheel of a four-wheel drive, or we could go inside and…"

Victoria stepped aside looking dazed. I walked past her and waited, pushing the envelope into my inside pocket.

"I know you probably hate me, but to be honest, I don't really give a shit, so perhaps it will be easier if we remain civil, at least."

She didn't answer, and I followed her into a room that was as cold as the reception. I shuddered as Victoria glared at me. "I can't afford this house, Mr. Adams. Benjamin had cancelled our life insurance, and my company didn't take kindly to the publicity surrounding Darren. It reflected badly on me, and they were looking to lay people off anyway. I gave them a perfect excuse."

"You've lost your job."

Victoria nodded.

"I'm sorry."

"Yeah, I bet you are!"

I had been ready for a fight but she had disarmed me so effortlessly. "I don't wish you any ill, Mrs. Pascoe. None of this has been your fault. I just want to know what happened."

"What? So you can go to the police with a murder charge and get Darren locked up for another ten years?"

"I'm not going to the police."

Victoria frowned. "You expect me to believe that?"

"I mean it. I can't prove it wasn't an accident. Just tell me the truth."

I thought she was going to cry, and a part of me wanted to embrace her. I'd not seen a more pathetic, vulnerable woman in a long while.

"I know that Darren was devastated when his father walked out, and I know he got into bad company. He found out about Elizabeth. He knew that his father had a child with another woman." Victoria sighed, pressing her head into her hands, her elbows digging deep into her knees. "I never knew about Jenny for fifteen years," she said looking up, her face pale and drawn. "Then I found that letter. I went berserk—really. I totally lost it! I always knew that Benjamin was a charmer, but I trusted him. I trusted him totally—he was a professional."

"How did you find the letter?"

"I didn't. Darren found it at Nana Pascoe's—that's what he called Ellen. It was at the bottom of one of the drawers—don't ask me what he was rooting for. When your life falls apart you don't ask questions like that."

Victoria clasped her hands tightly, as if she were quite literally holding on. "Darren was distraught, of course. He didn't tell me about the letter—not at first—but he couldn't even look at his father. I just knew it had something to do with another woman.

"Darren couldn't hold it in...all that hatred and disappointment. He threw the letter at me and ran out of the house. I didn't see him till late that night."

"It must have come as a shock. I mean, to find your husband has a teenage daughter."

Victoria winced, as if she was hearing the truth for the first time. "It was as if he had a secret life. I asked him if he was seeing her—supporting her, you know, buying her presents and that kind of thing."

"He wasn't," I replied sharply.

"I know, but I couldn't live with it. Some women could. Benjamin moved out, and Darren just fell apart." Victoria shook her head. "He became a different boy. He started getting into fights at school. I couldn't get through to him—he just sat in his bedroom every night playing video games—it was awful. Of course, initially he poured all his venom upon his father but then things began to change."

Victoria shifted awkwardly. "He started to talk about...your wife."

"Saying what?"

"He said that he wanted to kill that bitch."

I suppressed a sudden surge of anger that rose within me. "Well, he did, didn't he?"

Victoria looked away. "He didn't set out to kill her—he just wanted to frighten her—it was Taylor's idea. He was a nasty little fucker. I'd gladly strangle him with my bare hands!"

"What do you mean, *frighten*?"

"He had a photograph of your wife, from some event in the local paper...Elizabeth and Jenny Adams. I think it was a guitar recital at a school concert or something like that. Anyway, when they hijacked that car, Taylor had traced the face to an address and suggested that they drive by and brick your window...that was it. Two pissed kids were going to lob a brick and drive off."

"So what happened?"

"They were revving at the bottom of your street and Darren saw the ice cream van. He told me that he started driving slowly— he knew there would be kids around, so they just cruised. Then Darren saw your wife step out behind the van. He recognised her, and I think he panicked and somehow lost control. He put his foot on the gas and..."

I stared at this woman. She was trying to make a victim out of her son.

"He wouldn't have tried to kill a toddler—he wouldn't, you have to believe me!"

"But he aimed a fucking four-wheel drive at her, didn't he! He *aimed* at them—a mother and child! I can't believe you're trying to make excuses for him!"

"He didn't aim! It wasn't murder," Victoria protested, her eyes filling with tears "It wasn't!"

"Yeah, right. And you believe your son—okay, I get that. You'll believe what you want to believe, because getting your son back as soon as possible is all that matters. Well, guess what, Victoria, I'll never have Hanna back. I'll never have Elizabeth back."

I stood, towering over the woman who seemed to cower as if my words were fists raining down on her. Victoria looked down at her hands, still resting on her lap—still firmly clasped.

"What are you going to do now?" she asked meekly.

I shrugged.

"You're going to tell the police?"

"What would be the point?"

"Thank you."

"Oh, please don't. I'm not doing it for you or Darren."

I walked over to the window and stared out. The late-afternoon sun cast long shadows across the houses as uniformed teenagers walked in small groups, chatting and laughing loudly. "I'm doing this for Elizabeth, for Hanna…"

"I know. I understand that," Victoria said weakly. "If I could change anything—anything—then you have to believe me, I would."

"But you can't, can you?" I said, continuing to gaze out at the school kids, wishing Hanna would have followed in their footsteps. "It wasn't your fault. As much as I hate Darren—and your husband—I cannot blame you."

"I could have handled it differently," she answered.

"How?"

"I should have tried harder. I could have saved our marriage—tried to work things out—but I just couldn't get my head round the fact that my husband had a teenage daughter to another woman. I shut Benjamin out of my life until it became impossible for him to stay. I let him go and lost Darren in the process."

I turned. Victoria was still staring down at her hands. "You couldn't have known how badly he would react."

"But that's it! I should have known. Darren idolised his father. Our relationship was always uneasy after Benjamin left, and I lost control. He wanted to go and stay with him but that just wasn't possible. Then he wanted to go and stay with my sister. He would have lived anywhere but with me."

"You have a sister?"

"Yes, three years younger. She and her husband ran a farm down in Devon. My God, Darren used to love it, you know, helping with the animals, up to his neck in mud. He would spend four weeks of the summer down there. He even learned to ride horses. I think he would have been quite happy to spend his life with those animals."

"So why didn't you let him stay with them?"

"Because he wanted us to move there and his father wanted to make a fresh start—the three of us. My sister had a barn on their land which we could have converted. Benjamin was talking about joining a local practice—you know, fewer hours, more quality time together. I persuaded my sister to discourage him. It was my fault—I was selfish…I was just thinking about my own career." Victoria began to sob. "And now I have nothing—nothing to live for—nothing and no one!"

I had asked for honesty, but I didn't want to break a woman who had, beneath the frosty exterior, always blamed herself for everything that had happened to me.

"Look," I said softly. "If I hadn't been such a bastard—if I hadn't had an affair—then my wife would have never needed to seek therapy in the first place..."

Victoria dabbed her eyes. "Ifs and buts. Benjamin was a professional who abused his position. Your wife was vulnerable." She looked up at me, "If you had not had that affair, or if Benjamin hadn't met your wife, you would not have Jenny. Your life would have taken a different direction. You probably wouldn't have had Hanna, either. You could have never known what your actions would lead to."

Victoria looked back down at her hands. "I knew that my son would not be able to cope with a broken home. I could smell trouble, and if I had found it in my heart to forgive, or if I'd allowed Darren to stay with his aunt on the farm...you would still have your wife and Hanna, and you would never have found out the truth about Jenny."

We talked about actions and consequences, about the butterfly effect and our innate helplessness. I left Victoria Pascoe at her door that afternoon waving briefly as I climbed into my car. She smiled, yet her eyes betrayed her. Something inside told me I would never see the woman again.

***

On my way home, I had pulled over and called Josie from my mobile. She had listened intently as I repeated word for word the conversation I'd had with Victoria Pascoe. I'm not sure if Jo knew how she was supposed to react. Was it appropriate to sound pleased that I'd discovered the truth?

"Are you going to tell Jenny tonight?"

I'd already decided against it. "I'm going to make an appointment with that woman at the hospital—the one who's on her case. She'll know how to approach the whole thing. Besides, they need to know that the woman in Jenny's head actually exists—I'm going to enjoy that bit!"

Josie laughed. "Don't go sounding too triumphant, Rob. Just remember, you want to get her out of that place—not end up in the next bed!"

I wanted to bring Jenny home, more than anything else. In my heart, nothing had changed. I knew the truth, yet she would always be the girl I'd watched as she grew up—always the girl who ran into my arms as I walked through the door. Jennifer Adams could never lose her place in my life, but she was Benjamin Pascoe's child—it was a biological fact. Yet she'd never known him, never loved or cried for him, never listened as he read her the tales from *Alice in Wonderland* until her eyes began to flicker and close.

I feared that the knowledge might tear us apart. I dreaded seeing that distant look in her eyes. Would she find something in her own heart for the man she had never known? Would she grieve his death? I imagined her sitting with Ellen, listening as the old woman regaled her with stories of her son while flicking through old photographs. Would those visits become more and more frequent? Would Jenny long for her grandmother's company? Would Ellen be the link that allowed my precious girl to reach out and touch her father's memory?

I tried to push the thoughts from my mind, driving through another spell of heavy evening rain, pulling my collar up as I ran across the car park towards the hospital entrance. My mind was already playing tricks. By the time I stopped outside Jenny's door, I could almost hear Ellen Pascoe's voice. *And did I tell you about the time your father...*

No! Really? Oh how sweet...and he's so handsome...not like Robert. Do you think I have his eyes, Nana? Do you?

I burst in, convinced I'd find my daughter with the old lady. *Hi, Mr. Adams. Nan was just telling me about my dad...*

Jenny looked up, slightly surprised by my enthusiastic entrance.

"You're alone!" I said, breathing hard.

"Of course. Why shouldn't I be?"

I hugged her so hard that she thought I was drunk and tried to push me away. "You'll have to stop doing this, Dad, really!"

"Doing what?"

"Drinking! It's not helping."

"Hey, not a lip has passed my drops!" I joked and breathed hard in her face. "See?"

Jenny grinned. "Okay," she said cautiously. "But you're behaving kind of...weird."

"Maybe I'm just happy to see my beautiful daughter."

I imagined Josie cringing in the background, and my father shaking his head in disbelief. I sat down, counted to five, and clawed back my sanity. "Anyway, how are you?"

Jenny smiled. It was the old smile I remembered. The one I had not seen since that day our lives were changed forever.

***

Twenty-four hours later, I found myself sitting opposite Dr. Grace in her new office overlooking the hospital grounds. The desk was cluttered with papers that left me wondering if I'd been catapulted back into the age when Bill Gates was just a twinkle in his father's eye. Dr. Grace smiled, trying to find a place to stand her cup. "I must get round to sorting this out. I'm afraid I have a bit of a reputation for a lack of organisation." She looked up. "Are you sure I can't get you a drink?"

I shook my head. My nervousness was unfounded but it was impossible to relax even in a chair that was so comfortable it almost sucked you into a state of unconsciousness.

"Well, let's see," she said, punching something into her PC. "Jenny's been...yes...we're pleased with her progress." She turned away from the screen that shed an unflattering blue cast across her features. "The nightmares have stopped, as you probably know. Also, the voices."

I took a deep breath. "There's something you need to know…"

Dr. Grace lifted her cup and replaced it without taking a sip.

"The thing is," I began awkwardly, "there have been some developments…those voices…the woman in the dreams…We traced her. She existed."

The doctor's eyes widened.

"It was through the church—the one that Jenny…you know…"

Dr. Grace nodded. "Jenny told us about Reverend Allington. I know you were following a lead, and she was quite excited that you might have been close to proving the existence of this Amelia woman."

"It's a complicated story," I said, wishing I'd taken up the offer of a drink as I took her back to the beginning—the phone call from the minister and those first letters I discovered in his attic. The story unfolded easily, yet it felt as if I was trying to convince a complete stranger that I'd been abducted by aliens. My palms sweated and my throat felt like sandpaper as I finally revealed Jenny's bloodline.

Dr. Grace studied me silently as I admitted how my affair with the travelling hairdresser had sent Elizabeth falling headlong into the arms of Benjamin Pascoe. I didn't know how often they had slept together—it hardly mattered now. Jenny was conceived, Benjamin Pascoe's daughter, Darren Pascoe's half sister, Ellen Pascoe's granddaughter…

If there was an element of doubt that Jenny was not mine—the truth now felt like a knife twisting in my belly. For the first time, I'd told the whole story from beginning to end like a narrator taking his audience with him, and I had been listening to myself, swept along with the tale through to its awful conclusion. It was real. It was unbearable.

"This is…" The doctor paused, shaking her head. "I don't know what to say, Mr. Adams. I mean, you've had such a difficult time…"

She scrawled something on a notepad.

My mobile rang, playing out a jazz riff. I killed it, and Dr. Grace smiled. "I have studied psychology for years, Mr. Adams, and I'm still learning."

"But doesn't this change everything? I mean, those voices—they're not just in her head. She can't have imagined them."

Dr. Grace nodded, scribbling something else on her notepad. "There are those who believe that we carry the weight of our ancestors on our shoulders, passed down through generations and locked into our subconscious. It has been known for a child to draw or paint images or scenes—a house or a face—from their ancestry. We cannot really know how this happens, but we have to accept that it does."

"But it means that Jenny isn't losing her mind, surely?"

"*Losing her mind?* That's a rather unfortunate term. No, Mr. Adams, Jenny is with us because the voices—or the dreams—are causing abnormal behaviour. We need to reach a point where she is no longer influenced by those voices. Jenny needs to be free of them."

"So it doesn't matter to you if Amelia exists or not?"

Dr. Grace shrugged. "I'm not saying that it doesn't matter. It doesn't alter the goal, that's all." She smiled warmly. "But I think it might be a good idea to allow Jenny home…maybe for a weekend?"

I wanted to hug her. She was quite simply the most wonderful woman on the planet. "That would be…well…fantastic."

She laughed. "Good. You're obviously comfortable with the prospect."

"Comfortable? That doesn't begin to—"

"Mr. Adams, I'm delighted that you still feel the same affinity with Jenny, but I would advise caution. I'm not sure how she will react to the news that you are not her biological father. We might need to help her work through this." The doctor eyed me with suspicion. I seemed to be dealing with this with unnatural ease, and it was making her feel uncomfortable. It made *me* feel uncomfortable, because I still felt I was watching someone else's life unravel, not mine.

I could feel the clouds forming. I was who I was…the son of a good and righteous man with a mother who remained faithful to her son and husband. I had sweet memories to which I clung. But Jenny was about to discover that she had lived in ignorance of a truth that would shatter her world and taint every memory she had.

Chapter Twenty-Seven

A T FIRST, SHE just stared. Not at me. Not at any one or anything. I sat by her bed and waited, like a talent show finalist waiting through an eternal silence while the producers left them dangling for the entertainment of the public. "I'm sorry," I whispered. There was nothing else to say.

Jenny didn't answer. A tear trickled down her cheek.

"I just want you to know...I love you. You are my daughter. In my heart, nothing changes."

Silence.

"Jenny?"

She turned, staring through me. "You can go now."

Her eyes were lifeless. "I can't leave you."

There was a polite tapping on the door. Dr. Grace poked her head in. "Everything all right?"

Jenny looked up, unsmiling. "He's just going."

Dr. Grace frowned as I stood. Jenny slumped back onto her pillow, turned on her side and covered her head.

"You really want your father to go?" she asked softly.

Silence.

"Jenny?"

My daughter pulled the sheet from her head and glared at us with something that resembled hatred. "Well, my father isn't here. Isn't that what you've just told me? My father is dead!"

"But that isn't—"

"Please! Leave me alone. I just can't be arsed with you...or anyone!"

"But Jenny—"

She and pulled the covers back over her head. "Just go! Please!"

Dr. Grace looked at me and nodded towards the door.

I remember walking down the corridor with her hand on my arm. I remember sitting in her office with a hot cup of tea because, for some reason, I couldn't face coffee. I remember the guilt enveloping me like a swirling black mist, and in that moment, I realised that if Jenny could not accept me as her father, I had no daughter.

***

I picked Josie up at The Keys after she called and insisted on taking me out for a meal in town. "I thought you might need to talk," she said. "So you drive and I'll pay."

It sounded good to me—better to have a belly full of pasta then a head full of demons. We settled on a small back street Italian restaurant that served the best pasta for miles, according to Josie, who was married to the world's greatest authority on Italian food. A young man with greased-back Elvis hair led us to our table in the far corner and lit the candle as we took our seats.

Josie had said little throughout the half-hour drive. It was easier to talk over dinner, when eye contact was just as important as the words on our lips. "This is all about you tonight, Rob," she said, glancing up from the menu. "You've got to tell me how you feel. I mean, how you *really* feel."

The truth was, I wasn't sure how I felt. Jenny was just a kid in shock, and I knew that time would heal.

"This whole thing with Amelia could bring you together," Josie said. "And as heartless as this may sound, her biological father is dead. She's not going to be looking to form any kind of relationship. You don't have any competition. It's just you and her."

Jo was right. Everything had changed, yet, at the same time, nothing had changed.

"This whole Amelia thing is an adventure, and you're both in it together. It will stop you both over-thinking the whole biology-versus-nurture shit. She's your girl, and you both know it. Don't push it, just be there."

I ate everything on my plate while Josie polished off the last of the wine and she smiled as I looked longingly at the bottle in the ice bucket. "I know, hun," she said, reading my mind. "But I don't think alcohol would be such a good idea tonight."

I nodded. Wine was always good on the lips, particularly with pasta, but it had a habit of lifting me to great heights and then dropping me quite suddenly into a pit of gloom. Even when life was good, with the help of alcohol I'd somehow manage to find the cloud behind the silver lining.

I climbed behind the wheel of my car, greeted by the scent of Jo's perfume. I breathed in deeply and glanced over at her. She turned and smiled. I kissed her gently on the lips, wanting more but knowing that the tenderness that existed between us would always be there. I could wait.

She smiled. "You okay?"

Josie was good for me. I wanted to tell her but couldn't find the words. Facing Jenny wasn't going to be easy, but if she needed time then that was fine. Time was something we both had.

We chatted lightly on the way home. It was all about the good times. New Year's Eve at The Keys and the characters that had frequented the place over the years. Smiler Sam, who had a grin so wide he looked like a Muppet. Then there was Tricky Dicky, who regaled his many friends with tales of sexual conquests. His ability to attract scores of young attractive women baffled almost every one of the regulars until they found out he was a closet gay.

Josie laughed when she recalled Donkey Tom, whose party trick involved revealing his male appendage to anyone interested. "We could have made money out of that guy," she said. "If he hadn't nearly closed us down!" That was another story, even though it hadn't been so funny at the time.

I glanced at Jo, who had fallen silent and was staring into my rear-view mirror. "Turn right," she snapped suddenly. "Here!"

"What? Why?"

"Just turn!"

I floored the brake pedal, spinning the wheel and sending the car screeching into the corner. "Shit! Why did you do that?" I said, regaining control of the wheel.

Josie was still staring into the mirror. "Just drive. I'll tell you in a minute."

"Are you on the run, babe?" I joked as a black cat ran across our path.

Josie looked serious. "Pull in," she said, almost in a whisper. "Here!"

I swung over to the kerb behind a parked truck. "What's going on?" I said as Josie continued to stare into my mirror.

"Just wait. A car will pass us in a minute. Just keep looking ahead—don't turn."

A red Fiat moved slowly alongside before continuing down the road and turning off at the next junction. "That car has been following us," she said. "I noticed it pulling out from a parking space when we left the restaurant. They kept close all the way…" She paused. "Who the hell would be following you, hun?"

My heart was still thumping after my rally-car turn. I couldn't think. It had to be a case of mistaken identity.

"Let's hope you haven't got a look-a-like who's on someone's hit list," she said with a girlish giggle. "You need to keep your eyes peeled. Beware of the red Fiat!"

**

After lying awake for several hours, wondering who would want to be trailing me around in the early hours of the morning,

I fell into a restless sleep in which I found myself standing at the window watching Hanna and Elizabeth standing behind the ice cream van. They were waving, laughing and unaware that I was screaming, *"Run! Please run! You're both going to die! Please... run!"* But I couldn't change the past—not even in my dreams. The sound of screeching tyres filled the room, reverberating, tormenting. *They are going to die! Look! Look! Look!*

I woke just before Pascoe and Taylor ploughed into the back of Mr. Whirl's pink-and-white ice cream van. My body was covered in sweat and my heart was thumping hard. I took several deep breaths and took a gulp of water from the bottle on the bedside table. It was light. Small mercies. I was okay to shower, dress and make myself a coffee while catching up with the news. Normal people who were leading normal lives would be doing the same thing. *See? Everything is okay.*

But it wasn't. The boy who had killed my wife and little girl was Jenny's brother. How was she going to live with that? How was I going to live with that? Pascoe was *family.* The whole idea of planning my speech at the hospital was little more than foolishness. I was old enough to know that conversations took their own course and there was always the possibility than Jenny would still not want to see me.

I called Sebastian just to hear his voice—the source of calm in the centre of a storm. The old man listened as I related the events of the past few days.

"So there is a link," he said, obviously shaken. "It must have come as a terrible shock."

I felt myself choking back the tears as I tried to reply.

Tint stopped me. "It will be okay—she belongs in your heart, and you belong in hers."

His words carried the weight of a man gifted with wisdom. It wasn't so much the content of his counsel, it was the delivery. Not so much about the bullet, more about the weapon from which it was fired. I could imagine the old man could convince me that he was the son of God if he'd been given enough time.

***

The hospital corridor leading to my daughter's room was thankfully long, and by the time I arrived there, I'd decided on a breezy entrance. Jenny was listening to music on her iPod, wired up and in another world. She looked up as I stood tentatively in the doorway and smiled. The relief was palpable. She pulled the wires from her ears.

"Hi," she said softly.

I nodded and walked towards the bed, unsure as to whether I should even attempt a kiss. Jenny reached out her hand, and I took it.

Tears formed in my daughter's eyes. "I'm sorry, Dad—I just can't get my head around this." A tear escaped and trickled down her cheek. "To find out you aren't who you think you are—that's bad enough—but the Pascoes! Oh my *god*!" she hissed.

"Nothing's changed in here," I said, patting my chest. Sebastian's words sprang up in my head. "I can't think of you as anyone other than my daughter. You always have been and you always will—"

Jenny reached up and threw her arm around my neck and began to weep.

We held each other, welded together in a love that I knew, in that moment, no one could break. She kissed me several times on the cheek before sinking back into the comfort of her pillow.

We talked, yet I don't remember anything beyond an embrace that told me nothing life could throw up was going to defeat us. We were a team.

On my way home, something made me take a left turn down Hey Park Road, heading towards Victoria Pascoe's house. Maybe I just wanted to tell her that there was no ill feeling. Maybe I just wanted her to know that things were good, but when I arrived, there was no one at home.

I turned to find a young woman with a baby in her arms, standing in the gateway. "You lookin' for Mrs. Pascoe?" she asked.

I nodded.

She looked at me. "You ain't heard, then?"

"Heard what?" I asked, already fearing that the woman didn't have good news.

"She hung herself this morning—jus' like her husband did. Terrible, it was. You just don't expect it to happen in your street!"

I froze, rooted to the spot.

The woman looked glumly at her baby. "Don't know how parents can do that to their kids, to be honest. It's not fair—that Darren one is already off the rails. Can you imagine…"

I found myself muttering something of an apology as I pushed past her and climbed behind the wheel of my car. Darren Pascoe would be called away from whatever he was doing. They would have sat him down, wearing their masks of concern, to inform the teenager that he was never going to see his mother again. Another young man was heading for the social scrap heap—drugs, crime, more drugs. My daughter's half brother. *Family.*

The drive home was something of a blur. My mind focused on an image of Victoria Pascoe's lifeless body being carried away. It would probably make the local papers and, somewhere along the line, Darren would be mentioned. A snippet of news in a moment of time. *Did you read about that woman hanging herself? Her husband committed suicide a while back. Feel sorry for that kid.*

That would be it; the conversation would turn to the weather or the next holiday. The world would continue to turn, but not for Darren. He would have probably heard by now, and I wondered how a kid managed to deal with shit like that. I called Josie.

"You know something, Jo?" I said, still trying to digest the news myself, "For a split second, I actually felt sorry for that Pascoe kid."

I'd wanted to believe Victoria when she'd told me that Darren had never intended any harm. He was just a screwed-up kid who wanted to vent his anger. I wished he had put a brick through my window. I wish he had swerved clear just as Elizabeth had stepped into the road. But our lives changed forever. I remembered the day Jenny came home wearing a t-shirt emblazoned with the words 'shit happens'. "You can take that off now!" I'd snapped as she walked through the door. Maybe I should have let her keep it, because whatever anyone thought of the sentiment, it was the truth. Shit did happen.

***

I drove up to Tabwell the following day determined to find the Stanwicks' home. The library was the obvious place to start, and the woman at the desk greeted me with an officious smile.

"Can I help you?"

I nodded and explained that I was looking for some local history—"The location of The Stanwicks' home. They lived there in the late eighteen hundreds."

The woman's grinned, looking rather pleased with herself. "I think I can save you the trouble," she said. The place you're looking for is The Crest Hill Rest Home."

She must have seen the look of surprise on my face and seemed more than happy to chat.

"It's quite well known locally—believed to be haunted—and has changed hands several times. The Morton family bought it from the Stanwicks and then I think it became a hotel…then a rest home. The ownership changed hands about five years ago. The Farridays run it now. Do you want the address?" She jotted it down on a slip of paper for me, and I thanked her and left.

I drove along the tree-lined road imagining the horses and the carriages of a bygone age. There was still enough of the past about the place to make it easy to imagine life in the eighteenth century, and as I pulled up outside the gated rest home, I could almost see Reverend Allington striding up the driveway with evil in his heart.

I sat looking at the large mansion house with its freshly painted cream walls and manicured lawns. The Farridays certainly looked after the place, and I imagined not much had changed in the general appearance since the days when Amelia Root resided in its attic. The thought chilled me. It was as if I'd stumbled into Jenny's nightmare.

Even Josie sounded suitably impressed when I called her from my mobile. "Jesus! That must feel really weird," she said, almost in a whisper. "How do you feel?"

"It's surreal," I said, glancing up at the house. "And a bit scary, if I'm honest."

Josie laughed. "Hey, I'm scared, too—and I'm sitting here with a bar full of drunken women trying to get a mouthful of the male stripper. I'll have to go, hun, before we go totally pornographic!"

I told Jo I'd call her tomorrow and fired up the engine. I can't remember the drive home, my mind focused only on the Stanwicks' home and the girl they kept imprisoned there. She deserved a grave, an epitaph in remembrance of her life, however short and wretched it had been.

**

I called the rest home the following day and made an appointment. Mr. Farriday took the call, and I told him that we were looking for a suitable place for my elderly mother, claiming Crest Hill had been recommended by a good friend. Farriday told me that Saturday would be fine, which meant that Jenny could accompany me. At some point, we would have to come clean, because I didn't imagine that many people asked to see the attic when viewing the home, but Farriday sounded like an easy going, pleasant character who might at least make an effort to help.

Jenny looked tearful when I called in at the hospital. I told her about Crest Hill Rest Home, and she managed a weary smile but she needed time.

Dr. Grace accompanied me back down the corridor. "Being told that you are not her biological father will have hit her hard," she told me. "She'll have good and bad days—good and bad moments, actually. She will be feeling betrayed by your affairs—both yours and her mother's. She's old enough to be affected by the knowledge that she's not a product of a loving relationship—more of an illicit alliance born from your relationship with another woman."

I picked Josie up from The Keys that night, after opting for a coffee and a catch up at Tammy's. She climbed into the passenger seat and let out a long sigh.

"So what happened with the stripper?" I asked.

Jo rolled her eyes. "No more fucking hen parties! That's it!"

"I take it things got out of hand?"

Jo shook her head. "It was what they had *in* their hands that was the problem," she said without a flicker of a smile. "The bride was about to go down on the guy while her mates filmed it! Honestly! And they talk about blokes!"

I grinned. "I bet you were popular!"

"I nearly got lynched. They accused me of ruining the show. The stripper managed to calm them down, and when they were leaving, the bride's sister thanked me for putting a stop to the whole thing." Josie fastened her seat belt as we moved off. "I can't believe it. That girl would have regretted it for the rest of her life—and it would have been on her mate's phone, too."

I had coffee and garlic bread; Jo went for chocolate, her resolve broken the moment she saw the cake under the glass. "It's begging to be eaten," she told me. "How can I refuse?"

"Go for it!" I laughed, "We can eat healthy tomorrow!"

Jo threw me a mockingly indignant look. "I'll have you know I've lost another two pounds!"

I told her she didn't need to and that she was perfect as she was. I meant it.

We sat for over an hour talking about the Stanwicks' house, Amelia, and ghosts. Conversation was always easy, and eventually, we started reminiscing. It was good that we had a history. The woman by my side had not come in out of the cold; she was not a stranger with baggage I knew nothing about. We had been friends, and although I had never believed that friends made good lovers, maybe Josie was the exception.

We left Tammy's at close to midnight, and as I started up the engine Josie touched my arm. "Look, hun—over there." I followed the direction of her eyes. "The car," she whispered.

The red Fiat was parked up in the far corner of the car park. I stared hard but couldn't make out the face of the occupant. Josie's eyes were better than mine.

"There's two of them," she said.

"Male or female?" I asked, my heart beginning to race.

"Can't tell…just shapes," She replied. "Best just drive. Stop over with me at The Keys."

The Fiat followed but turned off before we reached home. "I'll make your bed up," Jo said as we parked up. "Best not take any chances. Your life is complicated enough."

I laughed but wasn't sure why. There was no reason why anyone should be taking an interest in my whereabouts, but the mistaken-identity theory was starting to bug me.

"Promise me you will never, ever even think of approaching that car, Rob," she said as I was turning in, praying for a decent sleep.

"No chance, babe," I said. "I'm too much of a coward."

Josie kissed my cheek. "That's one thing you ain't, hun," she said. "Get some sleep. You've got a big weekend coming up."

Chapter Twenty-Eight

I LOOKED OVER at my daughter as the Stanwicks' former home loomed up from behind its tree-lined driveway. "This is it," I said. "This is where Amelia lived."

We watched as the gates eased open with a series of creaks and clangs, wondering if this really was the end of our journey. Jenny looked up, searching for an attic window. We were both thinking the same thing.

A young domestic in a pale-blue uniform answered the door and waved us in. "You're here to see Mr. Farriday?" We nodded and followed like obedient children as she weaved through a room of tables laid for dinner.

"Do you think Amelia ever saw this room?" Jenny whispered as we passed a couple of elderly ladies sipping tea in the corner. The thought chilled me. I almost expected to find her waiting around the next corner.

Brian Farriday was sitting in an office that would probably have been nothing more than a storage cupboard when the Stanwicks had lived there. He acknowledged us with a brief hand gesture and continued with his phone call. He was a rather lanky, awkward-looking character, with deep-set eyes and a receding hairline, who would have looked more at home in a sit com than running a home for the elderly.

Jenny stared at the photographs, postcards and health and safety notices pinned to the walls. Could the spirit of Amelia still be here?

Farriday replaced the receiver and apologised. "Never a minute, I'm afraid." He stood and closed the door. "To be honest, I'll be glad to get shut of the place." He smiled. "We've just had the outside painted but I'm afraid it's falling apart."

I looked at him quizzically. "Really?"

Farriday sighed. "There's a lot of repair work on an old place like this, and when it's full of old people, you can't really start pulling their home apart."

Jenny frowned. "But I'd heard it was haunted."

Farriday laughed. Thin lips. White teeth. "Oh, some of the old folk tell us they hear things, but medication and dreams play a big part in it, I would guess."

"But it does have a history of weird stuff going on," Jenny insisted.

Farriday grinned "Well, the Morton family had the attic room bricked up," he said. "But you don't have to worry. Your mother will be safe—"

"Bricked up? Why?" My heart sank. "Look," I continued, deciding that it was time to come clean, "we're not looking for a place for my mother—or father. They're both dead. We're here about the attic."

Farriday frowned. "The attic?"

"This is going to sound really bizarre, but we need to see that room."

"You can't. Like I told you, it's bricked up."

Jenny looked at me, then at Farriday. "We would pay to open it up."

Farriday shook his head. "Open it up? Are you kidding me?"

Jenny slumped back in her chair. Farriday saw the look of disappointment. "Look, I'm sorry, but I can't just start knocking walls down at the whim of two people who have just walked in off the street. I don't know you from Adam!"

"We'd also pay to have the door bricked up again," I replied.

Farriday shrugged. "I'm sorry, this whole thing sounds crazy to me. Why are you so desperate to see a dingy attic? I really don't understand."

Jenny and I looked at each other. "It's your story, sweetheart— you tell him."

***

We followed Farriday up the stairway as he rattled a bunch of keys like an irritated jailer. "I'll show you the door. It still opens, apparently.

"I thought it was bricked up."

"It is—behind the door."

"So that should make it easier to knock down. It—"

"No," Farriday snapped, quickening his pace.

We reached the top of the stairs, breaking into a trot in an effort to keep up with our host as he strode ahead past a series of open doors, each room occupied by domestics, dusting and changing bed sheets. The grandeur of the Stanwicks' house had been lost under plasterboard and pipes. Rooms had been turned into bedsits, oak-panelled doors had been painted and the carpets were going threadbare. I wished I'd taken time to find out if any photographs of the old place in all its glory actually existed. The time when little Amelia lived with her weak mother. The times when Sarah would climb those stairs with a heavy heart.

Farriday spun to the left, and we soon found ourselves following him up a much steeper and narrower stairway. My heart began to pump harder.

"It's just up here," Farriday told us. "Although there's not much to see."

The attic door was probably the only thing in the whole house that hadn't been painted. It remained in its original state. Old panelled mahogany. Farriday fished for the key.

"Why is it locked? You can't get in!"

Farriday rolled his eyes. "Superstition," he replied. "Not mine—my wife's."

"So she believes in spirits, then?"

Farriday nodded. "She's convinced they exist—unlike me."

The key twisted in the lock. "There you go," Farriday said stepping back. "Take a look."

Jenny stepped forward. We both held our breaths. What would be waiting on the other side?

"Go on," I urged as Jenny hesitated, her hand resting on the brass door knob. She twisted and pulled. The door creaked and strained as my daughter pulled it towards her. A blast of cold air hit us, the musty scent of old wood and damp walls. Yet, sure enough, there was nothing but brick.

We stood in silence, looking at the wall, as if at any moment it would part like a theatre curtain as the show began, but there was no sound or movement. Even the chill had evaporated, along with the musty scent of Amelia's home.

"Well, this is it," Farriday said. "Your story was fascinating, but I'm afraid I can do no more."

"Can't or won't?" Jenny snapped.

Farriday glared, clearly vexed. "I'm sorry. I won't."

***

Jenny seemed remarkably at peace as we drove home. "I thought you'd be disappointed," I said as we pulled up outside the house.

Jenny smiled. "He'll change his mind," she said. "Just wait and see." Jenny could tell I wasn't convinced. "It'll gnaw away at him," she continued. "Okay, he doesn't believe in spirits, but I bet he's the type who won't like people keeping secrets—he'll want to know what's really on the other side of that door."

I didn't see a man like Farriday giving in under pressure. We had done the right thing in leaving with a handshake and our number scribbled on a post-it note.

"I know how you feel about that room, Jen, but you have to be prepared—"

"I need to be in that room," she said as we walked through the door. "I've got to believe that Farriday will change his mind."

I sensed that Jenny didn't want to pursue the subject any further. She flicked on the TV. We were trying hard, and I never doubted that Jenny loved me, yet there was a wall between us as impenetrable as the one keeping us out of Amelia's room. She wasn't mine—and I wasn't hers.

The TV became our focus, allowing us to avoid any meaningful conversation. I grabbed the remote and killed the sound. Jenny shot me a look. "What are you doing?"

"We need to talk."

Jenny groaned. "About what?"

"You know what."

"There's nothing to discuss."

"I need to know how you feel." I could hear my father again—*easy, my son...easy.* "You'll always be my girl, Jen. I couldn't feel any differently towards you, even if I wanted to."

Jenny continued to stare at the TV screen. "Are you seeing Josie?"

The question came like a surge of electricity through my body. "How do you mean?"

Jenny turned and glared at me. "It's a simple question."

"Josie's married."

"So were you. But it didn't stop you screwing the bitch?"

I felt like a deflated tyre, my spirit leaking from every pore. "We're friends. She's been there for me."

Jenny smiled sarcastically. "The age old prelude to an affair."

"But I don't understand where this is going?"

"Okay, the bottom line is this. You fancy the pants off Josie, it's so obvious. You don't have any ties, you don't have a wife, you don't have any children." Jenny looked at me with venom in her eyes. "So why don't you and Josephine piss off into the sunset and leave me and my murderous little twat of a half brother alone!"

If I'd had an answer, I could have barely voiced it. Jenny grabbed the remote and turned up the sound. *Back off, son, you're done here. Let her rest.* So we sat watching a movie neither of us had the energy to follow, and that night, as Jenny rose and signalled that she was going to bed, I told her that I loved her. I loved her more than anything else in the world. She turned away without answering, and I listened to her footsteps on the stairs. At the end of the tunnel, the light that kept my hopes alive flickered and died.

***

Up to that moment, the weekend had been neither a success nor a failure. We had been comfortable together without being close. I returned from the hospital that Monday feeling deflated, like a father returning his child to her home after spending a few short and precious hours together. The house was empty once more.

I was about to call Josie. In fact, my hand was on the receiver when the phone rang. It was Farriday.

"Mr. Adams? I have been talking to my wife about that attic room…" He paused. "I'm afraid she has overruled me." He laughed. "You know what women are like. Once she heard your story… She's fascinated by ghost stories although she'll probably sleep with the lights on in future."

Jenny had been right. It was something more than optimism. It was knowledge.

"Anyway, we are getting our odd job man to open up the doorway—probably at the end of the week. Laura—er, my wife— wants to keep the door locked until you're ready."

I replaced the receiver after thanking him profusely. Suddenly, the place didn't feel so empty. I called Sebastian, who sounded as upbeat as I felt.

"Come on over," he said brightly. "I've someone I'd like you to meet."

***

The German shepherd pup yelped excitedly at Sebastian's heels as I followed them into the lounge.

"I've called him Ricky," Sebastian told me. "I couldn't have called him by any other name." The old man looked truly pleased with his new companion. "How about a shot of whisky in your coffee?"

It was a kind of celebration I suppose, for the two of us had turned a corner. I just wasn't so sure what awaited me on the road ahead.

Jenny was convinced that Amelia's attic home would hold the truth within its walls, but what would happen if the room she had visited in her dreams refused to give up its secrets? Where would we go from there?

Sebastian listened intently and then asked, "Exactly what are you expecting?"

I shrugged. The old man was going to tell me, obviously.

"You have to leave yourself open. You have to feel the place. Jenny has never been wrong—there will be something in that room."

"Amelia?"

"Who knows?"

Maybe that was the thing I feared most—more than finding nothing at all.

"You need to remember," the old man continued, "Amelia requires a resting place...a proper burial. Once you have found the body, Jenny will be free."

"But that's what I don't understand. Why should a spirit worry about a decayed shell?"

"It is not so much the body, it is the manner of her death. She lived and died with no recognition, whereas the man who raped and brutally assaulted her lies immortalised in the house of God." Sebastian shot me a look. There was anger in his eyes. "I don't think I'd be able to rest in those circumstances, do you?"

He lifted a whimpering Ricky onto his knee.

"Remember me telling you about the student who died in a road accident?"

I nodded.

"He appeared to me within an hour of his death, simply to tell me that I had been wrong. All those things of which I'd been so convinced. There was no God, no life after death. It was as if he could not rest until he had let me know." Sebastian smiled. "Amelia cannot rest, either."

***

I left the old man's house imagining an irate spirit languishing behind the wall of the Stanwicks' attic, waiting to unleash its fury upon the world. Jenny brightened when I told her about Farriday's call that evening, but there was no verbal reconciliation. I spoke to Dr. Grace about the possibility of allowing Jenny home again at the weekend. She seemed hopeful.

"Jenny seems healthy—her blood pressure is normal, and she seems relaxed. We are looking to discharge her within the next few days." Dr. Grace smiled. "We will be referring her for therapy, but providing she doesn't lapse back into this erratic behaviour, she will probably be better at home with you."

***

My mobile bleeped as I poured myself a fresh orange juice. It was a text from Josie.

Hey, you! Just learned to text. you are my first. How are you?
I punched in a reply. *Well done! How long did it take you?*
Ten minutes on, my mobile bleeped again.
About 30 mins! Haha!
Jo's message made me smile. She had never taken to her mobile and never bothered with social media. I kind of loved that, and for the briefest of moments, I'd forgotten all about Amelia Root.
It's an age thing! I punched back.
Two minutes later, my landline rang.
"Who's a clever girl then?" Josie crowed before I'd had time to say hello. "Meg's knocking me into shape!"
"Who's Meg?"
"The new barmaid. She gives a whole new meaning to the word *streetwise*. She's going to be really good for the place!" Jo paused. "Anyway, is there any news?"
I told her about Farriday and the attic room, but halfway through she stopped me. "Look, hun, why don't you come on over? We'll have supper."
It sounded good to me. I needed to think aloud, let my thoughts escape, and Jo was just the person. Besides, she served a mean cheese toastie, and no one could beat her milky coffee.
"See you in ten," I said, replacing the receiver and running a comb through my hair. That tired, middle-aged man stared back at me, and I wished to God that mirrors could lie.

***

The Keys was quiet. A few couples propped up the bar, and the girl I presumed to be Meg was serving up an exotic-looking green cocktail. Jo had been right. She would be good for the place. Meg was straight off the cover of a glossy magazine. Blonde, blue eyed, perfect white teeth and a smile that could chase the clouds from anyone's sky.

Josie killed the sound on the TV. The smell of the toasties and coffee drifted along the hallway. "I figured you might be glad of some company," she said, sitting opposite and revealing an eyeful of shapely leg. She smiled. "You've seen it before, hun."

I blushed, wondering what she would have made of Jenny's suggestion that we should disappear into the sunset. Maybe it wasn't the right time.

"So, you'll finally see Amelia's room—that'll be weird."

I nodded. "Sebastian says I should keep an open mind."

"And what do you think you'll find?"

That was the billion-dollar question. I shrugged. "I just want all this to end, Jo. I really do. It's messing with my head."

"How are you and Jenny getting on?"

"Slowly," I replied.

Jo raised her eyebrows. "That bad, huh?"

"It's not going to be easy. I mean, the whole thing between Elizabeth and Benjamin Pascoe—it's a bit of a bombshell, to put it mildly. The poor girl suddenly finds out she's related to Darren!"

Josie rolled her eyes. "Not exactly the brother you'd choose from a catalogue."

"Jen always thought she was from a stable home. You know— the whole loving family thing—two parents who loved each other unreservedly."

There was a look of maternal concern on Josie's face. She stood and patted my shoulder. "I'll go and get supper."

I wondered, and not for the first time, what course my life would have taken if I'd never met Melissa. Would we be living a contented suburban life with two-point-four children? I didn't know, but two things were certain; Darren Pascoe would have never hooked up with Taylor, and Jenny would never have been born.

Josie returned with a tray. Steaming cheese toasties and milky coffee.

"Marry me!" I said, laughing.

Josie smiled wryly. "Don't be raising my hopes, sunshine!"

***

James Taylor played on the radio as I drove home. Lou hadn't made an appearance all evening, and part of me felt uncomfortable. Was he waiting for me to go? The other part of me didn't give a gnat's arse. I'd wanted to stay, sharing my thoughts well into the night until we'd both fallen asleep in each other's arms, but when Josie had yawned and glanced at her watch, I thanked her for the supper and left.

When I arrived home there was a message on my answering machine. It was Dr. Grace. "Mr. Adams?" the voice was kind but officious. "Could you call me? Thank you."

After three minutes on hold, I was put through to the doctor who informed me that they were happy to allow Jenny home at the weekend. I punched the air, turned Frank Sinatra on high, and poured myself a rum and dry ginger with a ladle of ice. Jenny was still Benjamin Pascoe's daughter. Darren Pascoe was still her half brother. I still missed my wife and child, and if the bathroom mirror was not lying, I still looked like an old man. But at the end of the long dark tunnel, there was light again.

On my next visit, Jenny and I discussed the forthcoming weekend, skirting around the issues that we should have been talking over. We had, it seemed, one thing in common: the desire to find Amelia. But I feared what lay ahead should we succeed. Would Jenny slowly drift away from me, meet a boy, shack up, have children of her own? Would I still be in her life?

"I was thinking," she said as I was leaving. I turned, one hand on the door. "Maybe it would be better if you didn't come in again…leave it till the weekend."

She looked away, unable to look me in the eye. I wanted to shake her. I wanted to scream my protest, but all I could manage was a cursory nod. I'm guessing she didn't look up until she heard the door close.

I called in on Dr. Grace on the way out, relieved to find her sitting at a cluttered desk. She greeted me with a smile and offered me a seat.

"Jenny doesn't want to see me till the weekend," I blurted out before my backside had touched the chair.

She smiled kindly. "It will take time, Mr. Adams. I can assure you that Jenny is trying to work through this. Maybe she just needs some…" Dr. Grace paused. "God, I hate this word, but maybe she needs some *space*." She tapped something into her computer and peered at the screen. "Damn! Look, I'm really sorry, but I have to be somewhere."

She stood, gathering her personal belongings: keys, black clutch bag and a lined notebook. "I can't get out of this…again, sorry—with a capital S."

I shrugged. "It's okay. I'll see you Friday."

***

The week dragged on, feeling more like a month. My head was already in that attic room, and my macabre imagination was fuelled by a bottle of rum and several cans of premium strength beer. Josie reminded me that I hadn't shaved and then stood over me, while I ran a razor across two days of stubble, before dragging me to a salon in town. She settled in with a magazine while a girl called Rosie cut my hair and trimmed my eyebrows.

"How about putting some colour in those locks? And a facial scrub would do you the world of good," she told me as we drove back to The Keys. I sighed wearily. "You're looking older than you are, hun, and if you look old, you'll feel old."

"I'm tired," I told her, "and a bottle of hair dye won't change that."

Josie flicked on the indicator and swung the car into The Keys. "Fine. But do you really want to look like an old wreck? You honestly think that will help Jenny?"

By the time Friday came around, I'd been scrubbed, massaged and coloured. My trousers fitted better and although my head was still in a mess, Josie had a point. At least I now looked like a functioning human being.

***

Jenny did a double take when I picked her up at the hospital. "You look well," she said with an air of suspicion in her voice.

I guessed she thought the makeover was for Josie's benefit, so I just smiled and changed the subject, telling her that I'd called Farriday that morning and the wall was down. Nothing remarkable had happened. The workmen had taken the money they were owed and left the premises.

"He's going to meet us at midday, tomorrow," I said as we drove home. "So I thought maybe we could start out early and grab ourselves a bite to eat."

Jenny nodded, preoccupied with what lay ahead, almost as if she knew. "Sounds good. I'm starving. Fancy a huge portion of greasy fish and chips?"

I wasn't hungry. The alcohol had worn the lining from my stomach, but this was the old Jenny and I wanted to keep her. "Sure—and how about some thick white bread with lashings of butter?"

My daughter laughed. *My daughter...she would always be just that.* "Cool!" she said.

We sat watching an afternoon chick flick on the movie channel with two large colas and a mountain of fries with fish the size of small sharks. We fell asleep, our stomachs full, waking only as the credits rolled. We both had that *what do we do now?* look in our eyes. Neither of us could even think about food, and the TV was dire.

"Fancy a walk?" I asked. To my surprise, Jenny agreed.

We wrapped up against the brisk, cool breeze and took to the nearest public footpath just a mile away, both silent, our minds preoccupied with our visit to Amelia's attic. When it began to rain, we huddled together beneath Jenny's pink umbrella and laughed at our misfortune. After the past year, being caught three miles from home in a light rainfall could hardly be considered as a challenge to our character.

***

Neither of us had bothered catching up on the weather forecast, so we hadn't been aware we'd walked through the beginning of a storm which was going to sweep across the country over the weekend. That night, the light rain turned into something else. Ninety-mile-an-hour winds whipped the trees and sent bins skimming along the roads like stones across the surface of a pond.

We set off in the morning, ignoring the Met Office's warning against any unnecessary journeys. The weather had deterred the casual shoppers and weekend drivers, leaving us among the workers and the foolhardy for company as we headed through the driving rain with the windscreen wipers thrashing maniacally. When we pulled up at a set of lights, just three miles into the journey, I happened to glance in my rear-view mirror. The car behind me was, as far as I could tell, a black Ford. But behind that, a vehicle I had come to recognise was clearly visible as it attempted to change lanes.

"What are you looking at, Dad?" Jenny quizzed.

"Nothing, sweetheart. Just thought I'd spotted someone I knew."

Jenny returned to the game on her phone. I couldn't tell her about the red Fiat. Not yet.

By the time we arrived at the rest home, the wind had dropped, but the grey skies seemed heavier than ever—so heavy, in fact, that it was hard to imagine that there was anything beyond them.

"This place looks like something out of a Dracula movie," Jenny muttered as we pulled up. I killed the engine and waited. The rain was driving hard. We pulled our coats over our heads and made a run for the door without the umbrella.

Farriday was waiting for us in the hallway. A woman dressed in a navy blue suit stood beside him, only slightly shorter but at least a decade younger, her blonde, streaked hair, tied back from her face.

"That must be Mrs. Farriday," I whispered to Jenny as we approached.

"She's pretty," Jenny said under her breath. "Look at those eyes."

Farriday held out his hand. Mrs. Farriday smiled warmly. "Good to see you both. This is Laura, my wife."

Laura nodded. "Can I get you a drink? Tea? Coffee?"

We agreed, despite not wanting to delay our visit to the attic a moment longer. I figured that Laura had a few questions for us, and to appear unduly hurried might seem discourteous.

We were ushered into the Farridays' private quarters, a spacious and modern room with a huge plasma screen TV.

"Please, take a seat." Mrs. Farriday gestured towards a large leather couch. "Then you can tell me all about that attic."

Jenny and I looked at each other, rolling our eyes as Laura disappeared before reappearing with our coffee. "I'm afraid my fascination with ghouls irritates my husband, so I don't really get to watch those ghost hunting programmes on the TV." She glanced at Jenny, who was pale. "I'm sorry. That sounds rather flippant. This must be tough on both of you. I mean—you must have been desperate to come here and…you know…"

Jenny smiled and nodded.

"Anyway, Brian told me about this woman… Emily?"

"Amelia," I corrected.

"That's it, Amelia. She lived in the attic?" Laura sat down, her eyes flitting from Jenny to me and back again. I told her the story—at least, the part I knew would satisfy her curiosity. Laura kept looking at Jenny throughout, as if unable to accept that she had a real life ghost hunter in her home. If she had, for one moment, thought that we were just a couple of crackpots, it didn't show. There was no trace of disbelief in those eyes.

Finally, I stood. "Is it okay if we take a look?"

Laura blushed. "Oh, I'm so sorry. Of course."

Jenny tapped my arm. "Is it okay if we go on our own?"

Laura didn't look that keen to follow us anyway, but Jenny wanted to be sure. "I'll take you to the stairs. Just make your way back here when you're ready."

She gave us both a slightly doubtful look that questioned if we should be really entering the room without a priest. Jenny read her mind. "It's cool, honestly. You don't need to worry. No matter how long this takes, you don't need to check on us. We'll be okay."

Chapter Twenty-Nine

THE FARRIDAYS HAD left the door unlocked. Jenny and I stood for a moment, my hand resting on the handle. My heart thumped hard in my chest. "Why did you say that to Farriday's wife?" I asked.

Jenny shrugged. "I dunno. Maybe I just don't want her snooping around and disturbing something." Jenny smiled. "Amelia is a benevolent spirit. She means no harm."

I wasn't sure. Jenny had stabbed me, slashed her wrists, and trashed a church. She seemed like a spirit with anger issues to me. This time, there would be no brick wall awaiting us. Only the room. I looked at my daughter. *My daughter.* She took my hand and squeezed hard. "But I'm still frightened, Dad."

Dad. The word meant so much more now, and I wanted to draw her into my arms and hold her. I wanted to tell her how much she meant, but it wasn't the time.

"Me, too," I whispered.

Jenny smiled as tears welled in her eyes. "Here goes."

I turned the handle and pushed the door open. It swung majestically in eerie silence. Jenny gasped. This was it.

"I'm in my dream," she whispered.

There was nothing extraordinary about the attic room. A small window directly opposite was thick with grime, allowing in a little light—just enough to make out the table beneath it. We remained in the doorway while our eyes adjusted and then together we stepped forward.

An old mattress lay on the dusty wooden floor boards in the corner of the room, a tin bath alongside it. On the opposite side of the room, a trunk was pushed right up against the wall. I pulled the torch from my pocket. Jenny was shaking. I placed my arm around her.

"How do you feel?" I asked quietly.

"It doesn't seem real," she said. "Amelia sat at that desk. She sat on that chair."

"Are you up to looking in that trunk?"

Jenny nodded slowly.

The lid lifted easily. I flashed the torch across the contents of Amelia's life. Dresses, nightwear, a few old books from which she had been privately taught. I felt a heaviness in my spirit that I couldn't explain. Life had passed this girl by. This was all she had ever known. I was drawn towards the window and peered out through the grime.

How much the landscape had changed over years, I didn't know. The lawn stretched out below, lined by trees and overgrown shrubs. Amelia's father had once tended those borders, walked the lawn and maybe stolen a kiss from the lady of the house in the shade of the oak. I shuddered. Jenny stood, challenged by her surroundings. She was standing in her nightmare.

"I don't know what to do," she said in a hushed voice. "Why am I here?"

I peered back through the gloom. Even in the half light, Jenny looked an almost deathly white.

"If you want to go…"

The door slammed shut with a crashing thud as the attic window shattered. Shards of glass blew across the room, and I turned to see my daughter thrown backwards. In the blast of icy air, the stench of decay flooded my senses. I found myself kneeling over my daughter, my whole body shaking with cold and fear. "Jenny!" I whispered. "Jenny!" I cradled her head in my arms.

She opened her eyes. "I'm cold," she said. "I'm so cold."

It felt as if the blood in my veins had turned to ice. I was looking at my daughter's face but the voice was not hers. Nor the eyes. I touched her cheek. No one could be that cold to the touch and still possess a beating heart. "Who are you?" I said. "What do you want?"

The girl's eyes widened. "You're here now," she said, her voice barely audible. Her breathing quickened. I heard the death rattle. Amelia was going to take Jenny with her back to the grave.

"Where's my daughter?" I demanded frantically. "What have you done with her? Is that what you brought her here for? To take her? Why? Why?"

The faintest smile crossed her face. "It is over," she said. "You will know what to do."

"What do you mean?"

I could no longer see Jenny in the face I was staring down at. "What do you smell?" she asked.

I thought for a moment. "It smells like…"

I knew the smell. *Please…what is it…what is it?*

The girl looked at me; her lips moved silently. "Water… It's water."

That was it! Water. Stagnant water.

"What does it mean? What?"

The girl—Amelia—was fading fast. "It is where I am," she said. "It is where you will find me."

The girl I held closed her eyes. I felt the breath leave her body. Her heart slowed like a tired old clock, and she was gone.

I screamed, pulling Jenny up like a rag doll. "Oh, God, no! Jesus, no! Why? Why?"

I'm not sure how long I remained, kneeling on the attic floor, but my aching arms could no longer support the body. I lowered her back to the floor and stood, the blood draining from my head. The room began to spin, and I closed my eyes, bowing my head and taking several deep breaths. I had to remain conscious. I had to get my daughter's body out of this hole.

This had been the place Jenny had visited in her nightmares. Now it was my nightmare, but I would never wake up to find myself beneath a scented duvet. I had lost everything. *It's over... you will know what to do...* But I didn't. I didn't know what to do. Sebastian had never warned me. *The dead can't hurt you.* How often had I heard that?

Jenny lay, her skin clammy and cold. Now I could barely see her face through the gloom of the early evening. I screamed for help, crouched over my girl, unable to leave her side for a moment, lest she be taken from me, paralysed by my fear of returning to find the room empty, with no trace of Jenny—a girl, like Amelia, with no resting place.

"Mr. Adams? What the hell..." It was Brian Farriday.

My heart thumped so hard I could barely form a simple word. The door creaked open. Light flooded the room. I looked up to see two people silhouetted in the doorframe. Farriday had brought his wife. "Jesus... What's going on? What's—"

"She's dead!" I sobbed. "Dead!"

"Ambulance!" Farriday barked. "Quickly!"

I heard Laura's footsteps on the stairs.

"It's too late." I sobbed as Farriday knelt beside me, placing a hand gently across Jenny's forehead.

"What happened? What did you do?"

I realised there and then that I was going to be hearing that question over and over. The police wouldn't buy the story of Amelia Root. I was the only person there when my daughter died.

"She just collapsed," I said as Farriday withdrew his hand.

"We need some proper light in here," he said. "You stay there!"

I found no humour in the irony of the comment. I only wanted to wake. To wake or die.

***

Two paramedics returned with Farriday, who held a tungsten light on a pole. One of the men in green lifted me by the shoulders. "Leave this to us now, Mr. Adams."

I watched as they knelt over my daughter. "Can we have some light, please?"

Farriday called through from the end of a trailing wire. "I'm on it."

"She just collapsed?"

"Yes."

"Any medical conditions? Asthma? Anaemia?"

"No."

The tungsten bulb burst into life. "That's better." One of the medics muttered. I looked away. How could I face them? How could I look into their eyes as they told me what I already knew? When they told me my daughter had gone.

"Oxygen!"

I spun round as the larger of the green men placed a mask over Jenny's face. He looked up. "We have a pulse! She's alive, Mr. Adams. You daughter is alive."

I sat alongside Jenny in the ambulance, a foil blanket around my shoulders. I'd not even noticed how cold the attic room was or how close to collapse I had been. Farriday had grabbed my car keys and insisted on following the ambulance in my car.

"Don't worry," he assured me. "I'll be careful."

I didn't answer. I didn't care. My daughter still looked like a corpse. "Is she going to be okay?" I had asked the question several times, but the paramedic smiled patiently.

"She's a fighter," he said.

That wasn't an answer. It just meant that she wasn't going to take the Grim Reaper's hand willingly.

"Until we know what caused her to collapse, we really can't tell you much," he said.

They concentrated on keeping my daughter alive. I had nothing to give them. They asked again. Had Jenny any conditions, however minor? Any history? No. I had a healthy girl.

"Is there anything in the family? Heart conditions?"

I looked at the man in green. A robust, round pleasant face. A man in his forties. "I don't know," I replied. "Her father's dead."

The paramedic frowned. "But I thought you were her father."

"So did I…until a few weeks ago."

"I'm sorry. This is obviously awkward…"

"Her father is a man called Benjamin Pascoe. He took his own life," I replied, almost casually.

The medic looked as though he had just placed his hand in a hornets' nest. He patted my arm. The ambulance screeched to a halt, and the doors swung open. Farriday pushed the keys into my hand, and before I had time to catch my breath, I was following my daughter as they wheeled her down a linoleum-floored corridor. Next, I was sitting in a room with several others, flicking through a celebrity weekly, trying to focus my mind on some pop princess and her new groom as they opened their home to the photographers.

I wondered what my father would have made of the world's fascination with the rich, famous and often talentless. He had no desire for wealth. To him, possessions clouded the soul and dampened the spirit. All that man required was in his surroundings—the rivers, the mountains, the flora and fauna. Nothing man had created could ever match the beauty of nature itself.

I thought about calling Sebastian but changed my mind. What could he do? What could anyone do? I prayed, even though I wasn't much good at talking to a God I really wasn't sure existed, and even if He did, I'd pretty much blamed Him for everything. Even a deity might find it hard granting the wishes of a hypocritical bastard who wanted a favour.

If you're really there, just save Jenny. Please.

A doctor walked in. He was tall with thinning grey hair and heavy-rimmed glasses. "Mr. Adams?"

I stood, almost falling into him as he approached. "Jenny's stable," he said. But his dour expression told me that this was the sugar coating to a bitter pill. "But?" I said.

The doctor introduced himself. "I'm Mr. Lamont." He signalled that I should sit down. Lamont sat alongside me. "At this moment, your daughter is in a coma, but all the initial tests have come back clear. Medically, she seems in good health, and we can't find any cause for her condition."

I felt my stomach knot. My chest ached, and I could feel the blood draining from my head.

"Are you all right, Mr. Adams?"

I nodded, even though I knew he wasn't going to buy the lie.

"Are you up to telling me what exactly happened?"

I wasn't, but there was no option. They needed to know. They needed to know the whole story, and I didn't care if they believed it or not. Lamont listened sympathetically to the tale from the moment Elizabeth and Hanna had died to our confrontation with Amelia in her attic room. His eyes betrayed nothing. He smiled. "Thank you. We'll be running some more tests, of course."

"When can I see her?" I asked.

Lamont stood. "Soon. Someone will let you know."

I waited and drank more coffee. A young nurse appeared after one hour, and I followed her down the corridor and into a room where my daughter lay, tubed up and motionless. Lamont stood at the end of her bed. "You can talk to her," he told me. "About anything. It might help."

I pulled up a grey plastic chair and sat down. A pale hand protruded from underneath the bed sheet. I gave it a gentle squeeze.

"Hi," I said awkwardly. "It's your dad here… It's going to be okay, sweetheart." There was not a flicker. "Your granddad is watching you. He has faith… You'll be all right."

If she could hear my voice through the haze, I only hoped there was no lack of any conviction within it.

I talked about nothing that mattered for nearly an hour before Lamont returned and suggested I go home and get some sleep. It sounded like an order, so I didn't argue.

"If anything changes, we'll contact you straight away," he told me. "Just try to get some rest."

It was nine. There was a message from Farriday on the answering machine when I got home.

"Mr. Adams? Brian here. How's Jenny? We're really worried. Hope everything's okay."

I called back to thank him for his help before calling Josie, who insisted on coming over immediately. She arrived thirty minutes later, her face pale and drawn. "She'll be okay, hun, I know it. People come out of comas, and like you said, the doctors can't find anything wrong…"

She threw her arms around my neck and clung like a child. "She'll be back home before you know it."

I poured us a brandy and we sat talking till the early hours, trawling through the events of the day, searching for answers but finding none. After Jo left, I poured another large brandy and passed out on the lounge chair with the twenty-four-hour news rolling in the background.

When I woke, fully clothed, my head ached like crazy. It felt like someone was swinging a hammer inside my brain, and I swallowed a couple of pills before calling Sebastian. Thirty minutes later, I was standing on his doorstep, unshaven and still wearing my old slippers. Sebastian studied me for a few seconds.

"Things not so good, eh?" he said, ushering me in. I nodded, stepping into the hallway only to be greeted by an over-excited puppy.

Sebastian listened in silence as I told him about Jenny. His obvious concern troubled me. "This has happened before," he mused, glancing over at his wall of books. "There have been several cases recorded where the subject becomes an unwilling medium—a mediator for the spirit."

"And they've ended up in a coma?"

Sebastian nodded. "Jenny—or Amelia—said that you'd know what to do."

"But I don't. That's the problem."

There was a look of enlightenment in Tint's eyes. "I was right. Find the body, Robert. Find the body and you will get your daughter back!"

I stared at the old man, and our eyes locked. "You have the clues. What Jenny did in the bath, the stench of stagnant water in the attic room. The girl lies underwater somewhere."

"Somewhere close," I mused, thinking aloud.

Sebastian smiled. "I doubt she would have gone far, with Allington's blood on her hands."

***

I spent the following day in Tabwell's rather quaint library, just a mile from St. Jude's, but the local history books revealed nothing. Jenny's condition hadn't changed, and I needed to do something. I caught the attention of the librarian, who looked up from her screen and smiled as I ambled over.

"Are there any lakes in Tabwell?" I asked.

The woman looked at me as if I was stupid. "Lakes? Well, we have one."

"Local to the Stanwicks' house?"

"Stanwicks'?"

"Sorry—the Crest Hill Rest Home."

The woman smiled. "Oh, sorry, I remember you now. Right… well, our only lake is quite a tourist spot. It's not that far from the rest home. You could walk it in about fifteen minutes, I reckon." She paused and reached under the desk and handed me a leaflet. "This will tell you everything you need to know."

***

Tabwell Water was well sign posted from the main road through the town: picnic areas, woodland walks, trekking and the usual pay-and-display car park with a small café area in the corner. I pulled up, bought my ticket, and took the path leading through the woodland to the lakeside. Was this the path the Amelia had trodden as she ran to her death?

My heart sank as the vast waters came into view. If Amelia did lie in its murky depths, she would be there until the end of time. We would never find her body—not even with a team of divers. I sat musing for hours, almost hoping that a hand would appear from the water.

Children played at the edge as their parents looked on. A family sat at a wooden picnic table, wrapped up against the winter chill, determined to complete their outdoor adventure.

A young man in a green shirt with the words *Lakeside Ranger* emblazoned across his back in yellow letters watched on from the doorway of a small wooden hut. He was a glorified litter warden, I suspected. Probably with degrees up to his eyeballs but no prospective employer willing to pay anything above a Third-World wage.

I left, walking with a weight on my shoulders. My mobile rang. It was Farriday. "Mr. Adams?"

"Speaking," I muttered, taking to a wooden bench beneath an ominous looking tree that threatened anyone foolish enough to sit beneath its tangled branches.

"Listen," he continued. "You might be interested...I went back into the attic—my wife was fascinated by your story. We found some diaries..."

My heart jumped in my chest." Amelia's?"

"Yes. They were at the bottom of that old trunk."

"Can I see them?"

"That was the idea."

I paused. "I'm in Tabwell now. I can come over."

"Certainly. How's your daughter?"

"Still in a coma, but stable."

I climbed behind the wheel of my car and hit the play button on the car stereo. Frank's big band struck up 'New York, New York' and I briefly wondered how my sister was doing over there before turning my thoughts to what Amelia's diaries might reveal.

I drove over the speed limit, braking sharply as I passed each of Tabwell's many speed cameras. Considering it appeared to be the Ferrari capital of England, the owners were unlikely to get out of first gear on the local roads.

I arrived at Crest Hill minutes later. Brian greeted me at the door. "Robert!" he said. "I have the diaries in my office. Follow me." Farriday, like the minister of St. Jude's, was quick on his feet, and I found myself in a half-trot trying to keep up with him. Several elderly ladies, huddled over a card game in the dining area, looked up as we breezed past. I smiled, my mind on Amelia.

Farriday had not really given me any indication of how many diaries he'd found. There were ten piled neatly on his desk. Burgundy and black, leather covers. I stopped short. "Jesus!" I exclaimed, and I suddenly felt my father's wrath at his son's blasphemous tongue. "I thought you meant a couple! This is—"

"Fantastic!" Farriday said. "Someone should publish these."

So that was it. I was in the company of a business man who saw old people as a way of making a quick buck, quite willing to turf them out onto the street when his profit margins fell. His excitement had nothing to do with the uncovering of the attic's dark secrets but the money it might make for him.

He looked at me, uncomfortable with my silence. "I can dig out a box from somewhere, if you want."

"What?"

Farriday looked amused. "To put the books in—I presume you'll be taking them with you."

I stared at the stack on the cluttered desk. "But I thought you would be keeping them here."

Farriday laughed. "From what you've told me, these books belong to your daughter." I'd misjudged the man, in part at least. They were on his property, after all.

"My wife has read a few pages. Some of it is just basic day-to-day stuff, but it really gives an insight. I'm sure that you and Jenny will find it interesting."

It was good to hear someone talk about my daughter as if she was still with us, rather than in some kind of metaphysical hibernation.

"Thank you," I said, holding out my hand as Farriday took it in a vice-like grip that felt both warm and genuine. He left and reappeared with a cardboard box. Ten minutes later, I was on the road back home with my head spinning in anticipation.

I wondered where my daughter was. The anguished spirit of a dead girl had taken her body and her mind as she stood in that attic room. Where had she taken my precious child? What was going on in her head?

Chapter Thirty

THE DIARIES WERE stacked in order so I made myself a coffee and sat back with the one I considered to be the last Amelia had written, flicking through the pages until my attention was caught by the following entry.

I had never felt such love and truly believed that no man would be so heartless as to separate a mother from her baby. Yet Reverend Allington had torn him—yes, torn him—from my arms and left without so much as a word of kindness. I called after him, "Her name is Rebecca!"

I flicked through several more brief accounts.

My heart aches and will continue to ache for as long as I live. Rebecca. That is her name. The name that God gave her. She will always be Rebecca, and the thought that Reverend Allington might give her a new name in the presence of his congregation filled me with a fury. That is why I escaped my prison in the dawn light and took refuge among the trees behind St. Jude's church.

I waited, my anger unabated, as I watched the parishioners filing through the gates. Believe me, I knew what I was about to do would not bring back my child, but God was on my side, and I believe that it was His Spirit within.

"The child is mine!" I cried, walking the length of the aisle towards the font at which the reverend was holding my baby. "She belongs to me!"

The congregation murmured behind me but I never saw their faces.

"Her name is Rebecca!"

I felt breath on my neck and two hands gripping my shoulders, pulling me back. "He is a hypocrite—this man who preaches the word of God and then comes to my room and forces himself upon me!"

I was dragged backwards and thrown to the floor at the gates of the church. "You young wretch!" a bespectacled man with a complexion as awful as The Devil himself barked at me. "Don't ever darken these doors again."

I rose, brushing the dust from my clothing. "Do not concern yourself, sir. I have told the truth. Do you think I could ever find God in here when a servant of the Devil rules over you?"

I wandered home, returning to my room uninterrupted and lay on my bed till late noon, my body too weak to rise and my eyes too heavy to read any of the books Sarah had left for me. The reverend's doctor visited, not from any concern, but too oversee my full recovery and ease the conscience of his peer. I was told to rest, though I have no option. Sarah is all I have.

Intrigued, I continued on, turning the pages with the reverence a scholar would have for an ancient document.

Sarah has read to me from the Gospels each day, fearful lest I should be lost to her God. I ask many questions, most of which she has no answer to, all concerning my child and how any man who serves the church could behave in such a manner. I have exhausted my own mind. I am sick of spirit, though Sarah told me that revenge belonged to the Lord Himself. I'm not sure if that is true. I think of how the minister might explain himself to his Lord. But maybe God will not consider me at all. Was I created for this purpose alone? The thought appals me, and I try to put it from my mind. They are the Devil's whispers.

My heart ached for the girl, alone with her thoughts every night of her existence, her only experience of physical intimacy at the hands of a man who despised her. I turned over to find the following pages were blank. Amelia Root had never written another word.

Chapter Thirty-One

I FELT STRANGELY uneasy, almost as if the author of these diaries was unwilling to let them go. Maybe it was the chill of the late evening stirring the memory of that clawing cold I'd felt as Jenny collapsed into Amelia's world. I turned on the TV, relieved to hear the laughter of a studio audience ring through the house. I poured another coffee, almost black, and set out Amelia's diaries on the table. At last, her thoughts, her feelings—her life— were there in front of me. But I was looking for clues about her state of mind.

"Where are you, Amelia?" I whispered. "Where are you?"

The studio audience let rip in wild applause as I killed the sound and picked up another diary.

> *Sarah was late this morning. I'd washed early and began to read, my spirits lifted by the blue sky and light frost across the lawns. These are my favourite days, and Sarah took me walking in the grounds. Oh, the freshness of the air. I wanted to breathe deeper than my lungs would allow. My father was working, tending the roses, and he caught the most beautiful butterfly, holding it tenderly, anxious not to crush its delicate wings.*
>
> *"This is as much God's creature as the lion," he told me. I knew that. I saw the beauty in those glorious colours. I cried because I could not understand why God bestowed such a tiny creature with such glory and*

left me, his child, destitute. My father enquired as to what had caused my distress, and when I told him he took me by my shoulders and told me that he loved me and to be loved was more important than physical beauty.

Later on, in the woodland, he had picked up a small frog. "Look," he said, "a creature, devoid of beauty, but wonderful in the eyes of its creator." I laughed. Its eyes were like mine. I made a croaking sound. If I were green, I might be mistaken for a frog. Sarah read me a passage out of the Bible afterwards. Jesus healed the leper. Sarah said that Jesus could still heal and she prayed for me.

I should count my blessings. My father loves me and so does Sarah. I don't think that Mr. Stanwick loves my mother. She has the whole house, and I have only this room, yet I have love.

I felt her reaching out through the page and heard her voice. I was there, in that garden.

It is raining today, and Mr. Stanwick is returning at the end of the week. My heart feels heavy with the news of his arrival, for I know that I shall be confined to my room throughout the duration of his stay. My occasional adventures within the grounds will be forbidden, and my father will find work elsewhere until he goes. Today is as joyless as the darkest night.

I hated Stanwick—a cruel man whose bitterness had ensured Amelia's continued existence away from the public eye, yet she had managed to find comfort in the presence of her father and her governess.

The master of the house arrived midday and sent Sarah home. Sarah had been crying, I could tell, although she tried hard to be brave. I won't see Sarah until Monday, so I am alone for two days. I have several books, and my food will be left outside the door, as my mother is not allowed any contact with me while he is at home. The sun is shining and I long to see my father. Where is he?

I closed my eyes. Why hadn't her father come to his daughter's rescue? Fear? Poverty? Shame? I read on.

I read my Bible today. I found comfort in the 23rd Psalm. The Lord is my shepherd.

Somewhere in those diaries, I would read of the moment Allington took Amelia, ripping at her clothes and forcing himself upon her. My heart ached for this young girl, and an anger rose within me. My father had risen every Sunday morning with a song on his lips and in his heart. He would take his place in the church pew, not out of duty, but out of love for his God and his joy was infectious.

I saw a radiance in my father's face as he drew me to him. As a child, I felt I knew God through my father. When I went to heaven, I believed that The Almighty would look and behave just like Dad—I had never had imagined a greater being. Now I was reading an account of a man—a wolf dressed as a sheep or worse—a wolf dressed as a shepherd. A man who had preached the word of God with evil in his heart. I felt my father's rage like a fire within.

I couldn't sleep that night. The vast expanse of water that formed Tabwell's only lake stretched before me, a dark lonely grave that refused to surrender its secret. *Find the body. Release Jenny.*

It was a hopeless task. The lake was deep, murky and extremely cold. No authority would commission a team of divers to look for a body on the word of a girl with mental health issues. But I had to find her—somehow, some way.

I called Sebastian the following day. He had just purchased a coffee machine and seemed anxious to try his bag of fresh rich roast Brazilian beans out on someone. I walked into a house that smelled like a high street coffee shop, complete with hissing and gurgling sounds filtering through from the kitchen.

Sebastian arrived with a cup of something that looked suspiciously like the contents of Tabwell's lake.

"I'm not sure how that will taste—you don't have to drink it," he said, unable to disguise his pride at having mastered a piece of modern technology.

I sipped the liquid, finding it a little too mild but surprisingly acceptable. I nodded approvingly.

Sebastian grinned. "So, what's been happening?"

I told the old man about the lake, feeling that he was my only hope. If he told me that the pursuit of Amelia's body was a hopeless quest then it really was.

Sebastian shook his head. "You know, Robert? I can't help feeling that we are missing something, here." He saw the look of puzzlement on my face. "Forget about the lake—that's my gut feeling. We can't go diving, and no one else will entertain the idea."

"But if she's there?"

Sebastian smiled. "That's just it—I don't believe she is."

We talked some more, but they were the last words I really remembered. It had been easy to forget how Sebastian had come into our lives. It was a feeling—a gut instinct. A sixth sense. Was that sixth sense now steering us away from the lake? I prayed it was.

I found myself driving to Tabwell once more, stopping off at the library. The woman at the desk smiled warmly when she saw me approaching. "Did you find the lake?" she asked.

I nodded. "It's a nice spot but not what I was looking for."

The woman frowned, and before I'd had time to consider the wisdom of confiding in a complete stranger, I was relating the full story of Amelia Root and her demise, throwing in a few white lies to cover myself. As far as the librarian was concerned, Amelia had suggested in her diary that she was going to drown herself—it was easier that way. The librarian listened attentively as her computer's screen saver flashed up.

"So that's why I'm here," I concluded. "Looking for her body."

The woman grimaced. "Well, it's a fascinating tale," she said, tapping her keyboard. "But I'm afraid I can't be of much help if you're looking for a natural expanse of water." She paused. "And you don't actually know if she succeeded in…you know… drowning herself?"

I did, of course. But I could not bring myself to reveal how. "Pretty sure," I replied.

I was standing with my arms hanging by my sides, feeling totally helpless, as the clock ticked on. The librarian smiled sympathetically. She had work to do, and it didn't involve looking for skeletons. I thanked her and wandered over to the local history section. Maybe something would grab my attention—something I'd missed before.

In all the dramas I'd watched, this would be the point where the protagonist would find that vital piece of information that he or she required. Me? No such luck. There were plenty of books written by local historians. *Tabwell's Soldiers. Local Walkers' Guide* and *Tabwell's Artists.*

I drove home feeling defeated and called Sebastian the moment I walked through the front door. I thought I'd call in and unburden myself on the way to the hospital. On the way to his house, I fiddled with the buttons on the car radio until I found a song I liked; I think it was The Eagles. I can't remember the song, but it hardly matters because the station switched suddenly. Neil Diamond was on the second verse of his classic 'I Am, I Said'.

I tried to switch back but the radio seemed to have locked. It stayed on that channel for one line and then it switched again, and The Eagles were back on. I would have thought nothing of it if the temperature in the car had not dropped to what was pretty damn close to freezing. The heating was on three, which should have been—and up to that point had been—comfortable. I turned up the dial and blasted hot air through the car for a good five minutes. Now the car was warm, but the chill I felt was in my veins. Amelia had meddled like this before.

**

Sebastian smiled. "She's determined, I'll give her that."

Maybe there was something in the line—about frogs dreaming of being kings—but was it about frogs, kings or dreams? The old man thought but couldn't come up with an answer, and on my way to the hospital, I found myself praying to a dead woman. Maybe this was how it all started—the gradual slide into insanity.

If you have a teenager whom you think isn't listening to you, try talking to one in a coma. It's hard on every level, but I managed to find something to tell her about my visit to Tabwell and the library with the nice lady behind the desk. I imagined what my daughter might say: *Was she pretty? Did you fancy her?* I hated holding the power. I could say anything with no fear of a reply. I could call her mother names—I could tell her how wonderful Melissa was. Jenny would not even flinch.

I listened to some New Orleans jazz on the way home, waiting for Amelia to start fiddling with the controls again. She didn't. Why? *Why can't you just tell me where you are? What's with all the cryptic shit?*

I headed straight for the kitchen to check out the fridge magnet alphabet, but they were all lined up neatly in the correct order. I put a Tony Bennett CD on the hi-fi and poured myself a rum and ginger. I'd forgotten to eat anything, and the alcohol began to fog my brain before I'd drained the glass. I poured myself a second. I needed sleep but I feared the bed.

I had not made a conscious decision to drink myself into a stupor, but I fell asleep in the early hours, propped up on the couch with a half-empty glass in my hand, praying that my dreams would take me to Amelia.

They didn't. Instead, I found myself wandering through a meadow, breathing in the sweet smell of wildflowers. I listened to the birdsong and the crickets as I settled under a tree. In my dream, everything was right with the world although I sensed that I could not remain there for long. I was there for a reason, led by a spiritual force, and I waited, listening intently to the world around me.

I heard a croak, faint but unmistakable. I looked down at the tiny frog that sat on the bark, watching me with interest. "Hello, young fella," I said, reaching down to pick him up. The frog was lost in the palm of my hand. "You need to get back to your pond."

I woke with a start—almost as if I'd been hit with a thunderbolt. The frog had leapt into the long grass, his mission accomplished. The answer had been there all along and I'd missed it.

I found Amelia's diary on the kitchen table and thumbed through it wildly, my heart racing, until I came to the page and read the line over and over again.

> Later on, in the woodland, he had picked up a small frog. "Look," he said. "A creature devoid of beauty but wonderful in the eyes of its creator."

A frog. Of course. A frog, out of water…but water that could not have been that far away. The woodland I had visited in my dream was the place Amelia had walked with her father in the grounds of the Stanwicks' home. Somewhere in those woods, there was water—a lake or a marsh big enough to invite a frog, and hopefully big enough to swallow a young girl.

Chapter Thirty-Two

FARRIDAY SOUNDED ALARMED by my early morning call. It was only eight, but I could not wait any longer. The internet had not thrown up any information. I sidestepped the formal greetings, getting straight to the reason for my call. "Is there any woodland in your grounds?" I asked.

"There is some woodland," Farriday said, "but it's quite overgrown."

"Is there a lake or a pond there?"

"There is. We sure get the frogs—loads of them!" He paused. "Why do you ask?"

I could hardly contain my excitement. "That's where Amelia's body lies—at the bottom of a pond in that woodland."

I cut across the stunned silence. "I need the pond dredged—I need to find Amelia's remains."

"I'm sorry, Mr. Adams. The woodland is kind of in our grounds, but the council bought it several years ago with a view to making it into a nature reserve with walks and a picnic area, which would be open to our residents as well as the public."

"So why is it overgrown?" I asked, my heart sinking slowly into my stomach.

"They decided there wasn't enough money in the pot to develop it. I think they've kind of scrapped the whole idea."

After twenty minutes of trawling everything to do with Tabwell on the web, I managed to find a contact number for the local council and finally ended up talking to a Gerald Davey, who was something to do with the environment. Davey knew the woodland. It was known locally as Mosswood.

When I asked Davey if there was any water there, he laughed.

"There is," he said brightly, "hence the name *Mosswood*. It's not quite a lake but not a pond, either. We've had to fence it off in case any kids get into the area. It's quite dangerous."

I sagged despondently. What next?

Davey continued, "It's too expensive to develop and it's not on our to-do list, I'm afraid."

"So it's just going to be left?"

"Unless someone buys it…"

"Is that a possibility?"

"I'm afraid I can't divulge that information," he replied politely. "Why do you ask?"

I really didn't want to go into the whole story again, and I doubted Davey would have been impressed even if he hadn't come to the conclusion I was some kind of spiritualist crackpot.

"Just interested. Thank you for your time, Mr. Davey," I replied courteously.

I hung up. Another dead end. I sank back into the chair, exhausted and weary. My head ached and my heart felt like lead in my chest. I slept only to escape the pain.

***

Jenny lay silently as I told her about the events of the day, trying to sound upbeat but feeling as if I were walking through an endless tunnel. My body was tired but my mind was as active as a kid on a trampoline, so Josie and I ended up at the diner, drinking coffee and eyeing the cheesecake. It was a minute past midnight and Kerry, a woman in her mid-thirties who would still require ID to buy alcohol, brought us a fresh jug of water.

Josie smiled. We should have been the only people in there but I'd counted ten in total. "Thank God for insomniacs, eh?" she said to Kerry, who laughed politely.

"It's a haven for troubled souls," she said. "I'm not sure if we should be serving them caffeine!" Kerry spun on her heels and I found myself watching the rear of the year through a tight black dress.

Josie tutted and shook her head. "Men! Honestly!"

I opened my mouth, about to defend myself with a lie, but Josie grinned. "It's okay, you're a man. It's a condition—an untreatable one!" The smile faded as she reached over and placed her hand over mine. "You'll get through this, hun."

I'd told her about Councillor Davey and water in the woodland. I'd told her about the car radio, the song and the dream, the passage in the diary and my fading hopes. " I've got the insurance money. I could use that to get the pond dredged. If it runs out, I'd just go back to work."

Josie looked serious, as if she were going to say something she'd thought long and hard about.

"What is it?"

Josie shrugged. "Look, I know that you're doing all this for Jenny, I really do…"

"But?"

"You're pinning all your hopes on recovering a skeleton."

I didn't answer.

"Listen, Rob, I know that you really believe all this stuff, and maybe you're right. But Jenny's coma is a medical thing. Maybe you should be placing more of that faith in the doctors."

"They can't find anything wrong. They don't know why…"

Josie was still holding my hand. We looked like a couple having an affair, miles from our respective partners. "Look, I'm delighted that Amelia exists, but it doesn't mean that Jenny is possessed by her. Okay, I can't explain it—I don't know what's going on—

but she needs you there, by her side, not running around body hunting."

I glared at her, pulling my hand away. "That's what you think? I'm a bad father?"

"I didn't say that! You're a good dad—a brilliant dad, in fact—I just don't want to see you chasing shadows."

"Sebastian is no fool, Josie. He is convinced that Jenny's condition is related to Amelia."

Josie shook her head. "I'm not suggesting he's a fool, but he's a convert."

"Meaning?"

"You told me yourself, Sebastian was a tub-thumping atheist. Then he encounters a ghost and sees the light, just like St. Paul on the Damascus road! He's committed, Robert. Whether it's atheism or spiritualism, he immerses himself in his beliefs."

"It doesn't mean he's wrong."

"No, but it stops him looking at things logically."

"You don't know him. He isn't like that."

Josie shrugged. "Well okay, let's look at your prospects. Who do you think is going to dredge that pond?"

I shrugged. I had no idea

"Jenny will come out of this coma, and when she does, she will need you more than ever."

I felt my heart—my spirit—in the vice-like grip of that steel claw, closing, crushing.

Josie sat in silence beside me as I drove her back to The Keys, but when we arrived, she kissed me gently on the cheek and said goodbye. I didn't respond. Even her love failed to lift my spirits.

The rum bottle was empty. I'd returned it to the cabinet rather than putting it in the bin. I didn't want it staring up at me in the recycling crate, reminding me that I was drinking too much. I poured myself an orange juice and took myself off to bed.

Bob Dylan's autobiography lay gathering dust on my bedside table. I opened it at the page with the corner folded over and began to read, without bothering to undress, and woke six hours later, relieved to see daylight.

Josie had put a doubt in my mind. Was I really being irrational? Was Jenny's coma nothing more than a medical condition that had confused the doctors? I called Sebastian.

"Robert, slow down," he said as I emptied my muddled mind, rattling off a jumble of words with the speed of a machine gun. "You're not being irrational. I've studied the paranormal in conjunction with the science that I had placed all my faith in for so many years, and I still believe there are things that cannot be explained."

"But if we can't find the body then I can't get Jenny back."

The old man could hear the desperation in my voice. "Have you spoken to the minister at St. Jude's?"

"Would there be any point?"

"Well, they have wrongs to put right, don't they? You could argue that the church owed that poor girl a decent burial."

I suddenly felt like a foolish schoolboy standing in front of his headmaster. I'd never even thought of the church. But would they agree to become a part of all this? "I'll call him today. It's worth a try."

"If you go, you must take the diaries and the letter from the governess. He'll want proof."

I replaced the phone and poured myself a coffee. I called the hospital first; Jenny's condition hadn't changed. Then I flicked through my phone, found the number, and called St. Jude's.

Reverend Francis answered immediately. I introduced myself, but there was no need. He recognised my voice. He listened attentively to the whole story. The attic room, the letters, the diary. I was allowed to finish without interruption. Francis sounded like a man who had just been hit with a sledgehammer.

"You have this…diary?" he asked. "And the governess's letter?"

"Yes."

There was a pause. "Can I see them?"

I showered and shaved and was behind the wheel of my car with thirty minutes. I drove most of the way with a cheap rat-pack CD drowning the noise of the road. Tabwell, with its leafy roads and quaint buildings, felt like a second home. I could almost smell the money mingling with the scent of the fresh country air. Its casual easy pace embraced me as the Church of St. Jude's came into view.

Reverend Francis met me at the door of the church. He smiled, offering his hand. "Good to see you again, Robert," he said. But his eyes no longer danced with evangelical zeal. He was troubled, and I sensed that he really didn't want to hear what I had to say.

"I know this is a little sensitive…" I took my seat in the vestry that was still scattered with confetti from a recent wedding.

Francis shrugged. "We should all face the truth," he said. "Without it, we are lost."

I placed the large Manila envelope on the polished wooden surface of a table that was graced only with a single silver communion cup. Francis studied the envelope, pausing for a while before finally opening it. "Allington is an integral part of our history here," he said solemnly. "He founded the local school and spent a great deal of time helping the poorest people in the community." He opened the letter. "Now it seems that the man had a dark side."

His eyes flashed across the pages as we sat in silence. He held the pages between finger and thumb, as if the paper were contaminated by its very content. Darkness lay between the lines. A woman was reaching out from her grave through the words of her only confidante, seeking justice.

It was at least five minutes—minutes that felt like hours—before Francis looked up, his eyes fixed on me. "I wish there was something in here, something that would compromise the credibility of the witness, but I can find nothing."

"I'm sorry," I said.

Francis smiled. "You have nothing to be sorry for—unlike our friend, here." He tapped the pages in front of him. His smile vanished, replaced by a look of ministerial concern. "I can deal with this two ways," he said. "I can either leave this matter with God, who will judge this man according to his works, or take it upon myself and suggest that we have his remains removed from the church."

I was shocked. "You would consider that?"

Francis nodded. "Yes, but it would be a matter for the Church itself, not me. Unfortunately, finance often dictates. The cost may well guide the powers-that-be to decide that it is God and God alone who is the judge, and that after all, these are just human remains..."

"But he lies like a saint," I interrupted, "with an inscription!"

"Yes. That is a point I'm sure we—they—will consider—"

I didn't allow Francis to finish. "We need closure on this—for Jenny's sake. Amelia's spirit will not rest until she finds justice."

Francis looked troubled. "I understand, Mr. Adams. But, as a minister, I have to believe that Amelia has justice. Justice by the hand of God, not man."

"She needs a proper burial. She is a child of God."

"And you believe that her remains are in a lake somewhere?"

"Yes."

"But how can I help?"

I had thought about this on the way over, so I told him about my conversation with the council.

Francis frowned. "They obviously won't be using public money to go looking for a body."

"Not without some hard evidence, no."

Francis smiled. "Mr. Adams, if you're going to ask the Church for financial support, I'm afraid you'll be wasting your time. As you have said yourself, the word of a girl who claims to be in touch with a spirit would not carry any weight. Contact with spirits is generally frowned upon in ecclesiastical circles, as you probably know."

I had reached yet another dead end. Francis laid his hands on the table...I sensed a sermon coming. "She has her justice, Mr. Adams."

"But why is she...haunting my daughter?"

Francis shrugged. "I would love to have the answer." He replaced the papers back in the manila envelope. "But in biblical times, we would be casting out demons."

I remembered the stories well. My father had read from the Bible when I was a child; many of the passages would be considered inappropriate these days. Yet they always came back to me.

Francis returned my envelope and promised to get in touch. I drove home with a clock ticking in my head. How much time did we have?

Chapter Thirty-Three

SEBASTIAN ACCOMPANIED ME to the hospital the following evening, striding along the corridor in his black calf-length coat. I wanted him there; I wanted his fatherly presence and his sagacious wisdom. He stared at my daughter, compassion in his eyes.

"Where is she?" I asked.

Sebastian didn't answer.

"Is she with Amelia?" I pressed further.

The old man shook his head slowly. A single tear trickled down his cheek. "It is something I cannot explain."

"Explain? What?" "

Sebastian smiled, his eyes remaining fixed on my daughter. He reached out and touched Jenny's forehead. "Don't talk to her, Robert. Just watch and leave her be. She isn't ready. Not yet."

***

He calls my name—Jenny. His voice is frantic and I feel myself falling. He still calls me, but Jenny is not my name. My body aches. I find myself on a bed, staring at the sunlight streaming through a single window. I am pleased to see the light, having had my sleep disturbed by raised voices from below. I recognised the reverend's voice but could not, despite my efforts, hear what he was saying. I rise and wash with cold water, dressing and saying my prayers, kneeling by the window. I feel the warmth of the sun on my face and imagine that it is the love of God.

For the first time that day, I smile. I feel strong but that feeling of inner strength alarms me. I am vulnerable and physically weak, there is no record of my existence, I know this—and yet there is a power in my hand, a determination in my heart. I stare at Sarah's face. She is beautiful—I cannot bear to catch my own reflection. Yet it is no longer of any concern to me. I suddenly see what I have never seen before. I am privileged to have escaped this world.

***

Jenny's eyes twitched. My heart leapt. It had to be good, didn't it? The nurse smiled and nodded, and I prayed that Josie might be right and Jenny would come through this regardless of whether we found Amelia's remains. But in my heart, I knew otherwise.

Jenny's eyelids flickered again and, just for a moment, I thought I saw the faintest of smiles. It stopped me in my tracks. Maybe I had imagined the whole thing. Hope does that—playing tricks with your mind and screwing up your head. I had to stay focused.

I dropped Sebastian off and stopped at McDonald's. I sat in the corner with a coffee and a sin-burger, choosing the company of strangers rather than an empty house. I watched a young couple arguing in the corner while their kid played with a plastic toy, seemingly unaffected by his parents' disagreement. He was too young to be out at this time—too young to be subjected to a late-night fight. This was the new breed of parent, self-obsessed and ignorant.

I ate and drank up, passing the kid on the way out. Instinctively, I reached out and patted the kid on the head as he bit into his burger. "You enjoying that, buddy?"

His mother looked up and smiled at me. She could have passed for a sixth-former. The kid's father looked at his kid and then at me. "Mind your own fucking business, pal," he said.

I looked at him and shook my head, walking towards the door. I knew he was following. By the time I reached the car, he was on my shoulder. "Who are you fucking shaking your head at, you prick?"

Normally, I would have told the bloke that I didn't want a fight and tried to get into my car. I always considered flight to be better than fight. But I had been fighting for over a year now. I turned. His face was in mine, and there was the smell of stale ale and onions on his breath.

"You some kiddie fiddler or sommat—strokin' my kid's head?"

"I wasn't."

Out of the corner of my eye, I spotted a CCTV camera on the corner of the car park. I began to walk away.

"Oy, you twat, where's you goin'?"

Away from the cameras, you idiot. Come on...follow me.

The white removal van provided perfect cover. He grabbed my shoulder just as we moved into its shadow. "Don't you fucking walk away from me, you pervert!"

My heart was thumping and my blood felt like oil, boiling in my veins. This man was the type of bloke that spawned thugs like Taylor. He was scum, jail fodder, looking for a fight wherever he could find it. He had a kid—his kid, probably. I didn't. Hanna had been snatched from me and Jenny...

"You runnin' away, prick?" he said, his forehead touching mine and his saliva spraying my chin. I felt a rush of excitement, because this idiot thought I was easy prey. He knew I wasn't touching up his kid. He just wanted to lay into someone. He was too stupid to even wonder why I had walked away from my own car.

"I'm not running away. I just didn't want this meeting to be caught on camera."

"Wha...?" He spun round to check out the CCTV. My fist connected with his cheek just as he turned back. It was only the second punch I'd landed in my entire life, but it carried all my frustration and bitterness and knocked him out cold.

I felt the bone of his jaw crack and splinter under my knuckles as the pain ran like an electric current from my hand through the length of my arm.

I walked back into McDonald's and told them to call the police and an ambulance. There was an abusive drunk in the car park who had tried to attack me and I'd acted in self-defence.

I spoke to the kid's mother and apologised. She started to cry, but I knew she wasn't angry with me. "You should have killed the bastard!" she snapped. The girl was just some silly kid herself who hooked up with the bad boys only to discover that they didn't make good partners.

The bloke's name was Wayne. The ambulance took him in for an overnight check-up, and the police already had him on their records. They weren't even interested in checking the CCTV, since they ended up dragging him in for public disorder offences several times a year. The young constable told me that it was highly unlikely there would be any case against me. Wayne would be discouraged from filing any charges.

I climbed behind the wheel of my car exhausted but exhilarated. Wayne was trouble and I had taken him out. My hand throbbed but the pain felt good, and after washing the contaminated blood from my knuckles and taking a couple of painkillers, I slept soundly, wakened only by the ringing of the bedside phone. It was Josie.

"Hey, Jo," I said drowsily. "What time is it?"

"You're still in bed?"

I glanced at my watch, blinking hard until its face came into focus. It was eleven.

"You still there?"

"Yeah, sure. I…"

"Look, just wondered if you wanted to call in for a spot of lunch. Or breakfast."

I laughed. It was good to hear Jo's voice. "Sure…fish, chips and mushy peas would be great!"

***

There was no change in Jenny's condition. The nurse on the other end of the phone checked that she had my mobile number and I hoped they might be anticipating some good news, but as I drove over to The Keys, Wayne was still on my mind. The initial feeling of satisfaction at having landed a blow for the decent people of the country had subsided, leaving me feeling uncomfortable.

Had I really stepped over that scumbag's body so casually? Had I considered for one moment that I might have killed him? Until then, I had only dreamed of landing such a punch, knowing that confronted by the target of my inner rage I would never have raised an arm. This was different. I had felt no concern for Wayne, his wife or his kid. It wasn't that I hadn't considered that he might be dead, but in that moment, I couldn't have cared less.

I had no intention of mentioning the incident to Josie—or anyone else, for that matter. If the police were correct, it was behind me. If I was ever unfortunate enough to bump into another member of the underclass then I would walk away.

Josie hugged me as if I were a long lost brother walking back into her life after years away. I kissed her several times on the cheek before she finally released me. "You okay, sweetheart?"

I nodded.

"Look, Rob, I'm with you on this—even if I seem…"

I took hold of Jo's hand and squeezed it. "It's okay. Honestly."

Josie cocked her head to one side. "Still love me, then?"

"Jo, I could never stop loving you, even if I wanted to."

"Ditto," Josie said, her eyes flooding quite suddenly. "Anyway," she continued, pulling herself together. "Park your backside in the corner and I'll get you a drink."

I watched her walk away and wondered what would ever become of me if she never returned. I needed her friendship more than I needed her bed. Lou gave me a thumbs up and a smile from behind the bar, and I wondered how many men would have been happy to stand aside while his wife hooked up with a free-loading widower. Not many, I suspect.

Still, his smile seemed genuine enough to leave me feeling like a creep. Your average bloke would have been drowning his sorrows over a few pints with the lads and putting the world to rights, but if Lou was thinking along those lines, he certainly wasn't letting it show. Maybe one day I'd be leaving The Keys only to feel someone tap my shoulder. I would turn to find myself on the end of Lou's fist before waking in a pool of blood.

Josie returned, and an easy smile crossed her face. She placed a pint down on the table—ice cold and screaming to be downed with enthusiasm. "So, whatcha been up to, sweetheart?"

Well, I just knocked some lowlife's lights out in a McDonald's car park...

"Jenny's eyes kind of...twitched," I said cautiously. "But, you know how it is. They aren't getting too excited just yet."

"But that's great, hun, isn't it? I mean, the right direction and all that."

"Yeah, I suppose. If we were in a TV soap, you'd know she was about to wake up. But this isn't a drama, is it? It's life. Real life."

Josie smiled and nodded. "It's still a good sign, though."

I took a long draw on my ice-cold pint, the liquid almost burning my gullet. My god, if felt good.

"I went to see Reverend Francis at St. Jude's," I told her, replacing my half empty glass on the table. Josie raised her eyebrows. "Really? And what did you tell him?"

"Everything," I replied. "I took the letters, too."

"And?"

"He was genuinely shocked, but I'm not sure what he's going to do. It's up to the Church Council or whatever you call it." I paused. "But if it was up to Francis, I think he'd have the remains exhumed and tossed in the nearest river."

Josie grinned. "Well, at least he's on your side," she said, studying my gloomy expression. "What's up, Rob?"

"I just feel like I'm hanging. You know, waiting."

"Look, hun," Josie shot back in her best schoolmistress tone. "There's nothing you can do. It's not your fault. You can't shake your kid awake, and you can't dredge that friggin' lake, so waiting is the only option."

I was unconvinced.

"What? You're going to hire a diver and go looking?" Josie had that twinkle in her eye, and I started to laugh, but in my mind, I wondered if it might not be such a bad idea.

***

After three beers and two whiskeys, I left the car and took a taxi. There were no messages on the answer phone so I poured myself a rum, laced it with Coke from a half empty can, and threw in a handful of ice. The phone rang.

I reached over, pressing the receiver against my ear. I didn't recognise the voice.

"Mr. Adams? I'm from the *Tabwell Herald*."

The very name of the town felt ingrained within my spirit. "Yes?"

"Sorry, my name is Dennis Blakely. I'm a reporter, and I hear that you believe that there is a body in the Mosswood lake? Is that correct?"

"Who told you this?"

There was a pause. "I'm not at liberty to say, Mr. Adams. I just want to confirm the details."

"How much do you know?"

A further pause. "Then I would assume there is some truth in the story?"

"I asked you how much you know?"

"Enough to make this well worth reporting, Mr. Adams. It's a fascinating story. One that might put some pressure on...shall we say, the relevant authorities."

"Meaning?"

"I would like to meet you. Get the story from your angle. Nothing much happens here in Tabwell. It's kind of...slow. If Joe Soap changes his Ferrari it pretty much makes the front page."

***

The following afternoon, I was back behind the wheel heading for Tabwell. Dennis Blakely was going to stand me a light lunch at the Lakeside Hotel, which, as the name suggested, overlooked Tabwell Water, the very spot to which my librarian friend had directed me several weeks ago. I'd remembered the rather quaint hotel, with its manicured lawns sloping down to the path that ran the perimeter of the lake.

I followed the signs and swung onto the cobbled drive of the hotel, lowering the volume on the radio as it belted out a Stones number. It wasn't a rock 'n' roll hotel, that was plain to see. I was fifteen minutes early—time to get myself a soft drink and find a seat in the corner.

The bar door was to the left of the main reception. I was pleased at not having to explain myself to anyone. I felt invisible, and that suited me fine. This could all go horribly wrong. Blakely might be out to make me look like an idiot at best and an irresponsible parent at least. It wouldn't be difficult. But then, I was tempted to believe that I was meeting with a small time hack after a ghost story that would sell his paper and draw in some much-needed revenue from local businesses.

I knew about the press, but I had also read my locals; there was a different attitude. You kept the stories straight and kept the readers happy. Rule number one: don't shit on your own doorstep.

My mobile rang. It was Blakely to say he was pulling up in the car park and wanted to know where I would be. Corner window seat to the left of the main door. I was wearing a dark brown corded jacket and a cream shirt. He told me he'd be there in five.

I hadn't formed a picture of Tabwell's local hack in my head yet he still took me by surprise. He was slim, stood at about six-two and wore a suit which hadn't been bought off the peg. He was good-looking with just the faintest shadow of stubble, which gave him that Hollywood movie star look. His handshake was as strong as one would imagine.

"Mr. Adams," he said, grinning broadly and revealing that he had spent quite a bit of money on his teeth. "Pleased to meet you."

"Likewise," I replied. "Can I get you a drink?"

Blakely shook his head. "I'll go get some menus. Then we can talk."

If Blakely's physical appearance had unnerved me, his manner had allayed any disquiet. I watched as he chatted at the bar, drawing admiring glances and occasional giggles from the two young girls who served him with a lime and soda. He returned, unaware of the eyes following him.

"Nice kids," he said, glancing back over at the bar.

"You been here before, then?" I asked, making small talk.

"Several times. I eat here quite regularly. The restaurant is a little expensive but the bar meals are quite reasonable and really good." He smiled. "I think you'll agree."

He passed me a menu. It was limited; he told me the owners preferred to go for quality, but he was sure I would find something I liked. Blakely chose the grilled salmon and, wanting to look as if I, too, was a lime and soda man with a love of healthy food, went for the same.

"So, how long have you worked for the *Herald*?" I asked him.

He smiled, taking a sip of his soda. "A couple of years," he said casually. "It's small time, I know, but I don't want to get into the cutthroat national scene, so I guess this suits me."

I looked at Blakely. Okay, you couldn't judge a book by its cover, but this guy looked like a shit-hot go-getter with the looks and the charm to carry him a fair way before he'd even have to put his brain into gear. He looked the part—the image that the business world craved these days. I just couldn't see this man settling for life on a local paper.

He sensed my apprehension but obviously decided to ignore it. "Anyway, your story. It sounds fascinating," he said, pulling out a tiny recorder and placing it in the centre of the table. "Do you mind?" he asked.

I shook my head and he pressed the button. There was a loud, old-fashioned click.

"Right," he said. "In your own words, Mr. Adams. From the beginning…"

***

We were interrupted only by the arrival of the waitress taking our order and subsequently delivering the food. At that point, we took a break and ate heartily. The food was, as promised, beautiful. Apart from that, Blakely remained silent as I related the tale from the moment Elizabeth and Hanna died to our meeting at the Lakeside Hotel. When I was done, Blakely reached over and clicked the off button on the recorder.

"Fascinating," he said. "Absolutely fascinating."

"You think you've got a story?"

Blakely nodded. "You know, of course, that Allington founded a school here?"

I told him I was fully aware of the reverend's altruistic exploits.

"Not just that, but he founded a home just outside Tabwell which is now an exclusive retreat for victims of domestic violence. It receives extensive funding from businesses and local government."

I didn't know that. "You say *exclusive*?"

"Set in its own grounds. Rooms well above the standard you might expect. Because of its roots, they put a Bible in every room—funny, but that still puts troubled people at ease—even the atheists and agnostics."

"So it receives funding?"

"Yes. Because of its church affiliation, certain businesses like to be associated with the name, particularly as it is a rehabilitation centre, and everyone likes to be seen doing their bit for society."

"So why are you telling me this?"

Blakely frowned. "Allington has his name on a school and a refuge centre. I'm not sure that everyone will want that name besmirched. It's just a warning, that's all."

"But surely it would not affect the work? I mean, the centres wouldn't close. All this happened so long ago."

Blakely ran his forefinger around the rim of his glass, staring down at the table. "No, they wouldn't, Mr. Adams." He looked up. "And, of course, you're correct. All this was many years ago. But if this becomes a story—how the founder of the refuge and the school not only knew about a young girl virtually imprisoned in an attic, but raped her and stole her baby..." Blakely stopped. "His picture hangs in the foyer of the refuge and in the main hall at the school. They would have to go... Any reference to the man will be erased. I think there will be people who would rather you let sleeping dogs lie—you get what I'm saying?"

***

I drove back home thinking about Allington's legacy. How could a man who had involved himself in caring for his community have raped a young girl and callously taken her baby? What desperation would force such a man's hand? I hadn't asked Blakely when the story would run, so the moment I arrived home, I found the number of the *Tabwell Herald*'s desk and called it.

A young woman answered.

"Could I speak to or leave a message for a Mr. Dennis Blakely?"

A pause. "Who's calling, please?"

"Sorry, my name is Robert Adams. I've just been interviewed—"

"One moment, please."

I listened to Elgar for about forty seconds.

"Hello, Mr. Adams?" It was the desk girl again.

"Yes."

"Who did you speak to?"

"Dennis Blakely."

"You sure?"

"Yes. Why?"

"Mr. Adams, we don't have anyone of that name working at this paper."

I felt my chest tighten. "But I was just speaking..."

"Did he have any ID?" she interrupted sharply.

"I didn't ask," I replied, feeling foolish.

"Then I can tell you for sure, he wasn't from the *Tabwell Herald*."

I replaced the phone and slumped in my chair.

"There must be some mistake," I found myself telling Sebastian ten minutes later. "Maybe the girl who took my call was new."

The old professor sighed. "Or you've been warned off," he said, telling me something I'd already suspected.

"I'm not interested," I replied, feeling increasingly agitated. "I want my daughter back. It's as simple as that."

There was a pause. "I know, Robert, I know. But whoever this Dennis Blakely really is—he's already made the first move. He knows the story. He knows what you're about. He knows what you're trying to do."

I Googled Blakely's name but the search engine turned up nothing. I had to try, even though I knew that I'd probably been given a false name anyway. I called the paper again and asked to speak to someone who might be interested in my story. I was put through to the editor, a young woman called Helen Pace, who became interested when I mentioned my meeting with a phantom reporter who I'd suspected wanted the story buried.

She promised to get back in touch and, checking the battery on my mobile, I headed over to The Keys. Lou greeted me at the bar and we chatted for a few minutes before he invited me to let myself into the flat. Josie was heading into town with an old school friend. "A girly day's shopping and some posh nosh," he told me.

I felt a tinge of jealousy. I wanted her to myself. I needed a listening ear. I rapped gently on the door and entered. The TV was on. Down the hallway, I heard the shower and Josie singing over the sound of the water. I waited, picking up a magazine and flicking idly through its pages. There was an article about a girl who killed her father in self-defence. I began to read; the girl had never forgiven herself despite having suffered abuse for so many years.

I suddenly sensed someone behind me. I turned. It was Josie, wrapped in a white bath towel. She grinned, as if she knew exactly how irresistible she looked. "You been waiting long?" she asked, holding the towel tightly over her chest. I nodded, almost winded by the desire I felt. She saw it my eyes and reached out her hand and gently touched my lips. The towel fell to the floor.

"Jo, we can't," I said as she pulled me towards her.

But we could. And we did. I had no room for guilt.

We made love behind a locked door, silently entwined, our breathlessness drowned by the sound from the TV. It was over all too soon and we talked while Josie dressed and prepared herself for her trip. "I don't want you to go," I told her.

She smiled through her reflection in the mirror. "I have to, hun," she said. "But you know I'd rather be with you."

She turned. "Be careful, sweetheart. I know you're not exactly tangling with the Mafia in Tabwell, but it sounds like there's at least one person who would rather you didn't make a big deal out of this story."

"I don't think anyone's going to put a bullet through my head, do you?"

Josie grinned. "No, but just be careful, that's all."

I drove back home feeling Jo's call for caution was a little ironic; we'd just made love in a room above the bar at which her husband was serving drinks. What would Jenny think? I thought about my daughter. I knew where her body lay but where was her mind—where was her soul?

***

My heart beats in time with the footsteps I hear on the stairs. I know immediately that the minister is alone. He knocks and waits, but his anger spills before him. "Amelia!" he calls. There is hatred in his voice—the devil's voice. The door opens and I see him, his frame fills the doorway. His lips are moving but I hear no sound. His face, reddened with rage, looks as if it might burst open.

Sarah rises from her chair and moves to my side. I try, I try to read his lips but cannot. The only sound I hear is that of a rushing, fierce wind. The minister continues to move toward me, his hands outstretched. Sarah steps between us. Then I see her falling backwards. Now the reverend is upon me, his rage unabated. His hand is on my neck. I smell whisky on his breath as I fall back onto the desk at which I have learned all I know of this world.

I am going to die. I feel something on the desk…metal. The blade Sarah used for the apples she picked from my father's tree. The handle seems to roll in my hand as I fight for breath. I raise my arm high. Our eyes are locked. That hatred, I see it so clearly. For a moment, I leave the world, everything turns an unholy black. It is only for a few seconds, but the hands around my neck lose their grip. I open my eyes. Blood pours from the Reverend Allington's chest. The blade is embedded to the hilt. I withdraw it with ease and he falls backwards, his eyes staring in fear. Fear of dying—fear of his God. He splutters blood. I stand and watch the father of my child…a child I will never know, slowly drift away.

***

I woke the following morning and poured myself a coffee. My mobile flashed up a message. It was Josie.

Fancy coffee? Tea? Me?

I thought for a moment. Our previous physical encounters had never been planned, and for some reason, I liked it better that way. It felt more like a crime of passion, and I could ride the guilt. I punched in a reply. *How about dinner?*

Sounds good. Where?

I was hungry. Pizza sounded good. *Antonio's?*

Yum. 8ish

You're on!

It was a date. We would taxi there, eat pizza and maybe get a little drunk. I imagined the conversation drifting from Jenny to Elizabeth and my future without her. But I was to learn something about Josephine Pamela Duxbury that I could never have foreseen in a lifetime.

***

I stand, transfixed. Having seen little of this world, death has come to my room. Sarah holds a hand to her breast. She is pale, and I fear she will faint. Me? I have no future, not now, but then, have I ever had anything to live for, imprisoned in this place? An institution

308

awaits, or maybe the noose, I do not know. I follow my instincts and flee, my eyes fixed ahead, the thunder of my feet ringing in my ears.

No one sees me as I pass through the lounge with the knife in my hands. A fire burns in the grate. At last, I reach the door. How cold the autumn air feels. How wonderfully fresh and bracing. I am still running—running through the lawned spaces towards the woods where I would wander with my father.

I need to rest. I need time to consider. My life is in my own hands, and I have the right to choose, but first, I wish to sit and enjoy the freedom of my final moments on this Earth.

***

The house wine was good enough. We ordered a mushroom starter and two medium specials with extra toppings from the waiter. Jo had something on her mind, and I guessed what it was.

"The other day," I began tentatively, sipping my wine. "I…I should have felt guilty. But I didn't."

I waited. Josie smiled. "You shouldn't," she replied. "Not really."

Her indifference troubled me. "Don't you?"

"There are certain aspects of it—of what happened—that might seem a bit sordid, but…"

"A bit?" I said, unable to disguise my concern. "Lou's my friend. Okay, maybe not joined at the hip, but, well…I was still screwing his wife in *his* flat while he was serving drinks one floor down. I mean, that's a pretty shitty thing to do to anyone!"

Josie avoided my eyes. "There are things you don't know, Robert," she said softly. "Things I'm not sure I'm ready to tell you yet."

"What? Your husband doesn't understand you?"

A tear escaped and trickled down her cheek. "Lou is a wonderful man. He understands me perfectly, and I understand him. That's why we're still together. We're a good team—a partnership."

Our conversation was interrupted by the arrival of the mushrooms in garlic. The waiter seemed to linger longer than he needed to, almost as if he had caught something Josie had said and his curiosity was getting the better of him. Josie smiled. "Thank you. This is fine."

The waiter half bowed and left us.

"You were saying?"

Josie took a sip of her wine. "We're fine," she said. "That's all you need to know."

I frowned. "But how can you be so casual about us? We had sex, Jo."

"I know. Like I said, there're things you don't know."

I felt as if the book was being closed. No more questions. We drank more wine, ate pizza and managed to laugh, but the whole thing with Lou was bothering me. We ordered another bottle and talked about the old days. If Lou had not called Josie up, I'm not sure the subject would have arisen again. She took the call without a flicker of guilt in her eyes. "Hi, darling…"

There was a pause. "Yes, the cleaner is at the back of the cupboard. Okay…" Another pause. "I'm still in the restaurant. Won't be too late." Jo's eyes darkened. "Before you go, I think Rob needs to know…about us? You okay with that?" There was another pause. "Thank you. Love you, hun. Bye."

The affection was real. There was no doubt about that. Josie caught the look of confusion in my eyes and smiled.

"So?" I said, taking a gulp of wine that stung my pallet.

"I'm not sure where to begin." Jo looked wearily at the two huge slices of pizza left on her plate. "You see, Lou and I…well, we're partners…"

"I know," I replied impatiently.

Josie shot me a half-hearted smile. "I mean partners in the old sense of the word, before political correctness kicked in."

"What? Like business partners?"

"That's it. Well…in a way, but close friends as well."

"So it's not like a marriage?"

Josie drained her glass and replaced it. "Fancy a brandy?" she said. "I could use one."

I nodded. "Go on…I'm intrigued."

Jo sighed. "Lou and I have been divorced for over a year."

"What? But why?"

Jo smiled softly. "Robert, I'm not his type—"

"But you're beautiful—"

Josie smiled. "He doesn't go for *beautiful*—he prefers *handsome*. Robert, I'm trying to tell you Lou's gay."

***

The darkness envelops me like a shroud, hiding me from the world. I am cold, but the temperature is bearable. I have found a nook in the wood where no one will find me easily, although I'm sure they will come looking. Just a day, another day maybe—perhaps two. Hunger and thirst will have overtaken me by then, dampening the sense of freedom I am feeling.

I feel the water drawing me, an opening to a world beyond. My father told me that the water is deep and dark. We would often sit upon the bank and talk, but always I knew that I would have to return to my room. This time, I will be able to gaze at the surface, knowing that soon I would step through it into a better life.

***

"Gay?"

There were a thousand questions in my head.

Josie leaned over and took my hand in hers. "Lou came from a family that would never have accepted his sexuality—not in a million years. In fact, his father would probably have beaten him to within an inch of his life."

I frowned. "So he married you to what? Please his father?"

"He tried to live what they considered to be a normal life, and I mean normal in the sense that he would have a wife, two kids and a mortgage with an annual holiday in Spain."

"Is that what he wanted?"

Josie looked close to tears. "Yes. I know you're told to be gay and proud, but Lou just wanted an uncomplicated life."

"When did you find out?"

"We made love twice, but from the beginning, Lou started to make excuses, often only coming to bed when he knew I was asleep. Then I would find him curled up asleep in front of the TV at two in the morning. He was affectionate, but he began to embrace and kiss my cheek, avoiding my lips."

Josie's eyes filled with tears. "I thought he was having an affair. I was distraught. Of course, he denied it, and for a while, he really made an effort, but he could never get an erection. He even went with me to counselling…" The memories obviously brought back the pain. "It was there that he broke down and told me the truth. He was gay—he had known it since his mid-teens but lived a life of denial. He said he would give me a divorce, and that he would look after me financially, but I didn't care about money. I was devastated. If it had been another woman… Well, maybe we could have got through it. But if you're gay then that's it. You can't change who you are."

I ordered two brandies from a passing waiter, barely interrupting the flow of conversation. "So what happened? I mean, you're still together."

"I loved him too much. That's all. So when he said he still loved me in his own way, I clung to that, and after weeks in what seemed like a haze, we agreed to stay together as friends—as partners. Over the months—years—we slipped into this comfortable understanding. We divorced last year. No one knew—they still don't."

I could not comprehend such an understanding but then I'd never been in that situation. "So does Lou suspect us?"

Josie nodded. "I think he knows how I feel about you."

I stared at her. "You mean as a kind of platonic thing?"

The tears trickled down her face. "Robert, I've loved you for years—I watched you rear two children with Elizabeth, my best friend, and I sat next to her making small talk with a heart that ached for you. My one enjoyment was sitting on your knee during the club gigs, singing 'The Man I Love' while the audience laughed, thinking I was teasing you—but I meant every word." Now Jo was crying, and other diners were casting furtive glances. "So many of those songs—so many—I was singing to you, choking back the tears." She looked at me. "And you had no idea, did you?"

I shook my head. The waiter delivered the brandies and I asked for the bill. "Let's down these," I said. "I have an empty house and we have some catching up to do."

***

It was eight before we finally dressed and poured ourselves a drink. I cranked up the stereo as Frank sang 'I've Got You Under My Skin' and we danced. It felt good to hold another woman—a woman who truly loved me without condition, knowing that after all this time, I loved her equally. If anyone had told me the degree of strength I would draw from that love, I would never have believed them. We were a team now, and together, somehow, some way, we were going to get Jenny back.

***

I called Josie the following evening after arriving home from the hospital. I needed her now more than ever. Jenny hadn't stirred, and my insecurities bubbled to the surface.

"So what will happen now?" I asked, trying to sound casual. "Will you tell Lou?"

I heard a sigh. "I can't think about that right now. It's still going to be difficult to walk out. He's my best friend, Rob. I know it's kind of weird, but I just want you to hold on to the fact that we love each other, okay?"

I nodded, forgetting she couldn't see me.

"Okay?"

"Yeah, sure."

There was a brief silence. "Look, sweetheart, let's just get Jenny back on her feet. You've got me for life if that's what you want. Let's not rush."

I felt easier. It really didn't matter. Josie would always be a phone call away at most. We could share a pizza or a bed anytime we liked. I pulled a can of beer from the back of the fridge and turned on the TV, lost in thought.

Where are you, Jenny? Where the hell are you?

***

I am hungry and my stomach aches. The sun streams through the trees and I sit in the broken rays looking like one of those angels in the Bible. A fallen angel, maybe, but I'm not evil. I have killed a man of God who chose to serve the Devil, but I am not evil. I know this in my own heart. The sun warms me. Last night I heard voices—through the stillness I heard someone talking. There is a part of me that does not belong here. As if I am visiting this body. They were voices from another world, from which I have been torn. I have decided to wait here until I can wait no longer. Till the hunger makes death appear a blessed release. I will never see that attic room again—I will never wake in my bed with an aching heart, longing to see my child. I will be with my maker, from whom I will pray for forgiveness. I am confused but I have to believe that God is love.

Chapter Thirty-Four

HELEN PACE FROM the *Tabwell Herald* called to say they would be interested in running my story, asking if I could meet with one of their reporters the following day. I agreed, wondering if the article might bring Blakely out of the shadows.

After taking several gulps of lukewarm coffee, I made my way to the graveyard. I hadn't visited Elizabeth and Hanna's grave for several weeks, so I stopped off and bought a bunch of flowers from the local supermarket, pulling the old strands of decaying stems from the pots and replacing them with the new blooms. If Elizabeth could see my feeble efforts at flower arranging, she would have laughed.

I felt squirming in my gut—that unease that comes the moment you confront your wife after having climbed out of your mistress's bed. Josie and I were, in the language of social media users, *in a relationship.* Suddenly, the friendship that teetered on the edge for so long had plunged headlong into love and all the uncertainty that came with it.

I had believed that we would be friends for life. We were comfortable together, and if we fell out, forgiveness and reconciliation were never far behind. Would this be the beginning of the end? Would Josie find the man she had loved for so long to be a disappointment? Would I let her down? Would we grow tired and intolerant before finally going our separate ways? The thought appalled me. We could never rekindle our friendship, yet I could never envisage living without her.

Maybe Elizabeth could read my thoughts. I wondered if she would give us her blessing. If there was life after death, how would the dead feel about their partners finding new love? I mean, *really* feel? Freed from the mortal body, would you ever want to return the ailments and constraints of life in order to enjoy a physical union once more?

The questions remained in my mind as I drove home and changed, ready for the hospital. I was going to tell Jenny about Josie. I needed to tell her that everything would work out. She liked Jo. Then I would tell her that I was heading back to Tabwell in the morning, and if things went to plan, we would have her back with us very soon. I wanted to believe it, but life was continuing on its unpredictable course, and Blakely was never far from my mind. Who was the fake reporter? And, more importantly, what did he want?

***

Thunderclouds rolled over the horizon as I set off down the motorway the following morning, and if the *Tabwell Herald* wanted some ghostly pictures then they couldn't have chosen a better day. The sombre light had reduced even the prettiest of village greens to that of a rather unwelcoming, soulless and haunted space, and for a moment I imagined the spirits of the dead seated around its stone memorial.

I drove past the green and turned left, towards the town, and less than five minutes later, I pulled into the car park at the rear of *The Herald*'s offices.

They were nothing more than two properties knocked into one, the entrance on the corner of a narrow side street and the main road through the town. I walked through the doors and into a small well appointed reception, occupied by a young receptionist.

Suzy greeted me with an engaging smile and invited me to help myself to a drink from the state-of-the-art coffee machine in the corner. She was about five foot in heels, slender as a stick, and instantly likeable, possessing a natural warmth that put me at ease. It wasn't hard to see why they'd put the girl up front.

I'm not great with machines. This one was threatening to make a fool out of anyone attempting to extract a liquid refreshment from its bowels, and I managed to press for a coffee minus the sugar. Suzy smiled warmly and peered at her computer screen, contentment oozing from every pore. I waited, as nervous as I'd ever been in the dentist's waiting room, trying to remind myself that this was going to be painless. The door opened and Helen Pace strode through with her hand outstretched.

She would have got the part in a movie playing herself, should the opportunity have arisen. A slim brunette with a grey pencil skirt and pristine white blouse, even with her hair tied into a bun, and her eyes shadowed beneath heavy rimmed spectacles, she was quite clearly an efficient and competent woman. I guessed she meant business; any female who went to such lengths to disguise her looks had her sights set far beyond a local rag. She was friendly enough, but I knew that if my tale lacked legs, as they say, she wouldn't be considering my daughter's plight for one second.

"You'll be seeing Liam Vernon," she told me. "He's particularly good with the off-beat stories."

I'd just finished my coffee as a rather portly man appeared at the door. He smiled and held out his hand. "Mr. Adams? I'm Liam. I'll be talking to you about your...erm...experiences."

I looked at him, standing in his ill-fitting jacket and baggy trousers. He seemed to be a contented man in his late-thirties, although his thinning hair and lack of fashion sense made it difficult to be sure. I followed him down the corridor into a rather sparse room with plain white walls and fading brown carpet tiles. The only light came from a single window, giving the whole place a rather gloomy feel.

"We'll get some photos later. Our man with the lens will be with us as soon as he's finished at the tennis club." He glanced at me, lowering himself into the chair and signalling for me to sit opposite. A single wooden table separated us. "They're having a grand opening of their new indoor court. That's as big as it gets, around here!" He smiled, glancing at his surroundings. "It's a bit like a police interview room. I'm sorry."

Vernon pulled out a notepad from the desk drawer, along with a tiny recorder. "Okay, just stop me when you fancy another drink."

I felt myself tense. He was going to ask me to start at the beginning but I was already there, standing at the lounge window on a beautiful Sunday afternoon. Hanna raised her hand and waved. It was the last thing she ever did.

***

I find some berries and wonder if they are edible. Why should I care? I decide to leave them, wishing I'd listened when my father was explaining the shrubs and the trees and the fruit they bore. I wonder what course my life may have taken if I had been born into the family that had imprisoned me. If my mother had been allowed to love me.

Sarah always plaited my hair and told me I was beautiful, but God has not bestowed me with beauty, so why should I concern myself with my hair. Sarah scolded me for pulling out the plaits but I have no interest in my appearance. My hair hangs long and loose. As plain and as uninteresting as my face. I'm sure there are those who believe that God did not actually have a plan for my life. That we are not all his children. They would preach that those born out of wedlock are destined for the fires of hell. Are we an enigma to a righteous God? Are we rejected by Him while still in our mothers' wombs? I could not bear the thought that God would never hear my prayers or forgive my sins. Oh my God, please look upon me with mercy!

I suddenly feel His wrath—not in my heart, but in my mind. Is this His hand, driving me into the forest to take my own life? Have I been worshipping a merciless God who cared only for those in His fold? I feel a weight in my heart and begin to vomit. I know that the end is near.

Chapter Thirty-Five

B Y THE TIME I was done telling Liam Vernon my story, the sun had managed to poke its way through the rolling clouds and we made our way to Mosswood with our lens man in pursuit. I felt my blood run cold. Was this really Amelia's grave? Shafts of light broke between the gnarled branches of the trees as they clung to the last vestiges of their leaves, turning from shades of green to flaming red and primrose yellow, illuminating a carpet of soft brown decaying foliage.

We worked our way through the wood, following the pathways worn by the public over the years. Children had hung a rope from a large overhanging branch and Liam told me that the council had planned an activity area for the local kids with a few picnic benches. I was more concerned with the pond.

Danger signs alerted us to the water ahead.

NO ACCESS BEYOND THIS POINT

Barbed wire, surrounded the mossy bank sloping down to the black grimy surface of the water which was, I reckoned about forty metres across.

"It's unbelievably deep," Vernon told me. "Almost like a mine shaft."

We stood alongside the fence, staring out across the lake. "Is there any chance of finding a body in there?" I asked, feeling suddenly pessimistic.

Vernon shrugged and smiled. "It all depends on how much you want it."

"And how much it costs," added the photographer, who had said little since joining us.

Vernon smiled again and turned to his colleague. "Shall we get some shots, then?"

Finally, the photographer held out his hand. "The name's Phil," he said.

Phil took about ten shots with me looking pensive and a couple of others looking out over the water and smiling directly into the lens for the final picture. It all took no more than a few minutes before we made our way back, shook hands and parted. Vernon told me that the story would make the following week's edition and arranged to send me a copy.

***

Sebastian had left a message on my answering machine, which flashed ominously in the darkened room as I walked through the front door. I called him back, apologising for not having kept him up to date. I'd been too busy with Josie, although I decided not to add that to the list of excuses. He listened as I took him through the events of the past few days but offered no advice or opinion when I'd finished.

I dropped in on him the following morning. I could smell the coffee. "I've been thinking," the old man mused as I followed him into his lounge. "This Blakely character?" He turned as I nodded. "You might want to put some effort into finding out what he wants."

"Meaning?"

Sebastian's brow furrowed. "Who could have possibly told him about the body?" he asked.

I thought for a moment. "Only the minister—or Farriday."

"So, news either travels fast or this Blakely is somehow involved in the church or maybe the manor."

"You think Farriday or the minister might know who he was?"

Sebastian nodded slowly "If you can describe him accurately enough, it might be worth a try."

***

I punched the number for St. Jude's into my mobile and waited. The clock on the mantelpiece sounded heavy like the ageing heart of an old man. Sebastian watched me like a wise old owl as the reverend answered, sounding tired and rather distant. The sound of my voice did nothing to lift his spirits.

"I've talked to the elders," he told me wearily, "but to be honest, they sound as if they might opt to ignore the whole thing."

My heart sank. "What about the hierarchy? Surely they will not want the name of the parish besmirched?"

There was a pause. "You've been to the papers, I know. I've had a visit from our local reporter. I think they might wish to ride this out. We would, of cause, distance ourselves from his actions, pray for forgiveness on his behalf—"

"And what about the girl he raped? Will you pray for her? Couldn't you at least give her a decent burial?"

I could sense the tension in the minister's voice. "If it were down to me, Mr. Adams…"

I sighed loudly, making sure he could hear my frustration. "I know, but that doesn't bring my daughter back, does it?" I threw the phone down without having bothered to enquire about the mysterious Blakely. How many other men walked the path of righteousness with evil in their hearts? Allington was dead, yet his name lived on—a local saint. It was at times like this that I really wanted to believe in eternal damnation. A pit of fire where the likes of Allington would burn while their victims smiled down at them from behind the pearly gates. But Amelia was a tormented spirit, unable to rest until she found justice.

***

I arrived home just as the house phone rang. It was Kelly Dawson's mother. She tried to sound upbeat, asking after Jenny and suggesting that my daughter might like to spend some time with Kelly. I hadn't the energy to go into the whole spirit thing, deciding to keep to the medical facts. Jenny had collapsed inexplicably and was in a coma; her condition was stable.

A silence followed, and I thought, for a moment, that Mrs. Dawson had hung up. "Mr. Adams, Kelly told me what happened..." She paused. "I'm sorry. My daughter can be rather foolish sometimes—"

"I'm sorry," I cut in. "I'm not sure what you're talking about."

There was another brief silence. "The séance."

"I'm sorry?"

"Jenny wanted to contact her mother. Kelly said she could help her. It was all supposed to be fun..."

"What séance? When?"

"They had a Ouija board," she began. "Kelly must have had it for some time. We didn't know. They sell those things as toys now, but I'd have never had one in the house." She paused. "Anyway, Kelly asked if anyone was there, like they do in the scary movies. At first, nothing happened, not for a few minutes. Then your Jenny asked if her mum was there. Kelly said that there was still nothing. I think that's when Jen asked if there was anyone else from her family, and that's when things kicked off.

"Kelly thought Jenny was moving the arrow thing to spell Y-E-S. Jenny asked who it was, and I think the arrow spelled—" Mrs. Dawson paused. "What was it now? Two words... *Find me,* that's it! *Find me.*"

I felt my chest tighten. Jenny had opened the door. In that one single act, she had let Amelia in, and now she was paying the price.

"That's when the picture came off the wall," Mrs. Dawson continued, her voice breaking. "Kelly said they felt something sweep through the room, like a green haze that felt cold and smelled damp and–"

"Like stagnant water?"

Mrs. Dawson was taken aback. "Yes. What makes you say that?"

I'd heard enough. I needed to press the brake pedal on my speeding thoughts. "Just a guess," I replied. "Thank you for letting me know, Mrs. Dawson. It's not your fault. Kids do stuff and we can't be on them twenty-four hours a day."

"I feel so bad," she continued, ignoring me. "I hope Jenny is okay. Can you let me know?"

I hung up, promising that I'd keep her informed, and thought about calling Tint. I tapped out his number but replaced the receiver before it rang out. Then I called Josie.

***

"Wow! Holy shit. That's kinda scary, hun. How do you feel?"

"Like I want to meet up," I replied.

"The diner again?"

"Sure. It's our place."

We agreed to meet there rather than me driving to The Keys to pick her up from under Lou's nose. The whole arrangement still left me feeling uneasy, and I wondered if there was a latent passion that might be aroused when their unconventional partnership was threatened.

Josie ordered a skinny cappuccino and a slice of death by chocolate. "Gotta say, hun, even a sceptic like me can't argue with that. I mean, how would Kelly's mum know about the damp smell and the *find me* message? It's so weird."

I smiled. "Told you so!"

"Yep, okay, Mr. Smug Bastard. I haven't got an explanation. Is that why you called me?" Josie grinned. "I'll give you this one, Mr. Adams, but make the most of it. This will be the last time you get one over on me."

I felt the tension draining from me as she reached across and took my hand. My heart raced the way it had when I first met

Elizabeth; the way it had when I turned to see Melissa standing behind me at the cash machine. I'd always found Josie attractive but never had she looked so beautiful as that afternoon in Tammy's.

"Everything is going to be okay, hun," she said softly. "I can feel it. I can't explain how or why…"

Her words warmed me, and in that moment I felt the same assurance. Together, we were invincible. Jenny wasn't just mine; she was ours. That was how it was. That was how it was meant to be. I felt as if I was drawing on Josie's strength, day by day.

I called at Sebastian's place on the way home and found him cleaning up after the new puppy.

"Sorry about the smell," he said breezily. "He's pretty good, generally." The old professor paused and looked up. "Any news?"

I told him about the séance as he poured me a coffee.

"I have to be honest," he said after reflecting for what seemed an age. "It doesn't surprise me. I did think that Jenny might have thrown the door open at some point, or left herself open, at least."

He handed me a cup as I sat down. "Many kids—and adults of course—play at contacting the spirits, and it is nothing more than a game with few consequences. But occasionally, they succeed and it gets very messy."

"It doesn't get much messier than this," I replied.

Tint smiled wryly. "True, but things are starting to make sense. The jigsaw is becoming a picture."

That evening, I sat talking to Jenny, despite Sebastian's advice to leave her alone, but didn't mention the séance. Whatever she heard—whatever information seeped through to her subconscious mind—I wanted it to be positive. We were going to find Amelia. Things were happening. The article in the *Tabwell Herald*, the pictures by the lake. We were within touching distance.

***

I can hear a rustling in the trees behind me. It can't be Allington, but it hardly matters anyway, for my life is over and I am eager to escape into whatever awaits me beyond. I am confused, one moment convinced of my innocence, the next I begin to doubt. If only he would give me a sign. I fear the hell that the men of God preach from their pulpits but I fear life more. It won't be long now—it won't be long before the water swallows me into its murky depths and then I shall be free. I pity my child. What awaits that poor girl? What awaits her offspring? Will I return one day, a vexed spirit? I dip my foot into the water and feel the cold. Not long now…not long…

***

I spent the next few days with Josie, calling in to see my daughter each evening, waiting, hoping to see those eyelids flicker. But she remained motionless. I stroked her hand and kissed her forehead, praying that she would respond. I told her I loved her more than anything else in the world. She was mine. *Mine!* I whispered the words in her ear, wondering if they would echo through her subconscious.

The article in the *Tabwell Herald* carried two photographs of the lake with me, looking suitably troubled, looking across the surface. The whole place reminded me of something from a horror movie with the gnarled roots of nearby trees snaking into the water.

I called Jo, who had taken time out from the bar to read the piece, which was given the best part of the second page. "It's pretty good," she said. "It'll get people interested, and that's what we want."

Sebastian Tint said the same thing, but I had reservations. I thought about the bogus reporter who had failed to resurface. His warnings about a possible backlash haunted me, and I wondered how the parish would react to their tainted saint whose remains lay in their church.

I went walking with the old man and his excitable pup that afternoon, having spent the morning watching the news channel and drinking far too much coffee.

"I feel that we are in something of a calm before an inevitable storm," he told me as we turned onto a footpath that traversed the edge of several acres of farmland. Ricky strained at his lead. "I'm guessing the *Herald* will have several letters—or emails, I suppose—regarding the reputation of our reverend."

***

"People will believe what they want to believe," Tint had told me. He was right, of course. According to the editor, the *Herald* could have filled a whole edition with public reaction to the article.

"Most of it was positive," Helen Pace said. "But we have to have a balance, so there are a couple of replies you might find…harsh."

The *Herald* published six letters.

A fascinating story. They should find the remains of this poor girl and give her a proper burial.

Another wrote:

Why are we always trying to dig up the past? Who was this girl and why would anyone want to waste money trying to find a heap of bones?

But it was the last letter that caught my eye:

The Reverend Allington has long been regarded as Tabwell's Saint, and now Mr. Adams is seeking to besmirch his name. We cannot prove that these letters are genuine, and I trust that the people of Tabwell will treat this story with the contempt it deserves. I am disappointed that the Herald has printed the sensationalist clap-trap, and I hope Mr. Adams crawls back under his stone! Let the Reverend Allington rest in peace.

"Prick," I muttered under my breath as I tapped in Josie's number.

"Is that you, Mr. Adams?" she said breezily. "Are you calling from under your stone?"

"Yep, I'm looking for a new man of God to besmirch."

Josie laughed. "You'll burn in hell," she said, "and I'm guessing you'll have Allington for company."

I didn't believe in hell. Never had done—at least not the lake of fire the zealous evangelicals preached. Even my father had problems with the doctrine of eternal damnation, preferring to believe that hell was separation from God. But when you hated someone enough, a belief in hell fire was kind of comforting. I hated Allington, and if he was burning somewhere, that was fine with me.

***

I sat staring at Amelia's diaries. A young woman's life—her thoughts. Something, almost as tangible as a hand resting on my arm, prevented me from prying any further. Whether it was my own fear or a paranormal force, I couldn't be sure, but I left them on the kitchen table and poured myself another coffee. I'd vowed to cut down on the drink, having caught sight of an overflowing bottle bin by the back door. I'd have been embarrassed to put it out for the recycling wagon, so I'd split the contents into three separate heavy-duty bags and promised to give the soft drinks a go.

Life was much tougher without the whisky-induced sleep. I found myself waking frequently throughout the night, listening to every creak and groan, imagining that the spirit of Amelia might appear at the bottom of my bed at any time. There had been moments during the seemingly eternal sober nights when I'd longed to call Josie. Longed for the time when I would awake to find her next to me each morning, a time when we could sit around the breakfast table as a family, together. But without the assistance of the bottle, I sometimes lay in the darkness of my room and saw nothing but the lake that lay like an ocean between us and any happiness we might grasp from the wrecks of our lives.

Josie called to say she was meeting with the brewery guy, so I called in on Sebastian for a chat. He offered me a brandy but I refused. Instead, we took a walk; it was something Tint did every day, regardless of the weather. Two miles.

"It's like a drug," he told me as we set out. "I can't do as much these days, but until I lose the use of my legs, I'm going to keep going."

Tint listened as I told him about Josie and my dream of a future, wondering if the old man might just be able to reassure me. Maybe he would have a vibe or an invisible crystal ball into which he could gaze.

"There is no reason why you can't have a life together," he said thoughtfully. "But futures are built on good foundations. You mustn't push Jenny into accepting Josie, and if she becomes distressed, you must be patient. Talk to her about Elizabeth. Don't neglect her memory." Tint patted my arm. "It will take time, and the longer it takes, the better your life together will be."

I'd never considered the possibility that Jenny would not come out of her coma. Nor had I considered that she would not return to full health. Maybe it was a kind of coping mechanism that kicks in; I couldn't have handled the thought of losing her, but I needed Jo too.

She was a forty-year-old woman who would pass for a girl in her early thirties, even without make-up. She possessed a natural beauty and a good heart. I wanted it to work. I wanted a family, no matter how long it took.

I returned home to find the TV flickering silently. The room was cold and empty, leaving me with a heavy feeling that was difficult to understand. I shuddered. The room smelled damp—the kind of smell you'd find in an old house that had stood unoccupied for years. I walked through into the kitchen and was immediately hit by a sudden change in temperature. It was warm, the warmth I had become accustomed to. It felt like home.

Stepping back into the lounge, the stench of stagnant water stung my nostrils like acid, and I resisted the urge to let out a scream. *Amelia.* I wanted to run but something drew me in.

Sit down…there is something I want you to see.

The voice was in my head, but it was almost as if something or someone had planted the seed. I obeyed.

I sat for several minutes, staring at the TV, waiting for something to happen, listening to my heart thumping against my ribs.

What do you want? What do you want to show me?

The minutes passed, and my mind raced. Was this my imagination? Was I going crazy? I glanced at the family portrait on the wall, wondering if Elizabeth would point an accusing finger in my direction.

This is all your doing—you and that whore, Melissa!

But nothing moved. Then my eyes fell once more on Amelia's diaries. That's when I saw it. Jutting out from the pages of a volume at the top of the small stack was what looked like a bookmark. It was one of the diaries I'd already glanced through but I'd not noticed the picture.

Take a look…look and read.

I reached over and pulled the diary towards me. It felt heavy—heavy and cold. Surely it was just my imagination. This was nothing more than the ramblings of a girl. But it wasn't a bookmark; it was a photograph. I stared at the image and my blood ran cold.

***

The photograph was probably no bigger than two post-it notes. I knew the subjects. A swarthy-looking, well-groomed gent in a double breasted jacket stood beside a seated girl in a long pale dress. She stared out at me, almost as if she knew. Her eyes were large, yet within that face, I saw an ethereal beauty. *Amelia,* I thought. *We meet at last.*

My hands shook. This was the girl. The girl who had my daughter. The girl who had sat in the attic room. I knew that the man who stood at her side was the Stanwicks' gardener—Amelia's father. The photograph looked as if it had been taken in the grounds of the house, maybe close to the lake where her bones lay. I shuddered. The diary lay open at the page I'd pulled the photo from.

Read it... The voice was there in my head.

I picked up the diary and began to read, feeling the ice in my veins.

> *Friday 12th August.*
>
> *I awoke this morning unaware of what awaited me. Sarah brought the photograph, and now I am able to see my father whenever I please. He seems to be looking back at me, and when I smile it is almost as if he smiles back. Foolishness, I know, but there is no harm. Sarah seemed distracted, oblivious to my joy as I held the photograph for the first time. "I cannot stay long," she told me. "The Reverend Allington wishes to see you."*
>
> *I asked Sarah what the minister could possibly want with me, but she told me she didn't know, and I knew better than to challenge her, of course. I would find out soon enough. I spent the morning reading poetry, trying to recite the verse without referring to the page. I was halfway through a particularly troublesome poem when I heard a commotion coming from the floor below.*
>
> *I heard my mother's voice raised in anger, but her words were lost in an eerie echo. Thankfully, I did hear footsteps on the stairs and returned quickly to my*

desk. Sarah always knocked, and so did my mother on her infrequent visits. I waited, sensing a presence on the other side of the door.

"Hello?" I called.

The door opened. It was the Reverend Allington.

"Good afternoon, Amelia. You're reading, I see. Very good."

I smiled politely, wondering what the minister could possibly want with me.

"Do you read your Bible, Amelia?" he asked.

"Yes, sir, often. I love the parables."

He smiled, but there was a coldness in his eyes. "That is good. We are all put on this Earth in the service of our Lord and we must be obedient to his calling."

I closed my book, for it is polite to do so in company. "I'm not sure that the Lord has need of me," I said.

The reverend smiled. "He does, Amelia."

I averted my gaze, unable to look him in the eye.

"God works in mysterious ways." He paused, waiting for me to enquire as to what he could possibly have planned for me. "I'll come straight to the point, Amelia. Mrs. Allington is barren. She is unable to give me a child." He stared at me. "It is not God's will that a woman should be cursed in this way, but He has provided an answer." He looked at me, awaiting a response. "Do you understand what I'm saying?"

I shook my head.

"The Bible tells us that fornication is sinful, but I believe that it is only an abomination to God when it is borne from lust rather than necessity. God will look kindly upon a woman who bears a child for one of His servants."

His eyes bore into me, cold and unfeeling. My heart began to thump, and I felt beads of perspiration forming on the back of my neck "But I cannot—"

"You can, Amelia, and you will."

I can hardly bring myself to put to paper the thing that happened in what may have only been minutes but felt like hours. He took my hand and pulled me from my chair. I resisted and found myself shaking violently. This angered the minister. "Don't resist the will of God, you stupid child. The Devil will have you!"

I found myself lying on the bed, the reverend standing over me, unbuckling himself. "Open your legs, my child!"

I began to sob, but my refusal angered him more. His face was crimson, his eyes wild. Even now I feel the terror, I feel the betrayal. My own mother had allowed this. I called my father's name, praying that he might rescue me, but my cries angered the reverend even more, and he slapped my face hard. The pain stunned me, and in that moment he pulled my legs apart.

He didn't enter me out of love. His contempt was clear and I submitted, closing my eyes and biting my lip so hard that it bled. I could not bear to look up at the man but listened to his breathing as it became heavy and laboured. I tried not to cry but the pain was almost unbearable, although I knew that my protests would remain unheard. The taste of blood was bitter on my tongue as the reverend suddenly withdrew himself from me.

"That is it, my child," he said, buckling himself. "It is for God to work His miracle now. I shall return tomorrow and I shall expect obedience, my child."

With that, he left the room. I heard the door close, his footsteps on the stairs. When I knew I was alone, I began to sob, but no one came. There was blood on my legs, a throbbing pain in my groin. I cleaned myself with a wet cloth and sat at my desk, staring out across the sun-bathed lawns. I breathed deeply, imagining the scent of fresh meadow in the air beyond my window.

Sarah visited and found me in a state of great distress but I could not bring myself to tell her what had happened. As darkness fell, I took to my bed and lay motionless, imagining myself walking in the grounds, stopping to look at the flowers that my father tended. But the events of the afternoon weighed heavily, and I could still smell the reverend on my skin, recalling the pain as he bore down on me. I prayed that night. I prayed that I was with child, for the thought of him taking me once more tormented my soul.

I returned the diary to the other volumes and flopped back into my chair. Amelia, an able writer, had caught little of the horror she had endured, but I felt it. The pain, the loneliness and the betrayal of her ordeal gripped my heart, and I felt my spirit become as one with hers. The room was cold again, and my groin ached. I smelled old cloth and mothballs, fused with a faint aroma of stale perspiration, and as I closed my eyes, I was there in that attic. I began to sob.

The garden was in darkness as I wandered out into the chill of the evening air. I shuddered, again suddenly feeling that I wasn't alone. I peered through the gloom. Something—someone—moved. I instinctively took several steps forward and then I saw her.

The girl knelt, her hands resting on her knees. I took another step forward. The girl rocked gently, staring down at her clasped hands. "Father?" she whispered. "Is that you? Is that you?"

I froze. "Jenny? But how? How?"

I moved forward and suddenly I was there, standing over the girl. It wasn't Jenny. She was too slight—too small. Amelia looked up, her face ravaged by time, rotting flesh falling from bone. I screamed. "What do you want? Where is my Jenny?

The girl stared at me, unblinking. "My child will return to you," she replied, in a voice that echoed in my head.

"When? When?" I hissed. "When will she return?"

Amelia did not reply, looking back down at her hands as the remaining flesh fell from the bones and the skeleton crumbled into the earth.

I woke several hours later, my whole body weak and drained. My mobile rang. It was Josie.

"Where the hell have you been?" she said, "I've been ringing for hours!"

I checked my watch. It was nine.

"I'm just checking you're okay," she continued before I had a chance to tell her I'd taken a nap. It was more than that, of course, but I needed to talk face-to-face, so I told Jo I'd head over to The Keys for a beer. Josie sounded pleased.

"Want me to come with you to the hospital tomorrow?" she asked. "We could grab some food after, if that's okay?" That was when I realised I'd not eaten that day. I slept little that night, unable to erase the image of Amelia's face from my mind.

I was glad of Jo's company as we made our way to the hospital. Jenny lay, her body almost motionless, her mind in Amelia's world. I knew it, but could tell no one how. I had seen those eyes looking up into mine as I'd held her in that attic room, as I'd wandered into the garden in my dreams.

***

The water reaches my waist. I long to record these last moments just as I have faithfully chronicled my existence in the hope that one day someone will read them and pray for my soul...

***

My daughter's eyelids flickered. Josie pulled on my arm. "Come on, Jen!" she whispered. "We're waiting..."

Yet I knew. She wasn't going to return. Not yet.

***

The water reaches my knees, and I feel my feet sinking further into the mud. It is as if some unknown force is pulling me down, and I know with each step I may be plunged beneath the depths and into my grave. The Reverend Allington will rest under a headstone bearing his name, and I shall lie beneath the water, where no one will find me. Not yet. One day, maybe. A belief in God has been instilled within me, but right now, I cannot concern myself with anything other than the need to flee from this life. I take another step.

I am up to my waist now. It surprises me how quickly my body becomes accustomed to the cold. The lake—my escape from the hatred of those who would gladly cast me into hell fire with their own hands. The discomfort as I surrender my life to the water is nothing compared to the pain that awaits me if I choose to remain. I will not be missed. The doctor who took my child from me with such a cold heart will certify that the reverend died suddenly and the causes will be unknown. Men of God were called by their maker, not taken by the hand of a mad woman. I knew this. I knew also that my child would grow unaware that her mother lay at the bottom of a lake, her bones stripped of flesh by time, slowly sinking beneath the mud. I took another step forward.

***

Josie slipped her arm through mine as we crossed the car park at Tammy's. We had already decided on a healthy burger with fries—ninety-nine percent prime beef and one hundred percent potato.

"I'm taking it easy on the salt, how about…" Josie squeezed my arm, pulling me to a stop. Her eyes were fixed on the car park entrance, where a red Fiat pulled in.

I broke free from Josie's arm and headed in the direction of the car, my walk turning into a run.

"Rob! Leave it! You promised!"

I had. But my need to know overcame my cowardice. I had barely started my sprint before the Fiat screeched to a halt, reversed and spun away through the exit. We watched as the car disappeared down the road. Josie looked at me.

"Well, I don't think there's any doubt now, is there?"

I shrugged.

Josie shook her head. "That was really dumb, Rob," she said angrily. "We need to get the registration and report it, leave it to the police!"

"Next time," I said. "Whoever it is doesn't stalk people for a living. They're not clever enough."

If I'd not been so hungry, Tammy's would have been a waste of time, but I cleared my plate and downed two cups of coffee while relating the tale of Amelia's rape. Josie listened in silence as I found myself repeating the story almost word for word. I could see the sloping handwriting, seemingly unaffected by the harrowing ordeal of its author.

When we were done, our stomachs full and our hearts heavy, we left Tammy's, checking for red Fiats on the way.

"Looks like they're giving us some space," Josie said as we drove away. "But next time, hun, have your phone ready. Don't try anything stupid. Just take a photo, okay?"

I nodded.

Josie wasn't convinced. "Promise?"

"I promise."

I slept well that night. No dreams. At least, none that I remembered.

***

I awoke to the first frost of the year. The summer was drawing to a close and the Met Office predicted a harsh winter. The big freeze would probably hit late January and last well into February, with the south expecting several inches of snow. It was a good time to be a northerner.

I looked out of the window, wishing that Mr. Whirl hadn't pulled up with his happy-clappy music and enticed my little girl to buy one of his chocolate chip cornets.

The covering of frost did little to dress the stage of my little girl's murder. She should have been here with me, chattering away and asking when it was going to snow, but the house was silent. I switched on the TV and turned up the volume, but it failed to kill the emptiness. I drank coffee and tried to muster some kind of interest in what the newsreader was telling me, but nothing mattered.

I leaned back and closed my eyes, hoping that a short nap might help, but my escape was interrupted by a knock on the front door. Expecting a charity worker or a salesman, I was ready with my best *you've called at a really bad time* face, which Elizabeth reckoned would have Freddie Kruger cowering in fear. But instead of a badge-wearing fundraiser, I was confronted by an attractive teenage girl. Her face was vaguely familiar.

"Are you Robert Adams?" she asked.

I looked past her, my attention drawn to the car which pulled away from my driveway and moved slowly down the road. It was a red Fiat.

The girl studied me hard as the car disappeared out of view.

"I'm sorry," she said. "I can explain."

We stood peering at each other; she seemed as curious about me as I was about her.

"I'm sorry, but who are you? What do you want?"

"My name is Kayla," she replied. "Can I come in?"

I knew the dangers. It wasn't a good idea to invite a teenage girl into your home—particularly one who just arrives on your doorstep unannounced. But curiosity got the better of me and I stood aside.

"Thank you," she said as I closed the door behind her. The girl studied everything, the photographs, the paintings, the ornaments. It was as if they were all saying something to her—about me, about my life.

We sat facing each other on opposite sides of the room. Kayla looked uncomfortable, like a kid at her first job interview, fiddling with the tassel on her fleece.

"I take it that you're the one who's been following me for the past few days?" I began.

Kayla blushed. "I'm sorry. It's my auntie, it's her car and she's not very good at conducting covert operations," she replied with a nervous giggle.

I smiled, deciding it was best to let her do the talking.

Kayla shifted awkwardly, and her eyes filled. "Oh, God!" she whispered, fighting the tears. "I've practised my lines over and over again. I've imagined the whole conversation. I've had dreams—nightmares." A tear trickled down her cheek. "And now I'm here…"

I stared at her and suddenly remembered. "You were in the café," I said. "A few weeks back. Sitting in the corner?"

Kayla nodded, wiping away another tear. "The girl you were with? Was that your daughter?"

"Her name's Jenny," I replied.

It was almost a groan of resignation that escaped Kayla's lips. "This is all a mistake. I shouldn't be here. I'm so sorry!"

There was no way I was letting her go now, not without an explanation. "You've put a lot of effort into seeking me out. You might as well tell me what this is about."

The girl looked at me, her face stained with tears. "My name's Kayla," she said. "Kayla Ingram. You knew my mother."

I stared at her. "Melissa? Melissa is your mother?"

Kayla nodded. "And you're my father."

I felt a pounding beneath my ribcage. *But I'm Jenny's father. Jenny!* I wondered where she was.

***

I can hear the birds calling to each other. I'm not sure how long I have been standing in the water. The voice of my father in my mind... He calls my name. I take another step. I feel my feet sinking into the mud. Time means nothing now. I take another step, and the water covers my shoulders. The cold rises, my head is aching. I can no longer hear the voices. Does he no longer seek me? Did he think I would never venture into the woodland—the place he would bring me? The place he would teach me about the flowers and the trees, the frogs and the spiders? Am I alone again? One more step. Just one more...

***

The young girl peered at me through her tears as I tried to gather my thoughts. My mind raced. I didn't want to believe her. I wanted this whole thing to be some kind of hoax. A mistake. Yet I knew it wasn't.

"She told me all about you. About the…fling."

So that's what it was? A fling? A fling that had delivered a daughter.

Kayla was studying my reactions. "She told me how you wanted to marry her. How she ran away because she was scared of commitment. That was just the way she was. She never settled, but she said she never felt for anyone the way she felt about you."

My head was full of questions, unformed and racing around my mind. I couldn't find the words. My whole body felt cold and my hands shook.

"She found out she was pregnant six weeks after she quit her job at the hairdressers. She went to live with her sister in London, and that's where I was born. Then we moved to Ireland and mum set up her own hairdressing business. She wanted to tell you about me but thought you'd be better off without her."

"You live in Ireland?"

Kayla shook her head. "No, we moved back to London."

Kayla's eyes filled again. "It was the worst thing we ever did!"

"Oh? Why?"

Another tear tripped down her cheek. "It just was!" Kayla paused, wiping at her face with the back of her hand. "My mum got cancer. She wanted me to go looking for you after she'd gone."

"She died?"

Kayla nodded. "She wrote me a letter to give you. I went to live with my auntie—the one with the Fiat—and that's how it started." Kayla allowed herself a brief smile.

"You have the letter?"

Kayla nodded and pulled an envelope from her pocket. It was sealed. "I haven't read it," she said.

My heart quickened as I recalled the girl who had broken my heart seventeen years ago. It was still fresh. Time had not dimmed the memory.

Dear Rob,

If you are reading this then our daughter has found you. She's beautiful, isn't she? I am so sorry that our brief affair came to such an acrimonious end. I wasn't ready to settle down, and I could never have given you the life you wanted. I hope you see that you already had that life. I would have taken that from you and we both would have been unhappy. That is why I never told you about Kayla. I wanted you to repair your marriage.

Rob, she is a strong girl so if she has no place in your life, please be honest with her. I realise this will have come as a shock, and Kayla will understand this. I have told her that you are a good man and would have willingly given her the home she has always wanted. I did love you, Rob, and if I had settled with anyone, it would have been you. I'm trusting that you will learn to love Kayla as I am sure she will learn to love you.

Melissa x

I looked up to see Kayla waiting patiently. "If you don't want to know me, it's okay, I'll understand—honestly. This is a big thing and you already have a daughter and..."

I wanted to reassure her but I couldn't dismiss the doubt in my mind. "I just need to be sure, Kayla. I need to be sure that you really are my daughter."

Kayla's face fell.

"I'm sorry. That sounds awful. But what if your mother was seeing someone else—besides me? What if she thought I would make a better father than the other bloke?"

I felt as if I had just slapped her hard across the face. She looked stunned. "My mother never slept with another man," she snapped, "There was never anyone after you!"

"What? In sixteen years?"

Kayla nodded. "She always talked about you. There was no one else."

I'd always imagined that Melissa would have enticed another man into her bed within weeks of leaving me, never believing for a moment that the time we'd spent together had meant anything more than another fling. How wrong I had been.

"If you want a test then that's fine by me," Kayla said. "I'll understand."

I shook my head, even though a part of me thought it wouldn't be such a bad idea. I was still coming to terms with the fact that Jenny wasn't mine, and if Kayla was going to become a part of my life, I didn't want to find out that she wasn't mine either.

We exchanged numbers, and when I looked out of the window, I saw the red Fiat parked up outside. We hugged awkwardly, and I watched as the car pulled away. My phone flashed several seconds later. It was a text message.

Thanks, Dad. Let me know if you want to see me again xx

***

The painkillers didn't touch the headache which had developed into something closer to a migraine, and by the time I reached Jenny's bedside that evening, I felt physically sick. "You have a sister," I whispered, "and I have another daughter."

I almost expected Jenny to open her eyes, jolted back to life by the news that her family was growing, week by week. A half brother and a stepsister. But she didn't stir.

I couldn't face Josie or Sebastian and took to my bed with my head still throbbing. Melissa was right; Kayla was a beautiful girl and seemed smart, too. Any man would be proud to be her father, but her timing couldn't have been worse. I drifted in and out of sleep all night, unable to clear my mind and wondering if maybe I should have called Josie and talked the whole thing out.

By morning, it was clearly my best option, and I headed over to The Keys.

Josie's bright and breezy greeting lifted me out of the haze that had settled on my mind. Unable to focus on anything, I'd poured myself a coffee, turned on the TV and watched the news team trawling through the events of the previous day without hearing a word. They were nothing more than talking heads spouting words that meant nothing. They were voices. Just voices with nothing to say. I'm not sure Josie knew what was in store when she asked me if there was any news.

"I'll tell you when you've made me a coffee," I told her, managing to find a space on which I could sit on a couch covered in clothes and discarded soft drink boxes.

"I'm gonna have a real good clear-out today," she said. "Just throw those things on the floor."

I did.

Josie grinned. "You look beat up, hun. Not slept again?"

I shook my head.

"No news on Jenny, I presume?"

Again, I shook my head, but tears suddenly started to form in my eyes.

Lou popped in to say hello before hastily disappearing; dealing with emotions was not his strong point.

Jo passed me a mug of steaming coffee and sat opposite, pulling her housecoat across her chest.

"I know who the stalker is," I told her.

Jo stared at me. "No shit! Who?"

She sat almost motionless as I told her the whole story, but the expression on her face left me in no doubt that Melissa was going to get little sympathy, even if her life had been cut short by cancer. It only reminded Jo that I had cheated on my wife, and if I had cheated once…

I handed her the letter and the photograph. "She looks like her mother," she said dryly. "More's the pity."

I ignored the comment and watched as Jo read the letter, shaking her head as she handed it back. "So now you have a permanent reminder of your affair," she said angrily, "as well as a permanent reminder of Elizabeth's fling."

I nodded. Maybe this hadn't been such a good idea.

"You have really fucked up your life, Rob. All of this shit is down to you. Elizabeth is dead, Hanna is dead, both of Darren Pascoe's parents are dead…and you know what? If you have just kept your dick in your trousers, they'd all be alive!"

I felt a physical pain in my chest, and my stomach turned. For a moment, I swore I was going to throw up yesterday's food.

"And what is this going to do to Jenny? What? Have you even fucking thought about that? She's going to feel like a spare part. Every time you're with Kayla, every time you even talk about her, she is going to wonder how she can compete with your real daughter."

"It's not like that," I protested, still feeling that crushing weight under my ribcage.

"How do you know, Rob? You don't know Kayla. She could be a little bitch, demanding your time, expecting you to drop everything the moment she clicks her fingers. Don't tell me she won't, because you don't know. Her mother was a selfish cow, and what's in the cat is in the kittens!"

I wished I had an answer, but everything Josie said was true. I didn't know Kayla. I could only hope—and maybe even pray—that she was a girl who would one day be a part of a happy family, but right now, I foresaw only friction and heartache.

Jo glared at me. "So what are you going to do? How are you going to fix this?"

The truth was, I didn't know. "Kayla said she'd be in touch. She's giving me time to think."

"Oh, she'll be in touch, all right. Mark my words!" Josie stood, taking my half-empty cup. "I've got things to do. I'm sorry."

I looked up as tears ran down her cheeks.

"Just go, Rob. Please!"

When I reached the door of The Keys, Josie was several yards behind me—a safe distance. No hugs. No kisses. "It could work out well," I said, briefly making eye contact. "We could be a family."

Josie threw me a death glare. "A family? I don't know if I want to be with you anymore, Rob. I'd sooner stick with Lou than take a risk with a man who I could never trust. What happens when the next Melissa comes along? What happens, Rob? Tell me!" She paused. "You can't, because you're a man—a man who's managed to screw up his own life and leave a trail of shit behind him."

If I'd have been a more eloquent man I might have found a worthy reply. "I would never do that to you," I said weakly.

Josie stared at me with a look of utter contempt. "Oh, too right, you wouldn't! I'm no Elizabeth. I wouldn't sit in the corner crying. Believe me, if you ever messed with me, I'd make you regret the day you were born. And that's after the surgeons had sewn your dick back on!"

I climbed behind the wheel of my car hoping I never heard from Kayla again. There was too much history behind the girl. Too many painful memories, and I could not see how Jenny could ever be comfortable being around her. Josie was right. Maybe, as heartless as it might sound, it might be better if I explained to Kayla that I didn't want any contact.

***

By the time I saw Jenny that evening, my mind was made up. My real daughter was lying in front of me. She was my life, and

I was going to make sure that nothing came between us. I called Josie as soon as I arrived home. Lou answered and told me she was busy in the bar so I messaged her.

Jenny is my only girl. That's how it will stay. xxx

I waited anxiously but Jo didn't reply. She was still mad at me. Kayla would hate me too. What was I going to tell her? Sleep came as a way of escape, my mind spinning me into a deep dream-free slumber.

I couldn't face food. I looked at my reflection in the mirror; I'd seen healthier looking corpses, and the stale taste of coffee found me rooting through the fridge, where I found a carton of fresh orange. I pulled desperately at the tag and took several mouthfuls just as my phone rang.

"Mr. Adams?"

I recognised the voice from somewhere.

"This is Dennis Blakely. I interviewed you a while back, about the body in the lake?"

This was the *Tabwell Herald*'s mystery man. The reporter they knew nothing about. "I remember. The *Herald* had never heard of you."

Blakely was ready. "I know. Look, please don't hang up—I can explain. Can I meet you?"

I was intrigued and would have travelled halfway across the world to hear what he had to say, but it was clear he was prepared to meet me on my terms, so I gave him the address of The Keys. I had no idea what the bogus reporter had to tell me, but if it got Josie talking to me again then it hardly mattered.

Blakely told me that it was a good seventy-mile drive and we agreed to meet at lunch. I sat and stared at the moving pictures on the TV screen, my head still spinning. The painkillers made me drowsy. Sleep was a way out, and providing I avoided meeting Amelia in my dreams, it was all good. But I didn't so much sleep as crash headlong into oblivion, waking at midday with only half an hour to dress and get myself down to The Keys.

Blakely was waiting for me when I arrived. He was seated in the far corner with a glass of spa water and a lunch menu. He greeted me warmly with a handshake as firm as I'd remembered.

"I'm sorry for all the subterfuge," he said, grinning broadly, "but I think you'll forgive me when I've explained everything."

Josie hadn't made an appearance but left Lou to take our order. My appetite only allowed me a side snack of garlic bread, but Blakely was clearly a man with an empty stomach; he ordered steak but washed it down with nothing stronger than a glass of soda water.

"Never worried to much about wine," he said, handing the menu back to Lou. "And I wouldn't know a vintage if it slapped me around the face. Water keeps me fresh."

I was anxious to learn what this man had in store for me and wasn't interested in getting into a discussion about alcohol. He must have seen that quizzical look in my eyes.

"I'll get straight to the point," he said, resting his arms on the table and leaning in as if he was about to reveal something that no one else was meant to hear. "My father—well, my father's company—is purchasing Crest Hill Rest Home, and the woodland, too."

I shrugged. "So why did you want to know about the body?"

Blakely grinned. "Well, we are planning to convert the whole place into a leisure park. Not like Disney—it will be forest walks, outdoor activities for families where kids can get away from their iPods and TVs. We're going to have nature trails and picnic areas. The house will be turned into a hotel, and we will add a conservatory. That will be the restaurant, and we hope to eventually buy up another few acres of land beside the wood and plant more trees and build wooden lodges."

"Sounds brilliant," I said. "But—"

"I know. What does this have to do with you?"

I nodded.

Blakely took a sip of wine. "We are planning to clean up the pond and turn it into a picnic area. There will be fountains, and we will stock the place with fish. Giant carp—all the stuff kids love."

The man's enthusiasm for the project was clear, but he could see I was becoming impatient.

"I'm sorry. The point is, we will be dredging the pond. But by the time all the planning has gone through, work won't start for a good twelve months." Blakely smiled. "I'm guessing you won't want to wait that long."

I felt a proposal coming, but it was one that might cost me money.

"The thing is, my interest in your story is entirely personal. I'm addicted to ghost-hunting programmes. I just love all that paranormal stuff—always have. That's why I posed as a reporter. I've got a nose for bullshit, and I just wanted to check you out."

I shrugged, trying to suppress the anticipation. "Did I pass?"

"With flying colours. Even when I tried to scare you."

"So what happens now?"

Dennis Blakely drained his glass. "I've spoken to the Farridays, and they've agreed to let us send some divers in to search for the body."

I stared at him, waiting for the catch.

"Don't worry, Robert," he said, raising his empty glass. "This one's on me. It won't cost you a penny."

Chapter Thirty-Six

I WOULD HAPPILY have kissed him on the lips at that point. He was staring at me, waiting for a response, but all I could muster was a rather weak thank-you.

"Would you like to be there? When they look for the body?"

There was nothing that would keep me away. When this man, whose tailored jacket would have funded my whole wardrobe, had waved a wad of his father's cash, the flickering light at the end of the long, dark tunnel had burst into life. I was in the mood to talk. By the time we cleared our plates, Blakely had my whole life story. There would have been nothing to hold his attention, had I not gone looking for Melissa that morning, but that decision had turned an existence into a soap opera. We shook hands.

"I'll call you next week, before the dive." He left, turning at the door and giving me a thumbs up.

Josie stood at the bar, dressed to kill and looking my way. In that moment, all thoughts of Blakely and his divers were forgotten as I waited to see that smile that told me I was forgiven. But she turned, as if the very sight of me offended her.

My heart ached at the thought of losing her, but I didn't have the words to win a woman back. I stumbled like an infatuated schoolboy, tripping over his pre-rehearsed lines.

I sat for a while, staring at the menu, the empty plates and glasses littering the table. I had no stomach for a dessert but I couldn't leave—not with the cloud of rejection hanging over me. I had to know. I had to know if Jo was ever going to be a part of my life again. The words were there in my head, jumbled like a kids' jigsaw, but each time they formed themselves into something I could deliver, they evaporated.

It was hopeless, and the place was filling up with lunchtime diners. This was a table for four—a family—parents with their kids, grandparents with their grandchildren—people who hadn't managed to screw up their lives. They would be waiting for the loser in the corner to vacate his table and slither off home to his empty house and his empty life.

I pushed the menu aside, sliding back in my chair. There was no point in hanging on.

"Not fancy the ice cream, then?"

I looked up. Josie stood over me. She saw the pain in my eyes. "Babe, I'm sorry," she whispered.

It was like an explosion within. I stood, pulling her into my arms. "I'm sorry, too. I'm sorry for screwing up my life, I'm sorry for hurting you. I'm sorry for everything!"

I wasn't even aware that everyone had stopped talking, intrigued by our very public display of affection.

"They know," she whispered. "Lou has told everyone. He's happy for us."

I felt the tears welling in my eyes. It was now. Now was the time. "Jo, I love you," I said. My voice must have carried across the room. "I meant what I said—I want us to be a family." I broke the embrace, holding her hands in mine. I'd never been one for grand gestures, but I found myself pulling the ring from the empty drinks can and sinking to my knees. "Josie Duxbury…please say you'll marry me? Please!"

Jo gazed at me, her eyes bright. "Of course I will!" she beamed. "Of course I will!"

I pushed the tin ring onto the tip of her finger. She laughed as the whole place erupted into applause. "I don't think that's going to fit!" she said as we turned to see everyone in The Keys standing at their tables, whistling and cheering, clinking their glasses. I looked over at Lou. He was clapping, too. Our eyes met, and he smiled.

"I always knew," he mouthed. Then he rattled a glass on the bar. "It's Happy Hour!" he shouted.

That seemed to go down even better than my impromptu proposal.

Josie sat opposite me. "You look a little confused, hun. Happy but confused."

"It's just the response," I told her. "Everyone thought you and Lou were a happily married couple. They've taken all this pretty well."

Jo grinned. "There are quite a few strangers in here, hun," she said. "And our regulars suspected that Lou and Sammy are close, although they're not exactly a couple...not yet." She glanced over at the bar, "Let's face it, no one would know that Lou was gay, but Sammy? You'd have to be blind."

"So everyone knows the situation...with you two?"

Jo nodded. "Pretty much. We decided to make it public the other day, and word travels real fast in these quarters. There were a few raised eyebrows, but..."

"How long has Lou known?"

Jo shrugged. "He's known how I felt for a while, but we had a good chat last week."

"So what's going to happen?"

"We'll continue to run the pub together. We're good friends, Rob. That won't change. We love each other, if you know what I mean."

I nodded. That was fine with me. I was looking at my future wife. That was enough.

Chapter Thirty-Seven

I WOKE THE following morning to low thunderous clouds that threatened to deliver more than the gentle drizzle that greeted me as I looked out of my window. Nothing could dampen my spirits that morning, and although Jenny had looked like death, I believed she would be back. Josie may not have shared my conviction regarding the causes of Jenny's comatose condition, but she wanted to believe that the recovery of Amelia's body would bring the whole saga to some kind of close. That was good enough for me.

I had already decided to visit the grave. It may have been a guilt thing, but when a man is ready to move on he at least owes it to his wife to explain, even if she has passed over. I parked up at the cemetery and waited for the rain to pass. The black clouds rolled by and as the sky brightened I stepped out, an umbrella tucked deep into my waterproof jacket.

The jacket was the last thing Elizabeth had bought for me. We had taken a weekend break in Cumbria, determined to spend the time walking on the fells. Unfortunately, the weather forecast threatened continuous drizzle. They weren't wrong. It was pretty much like living in a cloud, so we found ourselves browsing the outdoor activity shops like seasoned hikers, and that was when Elizabeth presented me with a Gore-Tex jacket as an early birthday present.

That all seemed so long ago, and now I found myself in a deserted cemetery standing at Hanna and Elizabeth's grave in the hazy light, reading the inscription as I'd done many times before.

Once again, I began to weep. The pain rose within me, fierce and unstoppable. I loved Josie but I grieved for my wife, I grieved for my baby girl, and I sobbed with remorse for everything I'd done. I had failed her, broken her heart, and she lay there as a consequence of my actions.

I knelt on the rain-sodden ground for an hour until the tears stopped. I returned to my car just as the sun finally appeared from behind the thinning clouds. I felt cleansed and peaceful, almost as if Elizabeth had reached out from beyond the grave and laid a forgiving hand upon my spirit. Maybe that was just wishful thinking, but I knew that if she had to choose another woman for me—a woman to be a mother to Jenny and fill the gaping hole she'd left—it would have been Josie.

***

We shared lunch at Tammy's and ate well. I had the monster topped pizza, washed down with a beer, while Josie picked her way through a chicken salad, explaining that she wanted to look good in her wedding dress. We laughed our way through the meal, yet I was dreading a call from Kayla. It had to come at some time over the next few days, and I'd have to deal with her face to face. Josie made it clear that she'd support me in whatever decision I came to, but that decision was mine. I was on my own.

The call from Blakely came first. Three days after we had last met, he phoned to say that the dive would take place at the weekend. I spent the Friday night at Jenny's bedside, finding it easy to talk about Blakely and his men and the plans for the Stanwicks' home. It was going to be a place where the kids could play and learn. Amelia would have loved that. Family life—the very thing she had been denied. Everything that the Stanwicks stood for— the master's cruelty, the weakness of his wife, the subservience to the church—would all be brushed away, and the house would ring with the laughter of children, drowning out the cries of the young woman who once sat imprisoned within its walls.

***

I was greeted by Farriday in the grounds at the edge of the wood. "This is exciting," he said, with the air of a man who had offloaded all his troubles for a fair price. The skies were broody and grey, plunging the woodland into an eerie darkness, and the small film crew Blakely had hired was setting up lighting around the pond.

"I'd say this was more like a small lake," one of the crew muttered, adjusting the lighting pod.

Blakely welcomed me with his usual firm handshake. "I thought we'd use our guys to capture the moment," he said with a childlike enthusiasm. "For the record."

Just then, three divers appeared from behind a canvas screen set up between two trees. Two cameramen swung their lenses in the direction of the divers as they made their way to the water's edge.

My heart began to thump. Farriday had been joined by his wife, and they stood arm in arm, a little way back from the action.

Josie had chosen not to join me. "This is between you and your daughter," she'd said, kissing me gently and wishing me all the luck in the world.

The faceless divers in their black frog suits looked almost sinister as they waded up to their waists. Blakely turned to me. The smile had vanished from his face. This man may have had the money to indulge his ghost-hunting fantasies but he wasn't playing. "This is it, Rob," he said. "This is what you've been waiting for."

***

I take another step and sink into the mud beneath my feet. This time, there is no going back. The ground sucks me down into the murky liquid. The water swirls around my ears. I close my eyes and hold my breath but only to delay my departing. I sink further; now the mud reaches my knees. I cannot escape, and for the first time, the fear of death grips my heart. It is too late. I could not free myself even if I chose life. I feel the knife in my hand and slowly draw it across my wrist.

My lungs give up the fight. The foul-tasting water enters my body as I fight and choke. The light from the surface is beginning to fade as I leave this Earth, at last escaping the body that has imprisoned my spirit. Now I am beginning to feel a warmth. A heavenly warmth. I feel myself fading, fading slowly... Peace. Peace at last.

***

The skies grew darker as the crew, under Blakely's watchful eye, adjusted the lighting.

"Let's get this done before there's a fucking deluge," one of the cameramen shouted from under a giant umbrella which covered both him and the camera. One of the divers disappeared below the surface as the other two followed.

Blakely turned to me once again. "Fingers crossed, Rob," he said as the film crew swung their cameras towards the murky surface.

The first diver appeared after what seemed like an hour but was probably no more than a few minutes. "There's a shitload of mud down there," he called. "If there's a body, it could be under four metres of sludge!"

My heart sank. Blakely grimaced. "Just do your best, mate," he called back. "If we need to come back tomorrow, we will."

The diver disappeared as the other two surfaced with the same story. It could be a long search, and the light was fading. Two hours later, Blakely called it off.

"I'm sorry," he told me. "We'll start at first light tomorrow."

I shrugged, unable to hide my disappointment.

Blakely patted my shoulder. "I'm staying at the Albion Hotel. They've got vacancies." He smiled. "The room and the breakfast is on me. I insist. You're not driving home."

***

I called the hospital from the hotel lobby. There had been no change. Jenny was still comatose but stable. Blakely booked me in and escorted me to my room, just three doors from his own. The Albion Holtel was a five-star affair and like nothing I'd stayed in before. My room, with its hot tub, luxury lounger and a bath that could accommodate a football team, left me wishing that Josie was here, too. I joined Blakely in the bar that night, and we managed to down two bottles of champagne, finishing the session with a brandy coffee. The more time I spent with the man, the more I liked him. His fascination with the supernatural was almost childlike and quite endearing.

I killed the sound on the TV and called Jo from a bed that dwarfed me, taking her through the events of the day before attempting to describe the opulence of my surroundings. We talked until I found my eyes closing, the champagne beginning to take effect. Jo wished me luck, and I fell asleep in a room lit only by the flickering images on the plasma screen.

I met Blakely for breakfast the following morning and worked my way through a bowl of bran followed by a full English and three cups of coffee. Blakely believed in eating well and waded in like a man partaking in his last meal. "We've got the whole day," he told me defiantly. "If that body is there, we will find it!"

I trusted him implicitly. He was a man with high hopes and deep pockets. This was something he would tell his grandkids—the day he found the body of a ghost. It sounded odd, but to him, that's exactly what it was.

When we arrived at Mosswood, the three divers were sitting on canvas chairs drinking tea from Styrofoam cups. They greeted us with muted enthusiasm, aware of what lay ahead. They were peering through cloudy waters, for bones lying beneath the mud, long since stripped of their flesh. This was not what they had imagined when they took up diving. This was not a shipwreck populated by exotic marine life swimming through the portholes. That was probably why Blakely had agreed to pay them double the going rate.

It was over an hour before they took to the water. My hands clenched, plunged deep into my coat pockets, while I fought the demons that told me this was all a waste of time. What if we didn't find a body? What if she wasn't there? The time passed slowly. The divers resurfaced, one by one, shaking their heads before taking to the depths once again. By afternoon, my hopes were fading.

The cameras remained trained on the water, but their operators had long since lost interest. Blakely looked dismayed. Even he was giving up hope. A silence had fallen across the whole area. No one was talking. We were all thinking the same thing.

"I'm not giving up," Blakely muttered. But there was little conviction in his voice. I felt beaten. The light I'd seen at the end of the tunnel was, once again, nothing more than a flickering candle.

Two divers emerged, looking for a break. They took to their canvas chairs and poured two teas from a flask. And that's when it happened. Suddenly, the waters erupted. The third diver seemed to shoot up from the surface like a cork from a bottle, his face twisted in panic.

"Get me out!" he screamed, thrashing at the water like a drowning child. His colleagues threw down their cups and raced down into the pond. "Get...me...out," he panted, finding his feet and struggling through the mud.

"What the fuck?" one of the divers muttered, grabbing an outstretched hand and pulling the terrified man forward onto the bank. "What's up, Eddie? What's going on?"

The diver stood, fighting for his breath. "I saw it!" he panted. "I saw her! She... She came up...from the mud... She was coming for me, I swear!" Eddie's eyes were wide, peering out through the goggles. He slumped into the canvas chair. "I'm done here. I'm tellin' ya—I'm not going near that water."

The other two divers looked at each other. "You sure it wasn't a fish or something?"

Eddie pulled his goggles from his face, his eyes wide with fear. "What? A fish with arms and hands...and a face?"

"You sure you weren't hallucinating? You're dead beat, mate..."

Eddie was angry. "There's nothing wrong with me! I've been diving for fifteen fucking years, and I ain't seen nothing like that ever! Nowhere!"

Blakely stepped up, clearly shaken. "She's there," he said. "She was showing you were her remains were buried. Sometimes that can happen. I remember reading—"

One of the divers held up his hand. "Are you fucking serious?" he snapped. "You think I'm going back in there?"

Blakely stared at him. "Triple pay," he said. "And a thousand quid each as a Christmas bonus."

The two divers glared at Blakely. "Not for a million bucks, matey." They looked over at Eddie, who was sitting on the stump of a tree, his hands trembling. "Look at the state of him! That's heart attack material."

Blakely's shoulders dropped as he sighed loudly. "Look, wherever Eddie saw the girl, that's where she is. You just need to go deeper. There's a shitload of mud at the bottom."

The divers looked at each other, then the taller of the two said, "You've been watching too many movies, but I'll cut you a deal— triple pay and a thousand notes—cash?"

"You have my word."

The two divers, still reluctant, took to the water once more. We waited. Eddie sat, still traumatised by his experience, sipping his tea. Five minutes turned into ten. Then into fifteen. Then, suddenly, one of the divers surfaced and punched the air. "We've found her! She's here!"

Blakely threw his arms in the air "Yes! Yes! Yes!"

I stood in silence as the wave of relief washed over me. This was it. We had found her. "How long will this take?" I asked one of the divers.

"It's difficult to say. We have to remove all the sludge from around the remains before we can bring her to the surface. I'd go and get yourself a coffee or something."

But it wasn't coffee I needed. I wanted to be with Jenny. "I'm off to the hospital," I told Blakely, who stared at me in disbelief.

"What? You don't want to see the body? Why?"

The truth was, I didn't know. I just couldn't face it. I had no desire to see Amelia's bones. "Message me," I said, walking away. Blakely watched me, still wondering how I could possibly leave at a time like this.

Only fortune prevented me ending up in an ambulance. I ran two red lights and stopped inches short of hitting an old lady on a crossing. My mind was on my daughter, and the whole journey was something of a hazy memory.

Jenny lay motionless as I sat down beside her with a cold drink from the machine in reception. My phone kept dropping its signal, leaving me wondering if it might be better to sit in the corridor until Blakely called. I kept checking my watch. One hour turned to ninety minutes. Ninety minutes turned into two hours, and then suddenly my phone rang.

"We—got—" Blakely's voice dropped. "It's been a—job—we—"

"I can't hear you!" I yelled. "The signal is bad—have you got the body?"

No answer. I threw the phone halfway across the room and buried my head in my hands. The whole world seemed to stop and fall silent. I'd caught enough from Blakely to know that Amelia's remains were out of the water. Then I heard her voice. It was little more than a whisper.

"Dad?"

I looked up. Jenny was staring at me.

"Why are you crying?"

***

"You're back!" I screeched, loud enough to bring a passing nurse running along the corridor.

Jenny was still trying to focus.

"I'm here, babe!"

I wanted to pull her from the bed and hold her. I wanted to take her in my arms and never let go. But Jenny looked confused. Why was her father acting like a crazy guy? The nurse burst through the door.

"Oh my goodness!" she exclaimed. "This is wonderful!" Jenny just frowned.

"Yes thank you. But can one of you get me a drink? I'm so thirsty!"

***

I hugged the first nurse that responded to my calls. Jenny looked weary, but over the following days her colour returned and all the tests came back clear. Blakely assured me he was taking care of everything. The relevant authorities, including the police, had been informed, and copies of Sarah Bell's letter would be used to assist in identifying the remains.

"The company will cover all the costs," he told me. "Including the funeral." I thanked him, knowing that nothing I said would convey my gratitude. "But you might have to deal with the media," he warned. "This kind of story usually arouses quite a bit of interest."

I kept Jenny informed and she lay quietly, listening.

"I was there, Dad," she told me one evening. "I was there, under the water. I felt myself passing out beneath the surface. I know how she died. I was with her. I *was* her." Jenny squeezed my hand. "I felt myself rising to the surface. That's when I opened my eyes. The moment you found Amelia."

"Just as Sebastian told me," I replied.

Jenny smiled. "Nothing else matters now, Dad," she said. "As soon as the funeral's over, we can get on with our lives."

They were the words I thought I'd never hear. I kissed Jenny on the cheek.

"Dad?" she whispered as I opened the door to go. I turned. She blew me a kiss. "I love you."

"And I love you, too, babe."

I closed the door behind me and made my way back to the car, tears streaming down my face.

***

Josie cried, too. "I'm sorry I doubted you, hun," she told me. "It's just such a relief…"

"I need to tell her about us," I interrupted. "I want to be totally honest. It's only fair."

Jo wasn't convinced. "I'd hang on if I were you. You can't rush the family thing. It will happen, but you need to spend time together."

Maybe she was right, but my head was spinning. I had emerged from that tunnel, walking into a light that was blinding my senses. The relief was intoxicating, and I needed Jo to save me from myself.

"You're impetuous, Rob. Let the old wounds heal. Don't create new ones."

I should have slept well that night but I didn't. Kayla messaged me just as I was locking up.

Hi. Is it ok if I call tomoz about lunch time?

My heart sank. Kayla had all the weapons she needed to carve my life open, but I messaged back and told her that it would be fine. How do you tell your biological daughter that you have no room for her in your life? It wouldn't matter how I dressed it up; rejection is still rejection. I paced around the house like an expectant father, which was ironic because that was basically what I was. When the knock came, I actually jumped.

Kayla stood with her hood pulled up over her head, making her look a lot younger than her sixteen years. She grinned expectantly, having no idea what lay in store.

I made her a juice and sat opposite her. Kayla was still trying to read me. "I know this must be a big thing, and it will take time, but—"

"Kayla," I said, stopping her mid-sentence. "This is a really bad time."

Kayla's face fell, and I found myself telling her everything that had happened since her mother walked away, leaving me to repair my broken marriage. She listened, stunned. "So Jenny isn't yours?"

I shook my head. "And everything that's happened has happened as a result of my affair with your mother. I've got to do what is right by Jenny..."

"But she's not yours," Kayla said sourly, "I am!"

"She is mine," I replied, trying not to raise my voice. "I have raised her as my own. I can't think of her as anything but my daughter. Not after all this time."

Kayla looked down at her hands, clasped together on her knees. "So you don't want me in your life? Is that what you're telling me?"

"It's not that I don't want you—it's just that I need time with Jenny. Put yourself in her position. Wouldn't you be feeling a little insecure at the moment?"

Kayla glared at me. "How insecure do you think I'm feeling right now? My own father doesn't want me. Do you honestly think I'd want to come between you and Jenny? Do you think I'd try to take you away from her? I just want to spend some time with you, that's all. I'm not a threat."

She stared at me with anger in her eyes, waiting for me to reply, but all I could do was apologise.

Kayla stood up. "There's no point, is there? You're not going to change your mind."

Before I could answer, she had pushed past me, and moments later, I heard the door slam. I watched from my window as she walked down the path with her phone pressed to her ear. It was probably a tearful call to her auntie, asking to be picked up at the bottom of the road. I wished I could have gone after her and made things right. Could Kayla ever be a part of my family? Josie, me and two girls? Maybe one day. Just not now. *Let the old wounds heal.*

Sebastian threw up his arms in sheer joy when I told him the news. His uncharacteristic display of emotion warmed me. "I knew it!" he said. "I knew you'd find her!"

"It was touch and go for a while," I replied. "And that poor diver will be having nightmares for the rest of his life."

Sebastian smiled. "He'll get over it. He's probably telling himself he imagined the whole thing."

I'd called in on him after Kayla had left and we went for a walk. I needed some fresh air in my lungs—fresh air and a listening ear. I was troubled at having rejected the girl, and I was hoping the old man could somehow salve my conscience. He listened in silence, as always, waiting for me to finish. Had I made the right decision? Should I have accepted her and hoped for the best?

For the first time since we had met, Sebastian seemed perplexed. "I can't be your judge," he said softly. "Maybe you have done the wrong thing at the right time."

I looked at him. He smiled. "Some might say that rejecting your son or daughter is always wrong, but I have to agree with Josie. Jenny is very vulnerable at the moment. She'll need all your love and attention. Maybe, in time, you can contact Kayla—when Jenny is stronger." We approached the Dog and Gun Inn by the canal bank. "I think I could do with a drink. How about you?"

***

I arrived home half expecting to find Kayla on my doorstep, sobbing into a paper handkerchief. She wasn't. There were no messages on my phone and no missed calls to my landline. I grabbed some loose change for the car park and set off for the hospital, slipping a Bob Dylan disc into the car stereo and promising to make time to finish his biography.

I spun into the hospital car park, making my way across the grounds and through the reception. That was when the thought dropped into my head from nowhere. What if Kayla was sitting by Jenny's bed? What if she had introduced herself as my daughter— my real daughter? Fear gripped me as I hurried up to the ward and my hand trembled, resting on the door knob. I paused before entering.

Jenny looked up from her book. "Hi, Dad. You're early."

I sighed with pure relief. She was on her own.

"What's up? You look washed out," she said.

I laughed. "I'm okay. What's the book?"

She held it up. *Jane Eyre.*

It brought back memories of my schooldays, when we'd gone to watch the old black-and-white movie starring Orson Welles as Mr. Rochester. I'd been so impressed that I read the book and decided, at the age of twelve, to become a bestselling novelist. I think I managed two chapters written in the style of Charlotte Bronte before I realised I didn't actually have a story—something that is apparently essential if you want to sell books. I gave up and decided to become another Orson Welles instead, but that dream died soon after my first appearance in the school play.

Jenny threw her book onto the bed. "Guess what? It looks like I'll be home this weekend."

It was the news I'd longed for.

"I'll be able to go to Amelia's funeral."

I smiled. There was no way I'd leave her behind, even if it meant incurring the wrath of the doctors. Jenny had to be there when they lowered Amelia's coffin into the ground. The funeral would bring closure to our dalliance with the spirit world. An end to the nightmares, the cryptic messages on the fridge door, bogus songs and pictures that fell off tables. Life would return to normal—whatever normal was.

For Jenny, normal would be the two of us rubbing along from day to day, and although I still longed to tell her about Josie, approval would not come easily. Jo and I would have to play the good friends game for a while longer, and the late-night chats over coffee at Tammy's would be a thing of the past.

In the meantime, I would make plans. We'd book some time away, just the two of us, father and daughter spending some quality time in the sun, as far away from here and the home that had become a stage for a drama that was finally drawing to a close.

Chapter Thirty-Eight

SEBASTIAN WAS WATCHING a wild life documentary, surrounded by copies of *National Geographic*, sipping at a large brandy. I sat in silence, allowing him to see it through to the end.

"Some of these creatures are almost like things out of children's fairy stories," he said, his eyes fixed on the screen. "Unless you saw it with your own eyes, you wouldn't believe they existed."

Sebastian lived a life of isolation. He didn't seem to have many friends; at least, there were none that he'd mentioned, and he rarely saw any family. Yet he never struck me as being lonely. I guess his life was full—a man at peace with his books, his dog, and his documentaries. A man with an active mind and eyes that saw beyond the surface of a materialistic world. I envied him. I envied his wisdom, but most of all, I longed for the peace he possessed.

He flicked off the TV, turning towards me. "Thank you for that," he said. "I didn't want to appear rude but I love this stuff— even the sparrows and the squirrels that I see on my walks." He placed an empty glass on the table at the side of his chair, "Anyway, how are things with you?"

I told him about my plans for a holiday with Jenny, hopefully sometime after Christmas. The very mention of the festive season brought a grimace to the old man's face. "Ah, Christmas. I expect that's something you'll have to wade through once again."

I understood exactly what he meant. Elizabeth and I had found ourselves carried through December on a sleigh ride of anticipation, planning, buying and decorating, only to be unceremoniously dumped back into our routine amid a pile of empty boxes and bottles along with a maxed-out credit card and an empty bank account. I hated the week between Christmas and the new year; I hated the whole new year thing, and my resolution usually involved something to do with never touching alcohol again.

Needless to say, I'd usually broken that one before the end of January.

"I'll be glad when it's over," I told him. "I think Jenny will be glad to see the end of all this stuff."

Sebastian looked at me. "Stuff?"

"It's been pretty freaky, this spirit world. I just want to get back to normal."

Normal? Could I ever live with normal?

The old man nodded warily. "I must warn you," he began, "Jenny is sensitive to things. I'm not suggesting she'll be walking around talking to dead people, but she might find herself picking up on things other people don't feel." Sebastian thought for a moment, weighing his words. "Imagine you are in a room full of people. They're all talking, and when you close your eyes, all you can here is a murmur of sound. But just suppose that a short distance away there are two people. You want to know what they are saying to each other, so you train your ears—you begin to concentrate.

"At first, their conversation is lost. There is just a wall of sound, but slowly, you begin to decipher their words, you begin to hear." Sebastian paused, checking that I was following his train of thought. "Jenny wanted to contact the spirit world and speak with her mother. She made the effort. She wanted to hear." Sebastian gave me a reassuring smile. "It's just a thought—an off-the-cuff theory—and you may never experience anything like this ever again."

I mulled over the old man's words trying to recall a time when I'd trained my spiritual ears and eyes on Amelia. All I'd ever wanted was to prove her existence, and I could never deny the things I'd experienced, but now, I just wanted them to stop. No more faces in the trees, no more strange smells and sudden changes in temperature. I wanted to live in my world. The one I knew.

***

I picked Jenny up from the hospital early on Saturday morning. She looked slightly bewildered, gazing around at her surroundings like a girl who had arrived home after years rather than weeks away. I was anxious. Did she want a coffee? Something to eat? To maybe catch a movie?

She looked at me, and her eyes filled. "Dad, I know you want to help, but please don't fuss. I just need some space."

Space was the last thing I wanted to give her. If she had been a child then I'd have held her till she fell asleep. That's what I wanted—to hold my daughter and never let her go. Space? That meant backing off, leaving her to make a move while my heart ached for the contact that would reassure me everything was okay.

"She loves you, hun," Josie told me. "She told you that, so hang in there."

But I was scared of losing her, and while my head told me Jo was right, my heart refused to believe.

"She's back in her room," I told Sebastian. "All weekend!"

The old man told me the same thing. Jenny needed time.

The following Wednesday, Blakely called me suggesting we meet at the Lakeside Hotel in Tabwell. Jenny was welcome to tag along. The call was short; Blakely was driving and he would message me with a date and a time shortly. He did.

Hi Rob! Lakeside, Friday 14:00 ok?

Jenny looked nervous throughout the journey, having spent most of the week in her room, venturing down to watch some TV and make small talk. We had fifty miles of road to travel in a metal capsule. There was no bedroom to which she could escape, no space. Physically, this was the closest we'd been for several days. I decided it might be time.

"What's bothering you, babe?" I asked, trying to sound casual.

Jenny stared out at the road ahead.

I turned briefly. "Jen, please talk to me."

A tear trickled down her cheek. "I don't know if I can handle this," she replied.

"Handle what?"

She paused, trying to find the words. "There will be a coffin. I'll be looking at the coffin!" Jenny looked at me. "You don't understand, Dad. I died with that girl. She took me through the final hour of her life on Earth. I felt everything she felt— that longing to escape her miserable life. It was awful. I felt the mud drawing me down and the water filling my lungs. No one should ever have lived and died the way she did. I want it all to be a horrible dream—something I can forget. But I can't. I have to watch her carried to a grave, knowing what she went through— what was in her heart."

I wanted to stop the car and turn and look my girl in the eye. I wanted to assure her that, in time, everything would be okay. But I drove on, my heart as heavy as lead.

We arrived at the Lakeside fifteen minutes early. Blakely was waiting and waved us over from the table by the window. "I booked this one," he told us, shaking my hand. "And you must be Jenny," he said, planting a kiss on her cheek. He pointed towards the large bay window. "No point eating at the Lakeside Hotel without a lakeside view!"

We chatted while we waited for the waiter to take our orders. "This is on the company," he said. "So I wouldn't scrimp if I were you."

Jenny blushed. That usually meant she was in the presence of someone she found attractive.

The waiter left after filling our glasses from a bottle of overpriced wine. Blakely read my mind. I couldn't afford to a drink-driving ban on top of everything else. He smiled. "Why don't you two stay over—spend the rest of the day and do some shopping?" He passed me an envelope. "That will cover the meal and drinks. I'll sort two single rooms."

I tried to protest but Blakely held up his hand.

"Rob! Don't even try! Seriously."

I smiled and thanked him. Jenny looked as if she was going to cry again, but Blakely caught her.

"No tears. You both need the break," he said softly. "I can tell."

Jenny ordered fish and chips. It was hardly going to break the company bank, but my daughter was never one for what she called 'flash food'. I abandoned my original low-fat, healthy choice and decided that nothing on the menu would taste better, so it was fish and chips three times. The company finances were safe.

Blakely eyed his plate of food like a man who hadn't eaten for several days. He was the sort who would be comfortable with anyone—a kind of social chameleon who changed his colours with little effort. He slipped easily from the small talk to the business he really wanted to discuss.

"I've spoken to the folk at St. Jude's," he began, "and I don't think it would be appropriate to have her buried within their grounds."

Jenny looked up at Blakely and then at me.

"Would you agree?"

"Yes! Yes!" Jenny replied with unguarded enthusiasm. "She wouldn't want to be anywhere near that place!"

Blakely sounded wary. "It's all very sensitive, and I've had to tread carefully. Reverend Francis seems like a good man. I feel a bit sorry for him, to be honest, and I'm guessing there have been several other very good men who have been at the church since Allington died."

Jenny shrugged. "So what will happen to the centre he set up? I mean, it's still running under his name. They still think he's a saint."

Blakely was guessing like the rest of us. "I suppose that will depend on the parish council," he said. "But if you asked me to predict the future, then I'd say that it will be running under the name of the church itself, this time next year."

Jenny grinned. To her, that was a minor victory. "And what about Allington's grave?"

"That's up to them, too," Blakely replied. "But they may be less willing to exhume a body. Maybe they will erase the inscription and try to forget he ever existed."

Jenny pulled a face that suggested it wasn't enough, but it was better than nothing.

"It's amazing," Blakely continued, clearly delighted to be part of the whole thing, "to think that all this started with a dream. It's one hell of a ghost story!"

Jenny shuddered. "I'm just glad it's over," she muttered. "Or it will be, after the funeral."

Blakely smiled. "Okay, that's what I wanted to talk about. I was thinking of having Amelia buried in the grounds of the house. We would have a brief inscription on her gravestone, and visitors will have access to a more detailed history of her existence. It would be in a brochure. I was thinking of leaving one in all the rooms."

Blakely saw that Jenny looked uneasy. "Don't worry, I'm not going to give away too much…nothing of the family tree."

Jenny nodded. She was only walking this Earth as a consequence of Allington's actions. "It will just include the story of how Amelia was born to the mistress of the house after an affair with the gardener—like that famous novel—and how her birth was never recorded and how she was locked away in the attic, taught by a governess. It's classic stuff."

"I guess people will buy into the Lady Chatterley thing," Jenny mused.

"But this is true. That's why I think people will be fascinated," Blakely added.

He had seized the commercial aspect of Amelia's miserable existence, yet I didn't begrudge him anything. Amelia would have her grave and her story would reach thousands. I couldn't see anything wrong with that. Blakely was just a frustrated ghost hunter who had a little corner of his father's dream park. If he'd been a model railway enthusiast he would no doubt have had tiny trains running across the grounds.

"The lake itself will be named after her," he told us. "It will be a picnic area and the water will be packed with fish. Of course, there'll be fountains and a small waterfall—you can't have water without fountains! I'm going to light it from beneath—all different colours—so that families can sit round till late on summer evenings." Blakely beamed. "It will be beautiful. And, of course, you two can visit anytime—free of charge."

So Amelia was going to be something of a theme park attraction. I never saw that coming when I found Jenny in the bath or found her sobbing in the vestry of a church fifty miles from home. But the funeral worried me. I really didn't want a circus, so I asked Blakely exactly what he had planned.

"I have the Farridays' permission to use their land, but the service itself will take place at the local crematorium. I've asked Reverend Francis to lead the service. He wants to make it a kind of public apology." Blakely paused. "It will take place in two weeks' time. I think there'll be plenty of media interest."

Jenny stiffened. "How do you mean?"

Blakely was taken aback by my daughter's obvious concern. "It's one hell of a story, Jenny. Like I said before, who would have thought when all this started in your bedroom—"

"I don't want to talk to any reporters! I won't! It's not a sideshow!" Jenny's eyes flashed with anger.

Blakely looked as if he'd had his face slapped. "Okay, I'm sorry," he said quietly. "If you don't want to talk to anyone, then you don't have to. I'll tell them that you want to be left alone."

"And you honestly think they'll take any notice? When have those leeches ever done that?"

"They will. I'll make sure of it. They'll have their story. I've got everything I need from the first interview with your father. I'm not going to go into all the personal stuff."

Jenny backed down, but her eyes were still dark. "They'll start digging," she said. "You know what they're like."

Blakely smiled. "I wouldn't worry too much. I'll give them enough to keep them happy. The funeral will make the news and then it will all be forgotten by the following week."

I placed a reassuring hand on Jenny's arm. "He's right, Jen. Just get yourself through the day."

Blakely leaned across. "I'll pay for the two of you to get away for a couple of weeks. You can be on a flight to Mexico the following day if you want."

I looked at Jenny, who smiled and shook her head. "This is something I can't run away from. I need to be at home."

Chapter Thirty-Nine

BLAKELY WAS RIGHT. Amelia Root was news. The story appeared in the national press and even ended up on the local six o'clock news, but Jenny and I had been shielded from the attentions of the media. Blakely remained true to his word; he had given them everything they needed from the beginning to the end.

"A body, believed to be that of a young woman who died in the late 1800s, has been recovered from Mosswood Lake in Tabwell. Divers discovered the skeleton after the diaries of the woman were discovered in the attic of the Crest Hill Rest home, former home of the Stanwick family. It is unclear how the woman's body came to be in the lake, but it is believed that she may have taken her own life."

Pictures of Mosswood flashed across the screen as Jenny and I sat, transfixed. My heart thumped. It had all come down to this, from that first encounter with the girl in the attic, the dream, the nightmare.

"According to letters recently discovered, the young woman, Amelia Root, was the illegitimate child of Mrs. Stanwick, and her birth was never recorded. The diaries suggest she was kept locked away in the attic of the Stanwicks' home and taught by a governess, Sarah Bell. A funeral is to be arranged, and her body will be laid to rest in the grounds of Crest Hill Rest Home."

The papers carried a similar report, keeping to the facts. Of course, Blakely's net failed to catch all the sharks. We received the odd call—reporters wanting Jenny to give them a personal account—but I made it clear that we had nothing to add. They figured it wasn't worth the hassle and left us alone.

We were relieved they showed little interest in pursuing the paranormal side of the story. Blakely had thrown the wolves enough meat to keep them happy, although I wondered how long it would be before the article in the *Tabwell Herald* resurfaced. I was already wishing I hadn't told them quite so much.

Sebastian called me the day after the TV report. He sounded ruffled. "The not-so-Reverend Allington seems to have got off rather lightly, don't you think?" he said sharply. Before I could respond, he continued, "Not one single mention of the fact he raped that poor girl and stole her child! Why do you think that is? Do I need to ask?"

I knew what was coming next. The old man's anger and obvious frustration were barely under control. "Might I suggest that your Mr. Blakely is looking after his own interests? He hasn't told the media about Allington because he doesn't want to upset the parish, and he doesn't want to upset the parish because he doesn't want any opposition to his activity park project!"

I'd already worked that one out but there was something about Blakely that I really liked. Tint was right; Blakely had always been cautious when it came to besmirching the name of a local saint, but I knew he was quite prepared to wade in with the whole story when his park was up and running, and that was okay by me. Sebastian wasn't so sure.

"Look, Rob, I understand why the church would feel uncomfortable about this, and I know it will upset a lot of the local people, but he was a flawed man—a wolf in sheep's clothing, preying on a wretched, vulnerable girl. Personally, I would dig the bastard up and throw his remains in the local rubbish tip! Even a stinking, stagnant pond is too good for him!"

Even Josie sounded indignant when I called her later that day. "You gave the Tabwell rag all the information about that rat,

Allington," she hissed. "They ran the whole story and got their arses kicked by the local council, I bet! So they conveniently decided to forget all about it. Now they've found the body, it's just a sleepy old village full of old cronies who want to drive around in their posh cars and show up at a pretty little postcard church every Sunday and say thanks to God for their fat bank accounts! It's all very cosy, Rob, but it stinks!"

I could hear the murmur of conversation and the chime of clinking glasses in the background.

"I just hope the funeral throws up the truth about why that girl could never rest at the church. Why she's going to be buried in the grounds of her home!" Josie's voice rose above the noise behind her. "I know all this happened over a hundred years ago, but it's still a wrong that has to be put right."

I replaced the phone feeling I had just taken a verbal beating. Maybe Sebastian and Jo were expecting me to go running to the media with the whole story. I would have gladly done so but—and Jenny agreed—there was something pleasantly covert in Blakely's plan to get his activity park up and running before putting Allington's name in lights and revealing him for the bastard he really was. I also really liked the idea of the park—a place where families could spend time together. If only Hanna had been alive.

Chapter Forty

I F THE DAYS leading up to the funeral had not seemed so long, we might never have discovered what lay in our own loft space. Jenny decided that she wanted to look through the old photos and draw up a family history, scanning the pictures and putting them together on a publishing programme with notes and dates. I pulled out several boxes—the ones I knew contained all the stuff we could have marked with the words 'sentimental value'—and together, we began to sift through them.

Jenny laughed and cried a lot. Pictures of Hanna as a baby. Hanna in her frilly sun hat. Elizabeth and Hanna pushing Jenny into the pool in Spain. My daughter looked up at me suddenly, tears staining her cheeks. "How could you, Dad?"

"How could I what?"

"Melissa!" she said softly.

I shook my head, avoiding her questioning eyes. There was no anger in her voice. No reproach, just a genuine question, and that made it all the harder to answer.

"I was a fool," I replied. "I don't know what else to say."

She pulled another cardboard box towards her and pulled out a wad of old schoolbooks. *Jennifer Adams. Age 8. English Literature.*

Jenny smiled. Melissa wasn't going to come between us—not today. She opened the book, flicking through its pages, stopping suddenly. "Aww, I remember having a crush on the teacher... Mr. Taylor, I think. I'm sure I asked him to marry me!"

I killed the sound on the TV.

"Did he say yes?"

Jenny grinned. "He used to ask us to write about anything we wanted. Most of the kids wrote about their brothers or sisters, some wrote about their pets. There was this one girl who loved killer whales and had been to Florida loads of times. SeaWorld was like home to her, and she knew everything there was to know about marine life. I kind of thought she was cool."

Jenny picked up another book.

"I wrote lots about animals. I used to pretend I knew what they were thinking. Sometimes I believed I could actually read their minds. Mr. Taylor said I had a good imagination." There was a sadness in my daughter's voice, a longing for the way things used to be. She stopped at a page and began to read. "This was something I wrote about a dream I'd had…" she began, but her voice trailed off.

"Jenny?"

My daughter's eyes darkened. "Oh my god!" she whispered. Her eyes closed as if she could no longer bear to look at the pages in front of her.

"Jen? What's wrong?"

She passed me the book. I looked down at the page.

My Dream by Jennifer Adams

Last night I had dreamed I was standing in a room. It was not a very nice room. There was no carpet and not much furniture. It was like a room in a poor person's house because there was just a desk by a little window, and there was a bed in the corner and a wooden chest on the other side of the room. I got a real fright because there was a girl sitting at the desk, and when she looked at me, I saw she had funny eyes. They looked like they were popping out of her head. I have drawn a picture of her.

I stared at the pencil sketch of Amelia Root—a drawing of the face I had seen in the old black-and-white photograph only a few days ago. Despite her age, Jenny had captured the eyes, the hair and the mouth perfectly. Eight years ago, as a child, Jenny had her first encounter with Amelia. There had been no Ouija board, no séance. Just a young, innocent girl who had stumbled into another world.

"You can't remember this?" I asked her.

Jenny shook her head. "Nothing. It must have just been the one time."

I wondered why. Maybe, in her young mind, Jenny had blocked Amelia out. Perhaps the short description in her school book had been therapeutic. The face of the girl was out there for everyone to see and no longer locked away in her mind. Jenny took the book back and studied the sketch.

"She's been waiting a long time. Eight years."

I spoke to Sebastian that evening, anxious to hear what he had to say about the drawing. The old man didn't even sound surprised. "Children are more open to the spirit world," he said. "As we get older, our minds become crowded. Like I said, we need to tune our minds, block out all the other sounds."

"A single dream, though? Well, it's unusual, I must admit. More often than not, a child will experience a similar dream or nightmare more than once, but these are generally dreams about fictitious characters that they encounter during their lives. Amelia Root was real. That's the difference."

I was talking to a man who measured his words and only verbalised the things he really believed. That's why I trusted him implicitly. That's why I wanted him there at the funeral, along with Josie and Lou—the people who mattered in my life. But there was someone else who should be there. Someone with as much right as Jenny herself. That night, I picked up the phone and called Ellen Pascoe.

Chapter Forty-One

O N THE DAY we laid Amelia Root to rest, the whole country was bathed in glorious winter sun. Jenny had slept little and rose at four that morning. She was nervous and pale but resisted using any make up to disguise her complexion, reminding me that it was not a party. "I'm really not arsed what I look like. I just want to see that girl at rest."

I didn't pursue the matter, hoping that Josie opted for the same approach to the day. It would score a few points with my daughter if nothing else.

On the way to The Keys, I decided to test the water. "Jo's been a rock," I began, feeling like a nervous teenager dropping the name of his new love into conversation for the first time. "So has Sebastian," I added quickly. Jenny didn't respond. "Josie's been a good friend...when you were in hospital..."

Jenny looked up. "Good." she shot back, giving me one of those knowing glances I hated so much. "Look, I'm glad, but she's married, and I couldn't handle any more affairs at the moment. I've got a load of shit going on in my head—a brother I don't want and a so-called father who topped himself." She turned away, staring out at the road ahead. "Dad, I know you like Josie, but let's not do this now, okay? Not today."

When I glanced over at my daughter, I saw the tears running down her cheeks and felt a heaviness in my chest. Why couldn't I have left it? Why did my daughter have to tell me these things? Things that would be so obvious to any decent father.

I pulled into the car park of The Keys, killed the engine, and pulled my daughter towards me. In my arms, she began to cry. I felt her tears on my neck. She was mine—an Adams, not a Pascoe. I told her that I loved her more than anything else in the world and that I'd never, ever hurt her. Up until that moment, we had muddled through the pain together, both nursing wounds that were wide open and raw. But with that embrace, I really believed the healing had begun.

***

We arrived at the gates of Tabwell's crematorium just half an hour before the service began. Josie, Lou and Sebastian had chatted happily together thanks to Lou, who, after years behind the bar, had mastered the art of polite conversation. It suited me, because it left Jenny and I free to wallow in our own thoughts. As we walked towards the chapel, my daughter pushed her arm through mine. "Here we go," she whispered. "This is it!"

I was nervous. I didn't want to see another coffin, either.

The press was there, and a small outside broadcast team huddled together on the lawn doing a piece to camera while a crowd of inquisitive onlookers had gathered, along with several sober-looking ladies. I guessed they were probably regulars from St. Jude's; in fact, I'd have put money on it. Jenny was thinking the same.

"Pew polishers," she whispered with a wry smile.

I'd have also parted with cash just to know what they thought of the whole Amelia thing, although it hardly mattered. At least Amelia would not be carried to her grave down the aisle of an empty church. She was going home, not to a damp, dark attic, but to the grounds she had loved. We stood in silence, reflecting. Neither of us looked for unnecessary words. But then I heard a voice behind me. "Mr. Adams?"

I turned to see Ellen Pascoe. She took several steps towards us, leaning heavily on her wooden stick.

"Mrs. Pascoe, it's good to see you."

She smiled warmly from under the brim of a black hat that made her face appear even paler than I'd remembered. "I really didn't think you'd want me here, all things considered," she said, looking at Jenny. Her eyes began to flood quite suddenly. "And this must be Jenny."

A tear ran down her cheek and, for a moment, I feared she was going to collapse. "Are you okay, Mrs. Pascoe? Do you need to sit down?"

"No! No!" she replied impatiently, still staring at Jenny. "I can't believe it. You are even more beautiful than in the photograph."

Jenny smiled awkwardly as Ellen reached out and touched my hand. "I'm so sorry. This must be as difficult for you as it is for me."

It was difficult, but I wasn't going to show any weakness. "It's okay. You have every right." I looked at Jenny. "After all, she is your granddaughter."

Another tear coursed down the old lady's cheek. "I've been longing to meet you, Jenny," she said, looking into my daughter's eyes. "But I know you have your own life, and I would never expect to be part of it—not after all this time."

Jenny looked up at me and then at her grandmother. "Time doesn't matter," she said tearfully. "You're still my nan—the only one I've got."

***

The room was full as Francis took up his position at the lectern. The hum of conversation stopped and the congregation fell into total silence. The music began—Barber's Adagio for Strings. Jenny grasped my hand. This was her music. Blakely could not have chosen anything better, and we both felt the same wave of sadness, the same nervous anticipation as six bearers bore the oak casket down the aisle. Jenny's hand shook, and I felt the beads of perspiration forming on the back of my neck. We could have reached out and touched the coffin of the girl whose spirit had transformed our lives.

Reverend Francis stood in silence for a moment as the bearers stepped back, and I wondered if he had slept at all last night. Did the death of this girl weigh heavily on his conscience, or had time diminished the importance of her life? He cleared his throat and began.

"Brothers and sisters, we are here to pay our respects to a young woman we never knew. She had no life to celebrate and lived during a time of much ignorance. It is befitting that her body should find its resting place in the grounds she would walk with her father and her governess. The only people, it seemed, who really loved her..."

Francis skirted around the details, never mentioning Allington's name, yet his short address was respectful and warm. Even Sebastian failed to find fault, and as we followed the hearse to the grounds of the home, no one uttered a word. Amelia was not cremated. Blakely had wanted a coffin rather than a pot full of ashes, and when we arrived, Jenny and I crossed the lawns to the grave that had been prepared at the edge of the woods. Only a handful of people had followed on from the crematorium. Francis was waiting, the casket in place.

As we watched the coffin being lowered into the ground, Jenny placed her hand in mine. This was the end—Amelia's final resting place.

"I can't believe it," Jenny whispered.

Blakely glanced over, forcing a smile. There was, if I'm not mistaken, a tear in his eye.

We threw soil and roses on top of the coffin as Reverend Francis committed the body to God, knowing that within a couple of hours Amelia would lie beneath the earth. Blakely had given the young woman a funeral, and her life, however miserable, had been acknowledged.

Jenny and I said goodbye to Ellen. Jenny said she would call in to see her soon, but as the others drifted away, we stood silently, neither of us able to find the words to describe how we felt.

When finally it felt right to leave, the sky was darkening and we pulled the collars of our coats up against the late-afternoon chill. A middle-aged man in an immaculately tailored grey suit was waiting for us by the car. He looked impatient, his hands thrust deep into the pockets of his trousers. Jenny took my arm. Something told me he wasn't there to exchange pleasantries. He turned as we approached.

"Mr. Adams?"

I nodded.

"Are you happy?" he snapped.

"What?"

"It's a simple question. Are you happy with what you've done?"

"I'm sorry? Who are you?"

The man squared up, hands still in his pockets. "I'm Mr. Driscoll, a deacon at St. Jude's."

"So what exactly do you want?" I asked, realising that I wasn't going to get a handshake.

"I saw the article in the *Herald*—the one where you claimed to have been guided by the spirit of this Emily woman."

"It's *Amelia*," Jenny spat.

"I don't care what her name is, young lady!" Driscoll retorted. "I care about St. Jude's!"

I stared at him. "Good! I'm glad. So what can we do for you?"

"Do for me? Haven't you done enough?"

"Meaning?"

"The Reverend Allington founded a school that has educated children in this parish for over a hundred years. Children who had no shoes—no food! He fed them and, in many cases, clothed them. He worked tirelessly for this community, and his legacy is still here for everyone to see—"

"He raped a young woman—over and over again!" Jenny said, interrupting Driscoll mid-flow.

"How do you know this?" Driscoll replied, his face crimson with anger. "Because some spirit told you? Don't you realise that all spirits are of the Devil—masquerading as the souls of the dead? Don't you read your Bible?" I saw the undisguised hatred in his eyes. "No! I bet you don't even have one—yet you have the gall to come here, complete strangers, and destroy the reputation of a good man! And for what? A bit of cheap publicity?"

Knocking out a lowlife in a fast food car park was one thing—knocking out a church deacon in front of my daughter was something else, so I tried reasoning.

"Look, we have a written account from her governess, and Amelia's own diaries. It is proof, Mr. Driscoll. I'm sorry if the memory of your saint has been tainted, but it's the truth!"

Driscoll glared at us. "The woman was obviously crazy. She told lies. And how do you know that the letter from this governess woman was genuine? Truth is, you don't! Why have you done this? The Reverend Allington was a good man!"

Driscoll turned suddenly to see Reverend Francis approaching. The minister smiled, greeting us warmly.

"Hello, Mr. Adams, Jenny."

Driscoll said nothing.

"What's going on here?" Francis said, sensing the atmosphere immediately.

Jenny piped up. "Apparently, we have been doing the Devil's work."

Francis stared at his deacon. "Mr. Driscoll," he said firmly, "we have had this discussion before, and I've told you in no uncertain term that you do not—not ever—approach Mr. Adams or his daughter. Especially his daughter!"

Driscoll opened his mouth, about to protest, but Francis held up his hand.

"I don't want to hear another word. Mr. Adams and his daughter have been through hell these past few months, and to suggest that they have been working in collusion with the Devil to bring down a minister who lived over a hundred years ago is, quite frankly, ridiculous."

He stared at Driscoll. "You are a fool," he spat. "And you are making a fool of the church and all those who worship there, and that is something I am not prepared to tolerate."

Francis turned to us. "You, my friends, are welcome at St. Jude's anytime."

He kissed Jenny on the cheek and shook my hand. We pushed past a shell-shocked deacon and climbed into the car, waving at the minister as I fired up the engine.

Jenny turned, buckling up her seat belt and grinned mischievously. "Well, that told him!" she said.

We ate at the Lakeside Hotel before travelling home. It felt right to stay in Tabwell for a while longer, out of respect for Amelia. Jenny looked worn out, but throughout the course of the late afternoon, she caught my eye and smiled. It was a smile that told me she had found peace, maybe for the first time since Elizabeth and Hanna's death. But more than that, there was a warmth between us that filled me with a new hope for the future. A future I could believe in, and an end to the hell we had lived through.

***

We spent Christmas with Josie, Lou and Sebastian, dining at The Keys. New Year, however, proved as difficult a time as ever without my wife and little girl, but somehow we waded through the sadness and found comfort in our relationship, which grew stronger day by day. Jenny and Kelly revived their friendship but stayed clear of the Ouija board, while Josie and I placed our relationship on hold. Naturally, I kept in touch with Sebastian, and Ricky the pup soon evolved into Ricky the rather large, excitable dog.

Josie never took up with the shady club owner but started singing at The Keys on Friday nights. Her Tina Turner set had everyone up on their feet, and two local musicians—a bass player called Billy Rat (because of his pointy face and ears, presumably) and a guitarist called Dodgy Den (I didn't ask!) agreed to join her. She went live, ditching the backing tracks, and the following April, on Jenny's birthday, she put on a party at the pub. It was nothing more than an excuse to put on a show—a celebration of our new life together and it was a night neither of us would ever forget.

Josie sang, playing the room the way she had all those years ago, while Lou had laid on a spread that would have fed a small country. And the cake—the cake, in the shape of a classical guitar—was carried in by two young men dressed as Spanish waiters while Lou led us all in an out of tune rendition of 'Happy Birthday'.

The following day, Blakely arrived on our doorstep with Jenny's birthday gift—two plane tickets to Spain. He had a hillside villa, high up in the town of Mijas, overlooking the coastline of the Costa del Sol.

"It's yours for two weeks," he told us. With that, he pushed an envelope into my hands. "That should keep you in food." Inside was eight hundred euros.

I never asked how Blakely knew it was Jenny's birthday, and I didn't really care. The nightmares had stopped, and Amelia was at rest, but we were still rebuilding our lives. By the time the holiday came around, early that summer, we were ready for a break.

***

Blakely's villa, nestled in the mountainside beneath the walls of Mijas, was everything we had anticipated, but the view was beyond anything we could have imagined. We wandered around the village during the day, taking rides around the cobbled streets in the carriages and walking the perimeter paths overlooking the miles of coastline with its hotels, bars and shopping malls. On the final evening, we ate out at a restaurant as the sun set on the horizon and watched as the Costa del Sol burst into a carpet of lights beneath us.

We ate well and shared a bottle of wine. The money Blakely had given us would cover more than the cost of a taxi home, and we raised a glass to our benefactor.

Jenny laughed. "If I was a few years older…" she said.

I smiled. One day my daughter would meet someone, and I would watch her drift away. The very thought filled me with dread—that moment when your child moves on. Not so much a fresh chapter but a whole new book. I watched her as she ate. My girl had grown into a beautiful young woman, who looked up and caught my gaze.

She smiled and reached for my hand. "I had another dream last night," she said.

I felt as if my heart had missed a beat.

"I saw Amelia. She was in the woods. I saw her face, looking up at me." Jenny smiled. "She looked so peaceful, Dad. So beautiful."

It felt so good to be holding my daughter's hand—to feel the warmth of her flesh, to see her face, to look into her eyes and see the love. Maybe there had been a purpose—a reason for everything that had happened over the past twelve months.

Someone once asked me if I believed in fate. At the time, I wasn't sure if our lives were planned or merely shaped by a series of random events.

The truth is, we have to live with the consequences of our actions, and although my demons still lurk in the shadows, reminding me of that Sunday afternoon, I've learned not to dwell on the past or concern myself with the future. Heartache and loss are a part of life, yet there will always be things for which we can be thankful. If you have your health, enjoy it. If you have faith, embrace it with all your heart. Treasure your family, love your friends, and may God, whomever or whatever you perceive Him or it to be, always keep you safe.

THE END

About the Author

Graham West studied art at Hugh Baird college in Bootle, Merseyside, before joining the display team at Blacklers Store in Liverpool city centre where he spent seven years in the art department before moving on in 1981 to become a sign writer. He lives in Maghull with his wife, Ann, and has a daughter, Lindsay, and two grandchildren, Sonny and Kasper. Graham also plays guitar at weddings, functions and restaurants. He took up writing in 2000 and has had a couple of factual articles published in magazines. *Finding Amelia* is his first novel.

Coming Soon

A Rising Evil
Beyond The Dark Waters
Book Two

Two years later…

Jenny is living with her fiancé, Jake, Rob has settled down with Josie, and Darren Pascoe is at liberty and anxious to make amends. But when Jenny starts seeing Amelia again and both Amelia's and Elizabeth's graves are vandalised, Sebastian has a sense of foreboding that the family may again be in danger.

Beaten Track Publishing

For more titles from Beaten Track Publishing,
please visit our website:

http://www.beatentrackpublishing.com

Thanks for reading!

Lightning Source UK Ltd.
Milton Keynes UK
UKOW04f2147070917
308785UK00001B/29/P